for everyone who loves their love stories with a side of angst

and Dwayne "The Rock" Johnson

WHEN IT ENDS

A DARK APOCALYPTIC ROMANCE

PENELOPE BLACK

Cover Design: Cat, TRC Designs

PLAYLIST

"River" by Leon Bridges
"Roslyn" by Bon Iver, St. Vincent
"Dark Matter" by Seratones
"Don't Blame Me" by Taylor Swift
"Blanket Me" by Hundred Waters
"Work" by Charlotte Day Wilson
"Gone" by Blake Rose
"Safe and Sound" by Taylor Swift
"You There" by Aquilo
"Still Don't Know My Name" by Labrinth
"Litost" by X Ambassadors
"Black Mambo" by Glass Animals
"How Do You Like My Fish" by Drum & Lace, Ian Hullquist
"Cornfield Chase" by Hans Zimmer
"Dream is Collapsing" by Hans Zimmer
"As the World Caves In" by Sarah Cothran, Wuki
"Je te laisserai des mots" by Patrick Watson

AUTHOR'S NOTE

Please note that When It Ends is a dark apocalyptic romance and it has some darker themes some readers may find triggering.

Please message me if you have any questions: author.penelope.black@gmail.com
Happy reading!

1

AMELIA

"YOU COME HERE OFTEN?"

I pause the maze I was creating with the condensation on my vintage tumbler. The drinkware is one of the only memorable things about this aging bar-casino on the outskirts of Las Vegas. The overused and uninspired pickup line is the cherry on top of my shitty-day sundae. I've had just enough alcohol and too little sleep in the last two days to reel in my annoyance.

"Do you have a small dick?" I ask over my shoulder without turning around to see the face that goes with such a terrible line.

It's not the first time I've thrown such a crude question at someone. And nine times out of ten, it gets the message across succinctly.

I'm not interested. Move along.

Much to my surprise, laughter greets my question instead of curses or insults. It's a carefree sort of sound, like he just heard a surprising joke. It's enough to pique my interest, and I swivel the barstool to the right and look over my shoulder.

He's tall enough that I have to tip my head back to take him in. Wavy dark blond hair, long enough to pull back. The blinking lights from the bank of slot machines behind us highlights his in flashes, but it's too dim in here to make out the exact color of his eyes. But they're dark, alluring even.

His laughter tapers off, leaving only dimples to wink at me as if to hint at his mischief. He mock-wipes a tear from underneath his eye as he slides his hands into his pockets, leaving his thumbs hooked over the top of his dark-wash jeans.

A charcoal gray tee stretches across his chest, the once-white logo faded. I idly wonder if he bought it purposely distressed or if it's worn from use. I'm not discreet about my perusal, but this mystery man only tips his head to the side. Patiently waiting until I've had my fill.

Heat warms my cheeks, but it's not from being caught. I like that he's giving me space to ogle him, it's oddly endearing. I pause when our gazes connect.

The low lights from the bar don't do either of us any favors, I'm sure. And the blinking lights from the machines to his right give his beard—a day or two past a five o'clock shadow—a tie-dye effect. On any other man, I'm sure it would take down his desirability factor, but he gets another point in his favor because it only heightens everything about him.

He nods and shoots me a secret sort of smile. I almost kick myself when my own lips curl up in response. He takes it as an invitation and slides onto the stool next to me.

My brows hit my hairline at his presumption, but I manage to check myself when I realize that it's one of the only available seats at this little bar. And I did just check him out for two solid minutes.

My new seatmate signals to the bartender with a finger and a friendly smile. I sip my drink, letting the harsh burn of rum and Coke—heavy on the rum—coat my throat as I watch him interact with one of the two men behind the bar of Tennessee Pete's.

You can tell a lot about a person by the way they interact with people in the service industry. I've seen firsthand the way people treat waitstaff and baristas and bartenders. It doesn't matter how attractive this guy is, I'm not going to sleep with him if he's rude.

Wait.

Where did that thought come from? I wasn't—I'm *not* going home with anyone tonight. I'm just here for a few drinks, maybe a burger and fries, and then I'm crashing for a few hours before I finish driving. I'm on the last leg of my cross-country trek home. Sleeping with some random man I meet in an old casino slash motel isn't on my to-do list for the day.

I suck my bottom lip as the man next to me orders a whiskey sour with a smile and some small talk, gesturing with his hands. He does have nice hands though, big palms with long fingers.

Sipping my drink, I tilt my head and study him. He reminds me of someone, but I can't quite put my finger on who. A celebrity, maybe.

He flashes those dimples at the bartender, and little tendrils of lust sit up and take notice.

I suppose having a little fun never hurt anyone.

He half turns his body toward me. "So, do you come here often?"

"Are we back to that so soon?" I counter quickly with an arched brow. "Should I repeat my question now too?"

He smiles at me and drags his teeth into his bottom lip. "Is that an invitation?"

My nose wrinkles as I stare at him for a moment, mentally chastising myself. Sure, he's good-looking. Okay, so maybe more than good-looking. He's downright hot. That kind of attractive that would make you throw your morals out the window.

Kind of like what I just mentally decided a moment ago.

I am going to be so disappointed if he turns out to be an asshole.

I sip my drink and eye him over the rim of my glass. "Does that line ever work for you—the come here often one."

The bartender, an older man with salt-and-pepper hair, smiles and slides his drink across the lacquered oak bar. The stranger next to me snatches it in a smooth movement, the veins in his forearms popping as he grips the glass. He accepts the drink with a murmured thanks. "I don't really hit on women often."

"Wow. I don't even know how to take that."

"Nah, it's not like that, Blondie. More like I don't really hang out in casinos or bars."

I roll my eyes at the nickname. Having naturally dark blonde hair seems like it would be great, right? Except it's this in between color—lighter and brighter in the summer and darker and moodier in the winter. Or if we're living in a city that actually has seasons like we have for the past couple years. "Blondie, huh? Because I haven't heard that one before."

He dips his chin. "Alright, what's your name then?"

I smirk with just a touch of incredulousness, but it gives me an idea. I've been in a deep '90s movie binge lately. "Cher."

"Damn. What are the odds, Cher? I'm Sonny." He holds out his hand, but since there's not much space between us, his fingertips skim the fabric of my olive green tank top.

I can't help it. He's too charming for his own good. Or maybe mine. "What *are* the odds," I murmur as I slide my hand into his. His grip is firm but not overpowering, and he pumps our hands for a few seconds too long, his dark eyes twinkling as they hold my gaze.

"WAIT, wait. You're telling me the most embarrassing thing you've ever done is run around in the snow?" I arch a brow at him, my mouth pinched to the side in disbelief.

"Well, I was thirteen, remember? And they'd dared me to run around the house in my boxers. I still remember feeling that adrenaline rush of doing something dangerous *and* catching the eye of the hottest girl in the eighth grade. It was a win-win."

I laugh as I point a French fry smothered in cheese sauce at him. "That doesn't sound even remotely embarrassing!"

He grins and pops his own cheesy fry into his mouth. "Well, that's because you haven't heard the embarrassing part yet."

"You tripped! Lost your boxers! Shrinkage!" My voice increases in volume and glee with each guess, laughter tripping over my words.

Sonny shoots me a mischievous side-eye. "Where do you think this story is going?"

I lift a shoulder and swipe another fry through the addicting sauce. "Spill then."

He blows out a breath, his cheeks puffing out to the sides. There's an air of playfulness around him. It's a welcome respite from my usual type. He lowers his head and looks at me from underneath his long, dark lashes. "Well, you see, my granddad came home and nearly had a stroke seeing my lily-white ass running around the house—"

"Ha! You did lose your underwear then!"

He straightens with a smirk. "Did I mention I was thirteen? Jake Thompson bet Carl Hannoc twenty bucks that I wouldn't actually streak. So I doubled-down on both of them and walked out with eighty bucks. And an earful from Pops. He read me the riot act in front of everyone that night—before he let me put my clothes on."

The mental image of an eighth-grade Sonny running around and trying to impress his friends plants itself in my mind, and I can't stop the giggles before they're out. He chuckles along with me as he takes another fry.

We switched out cocktails for soda and greasy food an hour ago. For bar food, it's pretty good. The company helps too.

The cheese sauce drips down onto the edge of my hand. I'm not one for messy hands while I eat, but I'm having too much fun to care right now. I toss the fry in my mouth and halfheartedly wipe my hands on the crumpled up napkin next to me.

I shake my head a little. "I can't even remember anyone's name from eighth grade, let alone memories so clearly like that."

I guess that's not entirely true. There are a couple people I don't think I'll ever forget, no matter how old I am. I take a sip of my Cherry Coke, the bubbles fizzing on my tongue.

"So you were thirteen, and that was … how long ago?" I squint with a tilt of my head.

"You fishing for my age, Cher?" He smirks. "I'm an open book, baby girl. All you have to do is ask."

I pause at the new nickname, my brows slanting low over my eyes. I don't know how long we've been chatting, but either it's long enough for him to read me—which seems unlikely—or it's a throwaway pet name. One of those things guys use all the time because they can't remember the girl they're on top of.

Disappointment threatens to prick my bubble of fun, but I shove it out of the way at the last second. Two baskets of fries and a handful of drinks doesn't mean anything more than exactly what it is. And I won't be here long enough to find out if he's a player or not, so no skin off my back.

2

AMELIA

"IT'S BEEN A PLEASURE, Sonny, but you didn't have to walk me. I'm perfectly capable of making it the one hundred feet from the casino to my motel room." I pivot in front of the faded blue door, a crooked brassy number six hanging from right above the peep hole.

I catch a glimpse of my reflection in the curtain-darkened window of my rented room behind me. Hair unruly from hours of tossing it off my face, eyes bright with laughter, cheeks pink from all the subtle flirting.

It's been years since I've felt this . . . alive. Since I felt like *me* again. I banish all thoughts of the last time I felt like this. I'm not going to ruin a surprisingly good evening with sour memories. It's my last night before I'm back home.

I'm only four hours or so away, but I'd been driving for ten before I stopped. I got the room for the night and had planned on eating and crashing for a few hours before hitting the road again. But it's two o'clock in the morning now, and even though my buzz is long gone, I'm not driving anywhere tonight.

"C'mon, Cher. You should know me better than that by now. I'm not going to let anything happen to you on my watch. You never know what kind of people lurk around just waiting for a pretty thing like you to let her guard down."

My cheeks heat at the way his honeyed voice wraps around each word, slowly and with intention. I sway closer to him, my feet rooted to the cracked pavement. I wet my lips, my gaze honing in on his mouth and that perfect way it tips up on the left. "That's very . . . kind of you, considering I don't even know your real name."

"Would you believe me if I told you it was Sonny?"

A small laugh slips out, mirth stretching my smile wide. "Not even for a second."

He steps closer, the tips of his black sneakers touching the tips of my classic black-and-white checkered Vans. His warm palm slides against my waist, his touch light. "Go in your room, Cher, and lock the door behind you, yeah?"

My heart beats loud in my ears, competing to hear him over the almost lulling noise of traffic. A slow buzzing feeling crawls over my skin, and I tongue the corner of my mouth. I step back, the scratchy wood of the door catching on the soft cotton of my tank top. My shoulder blades press into the hard surface as I fish the keycard out of my back pocket. Without taking my gaze off of him, I swipe it above the doorknob. It takes a few tries but eventually, it beeps, and the lock turns over.

The mechanical sound shoots through the charged space between us. Instead of breaking the tension, it enhances it.

The pressure behind me falls away as the cool air wafts out into the night. I take another step backward, opening the door further. The darkened room behind me feels like it has a pulse, throbbing in tune with my heightening desire.

Emotions play across Sonny's face, half of it shadowed by the overhang above the walkway. One step, and he's just outside my room, his hands on either side of the door. His biceps flex under the strain, and his face remains intense. It's a stark contrast to the flirty smiles and dirty smirks from the last few hours.

"Goodnight, Cher," he murmurs as he pushes off the frame to stand firmly on the walkway.

Regret tastes acrid on my tongue, like cantaloupe a couple days past its prime. I don't want this night to end. Not yet. Blame it on hormones or the canyon of loneliness that awaits me, but the thought of this being over has my gut clenching.

"Wait." The word shoots from my lips like a cannon, halting Sonny midturn. He arches a blond brow and glances over his shoulder. I lick my lips. "Stay."

It's not a question, and I know the moment he slowly pivots around that he noticed my demand right away. His eyes darken as he regards me, waiting patiently.

I take those two steps that separate us and reach out, giving him plenty of time to stop or deflect. I curl my fingers in the soft fabric of his tee and push onto my tiptoes at the same time I gently tug him toward me. Our height difference isn't nearly as much of an issue as I thought it would be.

"I want you to come in, Sonny." My lips graze his with the barest touch, but it's enough to send a spark to my nervous system.

Our chests hitch in unison at the contact. Anticipation seeps from our pores, swirling around the two of us, tightening and pulling us together like ribbons. I swear it feels like the world stops spinning.

Three endless seconds pass before either one of us reacts. I don't know who moves first, but those three seconds were enough for each of us to flip a switch. There's no tentative exploration or soft, sweeping kisses.

Our mouths crash together in a violent consummation of passion. All lips and teeth and tongue fighting for dominance. His hands roam my body, his fingerprints burning little sparks into every inch of exposed skin.

I drag him inside my room with an arm around his neck, flicking my other wrist to send the door closed. I blindly fumble with the lock, never taking my lips from his.

Apparently those five seconds are too long, because Sonny grunts and breaks our kiss long enough to slam the deadbolt over. He doesn't hesitate for a moment, his hands gripping my thighs tight and hauling me up his body. My legs wrap around his hips, and his hands settle on my ass, his fingertips sliding underneath the hem of my jean shorts.

My lower belly tightens at the feeling of his very large, very hard cock centered up perfectly. My clit throbs already, making her demands known early tonight.

I wiggle closer and seal our mouths together once more, rocking as much as I can against him. The tip of his cock nudges my clit, the pressure nothing more than a tease, a carnal promise. One I intend to cash in on tonight, several times if the orgasm gods are feeling charitable.

3

AMELIA

I'M FLOATING SOMEWHERE between dreamland and consciousness. I hover there, willing myself to slip back into the delicious dream I was in. Thor and Captain America were taking turns bench-pressing me, and it was right about to get to the *good part*. But a persistent low buzzing noise chips away at my blissful dreamscape. And once it snags even a second of my attention, it catapults me into consciousness.

The first thing I notice is the heat. Ugh. I lived in the desert for five years, you would think I could handle a little heat, but I guess I've been away too long. This doesn't feel like the dry heat of the desert, it feels humid and sticky.

A soft snore rumbles against my ear, and my eyes fly open. It takes five seconds for me to take stock of the situation. Two more blinks, and the events of last night shudder into my consciousness.

I'm almost afraid to move for fear he wakes up. A huge part of me wants to see him in the harsh morning light, desperate even. There's no way someone so charming and funny and gorgeous could be *that good*, ya know?

No, best to keep last night's memory untouched by the morning's regrets and revelations. I tuck it away to revisit later when I'm sitting alone in an empty house for one too many nights.

A quick mental check later, and I'm gently peeling the scratchy motel sheet off of me. I blink a few times, letting my eyes adjust to the bright light of the sun shining into the two-inch gap in the curtains. Huh, I guess we gave quite the show to anyone who wandered by last night. With nimble fingers and slow movements, I untangle Sonny's arm from around me.

I hold my breath as I slide out of bed, my skin prickling with awareness. My heart thrums in my ears, a staccato beat demanding I turn around and take in the man who brought me to three orgasms last night. Maybe even wake him up for a farewell round.

Instead, I shove that lust down and look for my clothes. It seems I went to sleep in nothing more than his charcoal tee. Our clothes are scattered around the room, but after a minute of searching, I still can't find my thong.

Sonny groans a little, and like a heat-seeking missile, my gaze snaps to him.

Oh my god.

Holy shit.

He rolls over, hugging the pillow my head was on to his chest, and I get an unobstructed view of his back and shoulders. Tattoos crawl over his upper back and shoulders to wrap around his arms, lines and shading primarily in black with only a few pops of color. I distinctly remember running my tongue along the lines of one of his tattoos earlier. It just so happened to be over his lower abdomen.

His blond hair looks almost like a halo in the sunshine, spread out around his head, but I have verifiable proof that he's far from angelic. Unless we're talking the fallen kind.

I shift a little, my thighs rubbing together as very clear images of the way he palmed my neck as he fucked me from behind flash.

My phone vibrates in my hand, a reminder that the movers are at the new house.

Get it together, Amelia.

I shake off the mental gymnastics I could get lost in and give up the search for my underwear. I step into my jean shorts and shimmy them up my thighs and hips. Jean shorts without a cotton and lace barrier is never a good idea, but when you've spent the night letting a man you just met worship you, it feels infinitely rougher.

I think about stripping out of his tee and changing into my tank top, but something stops me. Call it nostalgia or hopelessly romantic or even selfish, but I want to take it with me.

It's silly considering I don't even know his real name.

But it's tangible proof that the girl I thought I lost years ago is still here. It only took one blond Adonis, three drinks, and a plate of cheese fries for me to realize it.

I shove my bra and tank top in my weekender bag I dropped on the table when I first checked-in. I allow myself one more glance, a lingering look to memorize the way his muscles carve the most alluring image, and then I'm out the door.

Wind whips sand around in mini cyclones, not hard enough to sting but with enough force that I know I'll find it in places I didn't realize sand *could* settle into if I don't get in the car soon. A sense of foreboding washes over me, coating me in a warning of what's to come. I shake off the dark feeling, I probably just need a nap and an iced coffee, not necessarily in that order.

This isn't the kind of place you need to check out of, so I walk straight to my dark blue SUV, affectionately named Nova. There's a fine layer of sand covering the entire thing, more collecting in the windshield wiper well.

It took me almost two years' worth of tips at the coffee shop to buy it, and the guy at the used car lot gave it to me for a steal. I'm fairly certain he thought it would help his chances with my friend, Alley.

It didn't.

Speaking of my best friend, my phone flashes an icon with her gorgeous face as a text comes up on my home screen. I toss my weekender in the backseat, on top of the two suitcases, and slide into the driver's seat.

"Jesus, that's hot."

My skin burns as it hits the overheated leather. It's not even ten o'clock in the morning, and already, my car is practically an oven. I make a mental note to get one of those windshield shader things right away.

I don't look at Alley's text yet, eager to get on the road. I'd kill for an iced latte and a breakfast burrito right about now. I know I didn't get drunk last night, but it's still more than I usually drink. It's easy to get carried away when you're wallowing in your own misery.

Damn, my thoughts got dark quick today.

Misery seems harsh. I'm not miserable.

I'm just not . . . content.

A lot of people turn up their noses at being content. Self-proclaimed social media gurus will tell you that contentedness is akin to laziness, but I don't view it that way.

When you grow up the way I did, never staying longer than a few years in one place, it creates a restlessness. I never let myself settle because it made it that much harder to leave.

And we always left.

I've only ever felt content—happy, even—in one place.

And in approximately four hours, I'll be back there for the first time in five years.

Thirty minutes, a vanilla iced latte and an egg and sausage burrito later, I pull into a parking spot outside the coffee shop. I'm too hungry to wait another few hours to eat. Thankfully, the roads aren't too busy considering it's pretty much the only road in and out of this part of the desert. But it's Wednesday morning, so that works in my favor.

I polish off the burrito in six bites and wash it down with half of my latte, letting the creamy nutty flavored espresso jolt me. My phone vibrates in the cup holder, and my dad's face flashes from the little icon.

Dad: Hey, kiddo. We're heading out to the site early since it's possible we'll encounter some high winds. Movers are already there and unloading. The property management manager is at the house overseeing everything. She'll leave the key on the counter in the kitchen. The garage door code is 0332.

I smile through my annoyance and remind myself that he's probably thinking about five other things as he sent this text. I tried to warn him that moving this week would be tough since he had to be on location two days later.

Well, today, I guess.

A sigh slips out before I can reel it in. There's no sense in getting upset about it. He's never been the warm hug and movie night kind of dad before, I don't know why I expected him to be one now.

Me: Okay. I'll see you in a week when you get back.

I wait for a minute, but he never replies, probably already moved on to whatever is next on his checklist. Because that's what I am sometimes: something to be checked off his to-do list.

I blow out a breath and try to let the disappointment roll off like water on a duck's back. Another sip of my delicious latte helps. I check my messages, remembering the unread text from Alley.

Alley: Happy birthday, you gorgeous girl. I can't believe you couldn't stay another week so we could spend your birthday together! Even though you broke tradition and moved across the country, I forgive you. I'll see you next month for our girls' weekend!! ilyyyy

Warmth settles inside my chest, the weight of disappointment from Dad burned away by her text. Thank god for Alley.

Me: Thank you! Wait until you hear what happened last night. I'll call you tonight. ly!

Alley: omg. Pls tell me you hooked up with like a bearded mountain man after he fixed your flat tire on the side of the road!

Laughter bubbles up, the emotion bright and weightless.

Alley came into my life in the best way. We had recently moved to New Jersey for one of Dad's projects, and I got a job at an adorable little coffee shop not too far from our house. She's the shift manager at Déjà Brew, and it took all of fifteen minutes for her to declare us *destined besties*. She has more energy than anyone I've ever seen, and she's always finding the silver lining in everything. I didn't make it easy for her either. When we first met, I was perfectly fine to keep to myself during each shift. Friendly but not friends.

She was chatting with a customer about a new sports romance novel, and when I recited one of my favorite quotes from the book, it was like her eyes grew three sizes and little friendship hearts shot out of them like a cartoon. It sounds ridiculous, but she just has one of those Disney princess faces—and the personality to match.

She's my best friend.

She's the only one in my life who really knows me, and I'm clear across the country now. So I'm sure, like every other relationship I've ever had, it'll fade over time. The irony of my situation isn't lost on me.

I used to have two other best friends. We were thick as thieves for years. I loved them.

I was *in love* with them—as much as any seventeen-year-old can be, at least.

But then I had to leave Las Vegas behind, and I didn't realize that included them too.

Futile disappointment haunts me, turning the last sip of my iced latte to ash on my tongue.

Happy birthday to me.

4

AMELIA

THE LOUD CLICKING noise of my blinker gives this Taylor Swift song an EDM vibe with a quick beat. I tap my fingers on the steering wheel as I wait for the red light to switch to green. I'd forgotten how busy traffic can be, even in the outskirts of Las Vegas. And how aggressive the drivers are.

I learned how to drive in this city though, and I'm sure their particular style will come back to me. Like riding a bike, right?

Nerves slide around in my gut, that familiar feeling like pants that are too tight. I'm uncomfortable, and sitting in traffic for a million years just hyping myself up over what will probably amount to nothing doesn't help anything. I swear I've been at this red light for three minutes already, which is practically an eternity in traffic.

Twenty minutes and three turns later, my late grandmother's house comes into view. Technically, it's Dad's house since she gave it to him when she passed a little less than a decade ago. I've always loved this house. It's the only place we've ever lived for longer than a few years.

And I met *them* here.

The Spanish-style two-story home is the closest thing I've ever had to a home. The soft beige stucco walls and terracotta-colored tile roof always reminded me of some kind of fairytale. Wrought iron balconies jut out from two sets of French doors facing the street. One of those is my bedroom, and the other one is Dad's study.

Tenderness ripples outward from my chest in soft waves when I spot the bright blooms dotting the balconies and the bursts of color in front of the house. Big white primroses, sprawling yellow chocolate flowers, cotton candy pink and dark rose hollyhocks, their stems standing tall and proud. Desert globemallow with bright orange flowers wink at me from underneath the bay windows on either side of the front door. Desert spoon, blue agave, weeping yucca, and golden barrels.

It looks exactly how I remembered it.

Some of the nervousness in my belly settles at the sight. They're all there. The same flowers and bushes and cacti that were flourishing when we left all those years ago are still here.

Janet's worth every penny Dad pays her to manage the property, and I wonder if he'll keep her on to help manage the landscaping or if he's going to take over from now on.

I ease off the gas and pull onto the street in front of the daisy-painted mailbox. My grandma and I painted it together when I was seven. Dad and I came to visit Nana after one of the many times Mom split, and we spent the weekend planting desert daisies and weeping yucca. Nana was an artist, so it was her idea to *spruce up* her plain gray mailbox with the bright shocks of yellow and white.

I'm pleasantly surprised the mailbox is still here. It's a silly thing to be sentimental about, the flowers are nearly faded from aging under the hot Nevada sun.

Throwing the car into park, I expel a breath. The house is a flurry of movement with four movers going back and forth between the moving van parked in the driveway and the house. The front door is propped open, and Janet stands next to the palm tree in a plum-colored pencil skirt and a cream-and-black-patterned blouse. Her head goes from left to right and over again, overseeing everything. She wiggles her fingers in a little wave, and I return the sentiment, but I don't get out yet.

I need just another minute, time to give myself the courage to look across the street. I don't know what I'm more afraid of seeing: that it looks exactly the same or that it's completely different.

I glance across the street at the house that sparks a fire of familiarity. It's more light cream than beige, just a couple shades darker than white. My eyes glaze over as memories assault me, one after another until a montage of some of my favorite moments in life play in front of my eyes.

Watermelon sluices over my fingers, leaving a sticky trail down my forearm and dripping from my elbow. The sun beats down on us, my shoulders sun-kissed and warm to the touch. It's unseasonably hot for early May, but unseasonably hot feels like an oxymoron when you live in the desert and we're staring down the barrel of summer. It's a great day to spend by the pool with two of my favorite people.

And another memory hits.

My neighbors and best friends, Cole Armstrong and West Campbell, laugh, egging each other on in the way only brothers do. They're foster brothers, but they act like blood brothers. Cole wraps an arm around West's neck, wrestling him to the ground while I read a book on a sun lounger.

And another one.

"Everyone thinks the phrase is 'blood is thicker than water,' but the real phrase is 'the blood of the covenant is thicker than the water of the womb,'" Cole says, lounging next to me on the couch with his arm thrown over his eyes.

I scrunch my nose up and look at him. "I don't even know what that means."

"It means we're brothers from a different mother," West says as he plops down next to me. "But that's not true either."

"I know, I know. Wayne is your foster dad. How, uh, how did you guys end up here with Wayne?"

They stiffen next to me, but neither one says anything for a long time. I decide I don't need to satiate my curiosity if it elicits such a strong response from both of them.

I blink, and I'm transported back again.

I push off the concrete with my toe, enjoying the way the hammock swings in the gentle breeze. Thoughts of the boys consume me, like usual.

We've been inseparable since I moved in during seventh grade. But things started to change a couple years ago, for me, at least. It's like we started high school, and suddenly, I stopped seeing sweaty gym socks and a messy bedrooms. Instead, I see the way West's hair flops across his forehead when he throws his whole body into a laugh. And the way Cole always positions himself between me and literally the rest of the world.

And over the last few months, there were times where I would've sworn one of them was about to kiss me. Times when they leaned in close, gently tugged on my hair. West even smoothed an eyelash off my cheekbone last week like some heartthrob in a movie. But nothing ever went past that.

I shove my unrequited feelings down and take another bite of the watermelon wedge. It's a summer snack staple at their house.

Before I finish chewing, warm arms band around me and scoop me up bridal-style. He takes three big steps, and then we're flying. Two seconds that feel like an eternity in the air, just long enough for me to plug my nose with one hand and wrap my other one around his neck, watermelon wedge forgotten on the patio.

I'm not even a little bit surprised it's Cole. He loves to sneak up on me and toss me into the pool.

We hit the water with a crash, and our combined weight sinks us to the bottom. I tighten my grip around his neck as he lets go of my legs to wrap both arms around my back. My legs wrap around his waist as he pushes us up to the surface. We break through with matching grins.

"Aren't you tired of always throwing me into the pool?" I tilt my head back so my hair dips into the water, giving more of my weight to Cole. My

eyes close against the bright rays of the sun as the water slicks my unruly hair away from my face.

"And miss the way you squeal like that and wrap your arms around me? Nah." He flashes a grin as he helps me back up. It's an expression he wears often—he's feeling entirely too proud of himself right now.

A few butterflies flutter in my stomach, a soft jumbled feeling that I've started associating with Cole and West. He holds my gaze for another moment, his fingers spread wide on my back.

"C'mon, Cole, stop hoggin' her." West stands at the edge of the pool, an easy smile on his handsome face. His cheeks look pink, and his sprinkling of freckles pop in the sunshine.

"Jump in, West." I wave him toward us with a wide sweep of my arm.

West backs up a few steps with his hands relaxed on his hips. He shoots us a smirk before he runs and leaps off the edge of the pool, wrapping his arms around his legs. "Cannonball!"

A woman with two little kids walks out of the front door, the sight of them scattering the memories away like leaves on the wind.

I can still smell the coconut sunscreen and taste the sweet watermelon on my tongue. The nostalgia tastes like blackberries in March—bittersweet.

I push open the door and leave everything in the car to meet Janet, pushing all thoughts of teenage crushes aside.

5

AMELIA

"JUST A DRIVING PASS TODAY, PLEASE."

The cashier at the pay station, which looks like a little house, leans over the open windowsill with a smile. "Ten dollars for the day or sixty for the annual pass."

"Ah, just the day pass, please. How much is it to hike?" I hand over my credit card, gripping it tight between my fingers as the breeze curls around my arm.

"Have you hiked here before?" she asks over her shoulder as she swipes my card.

"Yeah, it's been a couple years though." My sunglasses slip down my nose a little, the warm air pouring through my open window.

"Well, it's just like riding a bike, you know. And the Spring Mountains haven't changed, so she'll still be here when you come back. Hiking passes are seven and camping is fifty."

"I'll keep that in mind, thanks."

She hands me back my credit card. "Now there are lookout points in all the best views, but the parking is pretty limited. Please don't park on the mountain road, it's not wide enough for people to go around you. And don't forget to stop for a drink at The Lodge. Lunch isn't half bad either."

I smile and nod along with her advice, tucking my card into my wallet and plopping it on the passenger seat. "Will do. Thank you."

She tips her head toward me with a smile. "Have a nice drive."

"Thank you, you too." A self-deprecating chuckle punctuates my words. It's one of those automatic replies but when you pause for a second, you realize it doesn't make sense. Like every time an usher rips the bottom half of your movie ticket and tells you to *enjoy the movie.* And ninety percent of the time, I reply with a "thanks, you too."

I pull away from the pay station and roll up my window. Those five minutes with it down were enough to steam up my car. I turn up the volume and pull down the visor to block some of the sunshine. Air conditioning hits me in the face, and I relax further into my seat.

It really is beautiful here.

The steep, sloping sides with faintly rounded ridges and peaks. They're a formidable sight, awe-inspiring and intimidating. I know from experience some of the trails wind up quite high in the mountains. Those aren't the kind of trails you want to take alone, but maybe I'll come back next week and do one of the easier trails.

Rich earthy browns and reds surround me, broken up with muted greens and grays from cacti and Joshua trees. Giant, sweeping peaks that seem so close but are really so much further away than you would think. There's a whole section of wild yellow flowers on the side of Griffith Peak.

The woman at the pay station wasn't exaggerating, the road is just big enough for two paved lanes with a small gravel shoulder on either side. Which is fine when we're relatively close to the flatland, but if I remember right, the road doesn't widen much as it winds around and around the Spring Mountains. It wraps around all the way to the top, where an adorable little lodge rests. I've been here dozens of times before. It was sort of a tradition to grab a basket of fries and sub sandwiches to celebrate whatever hike we had just completed.

Nostalgia and grief hit me with needle-like precision.

Will everything here remind me of them?

The house felt too big and too empty today, and no matter how much I told myself it's foolish to hope, the disappointment I woke up with today is all the proof I need. I caught myself staring at the house across the street one too many times.

Our houses face each other, not mirror images, just similar in the way most of the houses in this neighborhood are. It was almost muscle memory to look out my French doors, toward Cole's balcony across the street. Only instead of beige window treatments, they're pink.

Unanswered questions swirl around my head, and not for the first time, I shove them away. I came here to center myself again, feel the cooler air against my cheeks and appreciate mother nature and her grandeur.

Breathtaking, impossible views.

That's my destination today.

I've always loved being outdoors. There's something so peaceful about being outside, regardless of where we were living. The sun on my skin, the way the earth feels under my feet—it all grounds me, offers me a connection.

So I forced myself away from the French doors and packed a bag with snacks, swung through my favorite coffee shop, and drove here. It's a national treasure, and Charleston Peak is the highest mountain around for miles.

The Spring Mountains are gorgeous in the mid-morning light with deep narrow canyons and rising cliffs. The hillsides are steep, and the summits are sparse. Wind sweeps across my car, a big gust that whistles against the driver's side window.

My ears fill with pressure the higher I go, and I fight the nausea climbing up my throat. The elevation here is unreal, and considering New Jersey is barely above sea level, altitude sickness is a real thing. I reach into my bag on the passenger seat and pull out some pretzels to help curb the nausea.

I slowly drive past all the lookout points, planning to stop on the way down. Thirty minutes later, The Lodge comes into view. It's a brown A-frame with a bronze tin roof and classic log cabin style. The French doors are gorgeous works of art. Thick wood with intricate carvings done on both sides, stained with a color that only enhances the natural wood.

Twenty-five-foot ceilings and windows on as many walls as possible, it's the perfect spot to grab a bite to eat or something to drink and sightsee for miles. Cabins for weeklong rentals surround The Lodge, otherwise, the landscape is largely untouched. Meaning it feels exactly like you're camping in the middle of a mountain.

Pulling into one of the few open parking spots, I turn off the car and push open my door. Cool air blows against me, and the view takes my breath away. I can see for miles and miles.

From this vantage point, the world feels more infinite. Perspective rolls in like a soft wave coming to shore.

I am but one speck in the universe, and when faced with such naturally-made magnificent elements, it's much easier to remember that. It's a comforting thought, if not morose.

With that realization resting on my shoulders, I spin on my heel and cross the parking lot. The twisted metal handles are cool against my palms, and the doors are just as heavy as I remember.

I slide my sunglasses in my hair as a grin tugs up the corner of my mouth when I look around inside the oddly-shaped space. A giant three-hundred-sixty-degree wood-burning fireplace is the statement piece in The Lodge. It sits directly underneath the peak of the original triangle architecture. When it's lit, it kicks out some serious heat, which is necessary when the sun goes down—or when there's snow up here.

The steeply sloped walls are exposed horizontal shiplap, the light colored wood brightening The Lodge and making it feel much bigger than it is. There's a surprising amount of seating available with four booths along one wall and two-top and four-top tables sprinkled in the rest of the space. Plus, the bar on the opposite side of the booths has at least eight stools. It runs the entire length of The Lodge, and the kitchen is behind it, right through the swinging wood door in the corner. I remember the almost banquet-style seating in one of the two additions they built. Both rooms are off of the left side of The Lodge, each with a much smaller wood-burning fireplace.

A waitress with dark Dutch braids and a black tee pauses a few feet away from me with a serving tray of sandwiches balanced against her shoulder. "Hey, welcome to The Lodge. Take any table you want and order at the bar."

She's on the move before I can even respond, beelining toward a table of four in front of the wall of windows looking over the valley. I exhale a breath, accepting the onslaught of nostalgia that hits me when I look around. I woke up today and decided that if I can get through all the memories and nostalgia in a day or two, then I can move on. It's like they've had a chokehold on me for years, the closure nonexistent.

Hopefully, this helps me move through the bittersweet memories a little quicker. And pretty soon, I won't be reminded of *them* every time I turn around.

I weave around the mostly empty tables and pull out a stool at the bar and settle into it. The bartender is a guy probably a few years older than me. His hair is the color black that almost looks blue and it lays across his forehead in little waves.

"Hey, what can I get ya?" He leans his hand against the smooth lacquered bar top.

Settling my elbows on the counter, I scan the liquor bottles and beer on tap. "I'll just take an iced tea lemonade if you have it. Oh, and a lunch menu, please."

"Here ya go." He hands me a laminated menu. It's a small selection, only the front and back of one piece of paper. "Tara just got in, and she makes the best Rueben sandwiches if that's your thing."

My lips twist to the side at his enthusiasm. "I'll keep that in mind, thanks."

He raps his knuckles against the wood twice. "Sure thing. Let me grab your drink and give you a few minutes to look over the menu."

I peruse the menu with one hand and idly twirl the end of a lock of hair with my other. I half expect Sonny to slide into the stool next to me, but that's the kind of stuff that happens in a rom-com, not real life. And definitely not *my* life.

6

COLE

"ALRIGHT, man, finish up, and let's get going." I clap my brother on the back and scoot my chair back.

My brother flashes me a smirk. "Going to shit now so you don't have to dig a hole?"

I cuff the back of his head, and he dodges my hand but not quick enough. "Dumbass."

"Aw, c'mon, man. Lighten up. It's a gorgeous day, and we're enjoying a drink before we take in the great outdoors." He throws his arms wide, swinging them a little like he's showcasing the room we're in. An entire wall of windows lets the warm desert sun in, warming up the restaurant.

"Yeah, yeah. Just finish your drink, and let's get going." I push in the chair and walk toward the hallway just outside this room where additional restrooms are located. My shoes scuff against the aging hardwood floors, another reminder of the character of this place. It's a landmark, really. And we've been here often enough to have some of our own memories buried in these floors and walls.

There's a buzzing underneath my skin, a persistent itch that's preventing me from enjoying myself. West's right. It's the perfect day for a hike in one of my favorite spots. I'm off for the next five days, and I don't have shit planned, besides this.

A staycation sounded great in theory, but I can only sit on my ass for so long. Idle hands and all that. I almost went into work yesterday just for something to do. But who the fuck goes into work while they're taking vacation time?

Psychopaths, that's who.

Instead, I smashed an entire white sauce pizza from Freddie's and watched a bunch of true crime shows. Maybe that's the reason I feel off today. Too much pizza and not enough activity. I'm sure I'll be paying for it in a few hours on the trails.

A photo on the wall grabs my attention just before the restrooms, and my feet slow to look at it. My chest tightens at the five by seven photograph in the white mat and thick black frame.

West and I come to The Lodge nearly every time we hike Charleston Peak. How did I miss this?

It's a photo of the Spring Mountain Explorers from six or seven years ago. I remember that day. West had signed us up to join this adventure club that went all over the state—hiking and camping and all that kind of shit. My brother had his arm around me, his hair styled into this floppy cut that hung over his forehead. He had that look for years when we were growing up.

But my brother's haircut is the last thing on my mind when my gaze collides with the black-and-white smiling face of one of the few people I hate.

Only I didn't hate her then.

My thumb traces the glass over the edge of her face. I can almost hear her laugh as she leaned into me, giggling at whatever joke West had cracked.

Pushing thoughts of that day and *her* away before I let them take root, I expel a breath and push open the door to the restroom.

A few minutes later, I toss the wet, crumpled-up paper towel in the garbage can as I leave the restroom. The handful of steps down the hallway that spills into the dining room are torturous. I refuse to look over at her smiling face again, or worse, at the lovestruck expression on my face as I stared at her like she hung the fucking moon.

Our table is empty, not even the dirty pint glasses or the empty basket of homemade parmesan chips we shared are left. I bet West is at the bar, settling our tab.

We usually alternate who pays, something we started doing when we were kids, and now, it's just habit. The low din of chatter greets me just before I round the corner into the main restaurant. My feet slow for the second time in ten minutes. My mouth parts, and my muscles clench in shock. I feel my eyes widen as my blood pounds against my temples.

Fuck, am I dehydrated already? There's no way that I'm seeing clearly. No fucking way.

She stands in front of my brother like a fucking siren with her long hair in waves down her back. It's longer than the last time I saw her, blonder too, though it's hard to tell from this far away.

I don't bother calling myself on my bullshit.

I'd recognize the shape and shade of her anywhere.

She fucking etched herself on my goddamn bones and then fucked off, never to be seen or heard from again.

Feverish heat sweeps over me when she rests her hand against West's bicep and tips her head back and laughs, the smooth column of her neck arching in front of his face. It's such a familiar scene, it transports me back instantly.

Mia tips her head back and laughs, the joyous sound wrapping around my barren and bruised heart and squeezing it tight. The good kind of squeeze, like when I finally fucking passed Geometry and Mia threw her arms around me and murmured how proud of me she was. She was worried I'd be left behind in the sophomore class when they advanced to juniors like the rest of the kids in our grade. I didn't care about any of that shit. I never did. All I ever cared about was her.

And my brother.

And there was the problem.

I loved her. And so did he.

But I also loved West like he was my actual brother.

And I can't bring myself to steal her away from him, even if it means I don't get her either. Fucked-up situation for a couple of seventeen-year-olds.

She looks over her shoulder at me, her eyes alight with laughter and her hand wrapped around West's neck. She sits on the arm of the couch in her living room, some forgotten movie playing on her dad's new fifty-inch TV. "Aw, c'mon, Cole. You gotta admit that was quite the show at lunch today."

I tip my chin up and roll my eyes, an exaggerated move. "Of course, Mia. I always wanted to see Briggs's and Greenwood's bare asses as I ate my spaghetti on the quad."

She huffs a laugh and settles her feet across West's legs. "Yeah, that I could've done without, but still, those guys are assholes. It's about time karma started repaying that debt."

I flash her a crooked smile, the same expression my brother gives her. I don't particularly think she'd care if she knew the reason behind their impromptu streaking session today, but West didn't want to tarnish her image of him—his words, not mine.

The girl literally held him over a toilet last summer when we got into Wayne's expensive vodka. That shit was dangerous because it didn't have the same harsh burn as alcohol—it just tasted like peaches. West still can't look at peaches without turning green.

But whatever. He doesn't want to tell her that those assholes were spouting off about our girl, saying she was begging for their pencil dicks and charging like her ma allegedly did, fine. We took care of the problem, either way, like we always will when it comes to her.

7

COLE

I BLINK, the memory assaulting my senses with all the grace of a fucking rhino.

There's no fucking way West would be all smiles if he knew what she did. He wouldn't be wrapping his arms around her, he'd be pushing her away.

I clench my jaw as I watch them embrace like long-lost friends and worse, reacquainted lovers.

Fuck me, and fuck her for making me clean up her shit. Again.

I stop at the other end of the bar, where it's partially concealed and order a beer. The bartender doesn't engage in the typical small talk, and if he does, I'm too preoccupied to notice. I toss a bill on the bar and take a gulp of the ice cold beverage. The foam sticks to my upper lip, and I swipe it away with the back of my hand, my gaze focused on the tiny nick in the bar top.

Drinking too much before hiking is a bad fucking idea. It's a good way to get dehydrated, but just like everything Amelia Christensen touches, this day is already fucked. So what's a little dehydration if it helps me get through this?

Time skips, and I'm in front of her with no recollection of walking the length of the bar or finishing my beer.

Her back is to me, her arms thrown wide as she pulls back from another embrace with my brother. I refuse to think of him as a Judas, even though a small part of me does. I thought we were in agreement in our hatred of her.

But then again, he doesn't have all the facts.

Maybe today is the day I remedy that little oversight.

Anger bubbles inside of me, unfurling into indignation. My skin feels like it's vibrating as I work to control the emotions erupting inside of me.

How fucking dare she show her goddamn face here.

My brother's hazel eyes meet mine over her shoulder, but I shut out whatever he's trying to communicate with me. Even sitting down, she's smaller than both of us. He doesn't give anything away, focusing his attention on her once more.

"I can't believe you're here," she breathes out, her head tilting to the right.

"Here I am," West replies with a grin. His eyes light up as he drinks her in.

"Where do you live now? And Cole? How is he? I went to my grandmother's house—my house now, but . . ." Her voice trails off.

It's the opening I was waiting for. I twist a lock of her hair around my fingers, and my lip curls up at the softness. A myriad of blonde and even a little strawberry-blond mock me, wrapped around my knuckle. Fucking figures. Just another way to pull someone into her lies.

It's like slow motion when she turns around. My fingers hover in the air for a moment after her hair slips free from my grip. My gaze flicks up toward hers, and I lock it all down.

The anger and betrayal and even the spark of joy pulsing from my traitorous soul. Especially the spark of joy. I remind myself what she did, extinguishing the little flicker instantly.

Apparently not fast enough though.

I watch in fascination as her eyes go from wide and bright, her laugh lines winking at me with her mirth, to shuddered and damn near crestfallen.

She never could hide her expressions from me.

It's one of the reasons I thought she was genuine, but it wasn't until after that I realized she's a fucking master manipulator. She should teach a fucking class on acting and follow it up with a course on how to make people believe the lies you feed them.

She turns around fully and slides off the stool. "Cole. What are you doing here? I—"

I take a small step toward her, the toes of my tennis shoes just shy of brushing against hers, and rub another lock of hair between my fingers. I know she recognizes the move immediately. Good. I want the reminders of our past life together to haunt her. If I have to live with the memories of everything we shared, so should she.

Despite her fallen smile and halted words, her head tips to the side, and her eyes are open and inviting.

Adrenaline explodes like a cannon, rushing through my veins.

No. She's not going to bat her doe eyes with lashes that should be on a fucking Disney princess and feed me a bullshit line.

So I do the only thing I can think of—push her away before she can sink her claws into either one of us again.

"I think the better question is: What are you doing here? Still running away from your lies, hm? Or have you come back with a new sob story so people feel sorry for the poor little girl who's ma would rather get fucked by strangers for cash than be around her daughter." I deliver my acerbic gauntlet with a neutral expression, my tone even despite the thundering of my heart. It takes her a moment for her brain to catch up with the rest of her.

"The fuck, man?" West murmurs, but neither one of us looks his way.

She sucks in a breath, a wall slams over her eyes and they lose the sparkle they had moments ago. "Still an asshole. I guess five years hasn't changed that."

I rock back on my heels. "Nah, I'm telling the truth, baby."

She knocks my hand away from her hair, shuffles backward a step, and bumps into the barstool. In the corner of my eye, I see my brother stand up, effectively caging her between us.

She cocks her head to the side with a little self-deprecating shake of her head. "I can't believe I thought—"

"Thought what? You could roll back into town after five years of fucking crickets, and we'd what? Pick up right where we left off?"

The sunlight casts a square of light across us, highlighting the sheen on her blue-gray eyes. A smattering of freckles wink at me in the sunlight across the bridge of her nose. Her lips are bare, naturally dark pink and plump, and I can still recall the way they feel against my skin.

She's so fucking beautiful it makes my chest physically ache.

And not for the first time, I fucking hate her for making me hate her.

AMELIA

CRUELTY BLEEDS from Cole's words, sinking their hateful barbs into my skin and refusing to fall loose, no matter how hard I try to shake them off. It's such a shock, a terrible juxtaposition to the previous five minutes with West that it takes me a moment to register.

My eyes well up, and I bite the inside of my cheek to stop tears from descending down my cheek. I would rather eat my own tongue than let Cole Armstrong know he got to me. I used to scoff whenever someone told me they thought Cole was an asshole back in high school. He was charming and kind, caring in a way that made me feel seen, special. We kept to ourselves, the three of us. Only occasionally hanging out with bigger groups of people for parties and stuff. But even then, we spent almost all of our time together. I never understood the label they slapped on him.

Until now.

This version of Cole is nothing like the one I knew. Armed with secrets I told him in confidence years ago, he's wielded them like blades. And with only a handful of words, he's rendered me speechless. I can't even wrap my head around why he's so—so *angry*. But I don't think I'm going to get any answers from him now.

I clear my throat and drop my eyes to my shoes as I straighten the hem of my tank top. I allow myself three seconds. Three seconds where I swallow my disappointment like a bitter pill and level my expression out to something neutral.

"Ames . . ." West hedges, his fingertips skimming the back of my arm.

I jerk out of his touch but flash him a watery smile over my shoulder to lessen the blow. "You know where to find me. If you want to talk or whatever."

I glance at Cole from underneath my lashes, keeping my expression as blank as I can, and angle my shoulders so I can scoot in between them without touching either one. I don't think I could stand it right now.

It's been years since I've been this close to Cole. Since I've seen the endless depth of his dark brown eyes, the mini starburst of amber just to the left of his pupils. I used to see a future in his gaze, an impossibly unconventional one that included the three of us.

But that was the childish fantasy of a girl who believed in happily-ever-afters.

And with each day that passed in silence, she faded further into nothingness.

8

AMELIA

ONCE I CLEAR the initial wave of hurt, I can admit that I naïvely hoped I'd see them again. Maybe across the street or by some divine intervention—like The Lodge. Maybe I even subconsciously picked the Spring Mountains and The Lodge on a hail Mary.

And even with my volcano of hurt feelings I've buried under iced coffees and jokes, I was fucking excited to see West stroll up next to me at the bar.

Thrilled, even.

Everything I had thought about saying, all of the unrequited questions I was going to demand answers for went out the window when his hazel eyes landed on mine. His pouty lips tipped up into a disbelieving smile a second before he called my name. And the next thing I knew, the scent of soft linen and aged leather surrounded me as he pulled me into a hug.

But all of that turned sour minutes later when Cole strolled up and cracked me wide open for anyone to see and hear.

I used to think so fondly of my time spent in Las Vegas, conveniently forgetting the bad stuff and the way our friendship just ceased to exist, despite my attempts to reignite it. Those were the best years of my life. And I had thought coming back here would feel more like coming home.

But my brief interaction at The Lodge calls me out more than anything ever could.

The house on Green Tree Boulevard wasn't home—*they* were.

Time hasn't been kind or cruel, she's just taken more than her fair share from me. Aged me in ways I wasn't ready for without regard to my own needs.

But she's not beholden to the mere whims of a teenage girl, she simply exists. Taking more and more with each day you grow older, each commitment forced upon you.

Like uprooting your entire life when you finally, finally felt settled in. Found a place where you didn't simply exist, you thrived. I was cherished in Las Vegas once.

Cole's right. It was naïve of me to think I could waltz into their lives and act like it hasn't been years since we last saw one another.

There was a time where they both promised to call, to visit. Hell, Cole swore he would write to me, something I know he hated from English class in high school.

But all of my letters and emails went unanswered.

Except for one.

One letter that changed everything.

And after I mustered up the courage to call and explain, their phones were disconnected. A few weeks after that, I caved and wrote one more letter. I explained everything and begged for their forgiveness. I'd never meant to come between them, that's the last thing I ever wanted.

It wasn't until I met Alley that she helped me see that I didn't do anything wrong. I was vilified for something outside of my control, for having feelings. Real, deep, I-want-to-spend-the-rest-of-my-life-with-you kind of feelings. And those assholes blamed me for it, even though they were both complicit.

I take another deep inhale of air and trap it in my lungs for a few moments, exhaling all of the bad energy this trip down memory lane always brings. Birds chirp in the trees to my right, adding birdsong to this peaceful spot. A group of girls a few years younger than me park their little white car next to my SUV in the little five-slot parking lot. Their laughter is loud as they get out of their car, slicing through the peace like a hot knife in butter.

I don't mind the intrusion. I watch the four of them strike a pose, throwing their arms over one another, the canyon in the background. The two girls acting as bookends work together to steady the phone as they snap a photo.

A warm breeze rolls over me, bringing the scent of lichen, moss, and pine. I inhale, the scent familiar and comforting. The hair on the back of my neck prickles, and I sit forward on the bench. Tilting my head to the side, it hits me a moment later: the birds stopped singing. I look to the tree, but there's only the group of girls and me here.

Unease churns in my gut, and I push to my feet. I take a few steps closer to the girls, a warning on the tip of my tongue. Of what, I'm not quite sure. Something doesn't feel right. I check the sky—not a storm cloud in sight. It doesn't rain often here, but even the smallest amount of precipitation on the mountain is dangerous. These winding roads are paved and carefully constructed, but they're still thin strips of asphalt carved in the side of a mountain range. It doesn't take much to wash them out.

It's on my second scan that I see it.

It starts small, a stone, probably no bigger than a half dollar, skips down the side of the mountain. It rolls off a little overhang and lands with a resounding smack against the small parking lot, ten feet from our cars.

"Oh my god, that rock almost hit my car! My parents would kill me if I wrecked it. C'mon, let's get out of here," one of the girls nearly shrieks, anxiety coating each syllable.

A handful of small stones skitter down the side, following the first rock's trajectory. Foreboding weighs me down, sitting like a fifty-pound kettlebell in my gut. This—this could be a rockslide.

The terrible thought is enough to spring me into action, my muscles coiling tight as I run to my car. I'm a second behind them, all of the girls clamoring into their car just as a stone the size of a baseball slams into the parking lot, closer to their car than before. I watch with my hand on the driver's side handle as the driver throws it in reverse and speeds down the mountain. The screeching tires yanks me out of my stasis.

Horror leaks from my pores as I watch an entire rockface detach from up above and slide down the side. It breaks into smaller pieces with every tumble and obstacle it overcomes. I dive into my SUV, my nerves getting the best of me as I quickly reverse and throw it in drive. I go as quickly as I safely can, alternating between watching the road and glancing to my right.

I haven't decided if it would be better to see it coming and have the smallest head's up imaginable to speed ahead or focus on the road entirely and pray that a giant rock isn't going to push me off the mountainside, where I would undoubtedly roll until the bottom.

I don't see the white car full of girls in front of me, so hopefully that means they're just taking the road faster than I am. In fact, I don't see any cars on the road—small miracles. I can't imagine being trapped up here, a sitting duck.

No sooner than the thought crosses my consciousness, a giant boulder slips free from the side of the mountain and crashes into the road. I slam on my brakes, arms straight and strained as I brace against the steering wheel and narrowly avoid a head-on collision.

Sweat coats me head to toe as my blood accelerates loud and fast in my veins. It whooshes in my ears, drowning out my playlist that's pouring from the speakers.

That was close—too close. I've gotta get out of here.

I take precious seconds to ease around the boulder, my driver's side tires crunching against the hard-packed dirt of the nonexistent shoulder.

I fumble with the air conditioning knob without taking my eyes from the road, blasting cool air on my face. My adrenaline is pumping so hard, nausea swims in my belly.

Visions of Cole and West getting flattened underneath a boulder or trapped on the side of the mountain somewhere flash before my eyes. My foot eases off the gas pedal as the urge to find them pommels me. They're on foot somewhere on this mountain, West told me as much. The thought of either one of them getting trapped or worse under a rockslide has my heart clenching in fear.

I may not understand them, especially Cole, but nearly all of my fondest memories include at least one of them. I wouldn't be able to live with myself if I didn't at least attempt to find them.

Divine intervention strikes again.

Movement up ahead catches my attention. I flick my gaze quickly to the right, expecting to see another boulder careening toward me, but instead, I see two familiar faces.

9

AMELIA

COLE AND WEST stand on the side of the road, waving their arms above their heads in big, sweeping gestures. Dirt streaks their faces, but I don't see any obvious signs of hurt.

I ease off the gas completely and brake, stopping in the middle of the road as they rush my car. Cole dives into the passenger seat, and West slides into the back seat.

"Jesus, are you guys okay?" My voice sounds shrill even to my own ears.

"Yeah, we're alright. But if you hadn't stopped, I'm not sure we would've been. You saved our asses, Ames."

I hold in the flinch at his nickname, just barely. "Well, I'm glad to help."

Cole slips his backpack from his back and shoves it by his feet. "Drive, Amelia. It's not over yet."

I hit the gas and the car jerks back to life, my gaze on a constant swivel between the road, Cole next to me, and West behind.

The next moments are tense as more pebbles and larger rocks tumble from ten feet away.

"Our car is in one of the lots coming up, just another five minutes or so," West says.

Before we reach it, a group of four men yell and wave their arms around on the side of the road. My foot instinctively lifts from the gas pedal, but Cole reaches over the center console and palms my thigh, pressing it down. I don't know what startles me more: the electrifying way Cole's hand feels on my bare skin or the fact that he doesn't want to help. The whorls of his unique fingerprints brand themselves on the sensitive skin of my thighs, his hands large enough that his fingertips hit my inner thigh.

I swallow, my mouth drier than the Sahara right now. "We could've helped them." My voice is quiet but firm. My eyes stay glued to the road, my back ramrod straight and my hands aching from my tight grip.

Cole shakes his head from beside me, slowly lifting his palm. "They would've overwhelmed us and taken the car."

I cut him a glare before refocusing on the road ahead of me. A peek out the window shows the mountainside intact. Maybe we're on the other side of it and it's not falling apart? "You can't know that."

"Right now, it's about survival. Or did you forget that too when you left us without a backward glance?"

I ignore the ire in his snark. "Of course, I didn't forget. We couldn't hike here unless we took that safety course. But I don't understand what that has to do with helping people in their time of need."

West leans forward between the seats. "He's right, Ames. This is the only road in or out, and as much as I want to help people, I want to help us more. I saw at The Lodge that they're calling for a dust storm tomorrow, and we can't be caught up here when that happens. Not even our tents are good enough to keep it all out."

I roll my lips between my teeth and sneak a glance at Cole. He's silent, brooding out the windshield with his arms folded across his chest. It only highlights his biceps straining against the fabric of his tight black tee.

"Eyes on the road." His low voice snaps me out of it and just in time.

"Oh, shit."

"Faster, Mia."

"Fucking hell."

The three of us shout at the same time. Up ahead, a sheet of rock, dirt, and shrubbery slips down the side, heading straight for the road. If it lands before we make it through, we might not be able to get around it. It looks like Mount Charleston is falling apart, literally, from the top down.

"Go fucking faster," Cole snaps as he reaches up to hold the *oh shit* handle above his window.

"I can't go any faster. I'll run us off the road." Panic laces every word, my sharp voice piercing the air in the car.

"Yes you can. You're an excellent driver, Ames. Just pretend it's junior year, and we lifted Mr. Barber's keys. You're the getaway driver, remember? Cole and I would lay the pranks and you'd be idling in the parking lot, ready to whisk us to freedom."

The smooth tenor of West's voice calms me more than his dash down memory lane. It's low and right next to my ear, almost like I'm sitting on his lap, and he's whispering words of encouragement directly into my brain, soothing me.

I exhale and will my body to rely on instincts. I had them once before, hopefully it's like riding a bike and I pick it all back up. Quickly.

My fingers tingle, and I flex and tighten my grip on the steering wheel. I block it all out—West murmuring in the backseat and Cole grumbling next to me. The mountainside crumbling down around me and any possible people on the side of the road—everything but the narrow strip of road in front of me.

I know the guilt and terror will come later, but I don't have room for it in my very narrow tunnel vision right now.

I lose all concept of time. It could've been minutes or hours, I'm lost to the journey down the mountain that feels treacherous and narrower than it did when I drove up it.

"It's alright, Mia. You can ease up now."

My head jerks back at the feel of Cole's hand on my forearm. I blink several times, and a veil of awareness shudders over me. I try to release some of the tension in my shoulders when I realize we cleared the mountain.

I glance to the left and right before looking in the mirror. The sight behind me from the too-small rearview mirror freezes my muscles on instinct. My mouth parts, and I pull off the side of the road, quickly throwing the car in park. I twist around in my seat, coming face-to-face with West.

The familiar shade of hazel stares back at me, his pupils blown wide with exhilaration. For a moment, I'm teleported back to a different time, when we were all different people. When the days were never long enough, and the three of us were something much closer than neighbors.

My breath hitches, trapping itself somewhere within the low swirling of too many emotions in my gut. My adrenaline will start to wane soon, and any minute now, my fingers are going to tingle, nausea will climb up my throat, and stars will paint my vision.

Cole pushes open his door and steps out, turning to face the mountains behind us. I follow his lead and step outside too.

"Holy shit," I whisper.

From this angle, you can see the mountain shedding rocks and dirt like some sort of prehistoric snake is going to emerge from the center.

"Call Gray," Cole snaps.

"On it." West slides his phone from his pocket and brings it to his ear.

I tune out West's murmurs and slip back into the car. Distantly, I recognize the signs of shock, the midst of an adrenaline high. I'll worry about the crash later. All I want to do now is go home.

Cole settles into the passenger seat as West ends the call.
But first, I have to drop them off.

10

AMELIA

IT'S BEEN A TENSE, quiet ride. At first, I was wrapped up in my own panic, my anxiety flying high. I swear, those near-misses took years off my life. I kept waiting for the crash, but it's held off so far.

"It's the cream-colored house on the left. Pull into the driveway, and I'll open the garage door," West murmurs from the backseat. "You can pull in my open spot, since I have no idea when I'll get my car back."

I adjust my grip on the steering wheel and shift in my seat. "Oh, that's alright. I'll just drop you off and be on my way."

"Don't be ridiculous, Ames. Come in for a drink, at least. We're here, we made it, and we're okay."

The wind sweeps across the open plains, rocking my car and sprinkling a fine sheen of sand over the windshield.

I bite the inside of my cheek and nod, already going through excuses to cut out early. "Alright. One drink."

I pull into the three-car driveway of their house. It's a two-story Spanish style with a darker beige exterior and gray Spanish-style roof tiles. A few cacti line the small gravel bed in front of the big bay window facing the street.

It's hard for me to imagine them living in this house. All of my memories are tied up in a different house on a different street.

The car isn't even in park before West pushes the rear driver's side door open and hops out. Wind and sand rush to fill the car in an instant. I watch as West pulls the collar of his shirt above his nose and mouth and pushes the code in the garage door keypad. He ducks underneath the rising door and disappears from view.

Their garage door takes its sweet time opening, and with every second that passes, Cole's emotion swells. I still don't understand what the hell his problem is, but as the wind whips against my window, I shove my curiosity down further.

I have other things to worry about besides the volatile emotions of someone who won't even look at me after he laid me bare mere hours ago.

I ease the car into the space next to a white pick-up truck and shut off the engine. Cole pushes open the door on a grunt but otherwise, doesn't even acknowledge my presence.

I follow behind him, my gaze transfixed on the way this smear of dried mud creases and crinkles as the fabric stretches across his broad shoulders. My arms and legs feel strange, both tingly and tight and weighted down.

Shit. The telltale nausea that means my adrenaline is crashing churns in my gut. I need to sit down and maybe eat some carbs.

Lost in the hypnotic stretch of his shirt and my waning energy, I walk right into Cole's back. My nose smarts from the impact and his glare over his shoulder does nothing to ease anything.

"Sorry." My voice is quiet as I cover the end of my nose with my palm. Someone once told me that helps ease the sting.

"Watch it. And don't track in." Cole barely spares me a glance as he walks into his house. The fresh scent of laundry hits me the second we step foot inside the mudroom. A row of iron coat hooks take up nearly an entire wall, hoodies and jackets hanging from each one. Shoes line up haphazardly underneath, and I fleetingly wonder if they live here alone. That's a lot of shoes for two people.

I don't voice my question. Even if I wanted to rock the boat that is a closed-off Cole, I couldn't. My tongue stays frozen in my mouth as I watch with rapt attention as Cole reaches behind his head and peels off his shirt. Inch by inch, his smooth, tanned, and toned skin winks at me. If I didn't have that conversation at The Lodge with him, then I might be inclined to act on my lustful thoughts.

As it is, he hates me. I'm not sure his reasoning, but it's apparent that he doesn't think highly of me anymore.

Which suits me just fine. Mostly. Because I don't like him much right now either.

And unfortunately for both of us, my lust doesn't give a shit that he was a complete asshole earlier. She's ready to revel in the knowledge that we barely escaped death.

I decide no matter how deliberate it feels, there's no way he's putting on a slow striptease for me. He's probably thinking about his narrow miss on Mount Charleston as he pulls his shirt off and tosses it in the top-loading washer next to the dryer. The white machines take up most of the small mudroom space.

Without a backward glance, Cole leaves. I shuffle from foot to foot, weighing my options. The wind has picked up considerably in the last twenty minutes. It's not safe to go out in a dust storm, but it doesn't feel exactly safe here either.

No, that's not entirely true. Safe isn't the right word. I'm not sure I know the perfect word to describe the maelstrom of emotions swirling inside me right now. But most of them are uncomfortable, like a pair of jeans that's too tight around your waist.

I blow out a breath and do my best to exhale all the tension. The wind whips against the windows above the washer and dryer, making my decision for me. One drink, then I'm hightailing it back home before it gets windier.

I toe off my shoes, lining them up under the first hook. I almost feel bad about shaking out my hair and brushing the sand off my clothes, but then I remember the way Cole looked at me—the way cruelty wrapped around his words—and then I realize I don't care.

Much to my spiteful heart's chagrin, not much sand comes off. Still, I do my best to sweep across my clothes so I don't track it all over their house.

"Here. Thought you might be thirsty."

I look up at the sound of West's voice and accept the bottle of water from his outstretched hand with a small smile. "Thanks."

The tips of our fingers overlap, both of us holding onto the ice-cold bottle for longer than necessary.

He smiles, and déjà vu hits me square in the gut. It's the same smile he aimed my way years ago. Every time we riled up Cole, snuck out after curfew, laughed too hard at whatever stupid movie we snuck into.

He was a smiley kid, always friendly and kind. I used to joke that he had to be extra sweet to make up for Cole's sour demeanor. But in all the years we hung out, I never saw him give this smile to anyone else.

This one was reserved just for me.

It's been years since I let myself consciously think about the gaping hole they left. How my world dimmed, their absence leaching laughter and joy from my life.

The loss of it feels overwhelming, and not for the first time, I wonder why they never looked for me. Why they only sent one measly letter.

He tips his head to the side. "C'mon. I'll show you around first and then we can grab that drink."

The sound of his voice stutters my thoughts back to the present. I twist the lid on the water bottle and take a deep pull. Like his words willed it into existence, wind whistles against the siding of their house, a soft whooshing noise from the sand and debris.

Their kitchen is bright and airy with white cabinets, shiny chrome appliances, and a mini white and gray quartz island. Three wrought-iron-style stools are tucked underneath the small island, with an overflowing bowl of fruit in the middle. An espresso machine sits next to a black blender underneath the cabinet by the sink, and nostalgia seeps in my consciousness.

Cole has been drinking espresso since he was sixteen. I wonder what else is the same about them.

"Here's the kitchen, then our dining room table, the living room," West gestures around with his hands as we walk the long expanse of their open-floor plan.

Their table is a perfect square, blonde oak and well-loved. A little flowering cactus in a small gray pot acts as a centerpiece, and gray cushioned chairs are pushed in around each side.

I catch the words *Mount Charleston* and *landslide* from the news anchor on the huge TV in the living room. West pauses behind a black leather overstuffed sectional and reaches over to grab the remote control.

My steps slow next to him, trepidation whipping around inside my ribs like the sand beating against the house. I chalk it up to the entire day.

He presses a few buttons, and the news anchors' voices fill the living room.

"An unpredicted rockslide occurred at the Spring Mountains today. Rescue personnel are en route, reporting the mountainside roads sustained some severe damage and the main roads may be blocked. This leaves any weekday hikers possibly stranded overnight." The news anchor tilts her head to the right, quiet for a moment. "Alright, I'm just receiving word that a sizable dust storm is imminent. For more information on that, let's talk to our weatherman, Raymond Slater."

A guy with too-white teeth smiles at the camera for a moment before he steps to the side. His navy-blue suit blends into the blue background for a split second before the map appears behind him.

"Thank you, Chelsea. So as you can see here, we're under a wind advisory for the next seventy-two hours. There's a supercell storm sweeping in from the west, which is pushing thirty-to-forty mile per hour winds with gusts up to fifty-five miles per hour." He gestures to the screen behind him in a sweeping upward arc. "The dust storm warning should end in about twenty minutes, so if you're planning to run some errands today, I'd recommend waiting until this evening when it settles. Now, if the storm cell shifts, we'll likely see rain tomorrow, maybe the day after, but otherwise, stay tuned to JSN weather for more updates."

I don't realize the tension coiled in my muscles until a commercial for a sporting goods store comes on, the volume twice as loud as the weather. Shit. I need to call Dad.

"Damn. If we get a lot of rain, we're going to flood," West murmurs.

"Oh, yeah. I'd forgotten about that." Flash floods are a real thing here, and it's one of the scariest things I've ever experienced.

He looks at me over his shoulder, a small smirk playing along the corners of his lush lips. "How soon you forgot, huh, Ames?"

My heart stutters for a moment. The smirk is a distraction, and it does its job well, momentarily distracting me from the ice coating his words.

"I never forgot you. Either of you." My voice is low but unyielding.

He holds my gaze for a moment, his smile slipping into a more serious expression I used to see on Cole's face. He nods, the movements little and slow as he pushes off the back of the couch. "I'm going to go shower this shit off, so make yourself at home, yeah?"

I bite the inside of my lip. "Thanks. I'll be out of your hair as soon as this"—I hook a thumb over my shoulder toward the window—"calms down a little. I'm just going to call my dad."

West walks backward, the playfulness back. "Oh yeah, and how is Papa Christensen? Still chasing stars?"

I smirk. "Something like that."

He pauses inside the doorway, his hands braced on either side of the doorframe. His flexing biceps distract me for a moment. "Hey, Ames? It's really good to see you again."

Warmth settles over me like a heated blanket, but he pushes off the doorframe and walks backward out of view.

"It's good to see you too," I murmur, a private, giddy sort of smile tipping the corner of my mouth.

11

AMELIA

THE NEWS STATION comes back on, the anchors speculating the best places to watch the upcoming meteor shower. I take a few steps toward their sliding glass door when my phone vibrates in my pocket. My screen lights up with my dad's smiling face, and I swipe to answer it.

"Dad?"

"Amelia? Oh thank god. I've been trying to call you for thirty minutes!"

I pull short at his tone. He's never been the warm and affectionate kind of parent, but he's never snapped at me like this before either. He has more of a hands-off approach, leaving me to do my own thing most of the time.

My shoulders hit my ears with his reprimand. I'm twenty-two years old, and nothing makes me feel smaller than my father's disapproval.

"I'm sorry. I didn't have service. I went for a drive to Mount Charleston—"

"You went *where*?" His voice hits an octave volume level I've never heard before.

The hair on my arm stands on end. "What's going on? I've been to Mount Charleston before."

"Yes, of course, but I just got word that there was a rockslide that trapped hundreds of people." Rustling comes over the line, muffled voices in the background.

My shoulders settle down into a neutral position again. He must have the news on too. "I know. I drove through it, but I got out okay. But, Dad, I was going to call you because the wind is getting bad out here. It looks like there could be a bad storm heading your way. The news is calling for a wind advisory and possible flooding."

"A little wind and rain are the least of our worries," he mutters over some rustling. "Are you home now?"

I fiddle with the cap of the water bottle, running my fingertip over the small grooves along the side of the cap. "No, I didn't make it home yet. I . . . ran into some familiar faces, gave them a ride home. But I'm somewhere safe."

"Good, that's good. Listen closely, Amelia. When the dust settles, which shouldn't be more than a half hour now, you need to get home and pack."

"Pack?" My brows lower over my eyes as I stare into their backyard without really seeing anything.

"Yes, grab your camping backpack and pack everything you'd need to camp for a couple days—no, a couple weeks."

My mouth dries with each hurried word in my ear. "I don't understand."

Sounds quiet on his end of the line, punctuated by the slam of a door. It's quiet, just the two of us breathing and existing together, much like our entire life. "I need you to listen carefully because what I'm about to tell you seems far-fetched and paranoid."

I lick my lips and unconsciously turn toward the corner of the room. My shoulders roll inward, and I mentally brace for whatever my father is about to say.

He's a man of science, I remind myself. He's not prone to hysterics. He's almost unflinchingly even-keeled.

"We came out to the desert to capture the meteor shower, that much is true. But my team and I have been working on a theory that this meteor shower, the one that's set to breach our atmosphere, is the one Frederick Burton wrote about hundreds of years ago. It's been a topic of contention for years in the industry. How can someone predict something that will happen hundreds of years after they die? It doesn't seem plausible, right? While Burton's journals have been meticulously preserved, and—"

"You're freaking me out, Dad."

"Yes, of course. Sorry, I'm getting off track. Look, Amelia, I don't know if he actually saw the signs all those years ago and predicted this change or if it's all coincidence. You know I don't believe in divine intervention, but I'm inclined to start. Because what we have concluded with enough certainty is that the coincidences are lining up, and—"

"Dad." His name snaps out like a whip, interrupting him again. If I wasn't so on edge, I might feel shitty about it.

He breathes into the phone. "Finem omnia, Amelia. Finem omnia."

"Is that Latin? I don't know what you're saying."

"It's the end, Amelia." His voice rises, not quite yelling but close.

I don't have his restraint or his even temperament, and my frustration and anxiety boil over. "The end of what?"

He's unfazed by my yelling, which speaks more to his preoccupation than anything. "Everything. Or almost everything. We don't know for sure. But what we do know is that this sort of apocalyptic end was written about in Burton's journals. It starts with the meteor shower, which itself is nothing spectacular, as you know the Earth passes through some of the same meteor showers every year. But the exceptionally high winds across the globe—and our impending dust storms. The mass rock slide of Mount Charleston. All of these things on their own are manageable, but together they point to something else."

"I don't understand, Dad! I'm not a science whiz like you are, so break it down for me. What are you saying? That the world is just —what? Going to end because of some wind and a rockslide?"

If my father had ever shown any interest in any mind-altering substances, I would think he took peyote while on his trip to the desert. Considering the most he ever indulges is the occasional brandy while he reads science journals for fun, there must be another reason.

"No, of course not." His voice cracks through the speaker, but it does nothing to hide his panic. "I'm saying all of these things have been laid out for years and years. And if we're to believe it, next will be these big supercell storms, earthquakes, hurricanes and tornadoes, and eventually, volcanic eruptions."

I choke on an inhale. "*Volcanic eruptions*?"

"Yes, Amelia. I know how it sounds, but listen to me. This is serious. In three days' time, the DHS will be sending out alerts to everyone who has been chosen. We are on that list. That's all you need to know for now. I'm sending someone to get you. The earliest he can get there is two days. From there, you're going to meet me."

My mind spins and nausea claws up my throat. "Chosen?"

"Jesus Christ, Amelia, listen to me!"

My dad's voice screeches in my ear, and tears prick my eyes. "Dad, are you . . . okay? Who's with you right now?"

"Oh for Christ's sake, I'm not crazy. Here, talk to Jerry."

There's some rustling on the phone before I hear my dad's partner's voice. "Amelia, sweetheart?"

Some of the tightness in my chest eases at the familiarity of his deep baritone. Jerry's more than a work associate, he's Dad's best friend. They've been friends since high school, went to college together, and started working for the same private sector. Him and his wife, Cheryl, have moved around the country alongside Dad and me. They cheered me on at my high school graduation, toasted every holiday with us, and even helped out when Mom left. He's like family, and I know I can trust him.

"Jerry. What's going on? Is Dad okay?"

I've never worried about my dad's mental health before, but the man lives and breathes science. I can't even fathom some of the theories he's worked on in his career. And I know he works for the government, but this seems . . . impossible. Unfathomable.

Crazy.

He sounds fucking crazy.

Jerry sighs, the noise loud in my ear. "Hal's alright. Even though he's trying to hide it, he's scared. Mostly for you. He made sure they would send someone for you before he even confirmed our findings."

"Who's they? Your boss?"

"This one came from the top, sweetheart. All of this is on the government's dime. They're taking it seriously, so I'm inclined to follow their lead. And right now, they want us on that ship or in their bunker, so I figure, worst-case scenario, we all take a couple of long drives to the west coast, maybe check out the digs on a fancy ship."

I lick my lips, my throat drier than the desert outside. "And the best-case scenario?"

There's a beat, a moment where my disbelief and confusion swell into something larger than I can feel in my body. Hope grows against my will, this tiny kernel reminiscent of childhood that begs for someone to tell me everything is going to be okay.

"Jerry, are you still there?"

"Yeah"—he clears his throat, this gruff, familiar noise—"I'm here, sweetheart. Listen, we gotta get going, so get yourself packed, and we'll call you tomorrow with the exact meet-up point, okay?"

Disbelief floods me. "So it's real then? This-this prophesy or whatever that the world is going to go to hell in a handbasket?"

Jerry chuckles, the warmth in his laugh eases my nerves. I feel like I'm a mass of live wires, writhing around inside and snapping at one another.

"It sure seems so. If it'll pan out like Burton says, that remains to be seen. For now, we're doing what they tell us."

"Okay." My response sounds hollow even to my ears.

"Get home and get packed. We'll call you tomorrow with an update," Jerry repeats.

"I-I can't. There's a dust storm right now."

"That's alright, just wait until it passes, and then go home." He's endlessly patient, his voice a melodic rhythm.

"Go home, get packed. Got it. Talk to you tomorrow." Dad and Jerry just info-dumped on me, and I'm struggling to process everything.

"Stay safe, sweetheart." Jerry ends the call.

12

WEST

I LEAVE Amelia in the living room and round the banister, taking the stairs two at a time to the top. Frenetic energy hums under my skin, from hiking *and* Amelia. There's a pep in my step, and a giddy thrill zips through my nervous system. I bet I can get her to stay for dinner. I'll ask Cole to make something, he's always been the better cook, and maybe dinner turns into after-dinner drinks on the patio. And if I'm lucky, maybe I can convince her to swim with me, for old times' sake. Our pool isn't as big as the one we had growing up, but it's plenty big for the two of us.

A smile stretches across my face by the time I reach the second floor. The rockslide was unprecedented, but it pales in comparison to Amelia Rose Christensen sitting in my living room right now.

I hear the plumbing kick on, the gentle whooshing noise coming from down the hall—Gray's bathroom. When I called him from the car earlier, I didn't divulge all the details, just told him the plan changed, and Cole and I were heading back home. I neglected to tell him we'd be bringing a guest.

And I forgot to tell Amelia we have a roommate too.

Shit.

Damn, I'm off my game today. Seeing her sitting at the bar was like a punch to the gut. I lost my breath and a weightlessness lifted me above the ground, I swear it. She's the one that got away, and I don't give a fuck if that makes me sound like a sad sap. It's true.

I let her slip through my fingers all those years ago, and I'll be damned if I let it happen a second time.

It didn't matter how many girls I flirted with in school, she never got jealous. She never staked her claim on me, no matter how desperate I was for it. She was always unflinchingly content to spend her days with me *and* my brother.

And maybe that's where I went wrong.

If I want Amelia for myself, then I need to have a little chat with my brother. And there's no time like the present.

I stalk down the hall, slipping inside Cole's room. His door is open, so he must've been expecting me. He steps out of his closet, straightening the hem of a green tee and glaring at me.

"Spit it out already."

I send the door toward the frame with a flick of my wrist. I don't think Amelia can hear us over the TV, but I don't want to take any chances, not with the bullshit Cole spewed at her at The Lodge.

Damn, that feels like a week ago, not a few hours.

I lean my hip against his dresser and look at him. "She's here, and she's not going anywhere if I can help it. So back off, yeah? Don't be such an asshole."

He scoffs. "Should I be more like you? Pretend we're seventeen again and so far up her ass we can't see the sun? Follow her around like lost dogs, begging for scraps? "

My eyebrows reach for my hair, and I whistle below my breath. "Damn, Cole. Don't hold back on my account."

His frown smooths out. "What do you want from me, West?"

I purse my lips and examine him. There's more here, something he's not telling me. I lift a shoulder. "Play nice, Cole. That's what I want."

He glances toward the door and pastes on a fake smile. "You

wanna play pretend with the princess before she abandons you —*again*? I won't stop you."

I roll my eyes. People always assumed that because I'm the outgoing one, the one who's quick to offer smiles and start friendly conversations, that Cole was the mellow one. When truthfully, the man is more dramatic than the local theatre group. "Yeah, well, maybe I wanted to get reacquainted with this new version of Amelia. It's been five years, man."

Cole tips his chin up, a muscle in his jaw clenching turning his fake smile into more of a grimace. "I won't be here to clean up her mess when she fucking bolts again."

I can count on one hand how many times I lied to my brother. Growing up the way we did, our word was everything. We had so few people who stood by their word—and Amelia used to be on that very short list. A sliver of guilt wedges itself between my ribs as I look at my brother in the eyes and lie to him again. "Fuck, Cole. I'm not talking about wifing her. Just a bit of fun, maybe some reminiscing."

A low, cold chuckle floats across his pristine room. "Yeah, okay, brother. You forget that I had a front-row seat to the two of you."

I bristle at his insinuation. "We were kids then. All I'm saying is it might be nice to see her again, get to know her and where she's been for the last few years. And if it leads to more, then . . ." I trail off, the implication clear.

The groaning sound of the water cutting off interrupts us. Damn. I need to take a lightning-quick shower if I want to beat Gray downstairs. He's notorious for taking his time getting ready, so if I hurry, I should be able to do it.

"I'll see you down there," I murmur, pushing off the dresser. I tap the inside of the doorframe twice as I leave, a little habit we picked up when we were kids.

I'm not worried about Gray, not really. We've been living together for years, and outside of Cole, he's the only other person I trust implicitly.

But he has a tendency to walk around in gym shorts and nothing else. And I don't want Amelia to get startled.

Sure, that's the only reason why you don't want Gray and Amelia to meet without you there, a snide voice murmurs in my mind. It sounds a fuckton like Cole.

I rush through the quickest shower known to man and throw on the first clean shirt and shorts I can find. Five minutes later, I'm in the hallway, and Amelia's voice drifts up to me. Her voice is shrill, panicked maybe. I'm bounding down the stairs before I think twice. I grab the box newel post and skip the last stair, rounding the foyer just as I hear Amelia muttering.

"Go home, get packed. Got it. Talk to you tomorrow."

13

AMELIA

"PLANNING A TRIP, AMES?"

I jump at the sound of West's question and spin to face him. The volume buttons dig into my palm as I squeeze my phone.

West reaches me in two long strides, and with a hand barely skimming my lower back, he guides me toward a stool at the island. "Shit, Amelia. Are you okay? You're pale. Here, sit down."

I slide onto the stool, the metal of the back cool through my cotton tank top. My mind whirls around in circles, and with every beat of my heart, the same message pounds against my skull.

Get home, get packed.

Home, pack.

I grip West's wrist, and his brows slant over his hazel eyes, they're leaning a muddy green right now. We're close enough that I can see the light brown flecks. His pupils dilate as his gaze flickers between my eyes.

"What is it, Ames?"

"We have to go, West. Right now. As soon as we can."

"Go where?" Cole asks.

My head whips to the hallway where Cole and another man

stand in the frame. I exhale a whoosh as I lock eyes with the third man in the room.

A very familiar pair of dark brown eyes, his hair laying across his forehead in waves, lighter in the daylight. A dark blue tee stretches across his chest, and I bet if I closed my eyes, I can still feel his touch on my skin.

It's a shock, to be sure, but maybe my synapses are all fired-out from my phone call with Dad and Jerry, because instead of freaking out, I'm strangely relieved.

"Hey, Cher. You come here often?" His face splits into a boyish grin as he feeds me the same line from a few nights ago.

My lips spread into a smile before I even think about it. "Is that the best you got, Sonny?"

Cole steps in front of Sonny, blocking my view of half of him. He folds his arms across his impressive chest, and my gaze snags on the way his shirt stretches along his pecs and shoulders. I never would've pegged Cole as a gym guy, but with the way he's unconsciously flexing, I bet he's there four times a week. I reel in my interest, reminding myself he was an asshole only hours ago.

"You two know each other?" His words crack in the air around us.

Sonny steps around Cole, never taking his gaze from mine. He crosses the room to stop in front of me, palms flat on the island between us. He leans in and smiles, those dangerous dimples of his popping. "Cher and I go way back. Ain't that right, baby girl?"

"*Baby girl*?"

"What the fuck is going on?"

Cole and West talk over each other, but I don't tear my gaze from the man in front of me. My grin widens as I tilt my head a little to the right. "I thought we agreed *baby girl* is played out."

"One of you better start talking right the fuck now," Cole snarls.

"Gray, what the hell, man?"

Sonny—Gray, I guess is his real name—bends his elbows, bringing his face closer to mine. If he wanted to, he could easily bridge the small gap between our faces in a heartbeat. I don't move an inch either way. My nails dig into West's arm, which I distractedly realize I have hold of still.

He clucks his tongue, the noise mischievous. "I seem to recall no objections were made the other night when I was—"

Cole clamps a hand on Sonny's shoulder and wrenches him backward. "You better watch your fucking mouth."

My head snaps to the fury in Cole's voice, and my ire rises up like the tide. I push to stand, letting go of West's arm and pointing an accusing finger in Cole's direction. "You don't get to play knight in shining armor. Not anymore. Not after the way you spoke to me at The Lodge." I don't bother bringing up the biggest transgression.

A barrier slams over Cole, his body practically vibrating as emotions simmer behind his eyes. I've never known him to hold his tongue on anything, so I'm surprised he's doing it now.

Sonny shrugs off Cole's hand. "So, Cher, tell me how you know my brothers here."

"Brothers?" I choke on the word and look between Cole and Sonny.

"Foster brothers," West murmurs. "But I'm more curious about this." He waggles his index finger between Sonny and me. "So you two know each other?"

"No."

"Yes."

Sonny and I answer at the same time, but I'm still staring at West.

West purses his lips. "Well, which is it?"

Sonny swipes his thumb across his bottom lip, his stare holding a hundred questions, none of which I can answer now, even if I wanted to. "Would a rose by any other name smell as sweet?"

I clutch my phone in my palm, the bite of the buttons grounding me. I rake my teeth over my bottom lip, his sweet, flowery words reminding me of all the poetic words he whispered in my ear as he fucked me hard. It was a carnal juxtaposition.

"What the fuck?" Cole whispers.

"Aye, we've met," Sonny says.

The TV switches back from its commercial break, the news anchor's voice snagging my attention.

"We've just received a video from the rockslide at Spring Mountains from earlier today. We want to urge parental discretion, as I'm told it's unsettling."

Shaky footage fills the screen, people yelling and rocks sliding down the mountain like innertubes on the ski hill back in Jersey. Whoever is filming starts running, and the camera wobbles, blurring the mountain coming down like some abstract version of the horrible events.

It's surreal to think we were *just there*.

The weatherman from earlier appears on screen, Raymond something or other. "Pardon my interruption, Michele, but we have a new development. The winds should slow down a bit, dropping from forty-five to thirty, but only for a short time. A supercell seems to be moving this way, so expect the winds to pick back up. A tornado watch has been issued for the area, starting in the early hours tomorrow and lasting through the evening. Stay with us here on JSN for all your current weather needs."

My heart stutters at *tornado.* Jerry's words beating against my skull.

"We have to go—*I* have to go."

"What's going on? You just got here," West says.

I push off the island and take a step back. I hold up my phone and wiggle it a little. "That was my dad—and his partner. He's—he's sending someone to pick me up"—I smooth my eyebrow with my free hand and try to remember what he said—"tomorrow or the next day, I—he's going to call me and give me more information." I look away from their probing gazes for a moment. "My dad's a geological scientist."

"A what?" Sonny asks.

I bring my gaze back to them and roll my shoulders back,

stuffing my mounting anxiety. "He works for the government, homeland security, I think. He studies meteorology, seismology, volcanology—stuff like that. And he just called and told me . . ."

"Told you what, Ames?"

"Look, it sounds fucking crazy, but my dad, he's sending someone to pick me up, to meet him and Jerry and his wife. We're being taken somewhere safe. Orders come from the top."

"The top *of what*?" Cole asks.

I stare at him. "The White House, I would imagine."

Cole scoffs. "Bullshit."

I lift a shoulder and nod. "I know how it sounds. But this is what my dad does for a living, so if he says we're in trouble, then I'm inclined to believe him." I bite the inside of my cheek and release it just as quick. "And I think you should come with me. All of you."

14

AMELIA

MY CHEEKS PINKEN as the moments stretch between us. I shift from one foot to the other, but I don't lower my gaze or take my words back.

Sonny slips his hands in the pockets of his athletic shorts. "Tell me what else your dad said."

He looks at me without judgment, his posture relaxed. It doesn't feel like he's patronizing me, but that's not the only reason I tell him. If Dad and Jerry are correct, and we're heading into some apocalypse, I would never forgive myself for not trying harder to get them to come with me.

"First the dust storm, then supercell storms, earthquakes, hurricanes, and tornadoes. And eventually, volcanic eruption."

There's another weighted pause, the air impossibly thick as I laid down the order of events. I lick my lips and explain further.

"The DHS—Department of Homeland Security—will send an automated text with coordinates to everyone who has been chosen. From there, Jerry suspects a bunker or some kind of naval ship, but I'm not sure. He said worst-case scenario, we'll road trip west."

"And best-case scenario?" West asks.

I roll my lips inward and shrug, shaking my head a few times. I don't know what to say, so I don't say anything.

"Alright. Let's go," Sonny says, nodding a few times.

"Really? Just like that?"

He looks at me. "Yeah, Cher, just like that. Your dad—he's an expert?"

"One of them, I suppose."

"Good enough for me. Let me pack some shit, and we'll head to your house until your dad calls."

Cole side-eyes him. "You're not seriously believing this, are you?"

Sonny looks at Cole and tips his head toward me. "I trust her."

"You barely know her." West narrows his eyes at him.

Sonny looks at me, his expression serious. "I know enough. I'm going to grab some stuff. Don't leave without me, yeah?"

"I won't, I promise. Jerry said to bring camping gear, I'm not sure if you have any."

Cole scoffs, but I don't let it bother me. I hold Sonny's gaze for a moment so he knows I mean what I said. He turns around and leaves the kitchen. The stairs creak with his weight as he runs up them, and then it's just the three of us.

West raps his knuckles on the counter of the island. "Alright, I'm in too."

"You can't be serious," Cole yells.

"Come with us, man. Let's say Papa Christensen is right, then what? You'll be trapped here, *alone*, when a fucking volcano or some shit buries you? That's how you want to go out?"

Anything I say will only be met with resistance, and I'm not going to let Cole's stubbornness kill him, even if he is an asshole now.

Three tense seconds later, he nods. "Fine. We'll go. And when this all turns out to be a big fucking joke—"

"Then you can throw it in my face with all the other bullshit you seem hellbent on hurling at me," I snap.

Cole storms out of the kitchen and stomps up the stairs, presumably to pack.

West steps closer to me and grasps my hand. "Wait here, okay? We'll go in fifteen minutes."

Some of the tension leaves my shoulders, and I let them drop a little. "Alright. I'll wait. But West?"

He shuffles closer. "Yeah?"

"I have a bad feeling. Las Vegas is a basin, if we get too much rain or worse, a flash flood, we'll be trapped here."

He throws an arm around my shoulders and curls me into his chest. I haven't been hugged by anyone other than Alley in too long, and I haven't been hugged by West in even longer. It feels good. Comforting and like I'm coming home. I bury my nose into his chest, inhaling his crisp clean smell.

"It'll be alright, Ames."

Even if my dad's predictions are wrong, there's a mountain of unspoken things between us still. But even that takes a backseat. I soak in his comfort, wrapping it up and reveling in it.

I pull away and give him a halfhearted smile. "You better get packed."

His fingertips trail down my arm and linger on my fingers for a moment. "I'll be right back."

THIRTY MINUTES LATER, the four of us are pulling out of their driveway. Sonny sits in my passenger seat, his big duffel bag in the trunk. West rides with Cole, who insisted on driving himself. I'm glad he took Dad's warning somewhat seriously, if their over-stuffed backpacks and suitcases are any indication.

My SUV is no match for the increased wind pushing against the driver's side, and I tighten my grip on the steering wheel to keep us from swerving in the other lane. The sky darkens, but it seems more from the sun setting than storm clouds rolling in.

I split my time making sure Cole's car is still in front of me and keeping up with the heavy traffic. There's a line just to get in the parking lot of the grocery store to our right. People must've heard about the upcoming tornado and flash flood watches. There's always a mad dash to the grocery store whenever inclement weather is on the radar, regardless of the city or state.

But we're in the middle of the desert. Most houses have a water filtration system in their refrigerator for tap water.

So whenever we get these watches or warnings, people flock to the grocery stores.

And water is always the first to go.

I worry my bottom lip at the thought.

I clear my throat. "We might need to make our own grocery run soon. Dad and I only moved in a couple days ago, and I don't have much. Plus, we might need some things for the road."

"Alright, Cher. We'll get it sorted with the boys when we get to your place."

I chance a glance at Sonny, his quick agreement easing some of my nerves. I'm not so worried that I miss how good he looks in my passenger seat though. He swapped his gym shorts for black utility pants, the kind that I know I have in a box somewhere. They're lightweight but warm and more pockets than you would think are possible. I make a mental note to hunt for those boxes first. A dark blue tee hugs his chest and biceps, and a backwards black baseball hat holds his hair off his face.

His olive green hiking backpack is wedged down by his feet. It looks stuffed full.

"So what did you, uh, pack?" I drum my fingers against the steering wheel, a staccato rhythm.

He rolls his head along the headrest and looks at me with a half smirk. "What does one pack when they're told it might be the last time you see your room, your bed, and your house? That this could be the end of everything as we know it."

I pull the inside of my cheek between my teeth and hold it for a moment. "I don't know."

"I don't either." He reaches down and pats the top of his backpack a few times. "But the boys and I hike often, so I had this ready to go. Your dad said camping gear, right?"

I nod, the low churning in my gut picking up speed. "Yeah. I don't know why though if we're supposed to be meeting him and going on some ship or in a bunker."

"I could hazard a guess. In here I have a compact sleeping bag and roll, a couple changes of clothes, some toiletries, my favorite jacket, my lucky water filter, headlamp, sunscreen, energy bars and a little food, satellite phone, my Swiss army knife, a few maps, though I doubt we'll need those. My duffel has more of the same, plus a tent that folds down into a small square."

My brows hit my hairline as the anxiety swells and sloshes against my insides. "My camping backpack is considerably . . . *less*."

"That's alright, Cher. I'm excellent at sharing."

I'm not sure if the innuendo is there or if I'm reading too much into it. I slow the car behind Cole's SUV, stopping at a red light. I can't control the fluttery feeling inside my chest now. It feels like the wings of a bird flapping in between my rib cage.

"Why are you doing this, Gray?"

He clutches his chest in a faux injury. "Ouch, *Cher*, pinning me with the real name so soon?"

"I'm serious. Why are you here?"

His brows slam over his eyes, his smile dropping. "Why wouldn't I be?"

"Because I'm a stranger, and you're—you're just picking up your life on a whim based on the word of a *stranger's* father."

"I trust you, Cher."

A flush settles over me. I feel like I'm being chastised, but it's a valid question. "You don't know me." I keep my voice even.

Sonny drags his thumb across his bottom lip, pausing in the

middle for a moment before he lets it slip free. "Nah, that's not really true though. Is it, Cher? We know each other well enough."

"We had *sex*, Gray. That doesn't mean shit when it comes to actually knowing someone," I snap. I don't know why I'm needling him. I'm flushed and anxious, and I don't know what the fuck I'm doing, but I can't stop. My breaths are coming in too quick, and my mind is swirling around too fast.

"Pull over."

"What?"

"Pull over, Amelia." Sonny's voice is authoritative, and before I even realize it, I'm on the side of the road. I throw the car in park, my chest heaving.

"What about Cole and West?" I hush out between breaths.

"I don't give a fuck about them right now. You're my priority."

He reaches over and pushes the hazard light button in the dash, and a second later, the amber-colored lights blink on. His hand slips down by my hip, and my seatbelt immediately loosens.

His warm palm comes to the back of my neck, and with the barest hint of pressure, he turns me to face him. I shift, tucking my right ankle under my left knee. His eyes look lighter up close, like a rich cup of coffee with lighter swirls of amber. His full lips part, and he's close enough that I feel the puff of breath against my lips. "Breathe with me, okay?"

He inhales and exhales to the count of three, never breaking our connection. On the second pass, I join him, and three rounds later, my chest isn't as tight, and the overwhelming feeling of worry isn't as heavy.

As if we planned it, we both lean forward, resting our foreheads together. My shoulders drop their tension, and I close my eyes against the onslaught of tears.

"I'm sorry," I whisper.

"Nothing to be sorry for." His voice is quiet like mine.

"It's just . . . I don't know what I'm doing."

"No one does. We're lucky that we have a head's up, even if it's only a few days' worth."

"I'm selfishly dragging three people with me on this—this wild *goose chase* from my dad because the thought of all of you dying feels like someone's ripping my intestines out. I mean, how fucking crazy is it that we're even having this conversation." I pause and wet my lips, the sad truth a weight on my tongue. "And I'm terrified if I didn't ask, I would end up dying alone. But I'm being selfish, and it just occurred to me that you all probably have other attachments that you'd rather spend your possible last days with."

"Aw, Cher, if you wanted to know if the boys had girlfriends, all you had to do was ask."

I can hear the smile in his voice, but I don't open my eyes. Not yet.

His thumb sweeps back and forth over my neck. "And as for me. I think you already know that answer."

My lips quirk up in a smile without my permission. I roll my forehead against his a little, putting our mouths closer together. "Tennessee Pete's was some of the most fun I've had in years."

"Of course it was. You spent the night with me. And I'm not even talking about the many hours I was in heaven between those gorgeous thighs."

My cheeks pinken, and I open my eyes. "Cocky much?"

We're too close to see anything clearly, but his eyes were already open. His other hand comes up and tangles in the ends of my hair, tugging on it gently. "Confident, Cher."

I pull back a little and roll my eyes. "Whatever you say, Sonny."

"There she is," he murmurs, not letting go of me yet.

I still and look at him, my heart racing again.

"I meant what I said earlier."

"About what?"

He smooths a piece of hair behind my ear. "About you. I know enough about you. Whether it's fucking crazy or not, you're saving us. If the DHS does end up sending out texts to the chosen ones like we're in some fucked-up movie, you really think three punks who aged out of foster care are on that special list?"

The denial is on the tip of my tongue, but I swallow it down. I know he's right, just like I know that if I wasn't my father's daughter, there's no way my name would be on that list.

Determination lines my gut. "If there's a list, I'll do everything I can to make sure your name is next to mine." He nods a few times, his brows dipped together. I resist the urge to smooth them out with my fingertips. "And Cole and West too."

15

WEST

"WHERE ARE THEY?"

I run my hand over my head, threading my fingers through my hair and tugging on the ends. The small sting grounds me. "Probably got caught at a red light on Calla Vista Boulevard. I swear those lights are longer on purpose just to stop those assholes flying through the residential streets that wrap around the city."

Cole cuts me a glare, his brows low over his eyes. "You got a problem with my driving all of a sudden?"

"Nah, man. I don't. Stop projecting your bullshit attitude on me." I huff and slouch in the chair a little.

"I don't have a bullshit attitude," he mutters. "I just can't believe we're doing this."

I tip my head back and look at the ceiling of my brother's black SUV. "Can't believe what part? That there's an apocalyptic natural disaster shit storm headed our way or that we're with Amelia again?"

I always knew I'd see her again, but never in my wildest imagination did I ever envision this scenario. And fuck did I imagine some crazy shit for when we saw each other again. I feel the goofy grin on my face, and before my brother can call me out on it, I wipe it off.

His gaze narrows on me before he relaxes his expression. "Can't say I'm not surprised."

My jaw clenches together, and even though I tell myself to let it go, I'm too stubborn to listen to my own advice. "About what?"

He looks at me, his expression free of scorn or anything else I expected to see from his surly tone earlier. "If you knew who she really was, then you'd never entertain the idyllic fantasies I know you've been constructing for hours."

Everything inside me freezes, my muscles clench and the very blood that flows in my veins, dams up with his words. "What do you mean?"

His lips twist to the side, and he glances out the front windshield before bringing his gaze back to mine. "There are things you don't know about her, man. Things that . . . might change your perspective."

"What kind of things?" A bead of sweat collects on the back of my neck, and I force my muscles to unclench.

There's no way he knows, I remind myself. No way. He's not good at playing the long game, never keeps secrets from me.

Well, except for one.

But he doesn't know that I know.

Right?

Hesitation crosses his features, bunching up his eyebrows and twisting his lips to the side before they smooth out. If I would have blinked, I would have missed it. The back of my neck flushes, and I angle the air conditioning vent toward my face as the silence stretches.

He blows out a breath, his cheeks puffing, and he readjusts his faded blue baseball hat. "Nah, nothing man. It's just a lot can change in five years. You know? A lot can change." His last few words are quiet, like they're meant more for him than me.

I exhale as quietly as I can and nod a few times to myself,

looking out the window to buy a few seconds. No sign of Amelia's SUV yet.

Now I know he's keeping something from me. But if I push him, then he might push back. And a confrontation with my brother is not on my agenda today. I have plans to win back my girl.

So I fall back on bullshit stereotypes.

"Yeah, like the world ending? That kind of change?"

Cole slowly tilts his head to glare at me, as if to say *really*?

I force a grin on my face. "Too soon?"

He shakes his head a little. "To joke about the untimely demise of civilization? Yeah."

My smile morphs into something more authentic. "Ah, so you're a believer now, yeah?"

He messes with his faded baseball hat, slipping it from his head to roll the brim into a U shape between his fingers. "I don't know what I believe anymore."

I don't know what to say to that, and I don't feel the need to fill the silence. Music quietly plays from the speakers and I try to relax.

He sighs and drags his palm down his face. "What the fuck are we gonna do if her dad's right? Let's say all this shit happens just like he said. There's no way her old man is gonna let us weasel our way into some government-secured ship. Then what?"

Panic slithers around in my gut, and I can't decide if it's from the idea of dying in some supercharged earthquake or being separated from Amelia so soon after I found her again.

"Then we figure it out. We'll have each other. And Gray. And we'll get through it just like we have been for the last ten years."

The quiet hum of a car punctuates my promise, and a second later, Amelia's dark SUV pulls into the driveway. I bypass my hiking backpack and grab my duffel bag from the backseat, pushing open the door and hopping out quicker than it takes to blink. Urgency pounds at my joints, pushing me to get to her before my brother opens his mouth and sours my mood further.

Amelia slides out of the passenger seat, and I reach her before she even clears the trunk. I scan her from head to toe. Flushed cheeks, glassy eyes, smile a little watery.

Something's wrong.

"How come Gray's driving?"

"I convinced her to do a fire drill at a long red light," Gray says as he rounds the back of her SUV with his backpack slung over his shoulder.

I reach out to her, my fingertips grazing her arm. "Everything okay?"

She glances from Gray to me before she nods, a small smile on her perfect, plush lips. "Yeah, I'm fine. Sonny was very . . . helpful. Come on, I'll let you guys in."

Gray parked her SUV on the left side of their two-and-a-half-car garage, leaving plenty of space between the front bumper and the shelves against the wall. Rows of boxes take up the rest of the garage, some stacks three boxes high.

I don't understand how the fuck a fire drill prank is helpful but alright. That reminds me. "How did you two meet again?"

Amelia pauses with her hand on the doorknob of the mudroom door and looks over her shoulder, a coy smile tipping up the corner of her mouth. She jerks her chin to the sea of boxes to our right. "Sorry about all the boxes. My dad had them put most of the boxes in here until he can get to them, because, well, you'll see."

Gray bounds the three steps and slips inside, but I can't make my feet move just yet. She evaded my question. Again.

"What do you make of that?" Cole pauses next to me, his shoulder brushing mine.

I roll my lips inward for a moment. "I'm not sure. C'mon, let's go inside."

As soon as I cross the threshold, familiarity brushes against me from all sides. It looks exactly the same as it did the last time I was in here, right down to the outdated calendar hanging above the little key rack next to the mudroom door.

The ancient washer and dryer that I used to sit on top of while Amelia scrubbed at stains over the laundry room sink. The girl used to be insane about keeping her all-white Vans clean.

The four-seater marble top island in the middle of their kitchen where the three of us ate too many meals together to count—most of which Cole cooked. The silver stovetop camping coffee maker that Cole bought and kept here because he couldn't stand the taste of the watered-down drip coffee from the pot her dad had.

Even at sixteen, he was a pretentious fuck about coffee. Age has only made him settle in his ways more.

"Damn," Cole whispers from next to me. He's surveying the room with the same nostalgic expression I'm sure I'm wearing.

"Yeah." I clear my throat a couple times. I wasn't anticipating this feeling of unbalance. It feels like, if instead of my SUV, I had to drive a go-kart. The mechanics are similar in theory but nothing is the same as you're used to.

"I thought you said you just moved back. This looks pretty lived-in." Cole raises his voice so it carries to Amelia and Gray in the living room.

Her hair slides off her shoulder as she looks back at us. "We did. Dad left a lot of things here when we moved. Most of the furniture was my grandma's, anyway."

"What are all the boxes in the garage then?"

She lifts a shoulder. "More of our things—including my measly hiking gear."

"I told you I'd share, Cher," Gray says.

She flashes him a genuine smile and my gut tightens.

She bumps her shoulder into Gray's, but she's facing us. "Thanks. I'm going to shower first, but you guys are welcome to help yourselves to anything. The fridge is pretty bare, so we might want to think about getting groceries if the weather holds."

"Don't worry about us, just take your time. Cole will find something for us to eat."

"You sure?" She tugs her bottom lip into her mouth, her brows dipping together as she looks at Cole.

He lifts a shoulder. "It's fine."

A genuine smile spreads across her face. "Alright then. There's a spare bedroom upstairs, and one of you can take my dad's bed. They both need new sheets, which should be in a box somewhere. But one of you will have to take the couch." She hikes a thumb over her shoulder.

"That's not a problem, Cher. We'll figure it all out, you go take a shower."

"You telling me I stink, Sonny?" She flashes him a playful glare, and fuck me, but I want her eyes on *me.* Not my best friend.

"Nah, you know how I feel about you," Gray murmurs.

What the fuck is going on.

"Let's see what she has." Cole claps me on the shoulder and steers me around, toward the kitchen.

It's an olive branch, and after all the many rounds we've gone with life today, it feels like a fucking win.

He shoulders off his pack and sets it on the floor by the table, beelining for the refrigerator. I follow suit, and when I turn around, only Gray stands in the middle of the living room, fiddling with the remote control.

I blow out a breath just as the fifty-inch TV comes to life, a news station reporting the weather.

16

AMELIA

I TOSS and turn for the tenth time in as many minutes. It's quiet—too quiet—and this mattress doesn't feel familiar anymore. I can count on one hand how many times I've had insomnia in my life. The feeling is as foreign as it is unsettling.

I've been trying to sleep for hours now.

After I took a shower hot enough to melt the skin off my bones and washed my hair twice, I pulled on some jean shorts and an old tee and walked downstairs. Cole, West, and Sonny were working together in my kitchen in a way that only highlights their familiarity.

Cole made tuna melts for us—the gourmet kind that had cheese, sun-dried tomatoes, artichoke hearts, grilled onions, and a few other things that tasted delicious. I'd forgotten how good of a cook Cole is.

Or maybe I'd blocked it out when all the thoughts of him and West made my heart feel like it was trapped in a vise.

The news played in a loop in the background with the volume low as we all ate around the island. Conversation was superficial, and even though West tried to drum up more and more things to talk about, I was too tired to offer much.

Exhaustion fell heavy on my shoulders like a weighted blanket. And after the millionth time I yawned, I reminded them where the linen closets were and excused myself to my room.

As soon as I crossed the threshold, my exhaustion fled.

Or more accurately, every time I closed my eyes, the laundry list of things I need to find and pack by the time we leave flashes across my consciousness. I'm nervous about forgetting something, and the worry is keeping me awake.

Sonny was right. What are you supposed to pack when it's possibly the end of the world?

My chest deflates with a sigh. I toss the comforter and sheet off and swing my legs off the side of the bed as I sit up.

I need to make a list.

Lists always make me feel better, like I'm in control again. And the accomplishment high I get when I cross things off my list is unmatched.

I welcome the cool air against my bare legs, my oversized tee pooling around my hips. I reach over and flick on the small lamp on my nightstand. A low ring of yellow light illuminates my room.

It's a time capsule of seventeen-year-old me in a lot of ways. The furniture, the window treatments, the paint color—it's all the same as it's always been. I was never the kind of girl who put up pages torn from a magazine on my walls, but I did keep stupid mementos from over the years. Concert ticket stubs and a few photos are still tucked into the frame of my mirror above my dresser.

It's sweetly nostalgic, and for once, it doesn't hurt to think about my life here.

I cross my room and slip my fingers under the vintage pull handles of my six-drawer mahogany dresser. It's one of those that requires a specific amount of pressure and holding it *just right* to jimmy the drawer open. It was my grandma's when she was younger, and even though Dad offered to replace it with something new ten years ago, I never let him.

After a few back-and-forth shimmies, the top drawer finally opens. A stack of pretty notebooks, some small notepads, neon sticky notes, but no pens. I shuffle things around, but I don't even find a lone pencil.

I bet Dad's desk has a bunch of pens and pencils and probably even a few fancy fountain pens, but it's a veritable minefield in there. One misstep, and a mountain of files and books and loose papers will tumble down. Dad's organization skills are specific to him, and he'd be able to tell you exactly where everything is.

But there's no way I could replicate it if I knocked something down.

Okay, that just leaves the junk drawer in the kitchen. I don't think we cleaned that out when we left, so that's my best bet.

Clutching my phone in my hand, I pad down the hall and tiptoe down the stairs, avoiding the three creaking stairs. I pause in the mouth of the hallway where it opens up into the open layout of the first floor, the wood floor cool against my bare feet..

I shake my head a little, my hair flutters around my shoulders, wild from hours of tossing and turning.

He's just one boy.

Well, man, now, I guess. Though if I could look back on my time with them here, there wasn't much boyish about either one of them, other than their age. I suppose living through tragedies will do that to any kid—age them up.

But still, he's just one man. And he's in *my* living room.

I exhale a breath and remind myself that he's most likely sleeping. It's the middle of the night, and I'm being ridiculous.

And when the little voice inside my head reminds me that Cole is a night owl, I brush it aside and slink into my kitchen.

A soft white noise machine plays in the living room, but otherwise, it's quiet. I think if I strain my ears, I can hear the deep rhythm of his breaths.

A pang of longing hits me so hard in the chest, that a gasp tumbles out before I can stop it.

How many nights did I accidentally fall asleep listening to the cadence of his slow, even breaths while a movie played in the background? Cole shared my love for '90s cult classics, and they both entertained my every movie request, never shooting my suggestions down.

I press a hand between my breasts, pushing the fabric against my skin and shuffle over to the little bank of drawers next to the stainless steel French-door style refrigerator. I tap the flashlight app on my phone and pull the top drawer open. The contents practically spring open once it clears. Takeout menus, old receipts, notes with Dad's jagged script, loose keys, extra garage door openers, a few random magnets, the school year calendar from junior year. Everything makes that shuffling sort of noise as I rifle through it, digging to the bottom.

"Damnit," I whisper.

"What are you looking for?"

I jump and whirl around, a shriek lodging in my throat. "Jesus, Cole, what the hell? I thought you were asleep."

He holds up a hand to shield his eyes from the bright light of my flashlight. "I was, but you're loud as hell. You always have been terrible at sneaking around."

The tips of my ears are warm as I lower my phone. "That's bullshit. I was always the best at sneaking around."

The asshole smiles then, and I can't decide what's more irritating his insult or the stupid sexy smirk on his face. He nudges me with his shoulder as he steps next to me.

"What're you looking for at two in the morning?" He wraps his hand around mine, angling my phone so light shines inside the drawer again.

My mouth parts, and I'm sure I'm doing my best goldfish impression right now. But what the hell is going on?

I study his profile in the glow from the digital display on the fridge next to us and the soft glow from the flashlight. His strong jaw and the bump in the bridge of his nose that I know is from Tim Perkins in sophomore year. And again in junior year.

"You're staring." He's quiet, but his words lack any real reprimand.

"Why are you being nice to me?"

He tilts his head, his hair falling across his forehead. It looks darker in this light, darker than it was five years ago, like maybe he doesn't spend his days lounging around a pool anymore. His gaze is open, and his face is free of the scowl he's worn since we reconnected. "Is this nice?"

"You're right. This isn't nice, it's just not complete asshole either. And before you get all worked up about it, I'm not complaining. Just confused." And waiting for the other shoe to drop.

"A ceasefire then," he murmurs.

My head tilts to the side, and my eyes narrow in suspicion.

He straightens up and pivots so our chests are aligned. "It's been a long day, and I couldn't sleep, so let's not make it a bigger deal than it needs to be, yeah?"

I pull the corner of my bottom lip into my mouth.

"Don't worry, Amelia, when the sun rises, it'll be like this never happened."

He delivers his promise of contempt with such a soft tone that my breath catches. I might hate myself for it in the morning, but the idea of pretending we're not at odds is too great. Being here, with him, has sent me in a tailspin, longing and loneliness warring with one another.

I nod, my decision made. "I couldn't sleep so I thought I'd make a packing list for tomorrow."

He moves some highlighters around and scoots a few flyers to the left, uncovering a little pad of paper and a pink felt-tip. He holds it between his index and middle finger. "Like this?"

I snatch it from his hand, and for a second, he doesn't relinquish it. We hold each other's gaze, a million things unsaid hovering between us.

"Thanks," I murmur, my voice barely above a whisper.

The air rumbles, and it takes me longer than it should to realize it's not a physical manifestation of our unresolved past brewing between us.

It's thunder.

Chills race down my spine at the audible reminder of what's possibly at stake. I shift from foot to foot, the cool air conditioning wafting up to curl around my legs from the vent to the right of us.

"Maybe I should start packing now, instead of waiting until the morning."

Cole turns to look over his shoulder, the windows above the kitchen sink are behind us, their blinds flipped up. "I'll help you."

"You don't have to do—"

"Don't. We're in a momentary truce, so take the help." He turns around to face me again. "Unless you want me to wake up Gray instead. Or West."

His dark eyes hold me captive, the gauntlet growing between us. I relax my face, working to lower my brows and shoulders.

"There's no sense in all of us being awake."

He smirks, this little half smile of victory that infuriates me as much as it turns me on. "Perfect. Where's all your hiking gear? Let's start there."

17

AMELIA

I PLUCK a pair of soft cotton shorts from one of my boxes in the back hall and wiggle them up my legs with my back turned to Cole. I slip on my favorite pair of sneakers and look over my shoulder to find his gaze on me. His brows are low over his eyes, but he doesn't give anything away. He never has, so I don't know why I thought he would now.

There's something almost mystical about the dead of night. The horror films always paint it as a fearful time to be awake, but it doesn't feel like it to me. It's the witching hour, when everyone else is tucked safely in their beds. It's a time rife with possibility. Where the lines get blurred and inhibitions are lowered simply because there's no one around to bear witness.

I wet my lips and turn away from his perusal, opening the door with one hand and flicking the light switch on with the other. Yellow overhead light illuminates the two-and-a-half car garage.

I scan the space and will myself not to get overwhelmed by the sheer amount of stuff in here. The stacks of square moving boxes take up most of the available space in the middle and shelves loaded down with boxes and bins line the three sides. Dad was never much for holiday decorations, but my grandma was. There are boxes in here somewhere that haven't been touched in years.

And if Dad's right, they'll never be touched again.

"Let's get started," Cole says from my left.

I scoot over a step and watch as he beelines for the shelves on the left side of the garage. He searches through a plastic chest of drawers and pulls out a box cutter.

Nostalgia squeezes my heart at Cole's familiarity. A cold, damp sort of melancholy settles around my shoulders, the feeling at odds with the warm temperature here.

What if is a dangerous game, one I try not to play too often. It only ever leads to heartache. Blame the witching hour or the possible devastation on the horizon, but I can't stop myself from wondering what would have happened had I not had to leave Las Vegas all those years ago.

Oblivious to my internal freak-out, Cole mutters to himself as he walks toward a cluster of boxes. I take it as my cue to get to work. I start with the stack on the opposite end from him.

I turn the box around completely, but I still don't find any words scrawled on the cardboard. Grabbing the edge, I rip it open and see Dad's clothes. The next three boxes are all label-less—and full of Dad's clothes.

I roll my eyes and step over to the next stack of boxes. I don't know why they aren't marked with a room or person, at least, but it makes this so much harder.

After another five minutes, Cole straightens up and glares at me.

"Jesus Christ, Mia. Why didn't you label any of this shit?"

"I didn't pack this," I snap, ripping open another cardboard box. We're in a sea of cardboard and packing tape, half-opened boxes littering any available space.

"What does that even mean?"

From the corner of my eye, I see him stand up and slam his hands on his hips, his body angled toward me.

I pull the tape back on another unmarked box and flick open the flaps. More of Dad's books. I tuck the flaps into one another and push it to the side with a huff. I straighten up and turn to look at him.

"It means that Dad hired a moving company to pack us up and then drive all of our belongings a thousand miles across the country. So other than the shit I personally packed and drove in my car here, I have no idea where anything is."

He glares at me, his brow low over his eyes. "So you don't even know if it's in one of these boxes?"

"No, I don't know," I snap at him. "But if it's not in one of these"—I shove a box with the toe of my sneaker—"then it's lost. And that means I don't have the *one thing* Dad said I *needed*. Which *means* that I'm totally screwed."

I naïvely thought that Dad would make sure all of this was handled the right way, but I should've known better. Dad has always—*always*—been wrapped up in his work, and he's had a foot half out the door for the last three months in Jersey.

No amount of mentally kicking myself will help me now. I tip my head back to look at the ceiling, letting the annoyance and frustration roll off of me. The sound of the rain tinkling against the roof catches my attention in the quiet between us.

After a moment, I look back at him. His expression is a weird mash-up of annoyed and sympathetic.

"Look, I appreciate the help, but you don't have to stay out here. I can handle the rest of the boxes on my own."

He folds his arms across his chest, drawing my gaze to the way his traps flex underneath the worn navy blue fabric. "We're almost done."

The wind picks up outside, whooshing through the night. Something bangs against the house, a loud crash that has me jumping a foot into the air, my heart hammering against my ribs.

I clench my hands into fists and look toward the closed garage doors. "What the hell was that?"

"Probably a cardboard box or something."

I lick my lips and relax my hands, my gaze still stuck on the little windows in the garage door. The rain falls in steady streams, turning my little glimpse of the neighborhood into a distorted version of itself. "Yeah, Mr. Birchwood's recycling probably blew over again."

It doesn't sound very convincing to me, but he doesn't say anything further, just leans down and rips open another box. Lightning twists across the sky, highlighting the neighborhood. I count the Mississippis in my head, a childhood game that never quite left me.

Ten Mississippis, so two miles. The storm is still two miles away.

Something flickers outside, movement or light or something I can't quite make out from here. In my peripheral vision, I see Cole push another box to the side and haul a new one toward him, but I don't take my gaze from one of the small windows in the middle of the garage door.

I step over a box, weave around another three, and scoot by a stack three-high, stopping right in front of the window. Cobwebs and long-dead gnats stretch across the bottom corners, but not even that stops me from pressing my face as close to the glass as I can get without physically touching it.

"What are you doing?"

"I thought I saw something." I let my voice trail off as if I could spook it over all the noise the wind and rain make.

Boxes shuffle across the concrete, punctuated by Cole's grumblings, but just two seconds later, Cole's standing next to me. "What did you see?"

"I don't know. Maybe nothing. But when the lightning lit up the sky, it looked like people were outside."

Saying it out loud feels like I'm giving credence to my fear. I wait for Cole to call me out, but he's silent next to me. I cup my hands around the side of my eyes, shadowing my vision from the garage light a little. But it's no use, it's too dark outside, and the rain doesn't help anything.

Like Mother Natures is listening, another bolt of lightning streaks across the sky. This one larger than the first, lighting the sky for longer too.

One Mississippi.

I suck in a breath. I hadn't imagined it. The neighbors across the street, two houses down, are outside in the pouring rain. They're ushering things from their house to their open car—suitcases, duffel bags, even a laundry basket full of something.

Two Mississippi.

"Who leaves in the middle of a storm?" Cole whispers.

Fear climbs up my body, starting at my ankles and slowly inching higher and higher.

Three Mississippi.

Foreboding raises the hair on the back of my neck, and nausea churns in my gut, a sure-fire sign my adrenaline has kicked on.

"Do you think"—I have to pause to swallow over the knot of unease—"do you think it has anything to do with what my dad said?"

Four Mississippi.

"Nah, it's probably just a coincidence. Let's just get your stuff, yeah?"

Five Miss—thunder crashes through the air, lifting the hair on my arms. It's so loud, the house rattles a little around us, the stuff on the shelves clinking together.

"One mile," I say on a hushed breath.

"What?" I feel his gaze on the side of my face, and we're close enough to touch.

"The first lightning strike was two miles away, and this one is one mile. One mile in a matter of a minute. The storm is getting closer, and it probably means it's getting bigger and—"

"That's not how that works, remember? The Mississippi counting game we did as kids isn't entirely accurate. Thunder is the sound of a nearby lightning bolt, but just because it's less Mississippis, doesn't mean the storm is getting worse. It's just lightning striking closer to us."

I turn to glare at him, and even though I knew we were close, I wasn't prepared for it. The tip of my nose nearly grazes his chest, close to his collarbone. I rear back a step and his eyes flare. "Since when did you become a meteorologist? And besides, that only proves my point that the storm is getting closer. And probably bigger."

He's looking at me with this soft expression on his face, the kind of thing you do when talking to someone freaking out. "Hey, it's alright. It's just a storm."

Another bolt of lightning streaks across the sky, this one even closer and brighter. It lights up the whole neighborhood for three whole seconds.

"One Mississippi," I whisper just as thunder rumbles. It's an all-encompassing sound that fills the garage, rattling the things on the shelves and shaking the garage door. The wind shifts, sending raindrops sideways against the door, the pinging noise reverberating in the open space.

"Cole." My voice is shrill, exposing my fear. I reach toward him, my fingers curling into the soft fabric of his tee just as the lights go out, plunging us into total darkness.

18

AMELIA

I SQUEEZE my eyes shut and spring them open again. Darkness still greets me, her arms open, her touch sharp.

But tonight, the darkness feels different. It's as if light has been yanked out of thin air, smothered by shadows.

The absence of sight only heightens my other senses. My fingers clutch Cole's shirt tighter, fisting the material until my knuckles rest against his chest. The hair on the back of my neck stands straighter, and my lashes won't stop fluttering. It's both hopeful and futile, like one magical blink, and suddenly, I'll be able to see again.

Despite the rain pounding relentlessly against everything it touches, the lack of sound is louder. Little things that you've built into your auditory library, so commonplace that you don't recognize it until it's gone. The low hum of the empty refrigerator in the corner, the gentle whirring of the air conditioning blowing through the vents, the ticking from my grandma's wall clock.

Even though I'm in the garage, I know they're not contributing to the usual cadence of the house.

And it's deafening.

"C'mon, Mia. Let's see if we flipped a breaker or something."

I don't loosen my hold on his shirt. "No, look. The houses across the street are all dark, even their porch lights are off."

He leans toward the window, looking left and then right. "Huh, okay. We'll let's go inside and call the power company, see if they can give us an ETA."

A second later, a beam of light from his phone shines on our shoes. It takes effort to uncurl my fingers from him, and if I didn't think it would ruin the tentative peace we have right now, I'd lean against him. Instead, I follow behind him as he weaves around the opened boxes.

I can't explain it. I've never been afraid of the dark or anything like that. It has to be a twisted response to all the stuff Dad said.

Before we reach the single cement stair to the mudroom door, it opens. A deliciously sleep-rumpled Sonny stands in front of us, his phone flashlight angled down. The athletic shorts are low on his hips, and I lose all train of thought at the sight of all that tan, tattooed skin on display. His muscles look bigger than I remember, which is impossible considering I *just* saw him days ago. Maybe I wasn't paying enough attention then.

But I am now.

"Cher? Everything okay?"

I close my mouth and nod. "The power went out."

He steps back and to the side to let us walk past him. "Seems to be raining pretty good."

"That's what happens when there's a severe thunderstorm," Cole snaps, his back to us as he storms into the living room.

Sonny glances at Cole before looking back at me. "What were you guys doing out there?"

"Cole was helping me look for all my gear. Apparently, the moving company didn't label anything."

Sonny sucks his teeth as he closes the door firmly behind me. "Damn. Want another set of hands?"

"Sure."

"No," Cole says at the same time.

Sonny leans over and mock-whispers, "Is this some kind of foreplay for you two? This back-and-forth, hot-and-cold thing."

I jerk back a step. "What? No."

"Absolutely not," Cole barks. "Mind your own business, Gray."

Sonny purses his lips before they twist into a smirk. He lifts a shoulder, his eyebrows rising too. "Methinks doth protest too much, but, eh, what do I know?"

His smile is almost conspiratorial as he winks at me. "C'mon, Cher. Let's take another look at those boxes."

I look in Cole's direction, though without any light, I can't see much. I don't know if I was waiting for him to protest, but whatever it is, he doesn't give it to me.

"You don't have to. We can wait until the morning," I hedge.

"Nah. I can't sleep when it's too quiet. Might as well stay up now." He tilts his head to the side and holds his arm out. "Shall we?"

A crackle splits the air before I can take a step toward him. It's loud, kind of like static on a radio. My heart skips a beat as I turn toward the little speaker Dad keeps on the kitchen counter by the mudroom.

I cross the room and stop in front of the small radio and cock my head to the side. "Did you hear that?"

"It sounded like—"

The TV in the living room blinks to life, cutting off Sonny's response.

"What the fuck?" Cole murmurs. "Is the power back?"

Before the last word leaves his mouth, I hear the gentle whirring of the air conditioning and hum of the refrigerator. "I guess so."

Sonny crosses the room and flicks open the blinds above the kitchen sink. "I don't see any light out here."

"Then why is the TV showing that static snow like it lost a signal?"

I hustle into the living room, hunting for the remote controls. "I don't know."

Static noise blares from the speakers, louder than I know the volume was at earlier. My shoulders reach my ears, and I wince. Cole points the remote control at the TV, smashing the volume down button, but it doesn't change.

"What the fuck is that noise?" West asks from behind us.

That recognizable ear-splitting noise that precedes an emergency message crackles through the speakers. A series of long tones and short beeps. The sequence elicits fear, a sharp sort of terror skittering over my skin.

"The following message is from the Nevada emergency system. Stay indoors if possible. Severe weather is expected to impact the state over the next few days."

The same pattern of tones and beeps sounds before the automated message repeats itself twice more. No one says anything until it stops.

And like we're unwilling stars in a paranormal movie, the power dips the moment the message is done.

My fingernails scratch against the fabric of the couch cushion clenched in my fist. The hair on the back of my neck stands on end, and the seconds seem to stretch into hours before anyone speaks.

The power dips once more.

"Shit," I mutter.

Two dips is fine, but if it happens again, then it'll automatically shut-off to protect everyone from power surges. Dad and I learned that the hard way a few times.

"That didn't sound like the DHS to me, that seemed more like a standard emergency weather alert," Sonny says. He crosses the front room to the bay windows that face the street. He lifts a blind with his index finger and leans in.

I have to clear my throat before I can speak. "What is it? What do you see?"

"I don't know. I'm looking for lights—flashlights or lamps suddenly turning on. It's hard to tell if people are awake, and if they are, what they're up to," Sonny says.

That recognizable tone blasts through the speakers again before a different sequence of beeps, spiking my already high adrenaline.

"The following message is from the national emergency system. The message is for Hal Gerald Christensen. Please proceed to site twenty-three in Santa Monica, California. Bring only what you can carry."

The monotone voice cuts off on the second time through.

The power dips the third and final time, and even though I knew it was coming, the darkness still shocks me.

"Shit," I hush out on a quiet breath.

Three flashlight beams cut through the living room, and I release the breath I didn't realize I held trapped in my chest.

Disbelief is a strange emotion. In a lot of ways, it's protective, shielding you from something you're not quite ready to face. But it also clouds me, fogging up my brain and making it harder for me to think.

"Now that sounded like DHS," West says.

"Why did they call your dad by name here, at this house?" Sonny swipes his hand over his mouth.

"Dad always used this house as his permanent residence, and all the other places we lived were temporary," I mumble, looking at Sonny for a moment before refocusing on the TV.

I take a step forward. "What's site twenty-three?"

"I don't know. Do you remember your dad saying anything about a site or a number or anything?" Sonny asks.

I shake my head, my hair sliding along my shoulders.

"Think, Mia," Cole bites out between clenched teeth.

I jerk at his tone. "No, okay? He didn't say anything about that. But I'll call him—and Jerry."

"Alright, it's time to go, baby girl."

I look at Sonny, my mouth opening and closing. "But I—I don't have my things. And I still have to call Dad."

"It's alright. I'll find your things, yeah? I know what to bring. You go upstairs and get dressed. Layers, Amelia, okay? And anything you can't be without. Medication, glasses, photos of your family. We'll call them from the car."

"I have a photo of my grandma and me on my dresser, and I don't wear glasses." It feels like there's cotton in my ears, my words sound soft.

He tucks my hair behind both ears, his dark eyes holding me hostage. "Alright, grab that then. Do you know if your dad kept firearms around anywhere?"

I blink, seven, eight, nine times before I can find my voice. "I don't know. He wasn't really the gun type."

Sonny doesn't take his gaze from mine. "Cole."

"On it," Cole murmurs as he goes into the garage.

"Satellite phone too. I have one, but two would be better."

"Oh, we have one of those . . . somewhere in the garage." I rub the spots above my eyebrows as if the pressure helps me think. "In Dad's red chest of drawers in the garage. It has a bunch of stuff he uses on excursions."

Sonny nods. "Cole will grab them."

"I'll grab first-aid and any food and water," West says.

"I don't understand."

"We can't wait for your dad to call or his man to meet us—if he's still coming. We have no idea what people will do now that they've been woken up in the middle of the night to the power off and an emergency broadcast. But if I had to guess, I'd say panic."

"Chaos," I whisper.

"Exactly, Cher. Chaos. And we need to get ahead of as much of it as we can. So it's time to leave."

My hands grip onto his shoulders, my fingernails digging into his skin. If it hurts, he doesn't show it. "But you're not dressed . . ."

"Don't worry about me. I'll get dressed as soon as I pack you up. It'll take me thirty seconds."

I nod several times, these quick, jerky movements that send my cotton-filled head soaring. "Alright."

Sonny's hands slide from my neck to my shoulders, and then he spins me around, nudging me toward the stairs. "Be quick, Cher."

It takes two slow steps before his words register and light a fire under my feet. "Quick, quick."

I take the stairs two at a time, dash down the hall, and round the doorway into my room. Urgency rattles my bones, fear seeping from my pores. I stand in the middle of my room and pivot on the ball of my foot.

"Clothes, I need clothes."

I didn't take the time to put away any of my clothes yet, all of them bursting out of the overstuffed suitcases on the plush bench at the end of my bed. Wrenching them open, I rifle through them, grabbing leggings, fleece leggings, shorts and hiking pants like Sonny had on earlier, tees, sweatshirts, socks, bras, panties—basically a fraction of everything I just packed up a week ago and drove here.

I shimmy my shorts off and pull a pair of sweat-wicking leggings on, trade my sleep shirt for a blue racerback tank top and a black hoodie, and stuff my feet back into my sneakers. I scrape my hair back into a messy bun and secure it with one of the ever-present black hair ties around my wrist.

I'm breathing hard, flushed like I ran five miles and not merely packed a bag.

I wrench open my closet door and pull down a duffel bag and a backpack and stuff my things in there with plenty of room to spare. I toss another pair of sneakers, praying Sonny finds my hiking gear with my boots and bigger backpack.

I don't know how much good chargers will do if the power doesn't come back on, but I throw them and my charger bank in my bag anyway. I slip my backpack on and duck my head under the long strap of my crossbody purse, pausing in front of the photos tucked into the mirror above my dresser.

My grandma, Dad, and me on my tenth birthday. Me, Cole, and West in front of Snow White's castle in Disneyland when I convinced them to go with me. And a candid photo of the three of us by their pool that their foster dad took. It's my favorite photo of Cole and West because they look so different. Cole has a happy, carefree smile, and West broods in the background.

I pluck them free and stuff them into the small pocket of my purse without another thought.

Standing in the middle of my room, I exhale and spin around. This room holds a lot of memories, and a big part of me aches at the thought that I'll never see it again.

"Amelia? You ready?"

I startle at the sound of West's voice. This room only means anything because of *them*. And god willing, they're coming with.

19

GRAY

CHER WASN'T KIDDING, she doesn't have a lot in the way of camping stuff, but I pack up everything she has, just like her old man said. And just like I told her, I don't mind sharing.

My knee-jerk reaction was to call bullshit.

Not on her dad's predictions, necessarily, but maybe his packing list.

If some combination of natural disasters are set to take us out, we need a hell of a lot more than some solar-powered lanterns and a tent. Those things are great, but they're shit against a tornado.

What we really need is more information. I hope for all our sakes, we get it in Santa Monica.

"Got some flares, flashlights, satellite radio and phone, and some batteries. No gun though. You really think we'll need one?" Cole asks from across the garage.

The three of us have gone to the shooting range a few times, nothing crazy, but enough for them to get familiar with holding a gun. My granddad taught me how to shoot when I was in middle school. For years, we spent every summer road trippin' from coast to coast. Most of the time, we were in the Midwest, meeting up with my granddad's road friends. He was a bit of a free spirit, always had a problem with authority, and taught me some incredible life lessons.

I still remember the time he caught me messing around with one of his shotguns. He said, "Don't aim a gun at a man unless you're prepared to pull the trigger."

The next day, he taught me how to respect the gun for the weapon. And then years later, I taught West and Cole the same thing.

I stuff some cold-weather gear in her backpack and straighten up to look at one of the very few people I still trust on this earth. "I want to say no, but if what her dad's predicting is right, then I expect it'll be lawless before long."

"I don't know, man. You really think society will fall that quick?"

I narrow my eyes, looking across the garage at nothing in particular. "I think we have no idea what we're capable of until we're pushed to those limits."

I zone back in to see him clench his fists, jaw set, and brow low. I'd bet my favorite Swiss army knife that he's thinking about his limits and a certain blonde-haired goddess.

I can't be the only one who feels the need to protect and possess her. And fuck, I only met her a few days ago. These assholes had her for *years*, and I know *them* well enough to know that she'll have all three of us in her corner.

And if shit goes sideways, she'll need it.

Fuck, we'll all need the backup.

He rolls his neck out from left to right and back again. "But we'll be on some government ship or something, so we probably wouldn't even be able to keep it if we had it."

I lift a shoulder and close her backpack. "Maybe, but there are a lot of different variables. We don't even know if there is a ship, remember? For now, let's just pack as much as we think we'll need. We can always ditch it if we have to, but I'd rather have it."

Cole nods and turns around to look through more shelves. It looks like a semi-organized mess, but he seems to navigate it easily enough. Although I know he doesn't have the same experience as I do when it comes to this kind of stuff, he knows enough.

"I'm heading in to change and grab my stuff."

He throws up a hand to acknowledge me but doesn't turn around. "I'm right behind you. I just want to look through this one more time."

A few minutes later, I'm dressed and walking through the mudroom door with my backpack in one hand and my windbreaker in the other.

"First-Aid kit is light. We might need to grab some supplies when we stop for food, which we have very little of," West says, handing me a small red nylon bag.

"Thanks, I'll take a look in the car."

I toss the First-Aid bag and my duffel in the passenger seat of Cher's SUV and start loading up the few boxes we're bringing with us.

Cole brushes past me as he slides a box in the trunk of her car. "You're with me."

I slide a cardboard box full of loose bottles of water and a handful of pantry items next to Cole's box of camping equipment. His shoulders tense as he waits for my response, his hands resting on the sides of the box.

I raise a brow at his odd behavior. "Alright."

He nods a few times, more to himself than me, and I wonder not for the fifth time, what the deal is between the three of them. I suppose I could always ask Cher. Despite the obviously fake name she gave me, which I smoothly turned into our personalized nicknames, she screams authenticity.

But the jealous, asshole part of me that still remembers what she tastes like when she comes, wants to know why the fuck my two best friends, veritable brothers, neglected to mention that they fell in love with the same woman.

Who lived across the street from them for years.

How is it that we've been living together in one house or another for damn near five years now, and I've not heard a single peep about Amelia Christensen?

I could understand not sharing while we were at the group foster home. We didn't know each other well enough then, and the other guys that lived there were the toxic kind of desperate. They would exploit their grandmas if they thought it'd give them a leg up. Not exactly the kind of people you share your secrets with. It was the longest nine months of my fucking life.

But then Cole and West aged out and asked me to leave with them. Stay in that shitbox with ten other dudes who hate life and want to drag everyone else down with them or leave with the two guys who always had my back?

It wasn't even a choice.

We left and never looked back, sticking together since then—a brotherhood of sorts.

So, no, there's no way either one of those assholes had forgotten about her either. And if they claim they did, they're lying.

Since I've never known either one of them to be liars either, it leads me to believe that something else happened.

I FLIP up the hood on my navy-green windbreaker. It's one of my favorite jackets—lightweight and warm as hell. But mostly, I'm just glad it lives up to its waterproof claims.

The rain falls in sheets, the wind blowing it from the left one second and the right the next. I huddle underneath the small overhang from the roof to the side of the one garage door we opened as I wait for West to reverse Cher's SUV out of the garage and down the driveway. I don't know why he's driving her car, but it doesn't really matter. I still think it's stupid as fuck to take two cars.

There's too much room for error. We're unwittingly playing a game we don't know the rules for, only the stakes. And the stakes are astronomically high.

It feels like we're tempting fate right now, taunting her even. And she's about to rain hell down upon us.

Once West clears the garage, I jog over to it and grab the handle at the bottom. Without electricity, the garage door motor won't work. Luckily, the workaround solution is easy enough. Pulling the little red handle hanging from the track inside shifted it to a manual mode, which means I can open and close it by hand.

I'm careful about finger placement when I pull it closed. I once saw a man grab his handhold in between the panels, not realizing that when he pulled it down, the space between panels was eliminated. Nearly took off the tips of his fingers.

With the garage door down, I jog down the driveway to Cole's idling car, scanning the neighborhood. Other than the neighbors leaving during the emergency message broadcast, it's still quiet.

I slide into the passenger seat and reach behind me to pull off my soaking windbreaker. Water droplets scatter across the dash, and I run a hand through my hair, pushing the wet strands off my face.

"You good?"

I buckle myself and look over at one of my oldest friends. "Yeah, I'm ready."

Cole leads, slowly taking the corners with practiced ease. The tension is thick in the car, his eyes squinting with the limited visibility. The rain seems to let up if only a little. It's still coming down quick, but at least we can see further in front of us now.

I turn on the radio and twist the knob, hoping for some information. Music and more music, which are probably pre-recorded sets. I continue searching the channels. It doesn't look like anyone has any power, not around here at least. It's endless darkness, with just our headlights doing their best to shine a path.

"So that was your old neighborhood?"

"Yeah. West and I mostly grew up there with Wayne. It's as good a place as any."

"Bullshit," I say with a smile, twisting the knob again. "I saw the houses there. They're nice, like really nice. Plus, it sounds like you two were close with her."

Cole shifts in his seat. "That's true. Wayne was good to us."

The wiper blades sing their speedy song as the rain picks up again. They work double-time to clear the water from the windshield.

It's fucking wild to be out right now, it doesn't feel like real life. Like maybe I'm trapped in a dream, and soon I'm going to wake up in my bedroom in the house I share with West and Cole, and this whole goddamn thing will have never happened.

Like *she* never happened.

"And Amelia? Was she good to you too?"

It's an innocent question, not intended to make him look like he swallowed glass. When I met Cole and West, they both had a chip the size of Montana on their shoulders. I bet she smoothed their rough edges, polished them right up.

"Maybe that's a better question for you," Cole grits out between clenched teeth.

I lean back in the seat, sinking into the heat from the seat warmers on my lower back. A glance to the side mirror shows Cher's headlights comfortably behind us. Good.

Driving in the rain is different than any other condition. It's dangerous in a way you don't realize until you're already in the thick of it. And since we don't get a lot of rain here, I wasn't sure how West would drive in it.

The wind gusts, pushing against our car as we get on the highway.

"Looks like that weatherman's predictions of a flash flood might come true. Hopefully we left in time and don't get stranded."

Cole adjusts his grip on the steering wheel, the tips of his knuckles turning white. "Are you not going to answer me?"

I sigh. I'm only surprised he waited this long before he demanded answers. "What do you want me to say?"

"I want you to tell me how you know her."

I roll my head along the headrest and look at his profile. He's pissed and trying to conceal it. But we've known each other too long for that shit. "Nah, you want to know how *well* I know her. Must be well enough if we even have nicknames for one another, yeah?"

"What the fuck, Gray."

Annoyance pricks the back of my neck and heat licks up my spine. Blame it on the circumstances or our impending destruction, but I can't hold my tongue a second longer.

"What the fuck is right, man. What's your deal anyway? She seems pretty fucking amazing, and yet you seem to hate her when you're not eye-fucking her."

"I do *not* eye-fuck her."

"Yeah, alright, man. Whatever you say."

"You don't even know her, Gray. Save yourself some heartache and don't get invested."

I arch a brow and twist the knob again. "Ah, so you did love her. I suspected as much. West too?"

He doesn't answer me, which is all the answer I need. I get no satisfaction from the confirmation, but it does bring up more questions. Before I get to voice them, our car loses traction.

I feel the difference immediately. The tires spin, but our traction is gone.

"Fuck, we're hydroplaning!" Cole shouts.

"Don't slam on the brakes!"

My warning comes a second too late, and Cole hits the brakes too hard. It sends us into a tailspin, skidding across the four lane highway. We're in a head-on collision course with the retaining wall.

"Oh, fuck, we're going to crash."

I try to brace and not tense up, which is fucking impossible. Our car slides to the left at the last moment, crashing into the little brick wall. My head slams against the window with a nauseating force, and everything goes black in a blink.

20

AMELIA

MY STOMACH DROPS, and my heart flies into my throat as I watch Cole's SUV slide across the four-lane highway. The dark SUV is a phantom in the night, swinging to the right and then to the left.

"West!" I scream his name as if he can do anything to stop what's about to happen.

It feels like I'm watching everything unfold in slow motion. One second, they're in front of us driving, our mini caravan creeping through the dark, empty streets. And the next, they slam into the brick retaining wall off the shoulder of the highway.

I can't tell if he overcorrected or if he just lost control completely, but nausea soars inside my gut and adrenaline floods my veins.

"Hold on, Ames." He checks his rear view and side mirrors before he crosses several lanes.

Our tires spin as they look for traction in the rain. It's raining too much and too quickly, the ground can't possibly soak it up. Any low points are in serious danger of flooding.

Thank God there are no other cars on the road tonight.

I only hope it's not going to be our downfall.

He slows the car down with gentle taps on the brake. Each small jerk gives the tires another chance to grip the road and not get locked up in rain. Thankfully, we don't hydroplane or spin out, and he pulls up safely ten feet behind Cole's SUV.

Before he can even throw it in park, I push open the passenger door and hop out into the rain.

"God dammit, Amelia, wait!"

I hear him, I do, but I physically can't make myself wait. Not even for a second. Cole and Sonny are in that car, and I don't think I've ever been so scared in my entire life.

Car accidents are no joke. Even a simple fender bender can turn deadly. And they just slid across an entire highway, hydroplaned like they're in a Mario Kart grand prix, and crashed into a wall.

And neither one of them are getting out yet.

If I wasn't so fucking terrified, I think I'd be crying right now. But as it is, my fingers feel tingly and my chest is tight.

I'm half-running, almost to Cole's trunk when I lose my footing. Slick silt and tiny pebbles give way under my shoe, and I'm cart-wheeling my arms for balance. I land against his back bumper with a thud, my ribs taking the brunt of the impact.

Pushing off the SUV with a grunt, I shove my hair off my face and pray to every god I've ever believed in—and even ones I don't—for their safety. The driver's side took the hit, and it looks like the car must've bounced off the wall upon impact. Because there's enough room for me to walk between the car door and the brick wall.

"Cole, Cole!" I scream his name. The wind steals my terror and carries it away in an instant.

I curl my hands around my eyes and lean into the window, desperate to lay eyes on either one of them. Both of them.

The windshield wipers are going like crazy, and still the rain drenches us over and over again. The interior dash is all lit up. Cole's hunched over the steering wheel, and Sonny's harder to make out, but I think he's leaning against the window.

My experience with car accidents is minimal, but they should be awake, right? Unless they're unconscious, which is never good, they should be awake by now!

I pull on the door handles, but they're locked. My frustration boils over, so I pull on the handle again and again.

"Damnit, Cole!"

Panic gets the best of me, overtaking my muscle coordination. I bang on the window, these open-palm hits that hurt me more than help anything.

"Amelia! Over here!" West's voice cuts through the pounding in my ears and the rain on my head.

Cole's headlights shine against the wall enough that I can see West opening the passenger door. I round the hood of the car and wedge myself between Sonny and West, leaning over a tilted Sonny.

"Amelia?" Sonny shakes his head a few times, blinking rapidly.

"Are you okay?" My hands flutter around his face and his shoulders, my gaze frantically scanning him. I don't see any blood or anything impaling him, but that doesn't mean there couldn't be internal bleeding or deep bruising. Sonny groans and grabs the side of his head closest to me.

"Jesus, fuck, that hurt."

"What hurts?" I almost snap.

"I must have hit my head. I guess, on the window."

"Where? Show me."

He goes with my demand easily enough, leaning into my touch as I gently probe the area around his head. The rain beats against my back, my clothes long since soaked through. I'm probably a minute away from teeth-chattering status, but that's easily remedied.

Severe injuries from a car accident are not.

Sonny grasps my hand in his, the one not cupping the side of his head. "Are you okay? Did you and West crash too? Why are you shaking?"

"No, we're—we're fine."

"Good. That's good."

"Mia," Cole groans my name, and my heart jumps.

I jerk toward him, leaning over Sonny without touching him. "Cole, are you hurt? Are you okay? What happened? Is your head okay? Are you bleeding?"

"Give him a minute and just breathe, Cher." Sonny's breath warms the chilled skin of my shoulder.

It's only then I realized how far I've leaned over. My knee is on his seat, my palm flat against the middle console, my face hovering a few inches in front of Cole's.

"Fuck me, always with the twenty questions, Mia."

My adrenaline is flying too high to feel the real indignation I normally would at Cole's grumbling. Instead, I feel startling relief like falling into your bed at the end of a long day.

He didn't answer me, but he snarked. And that lets me know more than any answer he could give that he's alright.

The tingling in my nose is the first indication. Then my sinuses swell. And then my eyes fill with tears. It only took six breaths for me to fall apart. Loud, gut-wrenching sobs slip from my lips before I can stuff them back in.

I look at Cole, surprised to find his wide eyes on mine.

"What the fuck, Mia?" he whispers.

"I—I just—I thought you guys were going to be dead." Tears slide down my cheeks, falling into the puddle I've left over the middle of his car.

"I'm fine. I'm fine, okay? You don't need to keep doing . . . that."

If I wasn't having a hard time breathing through my tears, I might laugh at the distraught look on his face. It reminds me of the time our neighbor handed him her squirming baby at the neighborhood block party while she raced after her toddler streaking down the street.

He looks a little bit like that, a deer in the headlights and uncomfortable as fuck.

I sniff. “I can’t stop thinking about it. There’s no one around and you—you just flew into the wall like that.”

“Hey, it’s alright.” Hands settle against my hips, and I don't know if it's West or Sonny.

The one thing I do know is that I’m totally freaking out. A myriad of emotions kaleidoscopes inside me, but the biggest emotion, that all-encompassing one that drowns out everything else, is fear.

Cole groans and turns to look at me, his head resting against the headrest. “I’m fine, Mia. Honest.”

A three-inch gash above his left eye comes into view, and just like that, my tears slow. Anger is quick to replace it. “Well you don’t look fine.”

Anger is a funny emotion, isn't it? It's a mask. One you pull out and wear every time you don't want to talk. You don't want to acknowledge how you're really feeling. And right now, I'm really fucking scared.

“What hurts, man?” West asks from over my shoulder.

“Fucking everything hurts. I just slammed into a goddamn brick wall. What do you think hurts?”

My shoulders inch up toward my ears as tension fills my body. He can’t be on death’s door if he’s acting like an asshole again, right?

The startling, maybe even sad, truth is that I’ll take his bullshit every day if it means that he’s still alive.

Because that's what we've come to now.

If Dad is to be believed, then everything gets weighed against that judgment. The stakes are so high, other things seem almost meaningless in comparison now.

“Can you move everything? Is anything broken?” I ask.

Cole wiggles his fingers and wrists, moves his legs from side to side, then rotates his shoulders. “I’m alright. Just this,” he says, touching his fingertips to his forehead.

"And you?" I look over my shoulder at Sonny. "Are you sure you're okay?"

His fingertips skim up my arm and over my shoulder, his palm resting against the back of my neck. "I'll be fine, Cher."

"Good. That's good. But I think we should go to the hospital."

"No, no hospital," Cole says, his breathing picked up.

"Don't you think you should get checked out—both of you?" I look from Cole to Sonny and back again. They both said they're alright, but it's probably their adrenaline talking.

"We've been driving for, what, a half hour? And in all that time have you seen another car?"

My sinuses start to tingle again or maybe they never stopped. It's hard to tell what the hell is happening. I'm overstimulated and running high on adrenaline.

And apparently, my tear ducts are like a leaky faucet. Once they're turned on, they won't stop. I swipe a tear rolling down my cheek. "No. But until we know everyone's okay, we're getting you two checked out."

"I'm fine, Mia."

"You're not fine! You can't even open your eyes!"

He lifts his head with effort, his eyes blinking several times until they stay open.

"Cole," I breathe his name with much more emotion than I meant to. I don't think he picks up on it, not really.

"My head is killing me, like someone slingshot my brain against my skull. But otherwise, I'm alright." He drags the last word out, like he's emphasizing it for my benefit.

"Whiplash?" West asks.

"Most likely." Cole nods once.

"You good, Gray?"

"Yeah, man. I'm fine."

"See, Ames?" West's fingers flex against my hips. "They're alright. We gotta get off the road though, okay. We can't stay here like this."

We're on a dark stretch of the highway. If I squint, I can almost see lights somewhere up ahead. I can't pinpoint where we're at right now, but maybe we'll get lucky and it's a twenty-four-hour clinic or something.

"Gimme five, and I'll be good to drive," Cole mumbles.

"Absolutely not. I'm driving," I snap, reaching for the keys still in the ignition.

"Don't be ridiculous, Mia. It's pouring out, you can't see shit in the dark and definitely not when it's raining."

Indignation swells inside of me, drowning out the truth in his words.

"Guys." West's voice just barely carries over the rain and wind.

"I can drive a helluva lot better than you right now. I'll follow West, and he'll go slow enough anyway."

"Guys."

"Like hell you're driving my car. Gray can drive."

"*Gray* cannot drive. I'm literally seeing a ring of tweedy-birds like I'm the fucking Wylie coyote right now, bro. I'm out of commission for a couple hours."

Cole huffs. "Like I said, give me a few minutes, and I'm good to—"

"Jesus Christ, you two!" West roars.

"What?" Cole and I snap at the same time.

West resumes his position behind me, leaning in the car. He temporarily blocks the rain, but his wet, cold front presses into my already freezing back, and shivers race down my body starting at the top of my head.

"We got a problem. The front axle is bent. She's not going anywhere."

I bite the corner of my lip. "Should we call a tow? Or maybe the cops?"

"There's no telling how long it'll take the cops to show up right now, especially since the emergency broadcast said to stay indoors," West argues.

"So what do we do then?"

There's a beat of silence before Cole blows out a puff of air. "We ditch it. Clean our shit out and pile in your car."

"We can get a new tire tomorrow and come back," I offer.

"This kind of repair takes a few days and a few more parts than we can get off the shelf."

"But you learned to drive in this car." My voice is quiet, remembering all the good times we've had here. Remembering the time I got fed up with waiting for him to kiss me so I climbed into his lap in the middle of a movie at the outdoor theatre.

And I kissed him.

Cole turns his head, our mouths only an inch or two apart, as if he's remembering all the things he's done in this car too. "It's just a car, Mia. Right now, we've got more important shit to do, yeah?"

"Hate to break this up, but Amelia and I have been standing in the pouring rain this whole time."

21

AMELIA

THE FOUR OF us pile into my SUV, our bags and boxes in the trunk and a few in the backseat. It wasn't a lot to transfer, and West and I managed in two trips. My adrenaline is fading now though, bringing with it shivers and nausea. My wet clothes don't help either.

I wrack my brain for something to say, anything to fill the empty space between us.

But that's not true, not exactly. The air around us is anything but empty. It's full of memories and traumas, secrets and lies, and so much desire I could choke on it. How can I still be attracted to them after the cutting barbs Cole tossed at me, or their combined silence for five years—or that goddamn letter?

The end of the world feels a lot more real when we're sitting in the nearly abandoned highway in the middle of a monsoon. No one says anything, and I wonder if we're all coming to grips with our new reality.

It's a second of suspended time. This dense, weighted expectation that expands and fills every available crack between us.

"I still think we should go to the hospital," I mutter. As far as breaking the silence goes, it could've been worse.

West shakes his head before I even finish my request. "It's too risky. An emergency room visit can tie us up for hours at a minimum. They probably lost power too, so they're running on generators. They'll be backed-up."

My knee bounces, and I pull the inside of my cheek between my molars. I know he's right, but not getting checked out or reporting the car accident just feels like we're going against the grain. Like we're on the run or something.

I feel restless, anxiousness and indecision plague me, curdling the sandwich we had for dinner.

I pitched my voice low, the relentless pounding of the rain against the roof of the car helping to conceal my concern. "I get it, but I'm worried about them. If they're hurt—really hurt—and we don't get them help, then it won't matter if we spent hours at the ER or not."

"Head wounds are notorious small bleeders, and this is just a superficial cut, Cher. Nothing some painkillers and butterfly bandages can't help. Ain't that right, Cole?"

I twist around in my seat, trying to convey every emotion in my gaze to him as West eases us out onto the road.

This pull I feel toward Sonny reminds me of how I felt when I first met Cole and West. It's an unexplainable connection, an attraction on a molecular level.

Sonny's gaze is soft, his smile tipping up ever so slightly in the corner of his mouth. Not enough to flash me that lethal dimple, but enough to soothe some of my anxiety. He reaches forward and tangles his fingers in the wet strands of my hair. "I'm fine, Cole's alright too. I promise."

"We're gonna stop at a motel to change and regroup. We're out far enough that we won't be trapped in a flash flood. Maybe you can finally get in touch with your dad, Ames?"

I nod and face the front again. "Yeah. If he still doesn't answer, I'll try the sat phone."

"I think there's a handful of motels about twenty miles ahead. I see some lights up in the distance, looks like they have a few generators going. I bet they'll have some vacancies," Sonny says.

"Where are we exactly?"

"We're just outside the city," West says, his hands wrapped tight around the steering wheel.

"It felt like we were driving a lot longer than that," I murmur.

West chances a look at me before he focuses on the road. "We were, Ames. But with these shitty weather conditions, it's taking us ten times longer than usual. We're honestly lucky we didn't hydroplane earlier too."

It feels like forever until the red speck of light grows larger. And soon enough, if I squint, I can make out the neon sign for The Night Owl Motel. Bingo.

West pulls into the parking lot of the motel fifteen minutes later and parks in front of room eleven. "Stay here. I'll go check it out, get us a room if they have any."

They really took the color red and ran with it. The roof is barely peaked with red tiles, but it extends past the building, shading the wrap-around sidewalk and the red-painted banister. Faded red stucco exteriors with various whittled wood animals decorating the space in front of each room. The white doors and white window frames are the only break from the ocean of reds.

The building looks a little weathered, but the Nevada sun can age a brand-new building in a few years, so it's hard to tell how long this single-story motel has been here. There are three other motels on this exit, but this is the only one with any sort of lights on.

Palm trees line the side of the motel and parking lot, their trunks swaying and bending in the storm. I eye a particularly large tree about twenty feet away from us. It looks a little too flexible, and a sliver of worry weasels its way into my nervous system.

I scan the other side of the parking lot, noticing only two other cars on this side, parked in front of the rooms closest to the lobby. I don't know how many rooms are on the other side of the atrium-style reception area, but I'd guess ten to make it even.

I'm kind of surprised that the rooms are dark. I know it's nearing dawn, and the sun should be cresting over the horizon in the next half hour—if we'll even be able to see it through the storm clouds. But if there are TVs in these rooms, which seems very likely, they would've received the emergency broadcast.

Maybe they slept through it? I suppose they could be at a casino. The gambling in this town is second to none, so part of me wouldn't be surprised if a casino turned on their generators and let patrons keep playing.

I lean forward and watch for West, angling the heat vent on my hair as I finger-comb it and keep an eye on my phone. It's face-up on my lap, taunting me with its dark screen. No notifications from Dad or Jerry. Or even the government automated message. I don't think I'll get one since the message on the TV was for Dad, but I don't want to miss it if I do.

Cole and Sonny are quiet in the backseat, and a quick peek shows me they're both leaning their heads back against the head-rests, eyes closed.

I knew stopping was the right choice.

Movement from the corner of my eye catches my attention, and I look out the driver's side window to see West jogging back to the car with his hood pulled over his head. He all but spills into his seat, slamming his door closed and throwing off his hood with a shake.

"I got us a room. Figured it was better than getting two since I'm low on cash," West says.

Sonny groans. "Fuck. I didn't even think about that. We need to hit an ATM."

West looks at Sonny in the rearview mirror. "There was a list of nearby places—restaurants, casinos, shopping. We should be able to find one there on our way out."

"Couldn't you have paid with your card? They must have some electricity if the lights are on—and that sign." I hook a thumb behind us at the giant red and yellow The Night Owl Motel sign. It's one of those with huge bulbs, probably why we could see it from miles away.

West looks at me. "There was no one inside."

"I don't get it. How did you get us a room if there was no one there?"

West shakes his head, his lips pursed. "There was a 'Be Back in 15' sign, but who knows how long that was up. I waited for ten minutes, rang the bell, called out, even checked the back room since the door was open. No one. The room keys were right there, so I snatched the one for room eleven and tucked some cash under the phone."

My eyebrows scrunch over my eyes as I slowly run my fingers through my hair again, trying to separate it to dry quicker in front of the vent. "Maybe we should keep driving?"

West offers me a serious sort of smile, an expression I'm used to seeing on Cole's face. "It's already paid for, Ames. In a little bit, we'll get back on the road. Hopefully, you'll have reached your dad by then."

TEN MINUTES and one hot shower later, I feel marginally better. I can't quite shake the bone-deep chill, but the dry clothes help. I mostly showered to rinse off the cold, almost slimy feeling of the rain, not to wash my hair or anything.

I don't bother looking in the fogged-up mirror. I already know my hair's probably a frizzy mess, but I don't see one of those little hair dryers, so it'll have to continue to air-dry in messy waves.

I leave the bathroom door open, letting what's left of the steam slither into the room. For a motel off the highway, the rooms are pretty cozy. Two queen-sized beds take up most of the space with matching red-trimmed blankets and comforters, a simple wooden nightstand on either side—including an oversized one between the two with a lamp and alarm clock. Gauzy cream and heavier, gray light-blocking curtains trim the window facing the parking lot. A mid-sized TV hangs from the wall, the screen showing a local morning news show with the volume on mute and closed caption on.

West sits at a small two-top dark wood table with matching chairs, staring out the window with his head in his hand. "Feel better?"

Sonny stands up from the bed closest to the wall and brushes his fingers along mine as I cross the room. It's an innocent touch, but somehow, it warms me more than the shower did. The bathroom door closes with a soft snick, and I take a seat opposite of West.

"Much, thank you. How's he doing?" I keep my voice low as I jerk my chin toward Cole propped up against the headboard of the bed closest to us. He's holding a bunched-up towel to his forehead, the very edges tinged pink.

West turns to look at me, keeping his chin in his palm. "Do you want the good news or the bad news?"

"Bad first."

He nods and leans back in his chair, his hands resting on his thighs. He must've changed into dry clothes while I was in the shower. "The bad news is your first-aid kit is pretty bare. So we're going to need to find a pharmacy."

My heart spikes inside my chest, a quick, sharp jump. And I clench my fingers into a fist, my nails biting into the palm of my hand. "Okay. What do we need at the pharmacy?

West looks at me, his lips pursed, dark smudges underneath his eyes. "The gash in Cole's head is superficial, but it's big enough to need a little help closing. I thought I had some of that skin glue, but I don't."

"What the hell is *skin glue*?" I feel my eyes widen, and I can only imagine how bugged out I look.

West and Cole chuckle, this stupid, harmonious male noise that has no business being so musical or attractive.

I shift in my seat and resist the urge to fold my arms across my chest. Embarrassment heats my ears, but I don't think they're actually laughing at me. I hope not, at least.

West cocks his head to the side, a soft smile tilting his lips upward. "C'mon, Ames. You know what that is. Remember that time I slipped trying to run into the pool, fell and busted my shit on the concrete? Wayne came out and cleaned up my knee, closed the gash with that little bottle of liquid bandage. Or what Wayne liked to call it: skin glue."

I try to sift through memories I've long stopped thinking about, my brow scrunching with effort. "I remember you falling, but I don't remember the glue or whatever."

"Well, that's what we need. And we should probably stock up on a few other things. You know, just in case."

"Okay. Hand me a list, and I'll run to those shops around here. There's probably a twenty-four-hour pharmacy. I'll grab cash from the ATM too, if you want to give me your cards."

Before West can voice the disapproval written all over the lines of his too-handsome face, the familiar emergency broadcast tones blare from the speakers.

22

AMELIA

GRIPPING the arms of my chair, I whirl around and stare at the TV with my heart somewhere in my throat. Cole sits up in the bed and braces a foot on the floor. Sonny stands in the open doorway of the bathroom, his hands anchored on the doorframe.

"The following message is from the Nevada state emergency system. Don't panic. Stay indoors. Wait for further instruction from your local government officials."

I feel the color drain from my face as the automated voice repeats the message two more times.

"What the fuck does that even mean?" Cole glares at the offending TV.

Urgency beats against me, and I shove to my feet. I look between the three of them, the hair on the back of my neck standing up. "I don't like this. We should go. Get the cash and the glue and then we leave."

Sonny taps the doorframe twice with his right hand. "Let's go, Cher. It's me and you."

"Wait a minute," West says, pushing to his feet. "I'll go and you stay here. You need to rest up."

Sonny rifles through his backpack at the end of the bed closest to him. "I'm fine, man." He pulls out a windbreaker and tugs it over his head.

"*I'll* go with her. I know what to get," West nearly growls through clenched teeth.

"We don't have time for male posturing bullshit," I all but yell at them. I'm breathing hard, my gaze feels shifty as hell as I look between the three of them. Only Sonny looks at me like I didn't just screech at them. West and Cole wear matching raised brows and parted lips. Once again, I'm reminded that despite no blood relation, they're brothers in all the ways that matter. The kind of mannerisms you pick up from living with other people for years.

Sonny holds out his hand. "Keys?"

I smooth my hair back, ignoring the way the waves spring back in my face and snatch my own jacket from the table behind me. My phones tumble onto the floor with a soft clatter. I press the button on the side to bring the screen to life.

No new notifications.

Shit.

The bad feeling in my gut intensifies, and I can't pinpoint where it's stemming from. I know we're waiting on a call from Dad, but something doesn't feel right. Not with the new emergency message. I pull up his number, my finger hovering over his smiling face for a second before I press it and put the phone to my ear.

It rings and rings and rings.

Finally, his voicemail picks up. "You've reached Hal Christensen. I am unable to take your call right now, so please leave your name, number, and a brief message and I'll return your call."

I sigh and wait for the beep. "Hey, Dad. It's me again. We're outside Vegas now, but we had to stop for a little bit. We'll be back on the road in a couple hours, heading toward Santa Monica like the DHS message said. Call me back. Please. I have the sat phone too."

I end the call and scroll to find Jerry's number. I tap his smiling face and put the phone to my ear again, hoping for a better outcome. The call goes straight to voicemail, but I don't bother leaving a message. Jerry's phone hasn't been on at all, and I can only hope that he lost it and it's not something far more sinister.

I sigh and clutch my phone against my chest.

West steps next to me. "No luck?"

I shake my head. "No, but here." I press the satellite phone against his chest. His hand comes up to trap mine. "Keep this just in case he calls back. If I'm not back in an hour, call him with this."

He shifts so he's in front of me, the tips of his black sneakers touching the toes of my white ones. "Alright. Keep your phone on you and stick with Gray, yeah?"

I slip my hand from underneath his and take a step back. "I will. Write down what else you need. I'm going to go grab something from the car."

I swipe the keys from the table and dash outside. The rain has let up considerably, only sprinkling right now. The lobby lights are still on, but I don't see any movement inside. That's a long fifteen minutes. I almost wonder if they're in one of those rooms.

Dodging puddles and stretches of standing water, I unlock the car and open the trunk. Cole looked kind of pale, and I'm pretty sure I saw a couple granola bars and bottled water back here. I make a mental note to grab food—any food. Hopefully the shopping center West was talking about has a grocery store or a little food mart. I'd even take gas station snacks at this point. I shove a few granola bars, four bottles of water, and some peanut butter packets in a plastic bag.

"Amelia," West calls as he jogs to me. "Wait up!"

I turn at the sound of his voice just as he stops next to me. His hazel eyes lean green today, like frosted sea glass. "Hey, what's—"

West steps into me, his fingers threading through my hair. He angles my face toward his in a move so possessive it steals my breath. He doesn't give me a second to catch it before he slams his lips to mine.

The plastic bag slips from my fingers, falling to the ground with a thud. I feel frozen for a second, marveling at the way it feels to have his lips on mine again. But when he swipes his tongue along my lips, it jumpstarts me. I part my lips and cling to his arms, holding him against me.

We're standing in puddles with drizzling rain falling around, kissing each other like it's the last time we'll ever see one another again. He groans into my mouth, the sound so carnal, lust seeps into my veins like lava, slowly rolling down. His hand tilts my head even further, and I push onto my toes, more than meeting him halfway.

It's not the first time we've kissed—not even the second—but it feels infinitely different than all the other times. We're different and life is different.

He kisses me like he's been waiting his entire life for this singular moment. He brushes his lips along mine with such controlled passion, my knees grow weak. He slows our kiss, pulling back to nip at my bottom lip with a noise from the back of his throat. It sounds almost like a growl, and it's the most un-West-like thing I've ever seen from him. But I'd be lying if I said it didn't turn me on. He swipes his tongue to soothe the bite of pain, and I press into him further.

I've dropped some of my inhibitions, my head cloudy with desire.

West pulls back again, this time more solidly, putting nearly six inches of space between us like he's reluctant to part.

My lashes flutter open, and he's all I can see. All six feet, two inches of him. His dark hair tousled and hanging across his forehead, his eyes glossy and half-lidded in their slow perusal of me. His tee stretches across his broad chest, his tattoos peeking out from underneath his shirtsleeves.

He's a fucking eleven. He always has been.

I skim my fingertip over my kiss-swollen lip. "What was that for?"

He hooks his finger around mine, tugging it off my lip. "I've been thinking about doing that for five years, and I couldn't wait another second."

I roll my lips inward to stop the nearly giddy smile from spreading across my face. "Good. I liked it."

"I know you did, Ames," he murmurs. "Be safe, yeah?"

I nod, my gaze tracking his as he scans my face. "I will."

He flashes me one of his real smiles before he leans down and scoops up the forgotten bag of snacks, turns on his heel, and walks back to the motel room. I close the trunk and slip into the driver's seat, Sonny's already in the passenger seat.

There's a canyon of things left unsaid between West and Cole and me, and for the first time in a long time, I'm feeling hopeful about closing that gap.

23

AMELIA

SOFT MUSIC PLAYS as I try to pretend like West didn't just surprise kiss the hell out of me—like I didn't let him because I *liked it*. I'm not sure if it's actual awkwardness bleeding into the car or if I'm reading too much into it.

The rain stopped, leaving her signature on this city—probably the whole state if the emergency broadcasts are to be believed. I hug the far left lane since half of the far right lane and the entire shoulder is under water. Hopefully our exit isn't too deep, otherwise we'll need to find another way off the highway. The last thing we need is to flood the engine because I drive us into a mini lake.

I chance a glance at Sonny, but he looks like he always does. Calm, cool, and effortlessly attractive. His dark blond hair is mostly tucked behind his ears, a few strands springing free. His fingers drum a rhythm to whatever song is playing as he keeps one eye on the map app on his phone.

A smirk spreads across his face. "You're staring."

My gaze snaps to the windshield and my neck straightens. "I was not."

"It's alright, baby girl. I like the way your eyes feel on me," he murmurs.

I feel the blush spread across my cheeks. I don't call him out on the pet name, and if he asked, I might even deny it, but there's something about the way his deep tenor curls around that combination of letters that sparks something wild inside of me.

I clear my throat. "How long until our exit?"

"One point three miles, on your right. If you can't get to the exit, then we'll take the next one in three miles."

"Okay," I say with a small nod, glancing in my rearview reflexively. "Do you think it's weird that we haven't seen any cars yet?"

He looks out the windows before giving me his attention. "Nah, it's early, and we're kind of in the middle of nowhere. I'm sure a lot of people are adhering to the message to stay inside too."

The exit lane slopes down on the right, so I cross the few lanes and flip my blinker down. The road levels out, but the shoulder drops drastically to some man-made ravine. The water must've rolled into here because it's higher than I've ever seen it off the side of the highway before.

"So, are we not going to talk about it?"

I ease us around the bend in the road, my shoulders tensing toward my ears again. "Talk about what?"

Sonny smiles. "Oh, it's like that then, huh? Gotta say, Cher, I've never been ditched quite like that before."

It takes a second for me to catch up. I thought he was talking about the kiss with West. It feels like a lifetime since we hooked up in the hotel. I shift in my seat and follow the signs for the little strip mall. I look at him out of the corner of my eye. "It wasn't personal, Gray."

"Damn, Cher, it sure feels personal when you make a gorgeous girl come with your hands, mouth, and cock—*several times*."

I stop at a red light and look at him. His grin is genuine, if a little brittle around the edges. "I'm sorry. I shouldn't have left like that. It's just—I'd never done that before."

He tilts his head to the side, one of his brows arching. "Are you telling me I was your first?"

My mouth parts and I sputter, "What? No."

He grins then, a full-on smile with those damn dimples and all. "I'm just playing, Cher. I knew what you meant."

I gently nudge his shoulder with my fingers. "It's just, I didn't know the protocol for a . . . one-night stand."

He snaps. "Ah, that's where I went wrong." He pauses, and I'm convinced it's just for dramatic flair. "I didn't want just one night."

I suck in a breath, startled but not at all surprised by his honesty. Warmth settles on my chest, and I tip my head back against the headrest, holding his gaze. "It seems fate has given us a second chance."

"You believe in fate, Cher?"

I lift a shoulder as the light turns green. "I'm starting to. Look"—I tip my chin ahead, toward a big brown sign close to the street—"looks like one of those bulk stores with a gas station. I bet they have an ATM inside too. And food. We need food, Sonny."

"Alright, let's pull in and see what we can get." He leans around to look in the back seat. "Do you have a blanket or anything? I think we should cover our gear in the trunk while we go in, just in case. And Cher?" He waits for my gaze. "We're going to load this SUV up, okay? So be prepared for that."

I worry my bottom lip. "Do we really need that much? I mean, if we're going to be meeting Dad soon, maybe we should leave it for someone who needs it."

"We're going to load up, just in case."

He doesn't need to finish the sentence. We both know what he's not saying.

Just in case Dad doesn't call.

"Okay. Tell me what we need, and we can split up, cover more ground—"

"No. No splitting up. We stay together at all times." His tone is unyielding, such a contrast from what I'm used to that it pulls a sharp gaze from me.

"Okay, we'll stay together."

He nods, but the tension doesn't leave his frame. "Our backpacks will make us stand out, but my pockets are deep enough to carry sufficient cash."

"Jesus, how much money are we pulling from the ATM?"

"As much as we can. We have no idea the currency rate or trade value when we meet up with your dad and his government buddies. We need to be prepared for anything."

I pull into the parking lot, my foot lifting from the gas pedal in shock. It's packed. Like Black Friday packed. "What the hell?" I whisper.

It's a huge store, rectangular in structure with a detached gas station. All six pumps have a line ten-cars deep. Cars are honking and people are waving their arms, yelling.

"Gray?"

"Find a spot over here somewhere. I'm going to call West. We didn't have the radio on, so maybe we missed something."

I pull into the store's parking lot, shaking my head at the insanity of what I'm seeing. Guilt slithers in, breaking up some of my disbelief. I didn't turn on the radio on purpose—I wanted to listen to something familiar, a playlist I made for the drive here. That was a mistake.

"Hey, yeah. Let me put you on speaker," Sonny says, reaching forward and turning the volume all the way down.

A second later, West's voice fills the car. "Someone leaked the DHS messages, uploaded them to social media a couple of hours ago. It didn't take long for it to get noticed. About an hour after it went up, people across the country commented their emergency broadcast messages. It's not local—fuck, it's not even our country! People from all over the world are reporting severe weather and natural disaster warnings."

"So what are they saying now?" Sonny asks, rubbing the spot of skin between his brows.

West sighs, the sound noisy through the line. "It means the government lost its element of surprise, and now people know about the fucked-up Noah's Arc they're trying to create."

"But that Noah's Arc is going to save our asses, so let's not shoot a gift horse in the mouth."

"It's don't *look* a gift horse in the mouth, Ames," West says with a chuckle.

I wave a hand in the air as if to brush his words away. "Whatever, you knew what I meant. So what does that mean for us?"

"It means we lost the advantage for our supply. Now every person is going to run to their grocery stores and gas stations."

I blow out a breath. "Yeah, we already knew that. It's insane here."

"Where are you? That mall I saw?"

"Nah, we found one of those membership warehouse club stores before we reached the mall, so we're stopping here first. But it's significantly busier than I thought it would be for this early in the morning. I'm hoping they'll have the first-aid we need though," Sonny says.

"Did the sat phone ring, West? Have you heard from my dad or Jerry?" I find a spot toward the back right corner and pull my SUV in the space. It's a tight squeeze, but I'm hoping we'll be in and out.

"No, I'm sorry. I've had it with me the entire time. I'll text you the moment it rings."

"Alright, man, we better go," Sonny says.

"Okay. Be safe. And Gray?"

Sonny looks from his phone to me. "Yeah?"

"Don't let anything touch her," he practically growls.

He holds my gaze and says, "With my life."

24

AMELIA

I LOCK the car and slip the keys in my coat pocket, zipping it closed. Nerves dance inside my body, sparking every few seconds. I link my fingers with Sonny's as we cross the parking lot. Every loud noise makes me flinch—a car honking, people yelling, the shrill noise of metal on metal when the carts get pushed into the cart corral.

Sonny tightens his hold on my hand and leans in to brush a kiss on the top of my head. It's a comforting gesture, and it eases a little of my anxiety. A young couple sprints through the parking lot, pushing an overflowing cart, their faces pale and stricken.

"What if they don't have what we need?"

He squeezes my hand once. "We'll figure it out. We just have to stick together. Ready?"

I nod, and we cross the threshold. The bright halogen lights cast an almost neon glow on everything, a stark difference to the gray skies. Sonny leads us to the cart holding area, and we grab one of the last few carts. Another reminder that the store has seen a lot of customers today already.

I curl my fingers tighter around the handle, letting the plastic dig into my palms. Sonny stands at the end of the cart, to the right, his left hand clutching the corner as he guides us.

We bypass the first few aisles with furniture and office goods, and I side-eye the few people in those aisles. They're loud and just shy of aggressive as they argue about printer paper and scotch tape. Sonny plucks a giant package of toilet paper off an endcap and tosses it underneath the cart without skipping a step.

He pulls us down the pantry aisle next. The two of us deftly maneuver around the four other carts in this aisle. Despite the calm, I can't stop shifting my gaze to everyone. I'm hyperaware, and I already know it won't take me long to get overstimulated. Fear is slowly crawling up my back, making the tips of my fingers tingle.

Sonny grabs what's left of the peanut butter—five off-brand, sixty-four-ounce jars—and dumps it into the cart. I don't say a word, even if I feel like my eyebrows are in my hairline.

Next is oatmeal. Two big cardboard canisters and five boxes of the individual instant packets. He taps the cart twice, and I look from his hand to his face. He lifts his chin and cuts his gaze across the aisle and then back to me.

Stay here.

I nod in acknowledgement and scoot my cart as far over as possible. I watch him weave between a couple in the middle of a hushed conversation and a man in his late-forties with a fierce scowl. I put my back to the big shelves behind me and plant my feet, eyes scanning the aisle and the people.

Sonny grabs an entire cardboard case of canned tuna and adds a few loose cans to the top before he turns around and walks back to me. He sets it in the cart with a thump, the cans rolling off and clattering against the metal cart. He goes back for more, this time grabbing a big box next to the tuna. It's that make-your-own packets with mayo and pickle relish—a bunch of things that have a long shelf life.

He drops that box in the cart and walks toward the end of the aisle, skirting around another two carts. I lean to the side to keep him in my sight. He reaches up high, a sliver of his abs flashing as his tee rises, and grabs boxes of herbal tea and something else powdered. Coffee maybe?

I was too busy watching him, wondering why he chose peanut butter and tuna and what he's going to grab next. I got distracted and stopped watching the people around us.

And that's where I made a mistake.

The guy with a scowl takes a step toward me, his scowl deeper than before. "Hey you can't take all that."

My shoulders tense, but my feet feel light, like I could take flight any second. I stare straight ahead. I don't know why, but for some reason, I'm convinced if I don't engage, he'll leave it alone.

I was wrong. Again.

"Hey, I'm talking to you. You can't take all that tuna." The scowling man reaches forward and clamps his meaty hand on the side of my cart and jerks it toward him.

Confrontation brews in this aisle as heads turn toward him at the sound of his raised voice. I glare at him, but it does fuck-all to deter him. He jerks the cart toward him again, a gleam of triumph making his beady gaze nearly sparkle. I try to keep my hold, but he caught me by surprise, and I can't keep the cart still.

The back of my neck feels flushed, and my heart pounds like crazy.

Sonny's at my side a second later. He drops his armful of food in the cart and stares at the man with an almost bored expression. His gaze goes from the scowl to his hand and back to his scowling face. "Problem?"

The man's scowl deepens, his frown lines forming rivulets in his face. "Yeah, I got a problem. You and your little girlfriend are being selfish assholes."

Sonny cocks his head to the side and slowly blinks. "Get your hand off my fucking cart before I remove it and I'll forgive the insult." Sonny's words are delivered low but with so much force and authority, my gaze snaps to him.

"The fuck did you say to me?" The guy curls his fingers through the little metal holes further and squares his shoulders. I don't think it's the intended image he means because it just pushes out his beer belly further.

Sonny steps closer, and I see the transformation happen before my very own eyes. He's got a few inches on this guy, and he uses it to look down his nose at him. His entire face smooths out and freezes in this sort of mask that only a man who's extremely confident in himself can ever wear.

"I'm gonna give you three seconds to get your fat, fucking fingers off of my cart and step away from my girl. Or I'm going to cut them off and shove them down your throat," Sonny murmurs low enough that no one else but us can hear.

The man rears back, fury rising like the red flushing his cheeks. "I'm going to fucking—"

"One. Two." Sonny reaches back with his left arm and pulls out a knife from somewhere. He keeps it low, gently tapping it against his thigh so the guy can see it.

It's long as it is mean, and the way he grips the handle tells me everything I needed to know.

This is not the first time he's handled this weapon.

I don't know what the fuck is going on with me. I should be running scared right now, instead, I'm decidedly *not*. The tingles have spread from my fingertips and settled somewhere much, much lower.

I watch the color drain from the guy's face as his hands fly up into the universal surrender position, palms out. He stumbles back a few steps. "Jesus Christ, you're fucking crazy."

Sonny tucks his knife away, back to wherever it was in a flash, the rest of the customers none the wiser. He flashes him a grin—all teeth. "You know what's fucking crazy, man? Thinking you can put your hands on something that doesn't belong to you."

The guy backs up again, his ass bumping into his cart. He turns on his heel and practically runs down the aisle with his cart without another word.

Sonny waits until he's around the aisle before he looks at me. "You okay?"

I blink a few times. "I'm fine."

"Good." He steps closer and leans down in one fluid movement, tucking a lock of hair behind my ear. He follows the strand down, along my shoulder, down my back, where he toys with the ends. "I didn't scare you, did I, Cher?"

I tilt my head so our faces are aligned, and my nose brushes his. "I'm not scared."

"I would never hurt you," he murmurs, tugging gently on the end of my hair and tipping my head back further.

"I know." My breath hitches in my chest.

He wets the corner of his mouth with his tongue. We're so close, yet neither one of us makes the first move. Sweet anticipation claws at my gut, desperate to be fulfilled.

Sonny rocks back on his heels, putting distance between us again just as yelling from somewhere nearby picks up.

If he didn't flash me those stupid hot dimples, I might not be as forgiving. He shoves one hand in his pocket and grips the end of the cart with the other, whistling under his breath.

I steal a few glances around us, but either no one caught the whole thing or they're too busy to care. Either way, we cruise through the rest of the aisles with ease. Twenty minutes later, our cart is full. Bags of dried beans, lentils, and rice, jars of honey, and enough boxes of energy bars to last the four of us years. Bottles of vodka, bags of dried jerky, jars of bouillon cubes, and three boxes of canned goods. Instant coffee, powdered milk and peanut butter, boxes of pasta. A few fresh fruits and several cases of water.

And eight prepackaged fresh ham and turkey sub sandwiches.

I eye the last few things—they definitely don't fit the non-refrigerated theme he was going with.

He catches my eye and smiles. "We'll eat the sandwiches and

the fruit when we get back." Right on cue, my stomach grumbles, and I pull up short. "You alright, Cher?"

"Yeah, I'm fine. Just realized that I've been up for twenty-four hours, and I can't remember the last time I ate."

Sonny's gaze scans my face. "We're almost done."

I wave a hand in the air. "It's fine. I didn't realize it until I saw the sandwiches, but yeah, I am hungry."

He fishes out one of the sandwiches and walks it back toward me. "Here, you eat this and I'll push for a while."

Our fingers brush together, lingering like we're a couple in a regency romance. I pull my bottom lip in my mouth and tug the sandwich free.

"One more aisle, and then we're out of here."

I tear open the cellophane wrapper, peel the waxy wrapper off the top half, and take a bite that's too big. You ever start eating and then realize you're starving after the first bite? It's like you can't consume the calories fast enough. Yeah, it's a little like that for me right now.

Sonny chuckles at my enthusiasm as he leads us down a random aisle of things. He tosses a mini sewing kit in the cart. Disinfectant wipes and hand sanitizer, a small propane tank, a dozen lighters, and lots of antibacterial soap. They only have the bulk-size over the counter medication, so we have more than enough various pain relievers, cold medicine, allergy medicine—basically a million things I never would've thought of.

I crumple up the wrapper just as we get to the checkout. Like I just woke up from some sort of hunger-induced fog, I blink and the noise and anxiety starts to creep in again. The lines are ten-deep at each register, the combined energy of all these people swells larger and more volatile with every passing minute. I lean into Sonny, and he tosses an arm around my shoulder, pulling me in close and brushing a soft kiss along my forehead.

For how busy it is, we're checked-out relatively quickly. I don't think we spoke more than five words to one another the entire time in line. I was too on edge, my head on a constant swivel, eyeing everyone around us. Worried someone would try to take our cart or an employee would refuse us.

We cross the parking lot quickly, a long line of cars waiting just to pull in the lot. Sonny unloads and reorganizes a few things quicker than I even thought about doing it, and a few minutes later, we're back in the car.

"Where to now?"

25

GRAY

"THERE'S A PHARMACY UP AHEAD, on the other side of the gas station. We need to grab some things and get back." I gesture out the windshield, my gaze drawn to the shitshow at the gas station.

"Should we stop for gas first?"

I glance from Cher's white-knuckled grip at ten and two to the chaos at the eight pumps.

An itch feathers across the back of my neck. I don't doubt my ability to protect her, but sometimes it boils down to numbers, and I don't like the amount of aggressive people currently surrounding the gas station.

I force nonchalance in my voice. "Nah, we have a couple full cans in the trunk. We can stop once we get the boys."

"Okay," she says as she drives around the little access road that connects a bunch of stores.

You know there's a specific energy in the air before a storm, a sort of tangible static? That same kind of feeling crawls all over me now. I glance from the backed-up gas station to my side mirror and the overcrowded parking lot and back again.

"Call me paranoid, but I think we're going to run into some . . . speed bumps soon."

"Speed bumps?"

"I'm hoping they're speed bumps and not roadblocks."

Her brow crinkles in this specific way that my fingers itch to smooth out. "Literal speed bumps?"

"Nah, Cher. I mean trouble. I think we're going to run into some trouble soon. Seems strange to me that so many people aren't heeding the weather warnings, ya know?"

Cher's phone rings through the speakers, cutting off whatever she was going to say next. West's number flashes on the screen, but not a contact name or photo. An interesting piece of information in their ever-expanding puzzled history. She presses a button on the steering wheel, and his voice fills the air before she even says hello.

"Where are you?" The urgency in his voice is palpable from three words.

"West?" she asks.

"Where are you, Ames? Is Gray with you?"

"I'm right here, and we're in the car."

He sighs. "Good, that's good."

"What's going on, West? Did Dad call?"

"No, shit, I'm sorry, Ames. I should've led with that. Listen, you guys need to get back now."

"We're almost done. We're pulling into the pharmacy now," she says.

"Scale from one to ten, how vital is it to stop there, Gray?"

I think about what he's really asking me, mulling over everything I know and weighing it against the probability that we'll need it. At the end of the day, even if we meet up with Cher's dad, we're not guaranteed access to this illusive ship or bunker or whatever the fuck it is. You better believe I'm going to try like hell to stay with her, not just because I don't feel like dying, but Amelia's the kind of rare species that men will do anything to covet.

She needs someone to watch her back—and maybe even her front. Luckily for her, I'm very good with a knife.

"Gray?" West presses.

"I was thinking. Eleven, West. We need it, especially for Cole right now."

"I'm fine, asshole. Don't go sticking your neck out on my account," Cole snaps. They must be on speakerphone.

West sighs. "Shit. Okay. Just—get what you need and get the fuck out, okay? If they don't have it, we'll find it somewhere else—together."

"Tell me what's going on." My tone brokers no argument.

West sighs, and I imagine him running his hand down his face before he pushes his hair off his head. He's predictable in his frustrations. "Because of the leaked DHS messages we told you about earlier, there are now videos of damn-near riots happening around the country. People are acting like a *zombie apocalypse* is imminent, so the violence is off-the-charts. The original video is at five million views now."

"What does that even mean? Zombies?" she asks, pulling into the parking lot of the pharmacy. It's not as busy as I was expecting, which is good news for us.

"It means that people are freaking the fuck out," Cole says with a huff. "And people do stupid shit when they're scared. They're turning on anyone they suspect got a message, calling it a *golden ticket* like we're in some fucked-up Willy Wonka apocalypse, and these messages are one-way tickets to safety. The videos online are insane, and it's only been a few hours. Imagine what could happen in twenty-four hours—or forty-eight?"

"Park here," I say, gesturing to a free space closest to the exit to the street. Cher swings us into the spot and throws her SUV in park. "We're at the pharmacy, and it doesn't seem busy, so we gotta get moving. What else do we need to know that can't wait?"

"I don't know, man. People are turning on friends, neighbors, *strangers* at the gas station. There was a video from Texas of an entire gas station going up in flames like someone bombed it after a fight broke out over rationing gas cans."

"What the fuck?" Cher breathes out with wide eyes.

"From what we can tell, everyone is fair game. The original whistleblower account claims anyone who wasn't given a *golden ticket* would be barricaded indoors like the emergency broadcast said," West says.

Cher sucks in a breath. "So because we're out, we're targets? Is that what you're saying? There's no way to prove that we"—she lowers her voice and glances around—"got the message anyway."

"It's paranoia, mass hysteria . . ." West trails off.

"Chaos." I look at Cher.

As if she can feel my gaze on her, she turns to look at me. I know by the pursed lips and hardened gaze, she's remembering the little run-in with that entitled fuck at the store. I look for any fear or revulsion with bated breath. The last thing I want to do is hurt her or break her trust, but she has to know that I'll protect what's mine.

And make no mistake, Amelia Christensen is mine.

"Looks like you were right, Gray. Society seems to be starting its descent into hell early," Cole says, his tone resigned.

"We'll call you when we're back in the car. Last call for anything from the pharmacy." I hold her gaze, but my words are for them.

"We're fine. And Gray?"

"Yeah?"

"Don't be a fucking hero, yeah?"

I smile even though he can't see me. "Never am."

Now it's Cher's turn to map the pores on my face, her gaze hot. She ends the call with a press of a button. "You are, though. A hero, I mean."

I reach over and grasp her hand in mine. "Only for you, Cher. Only for you."

AMELIA

"SAME AS BEFORE, Cher, stay with me," Sonny says, tightening his hold on my hand.

The romantic inside of me skips at the simple touch. I can't help it. Hand-holding is one of my favorite things, it's deceptively affectionate. Not reserved exclusively for romantic affection, but just general love and care. And that's one thing I've always longed for more of.

The automatic doors slide open, air conditioning blasting us in the face as we walk through the second set of automatic sliding doors. Music plays quietly overhead, a song familiar but just out of grasp.

Sonny grabs two baskets and hands one to me before we skirt along the far wall of the store, slinking through the area with little makeup aisles and kiosks. Someone hums along to the music, coming from somewhere in the middle of the store.

He turns at the next aisle break and snags two backpacks off an end-of-the-year endcap. He rips the tags off both of them and hands me the Kelly green one. I unzip it and plop it in the basket.

The humming gets louder as whoever it is must be walking toward us. I glance behind us, but it's only chips and snack mixes on the shelves. We turn right down the next aisle, and the music overhead changes to an instrumental Christmas song.

The humming gets louder and louder until it stops somewhere close to us. Somehow the absence of the almost ominous humming is worse than the noise itself.

A prickle dances along the back of my neck, and my fingers reflexively squeeze. His feet slow until we stop in the middle of the aisle. The humming picks back up, and if I tilt my head just right, it sounds like they're following us, right on the other side of the aisle.

Sonny narrows his eyes and looks around, his jaw clenched.

"There were a dozen cars outside and no people inside. Where are they?"

I step closer to him and adjust my grip on the handle of the basket. It's plastic and shit as far as a weapon is concerned, but my sixth-grade gym teacher once told me I was scrappy for someone so short. And I've worn that backhanded compliment like a warning label for a decade.

"Stay close."

I swallow with effort, my throat dry, and nod.

My sneakers squeak against the linoleum as I pivot and glance behind us again. I half-expect to see someone—the person humming—breathing down my neck. But still, no one's there.

We stop in front of the medicine and vitamin aisle. It spans the entire back wall from the corner until the pharmacy.

He scans the area once more and lets go of my hand to grab the things that should've been in our first-aid kit without a word, tossing them in my basket and his. I organize them as best I can, splitting up the products between our backpacks.

Antiseptic wipes, gauze, various bandages—more things that I never would've thought of.

A thump comes from somewhere on the other side of the store, and we pause, our heads turning in union. Sonny turns around and tosses a few more things in the baskets, but I can't pull my attention from the store.

Where is everyone?

I haven't even seen an employee. Maybe they all left? No, that doesn't make sense. I shake my head, my hair brushing against my neck. If they left, they would take their cars. Right?

I bite my bottom lip hard enough for it to sting. Something feels off here.

He taps the back of my hand twice, which is curled around the basket's handle, and tips his head toward the pharmacy counter. I nod my understanding. I don't know why we aren't talking. We know there's someone else here, whoever belongs to the mysterious humming, but somehow, it feels safer to be quiet.

The hair on the back of my neck stands impossibly straighter. Goosebumps trail down my arms and my back. I don't like it.

We stop in the pharmacy's waiting area. Six chairs and a small coffee table to sit and wait for your prescription. A couple kiosks for brand name allergy medicine and one of those blood pressure machines.

There are two registers at the window, the metal chainmail gate pushed halfway up. We approach quietly and cautiously. My shoulders up to my ears with tension riddling the rest of my body. My steps feel wooden, almost hollow, and yet as heavy as weights.

Sonny scans behind us, big sweeping arcs from left to right, his mouth flat and his brows low, guarded.

I tug on the bottom of his shirt to get his attention. "What are we doing?" My voice is barely above a whisper.

"We need antibiotics, Cher." His pointed look at my obvious confusion is something I'm going to need to unpack later.

I don't know Sonny, not really. We met a week ago, and now our paths have crossed, tangled up, and forged a new path together in an inexplicable way. And I can't help but wonder if it was divine intervention.

Because if I were all alone, like I've been for so much of my life, I'm not sure I would've made it even this far. I don't know what he needs antibiotics for, but I would have never grabbed even half the stuff he got at the grocery, so if he says we need it, I trust him.

"Okay, let's go." I take a step so we're standing side by side. It's an intentional move, so he knows that I'm in this with him, that we're doing this together—that I'm *trusting* him.

A smile ghosts across his lips. It's gone before it even really has time to form, and he takes a half a step in front of me, angling his body in front of mine and strides toward the propped open door to the back end of the pharmacy.

He pushes it open with his fingertips and pauses. My heart

beats loud in my ears, anticipation swelling inside of me and mingling with a healthy dose of fear.

My adrenaline's pumping so hard and so fast. It's a wonder I haven't felt nauseated already.

Sonny turns left and heads straight for the big shelving units full of medicine. It's shelf after shelf of large, manufacturer-sized bottles of pills. Thank god they're in alphabetical order.

Not that it really matters for me, since I have no idea what most of them are.

Sonny plucks bottle after bottle with quick fingers, flipping them into my backpack and then his, only pausing to scan the labels around him. I angle my back to him so I can keep watch around us, make sure no one sneaks up behind us.

"Come on, come on," he murmurs.

"What is it?"

"We need prednisone, but it's not here."

"Maybe they don't have it?"

"No, they always have it. That and z-packs, and then we can go."

Now that is one antibiotic I recognize. "I know where those are. They're on the other side, by the door where we came in. I'll go get them."

Sonny's brows dip, and he sinks his teeth into his bottom lip for a moment.

"I'll be right back," I assure him. *I can do this,* my gaze says.

"You got thirty seconds, Cher. If you're not back—"

"I will be," I interrupt him. "And then we're done?"

He nods. "Yeah, then we'll get the fuck out this graveyard."

It's a dig at how empty this store is, but then why do I get chills down my back?

I can only hope it's not some divine foreboding.

I adjust the basket so it rests in the crook of my elbow and dash down the aisle back the way we came. There are a few shelves to the right of the door that leads to the waiting area. And that's exactly where my pharmacy kept it.

I know because I once waited twenty-five minutes in a pharmacy lobby just like this one when I had a sinus infection last year. New Jersey allergies are a real bitch in the spring.

I skid to a stop, my gaze flying across the shelves, looking for the familiar letter combination. I hope whoever decided on the complex names of antibiotics never knows the joy of a cool pillow at night.

The seconds tick away, urgency shaking my hands a little as I read the labels of the little plastic containers. Bingo. In the bottom right corner, there's an entire container of prednisone.

I don't know how much he wanted, so I bend down and grab it, upending the contents right into my backpack.

And then I hear a gunshot.

26

AMELIA

I PUSH TO MY FEET, whirling around with my heart in my throat. My breath is coming in quick, choppy pants.

I've been around guns before. Not much, but enough to recognize the sound when I hear it. Alley's dad brought us to the gun range a few different times. She was taking some self-defense lessons her father insisted on when she started managing the night shift, and I tagged along with her.

I loop my arm through the plastic handles and clutch the basket to my chest. My feet feel frozen to the floor, indecision plaguing me.

I swallow his name on my tongue. The need to shout for him is so strong, it batters against my teeth. But I know the dangers outweigh the slim possibility of benefit. If he isn't anywhere near that gunshot, I don't want to alert them to my presence—or Sonny's by calling his name.

I take three steps and then freeze. The register area is open, and if anyone is watching, I'll be spotted in an instant. An open target.

Fuck it, I think when I drop to all fours and push the basket in front of me as quietly as I can on the linoleum floor. I scramble across, hidden from view by the counter. Once I'm on the other side, I exhale the breath I didn't realize I was holding. My hair falls in my face, and I blow it off my sweaty forehead with a huff as I push to my feet.

"Sonny," I whisper-shout his name as I slink between the aisles. Silence greets me, the various white plastic medicine bottles mocking me. I keep my back to the shelves lining the back wall, taking quick, quiet steps toward the aisle I last saw him in.

"Gray."

Sonny's pant leg and sneaker come into view first, like he's rounding the corner in slow-motion. It takes a second for him to step out from behind an endcap at the end of the aisle.

I quicken my steps, relief settling my shoulders back down at the mere sight of him. "Oh my god. I was—"

"Amelia." His voice lacks any of the usual warmth. And his use of my real name doesn't go unnoticed. I pull up short six feet away from him as a stranger comes into view a half-step behind Sonny.

"Well, now would you look at that. It seems your girlfriend went and found us." The man's voice is scratchy and deep, the kind you would expect a Disney villain to have. Only he doesn't look tall, dark, and sinister. His blond hair shaved into a buzz cut, his jeans that are too low and big on his hips. His dirty white t-shirt that hangs loosely on his frame. He looks like some punk kid a couple years younger than me playing with his daddy's favorite gun.

"Do us all a favor, cupcake, and put the basket down."

I flick my gaze to Sonny, and he shakes his head in an imperceptible *no*. It's the direction I needed. I widen my stance and sink my weight into my heels, clutching my basket tighter. "No."

The guy's face contorts in rage. "This ain't some charity. You gotta pay for shit."

This guy doesn't elicit fear the same way that guy at the grocery store did, or maybe my adrenals are tapped. Or my adrenaline's almost run dry, and I don't have that healthy appreciation for fear right now. Either way, I tilt my head to the side and give him my best *bless your heart* look. "Sure thing. I'll be happy to pay for these. Are you a cashier?"

"Bitch, you deaf? I said put my shit down," he yells, raising a gun and waving it in the air next to his shoulder.

I can't hold in my flinch, recoiling a step. I scan Sonny quickly, searching for any obvious wounds. Maybe the gunshot was just a warning? I lick my lips and swallow, my throat drier than the desert we're currently trying to escape.

A low laugh tumbles from thin lips as they stretch into a wide, slimy smile. He looks mean as he narrows his beady eyes at me, scanning me from head to toe. "Oh you like that, huh?" He steps to the right, away from Sonny, and points the gun directly at me. "Are you going to take me seriously now, bitch?"

I don't take my gaze from the gun, stumbling back another step. My shoulder bumps into the shelves behind me, rattling the bottles. My thoughts stutter over themselves, the adrenaline I thought I didn't have roaring in my veins. I don't know what to do. I have a basket full of band aids and antibiotics. That's not shit against a gun. And we all know it.

I'm flushed, despite the air conditioning pumping through the overhead vents. Perspiration collects underneath my arms as I stare down the barrel of a gun. For the first time in forever, my mortality becomes very, very real.

With it, a clarity washes over me, sharp and unyielding.

I have too many things left to do in this life before I leave it. Too many connections to form—and *mend*.

Goals and dreams that have yet to be fulfilled.

And this asshole on a power trip isn't going to steal that from me.

Sonny's fingers flex wide and then fist, the movement catching my eye. He stares at me, all serious eyes and intensity, and then he flicks his gaze from me down to his shoe. Or hip? I honestly can't tell what he's trying to tell me here. I raise my brows quickly, glancing back at the guy waving a gun.

Sonny taps his left pocket with his index finger twice, and then I understand.

That must be where his knife is.

I dip my chin. He needs an opening to grab it, so I'm going to give it to him. Time to lean on that acting workshop I took two years ago.

I blow out a breath, angle my body to focus on him. "I am taking you seriously."

"Oh, I see how it is. You see this little thing and suddenly"—he waggles the gun again—"you're sweet as a cupcake. Dad was right, this little thing can be very persuasive." He almost murmurs that last part to himself.

"So, how much? We can go check out right now."

He brings the gun up to scratch against his patchy beard as he leers at me. His casual familiarity with the gun is freaking me out. He's too cavalier with it. You should have more respect for a weapon that can end someone's life in the blink of an eye.

"See, from what I hear, money isn't going to mean shit much longer. So I'm thinking we got to do a different type of compensation if you want to walk out of my place with that basket."

His disgusting, fat tongue sweeps out to lick along his lips, and it takes a concentrated effort not to shudder in disgust. His beady eyes narrow as they glide down my frame, leaving slimy trails of revulsion in their wake.

He sucks his teeth. "For a sweet little cupcake like you, it'll cost you a pretty penny."

On the inside, I recoil. I shrivel up and shy away from his revolting gaze. But on the outside, I take a step closer. I force my mind to blank, reminding myself to just get him to drop his guard. All Sonny needs is a moment.

I tilt my head to the side, feel my lips curl up into an inviting grin like I'm the puppet master, almost disassociating from my body. I sway my hips as I walk another two steps. "I think we can work something out. Don't you?"

His gaze lasers in on me, lowering his weapon and nodding several times. He swipes his tongue around his mouth obscenely. “Oh yeah, cupcake. We can work something out real nice.”

He takes a step to the side of Sonny, and this is it.

The opening Sonny needs.

The guy's attention is all on me, and Sonny pulls his knife from behind him, pivots, and brings it down handle-first on the guy’s head. A thunk punctuates the air, and it’s lights-out for the asshole with the gun.

It's over as quick as it begins.

He hits the deck like a sack of potatoes. Sonny grabs his gun, flicks the safety on, ejects the magazine out to check and then pops it back in and tucks it in the back of his pants. He moves through these motions so quickly, I swear if I would have sneezed, I would have missed it.

There's a story here—probably several stories. And I’m beginning to see bits and pieces of the real Gray. I only hope I have the opportunity to see more.

He stands over the guy, chest heaving and practical thunder clouds in his gaze. “You okay?”

“I can feel my heartbeat in my fingertips, but I’m fine.”

He smiles and eliminates the distance between us. He slips his palm onto the back of my neck and angles my face toward his. “You did good, Cher.”

I swallow against the emotion lodged in my throat. “I was scared.”

“I know, baby girl, but you were brave. And I never doubted you, not for a second.”

I don’t know if it’s the rush or the euphoria of being alive—hell, maybe it’s just because I’ve wanted to kiss him again since the moment I walked out of Tennessee Pete’s—but I push onto my toes and press my lips against his. He responds instantly, gripping the hair at the nape of my neck.

He devours me with the kind of passion reserved for reunited lovers, and I rise up further to deepen the kiss, throwing my arm around his neck. Another gunshot splits the air, and we pull apart instantly.

"Time to go, Cher. There's an emergency exit back here." He reaches around the endcap to grab his backpack and slings it over his shoulder.

I make sure my backpack is closed and put it on too. "Won't the alarm sound?"

"Not this one. Besides, even if it does, we don't have a choice. We can't go through the front. Ready?"

He holds out his hand to me, palm up. And I slide my hand in his, lacing our fingers together without hesitation. I have a feeling I'll follow him almost anywhere.

27

AMELIA

THE KEYS JINGLE in my trembling hands, and it takes three times for me to press the unlock button. Sonny's hand covers mine, plucking the keys from my grip. "I'll drive."

He walks to the passenger side first, crowding me as I slip inside. He pushes my door closed and rounds the hood of my car, his gaze constantly surveying everything. Commotion at the gas station captures my attention. The tension is so thick, I can feel it even with all the asphalt, shrubbery, and sheer amount of feet between us.

Sonny slides in, tosses his backpack in the backseat, and we're on the road in thirty seconds. The pharmacy grows smaller and smaller in the side mirror, until it's barely a speck in the distance. I don't know if I can say the same about the experience though. It feels so much more significant than a crumb on my life's résumé.

The drive back to the motel is a blur, the washed-out gray sky, the earthy-colored standing water. The roads are busy, but not as bad as I expected, given how many people were in that little shopping complex.

I let myself fall back into that space between the seatback and the window. The window is hard and cool against my fevered skin, but the angle is nice. If I let my eyes rest, I can almost pretend I'm on a fun road trip with a curated playlist playing from the speakers.

My lids drift shut at the gentle hum of the road underneath us.

"HEY," Sonny says, resting his palm on my thigh. "We're here."

I roll my head along the headrest and look at him with a couple slow blinks. "Oh, I was resting my eyes. I'm sorry."

Sonny's lips quirk up. "Did anyone ever tell you that you snore, Cher?"

My cheeks get hot, and I resist the urge to swipe any wayward drool around my mouth. "What? I do not."

His grin grows wide. "It's this cute little noise, sort of like a shuffling sound."

"Oh my gosh," I say through a laugh and swat at his bicep with the back of my hand. "Stop it."

His chuckle floats through the air, this easy sound that's light and bright. "It's alright, Cher. It's the universe's way of evening you out a little. Can't stack too many advantages and assets in one person. It's not fair for everyone else."

I look at him from underneath my lashes, a disbelieving smirk on my lips. "Are you flirting with me, Sonny?"

He squeezes my thigh in a quick flex of his fingers. "If you have to ask, then I'm not doing it right."

My laugh takes me by surprise. "And what are your assets, Sonny?"

His fingers swirl little patterns on the inside of my thigh. I've never wished for a skirt or pair of shorts so much in my life. "I think you know what my assets are, Amelia."

My smile slips from laughter into something fonder and softer. "Thank you, Gray. For being here."

"There's no place I'd rather be."

Acting on impulse, I lean over the middle console and press my lips against his. It's a soft kiss, not intended to take it further than this.

But I should've known by now that Sonny is anything but unexpected.

He meets my tentative exploration with passion I thought was reserved for behind closed doors. His tongue snakes out and sweeps inside my mouth, tangling with mine. His palm leaves my thigh, and a second later, he pulls back.

"We have an audience, Cher."

My eyes are slow to open, a lusty haze settling over my senses. He grins at me, a carnal promise on his kiss-swollen lips. I reach for him, desperate to feel his lips on mine again just as my car door opens. Heat swarms the car, heating up everything that wasn't already warm with desire.

"Everything okay? You guys have been out here for a while." West's voice is low, like he's speaking through a clenched jaw.

"We're fine, West," Sonny says.

Looking over my shoulder, my suspicions are confirmed. A muscle in his jaw ticks as his eyes narrow on Sonny. "Gray."

His name sounds like a curse from West's mouth. I can't help the small part of me that revels in his possible jealousy. When we were in high school, he had a constant rotation of girls on his arm—and in his bed. Or so the rumors went. He hung out with Cole and I all the time, but he didn't shy away from the many, many girls vying for his attention. Somewhere along the way, I stopped counting. And caring.

Or that's the lie I fed myself every morning for breakfast. It was easier that way.

But this reaction is new.

And worth exploring. You know, if we weren't facing the alleged apocalypse.

I'm still holding out hope that Dad and Jerry are wrong.

Speaking of which. I twist around and swing my legs out of the car. "Did Dad call?"

West drags his gaze from Sonny to me, his eyes softening instantly. "No, Ames. I'm sorry. But we should get on the road now. You guys didn't see the videos. I have a feeling it's going to get much, much worse."

I bite the inside of my bottom lip and nod. I don't feel guilty for kissing Sonny—*or* that West saw us. But a tiny seed of shame worms its way into my gut because the supplies Cole needs are in the backseat, and I was in the front seat thinking about how easy it would be to slide my hand into Sonny's pants.

I loop my arm through my backpack and push to my feet. "Let's take care of Cole first, then we can go. I'll call Dad again from the car."

West steps back but snags the backpack off my back. "Let me carry this."

"Thanks." Right before we walk into room eleven, the wind gusts. It swirls my hair around my face, creating a dark blonde veil. I push it off my face and see Cole standing in the open doorway.

"Took you guys long enough," he snaps.

I let his irritation roll off my back and step around him into the motel room. The cool air wafts over me from the big vents under the windows to my right. I pull out a chair and pat the top of it before maneuvering the other chair to face him. "Sit."

Cole huffs and folds his arm across his chest. I'm pleased to see the gash on his forehead already crusting over, but it needs to be cleaned. The bloody towel he used to stem the bleeding lays discarded on the table between us. "I can patch myself up."

I snort. "Sure. I remember the pillow you made in Mrs. Birchwood's class."

His shoulders pull back, and his top lip lifts in a snarl. "I was thirteen and stuck in a Home Ec class I didn't give two shits about."

I try to stifle my smile as the image of his terribly-stitched pillow comes to mind. It was a blue-orange-white tie-dye with black stitches along the edges. "Oh, believe me, I remember."

"Whatever. I don't need stitches, so I'll be fine with whatever you got," he says, holding his big hand out, palm up.

I glare at his hand before shifting to his face. "Sit down, Cole."

Sonny drops his backpack on the table next to mine, but I don't take my gaze from Cole. It feels like we're trapped in a battle of wills, and I'm feeling bold and angry enough to not back down.

That quick reminder of our past is enough to ignite the fire that kept me warm on all those lonely nights for the last five years. West doesn't wade in either, but I hear his low murmurs from across the room.

"Well?" I arch a brow. "Are you going to sit down or are you going to continue to pout?"

He sits down in the chair across from me, scooting backward a few inches and settling against it. His legs spread wide, pulling the fabric of his pants taut across his muscular thighs. I swallow against the dryness in my throat.

And I find a new reason to curse Cole's name.

The traitorous tingle in my lower belly warms places that had only just started to cool. I clench my jaw against the sensation and busy myself with getting the supplies out.

I clean my hands with antiseptic wash and scoot closer, leaning in to clean his wound. He's so much taller than me, that even sitting down, his forehead is too far away to comfortably reach. Shuffling to the edge of my chair, I wipe away the dried blood on his skin. I make a low sound in the back of my throat and extend my arm further to wipe the other edge.

"For fuck's sake, Mia. Here," he snaps as his big hands brand themselves against my waist. He hauls me to my feet, properly wedged between his thighs. My hand is frozen in the air, an inch from his head. "Are you going to finish or what?"

I know it's not even remotely the right context, but when his lips wrap around those six letters, all I can think about is *finishing* in a very different circumstance. As discreetly as possible, I exhale a long breath.

He tips his head back, just the barest inch, and looks up at me through his impossibly dark lashes. It's criminal how long and inky his eyelashes are. Spite and something a lot less hateful sparkles from his eyes.

It feels like it's been a lifetime since I was close enough to see the flecks of amber twinkle in his dark brown eyes without cruelty slipping from his lips. I sway closer to him without conscious thought, succumbing to the pull of the secrets trapped in his dark-eyed gaze.

His fingertips press against me, branding their unique patterns on my skin. My tits are mere inches from his face, rising and falling quicker with my labored breaths. His lips part, and the smallest kernel of hope takes flight.

A second later, it nosedives to the bottom of my gut when he blinks. He opens his eyes, a mask neutralizing his expression as his hands slip from my waist.

I refuse to let myself feel disappointed. I ignore him and make quick work of cleaning the wound, applying three butterfly bandages to hold the gash closed while it heals.

I haven't forgiven him for what he did, anyway. So really, this is best.

If my conviction sounds weak, well, I ignore that too.

28

WEST

I PRESS the button to open Amelia's trunk, the couple bags we brought inside the motel clutched in my left hand. "Jesus, Gray. How much shit did you get?"

He leans in and drops the new backpacks they came back with in the empty space between two cardboard boxes. A rattling noise comes from inside both bags.

I eye the offending pieces of material with a raised brow. "What's in those?"

He rearranges a few more things, maneuvering Cole's hiking backpack and making room for the duffel bags in my hand. "Antibiotics."

I side-eye my best friend. "You got an infection I didn't hear about?"

He straightens up and looks over my shoulder at the highway. "It's always good to be prepared."

"Hmm." It's a noncommittal noise, but it's the best I have right now. I'm at a loss of how to respond. Too many questions tumble around inside my head. How would we know which antibiotic to give? How would we even diagnose anything? How would we know the dosage?

And maybe the biggest question of all: how did they walk out of a pharmacy with a backpack full of antibiotics they definitely didn't have prescriptions for?

That aside, there's truth to his statement that I might not have accepted a week ago. I don't want to think about what it would mean if we found ourselves in a situation where we didn't have any supplies *and* we couldn't get access to them. At least we have some supplies.

Those videos Cole showed me fucked me up a little, and paranoia has become my constant companion since. I don't know what to do to alleviate it—or how to fucking deal with it. But the more I try to ignore it, the bigger it gets. Like some perverse balloon that grows larger instead of slowly deflating.

And the fact that there are considerably more cars on the road now than twenty minutes ago when they got back is making me fucking twitchy.

"We ready?"

"Find high protein pantry items. Beans and lentils will last almost indefinitely and sealed rice and canned goods will take years before they expire. Avoid produce and perishables unless you're planning to eat them right then. Check the dates on anything you buy, but all of these things in here"—he places his palm on a cardboard box—"will last you a long time. If you need more, look for food like this. Amelia will know what to get. That's why I went with her."

My heart pounds an irregular rhythm with every word he says. "Why are you telling me this?"

Gray looks me in the eye. We're the same height and similar build. Our personalities are deceptively different, but in a way that balances each other out. I consider him a brother, and I have for many years.

But I've never seen him look at me with the expression on his face. I don't even know how to describe it.

"I'm afraid we'll never connect with Amelia's dad, and you and Cole need to know this stuff."

My brows slam over my eyes. "You planning on going solo? Where's this all coming from?"

He looks into the distance behind me for a moment before giving me his attention again. "Nah, I'm not leaving her. But some things are out of our control. And I want to make sure she's not alone."

Indignation swells up inside me, puffing my chest and slamming my brows low. "I would never leave her alone in this world."

Gray nods, two slow jerks of his head. "And what if you had to choose? Her or Cole?"

Everything inside me shrinks down into a tiny ball of emotion. Too many to pinpoint just one, so it's easier if I do what I always do. I force a grin on my face. "You been reading those *why choose* novels again, Gray?"

He doesn't crack a smile. "I'm serious, West. I honestly don't know what the future holds. If we'll make it to some mysterious ship, or if it's an elaborate misunderstanding, and we'll all be back to normal in two weeks. But right now? Right now, it's a whole new world, and it's fucking chaos. The same rules don't apply. I know where I stand. Do you?"

I CAN'T STOP THINKING about what Gray said. It's been hovering in the back of my mind for the last fifty miles. I haven't really allowed myself to think about what's happening. Even in those moments of physical quiet while my brother and I waited on them, my mind was busy, too loud to let anything else in.

But I don't have that same luxury right now.

He's planted the seed, and the last hour of quiet has watered it endlessly.

I can't stop picturing some sort of post-apocalyptic hell on earth where Amelia gets stuck in a terrible life.

Could I do it? Could I essentially sacrifice my brother for her?

I glance at her through the rearview mirror, trace the long line of her neck when she tips her head back and giggles quietly. I watch the way her nose scrunches up when she's suppressing a laugh.

I think I could.

My brother snatched my chance with her before, but this time is different. The time and space between all of us was wiped out the moment the mountain fell. I've been given another opportunity, and I won't take it for granted.

"Eyes on the road." Cole's voice is sharp, low enough for my ears only.

I tighten my grip on the steering wheel and force myself not to look in the rearview mirror. Again. I don't bother defending myself, but I won't take all the blame. Those two in the backseat are fucking distracting.

"Do they need to sit so close to each other? And what could they possibly be talking about for the last two hours?"

I don't need to turn my head to know he's frustrated. I ignore the heat of his gaze on the side of my face. He's not the only one frustrated. I'll be damned if someone slinks in there and steals her out from under my nose—a-*fucking*-gain—brother or not.

"Why am I the one stuck driving," I grumble.

"Why don't you pull onto the next shoulder that's dry? I don't mind driving, and I don't think there's a rest stop for miles," Amelia offers.

I close my eyes in a long blink at the honeyed tone of her voice. What I wouldn't give to have her all to myself in the backseat for hours while someone else drove us to safety.

"Nah, I'm good, Ames. The sky looks like it's getting dark, so I don't want to stop unless we absolutely have to."

She leans forward between the two front seats. "I really don't mind, West."

I chance a glance at her. "You can take the next shift, yeah?"

She squeezes my shoulder before she sits back in her seat. "Alright. Let me know if you change your mind."

I nod and alternate keeping an eye on the traffic around us and the sky. I wasn't exaggerating. Storm clouds gather up ahead, and it's windy enough that you can see the clouds flying through the sky.

The closer we get to California, the more traffic there is. It's not surprising, there's really only one main road that's a straight shot from Nevada to the California coast. What's surprising is eighty percent of the traffic is on the other side of the highway.

"Are we sure we're going the right way?" Cole murmurs, eyes on the cars across the highway.

"The message for Amelia's dad said Santa Monica—"

"Site twenty-three, I remember," he interrupts. "But what the fuck does that even mean?"

I shake my head and glance at the traffic on the other side of the divide. "I have no idea. Hey, does it seem like they're slowing down?"

Cole cranes his neck to look around me. "Maybe there's an accident."

My lips flatten into a thin line. "Maybe. But why are so many people leaving California? We know everyone got a similar message to stay indoors."

Amelia's phone rings, playing through the speakers, cutting off any further speculation. The touch screen on the dash lights up with *Dad* and a little icon of Papa Christensen's face.

Amelia leans forward, over the middle console. "Quick, answer it, West!"

I press the green answer button immediately. The static on the other end fills the car, crackling and snapping.

"Dad?"

"Amelia? Amelia, are you there?"

"I'm here, Dad. We've been trying to call you for over twenty-four hours. Why haven't you answered?" She pitches her voice louder.

"What? Who's we?" Dad snaps.

I shift in my seat and share a look with Gray in the rearview mirror. A bad feeling sprouts inside my chest, and I wonder if this is the moment where we have to part ways. Amelia's brows hunch low over her eyes, and I don't think she'll give us up so easily.

I hope not, at least.

"Friends, Dad." The words are pushed past her teeth.

"Amelia. This is not fun time with friends. This is a matter of life and death!" His voice raises at the end, his irritation clear.

Fun time with friends I mouth and look at Cole, my eyes wide.

"I know it's a matter of life and death. I just had a gun in my face three hours ago." Her jaw clenches, her eyes narrowing. "You remember Cole and West, don't you? They lived across the street from us for all those years we lived here. And their . . . brother. The three of them have helped me."

My eyes cut to her at the mention of a gun. She glosses over the whole gun thing like it's nothing, a minor inconvenience. But it's not fucking minor, and my glare to Gray promises that we'll be having a chat about that real soon.

"Helped you—did you just say *gun*?" Her dad's voice hits fever-pitch, and I instinctively turn down the volume by two notches. "You know what? We'll talk about that when I see you. I'm about forty-five minutes away."

"Oh good. We're not too far behind you. We're about two hours from Santa Monica. But we don't know where site twenty-three is."

Her dad's words are garbled behind static and background noise.

"Dad? I can't hear you."

"Amelia—California—twenty-three."

"What? You're breaking up!" She's near yelling now, frustration making her words sharp.

"I said *do not go to California*!" Reception clears, and we hear him loud and clear.

Amelia gasps. "What?"

"You were supposed to wait for someone to pick you up! Why—why would you leave?"

Her mouth parts, closes, and parts again. She's blinking too fast, and I can practically see her thoughts tumbling over one another. "Because you told us to pack. And then the power went out, and after the emergency broadcast message that went out to everyone, the one personalized to you came on. It said Santa Monica, site twenty-three."

"God damnit, Amelia. Get the hell out of there!" her dad yells.

I don't think I've ever heard him curse before, and he just dropped two of them in a row.

Amelia's hands tremble as she tucks a lock of hair behind her ear, but I'm more focused on finding a break in the highway divider. We need to turn around.

"Why? What aren't you telling me?"

"The San Andreas Fault has been activated, Amelia."

29

AMELIA

I STARE at the little thumbnail of my father's smiling face on the touchscreen in my dash. I recognize the words he's saying, but I don't understand what that means exactly. My knowledge of the San Andreas Fault is limited to a few disaster movies West made us watch the summer he was obsessed with earthquakes.

I spread my legs wider, lean my elbows on my knees, and sink my hands into my hair. "Okay. Okay. That's fine. We can just . . . turn around, head back to Vegas."

"We're not taking this highway. There's no way we'll make it through. It's gridlocked heading back," West says. I'm not sure if Dad can pick their voices up through the spotty connection and noisy background.

"At least now we know why," Cole murmurs.

I hadn't really been paying attention to traffic, letting myself relax in Sonny's presence. But as I look at the three lanes of bumper-to-bumper traffic crawling along the highway, terror blossoms in my belly.

"We can't go back to Vegas. We could still get stranded if it starts raining again," West says.

"Well, you can't stay in California. Even if you don't get hurt, you'll be trapped behind road closures and destroyed buildings," Dad snaps. "You'll never make it to the bunker."

Okay, so I guess that answers that question—he can definitely hear them.

My head jerks up, facing the dash like he can actually see me. "Wait—what bunker?"

"This is what I've been telling you the whole time, Amelia! I need you to listen closely because I don't know how long cell towers will remain standing."

"What about our satellite phones?" I interrupt him. Talking over someone is one of Dad's biggest pet peeves, but honestly, we have bigger problems right now. And I need to know that if we get disconnected, I still have a way to reach him.

Dad sighs, the sound nasally and somehow shrill through the speakers of my car. "Possibly. I have no way of knowing what reception will be like underground."

The smallest kernel of hope is enough for me, for right now. "Okay. It's a possibility, at least. Tell us where to go, how to find you and this bunker."

"There's no *us*, Amelia. And I'm very sorry to say this so bluntly, but I don't have clearance for your friends. Jerry and I only have so many spots, and they're all reserved for family. I appreciate what you boys have done, but maybe it's best to part ways soon."

A dark whirling mass of desperation swirls inside my chest, growing larger and more destructive with each word from my father. He talks so casually—*parting ways* like this is a job that I'm leaving and he's giving the notice.

When really it's a death sentence. We're in the dark, less so than maybe the average person, but still so clueless about what's happening—and what's to come.

The thought of leaving them gives me hives—if hives were made of terror. Desperation swells, mingles with fear, and I open my mouth without thinking anything through.

"We're married."

Silence balloons around me, from the phone call and the three men surrounding me. It stretches, filling every available inch inside the car. The back of my neck gets hot, but I don't move. I don't tear my gaze from the photo of my dad's smiling face on the screen. Not even to check the expressions of the three very intense gazes I feel on me.

My dad breaks it first with a choking, hacking sort of noise. "Ex*cuse* me?"

I clear my throat and keep my gaze on the screen. "I got married. Three days ago." My hair prickles where it rests against my scalp, and I can't stop the panic-fueled words from spilling from my mouth. "Filed the paperwork and everything. My new husband has two brothers. And I'm not going in without them—*all* of them."

West jerks the wheel to the right. It's enough to tear my gaze from the screen to watch him cross three lanes of traffic. I careen to the left, but Sonny's sure grip stops me from tumbling too far. It's the first exit we've seen for miles, so I understand his haste. His hands grip the steering wheel tight enough to turn his knuckles white.

"When—when did you do this? We were just in New Jersey. And—and who exactly did you marry?" Dad practically barks his questions. I imagine him pacing, huffing in the way he does when he's annoyed.

I lick my lips and prepare to dig a little deeper. In for a penny and all that. "It was—"

"Me, sir. Cole Armstrong."

COLE

• • •

MY BROTHER'S head jerks toward mine so quickly, he takes the car to the right. We dip into another lane, and the car next to us slams on its horn long enough to make their displeasure known. It only takes a second to get us back within the lines as we fly down a smaller highway. We're desperate to leave California, just like the rest of the population, it seems.

My skin feels too tight over my muscles, stretched too far. Regret slaps me in the face with all the force of a bowling ball. I clench my molars so hard, I swear I hear them creak in protest.

But I'd bet my life savings that my brother is seething with jealousy right now.

And that's exactly why I did it. I can handle my brother's jealousy, but what I can't handle is him getting tangled up in her lies. If she'd named him, he'd get swept up in it. He'd lose sight of the fact that we're in a literal race against mother nature to survive.

And he might die for it.

That's not a risk I'm willing to take. Not when it comes to him or Gray. Though Gray seems just as enamored, he wears it differently than West.

Neither of them know who she really is, but I suspect none of us do. For them, I'll sacrifice myself so they don't get trapped in her web.

Of course, I can't explain that to them, not yet. West would brush me off like he did at The Lodge up on the mountain. And Gray would ask too many questions.

I clear my throat and pretend like her face isn't six inches away from mine. "Mr. Christensen, I don't know if you remember me. I lived across the street from you the last time you were in Las Vegas."

"Cole? One of Wayne's boys?"

"Yes, sir. That's me. My brothers West and Gray are here too. They were our witnesses down at the Little Big Chapel." I practically choke on the lie as it tumbles out.

"I—I don't know what to say. Is there something else going on, Amelia? This isn't one of those shotgun sort of things, right?"

Amelia sputters next to my ear. "What? Dad, no. Cole and I"—she coughs—"are in love." She clears her throat again. "But enough about that, please tell us what's going on."

"Yes, yes, of course. We'll talk more once we see each other. But Amelia? You need to get out of California right now. I'm not there, so I don't have an accurate reading, but our colleagues are predicting at least a nine point zero on the Richter scale when the fault goes."

"*What?*" Amelia gasps. "When is it supposed to happen? How much time do we have?"

I feel the color drain from my face as hope leeches out of me and fear swells. I lean forward and hit the dash in front of me. "Drive, West, drive!"

"Fuck, I am," he grits through clenched teeth, pressing on the gas more. The car jerks forward as he increases our speed.

"I don't know. An hour, maybe two. Maybe ten minutes—I don't know! It's a relatively new warning system they're still developing, but it's the closest we've ever come to predicting earthquakes." He pauses and background noise from wherever he is gets louder. "There will be aftershocks. Maybe even a series of catastrophic earthquakes, or possibly a complete breakdown of the entire fault line. But Amelia, I don't need to impress upon you the need for urgency, do I?"

"Fuck, Dad! Couldn't you have told me this earlier? A nine . . . a nine point zero will decimate everyone and everything unlucky enough to be in its target."

Goosebumps crawl over my too-tight skin with her words. Call it foreboding or fear or a fucking omen, but I can't shake the feeling.

"Stick to as many highways as possible, and for the love of god, *do not* stop under an overpass if the ground starts shaking."

"Where are we going, Dad?"

"The bunker is in Magnolia Park, Kansas. It's one of several government-grade facilities that have been regularly maintained and upgraded over the years. I'm told it's big enough to house a town's worth of people with scientifically-modified greenhouses for growing crops and a revolutionary water filtration system. Those are the two most important things if we're going to be underground, you know. Without those things, we might as well—"

"Okay, got it," she interrupts him. "Kansas. We can do that. Right, guys?" Her voice is so hopeful, it'd be too easy to step in and smooth out her fear.

"Maybe sixteen hours if it's on the west side? Twenty-two if it's on the east," West says.

I lean forward and pull up her GPS map on the touchscreen. I type in the city and a little white circle appears, like it's buffering or something. It clears a moment later, showing our destination. "Sixteen hours and twelve minutes. Without stopping, traffic, or road closures."

"So, realistically, closer to twenty-four hours," West says, drumming his fingers on the steering wheel.

I look from the quickly darkening sky to my brother. "Let's not worry about that until we have to."

"If something happens, you call me, okay? Me or Jerry. Use the sat phones. I want check-ins every three hours. And Amelia?" Amelia's dad pauses. "You have to get here by June first."

Amelia blows out a breath. "Okay. What happens on June first?"

"They close the doors."

30

AMELIA

"SIT BACK BEHIND COLE, Ames, and put your belt on," West demands as soon as the call disconnects.

I follow his command on autopilot, my knee bouncing with displaced anxiety. "I should be the one driving. I'm the getaway driver, remember?" My smile is weak, not that West can see it. His eyes are narrowed on the street in front of us as he weaves us in and out of traffic. He's driving like one of those assholes who thinks the normal rules apply, using the shoulder to pass cars that are going too slow for us.

Part of me wishes I could call out to them, urge them to go faster and get the hell out of the danger zone. But I don't have any real way to do that—and there's no telling that they would believe a random person anyway.

Not to mention, I don't know where the danger zone is exactly, but I'll feel better once we get the hell out of California. "Does anyone know where the San Andreas Fault is exactly? How close are we?"

"Isn't your dad a seismologist?" Cole asks in a tone that clearly says *shouldn't you know that*?

"Yeah, but that doesn't mean I know it," I snap.

"The San Andreas Fault starts on some beach on the Salton Sea and carves a path northwest, getting closer and closer to the coast. We're about an hour north right now," West explains.

"Which means we're still too close," Sonny says.

West nods. "We're still too close. Let's pray it doesn't hit until we're two more hours away. I'm heading toward Arizona and hoping for the best."

The radio plays softly as West flies down the highway, but it's otherwise quiet. The albatross around our necks is heavy enough, conversation would only weigh us down further right now. I shift in my seat, unable to get comfortable or stay still. There's a build-up of frenetic energy that I don't know what to do with.

Twenty minutes later, it starts.

The radio crackles to life, interrupting the song with an automated message.

"This is an emergency weather broadcast. This is an earthquake warning. Please take cover immediately. This is an emergency weather broadcast. This is an earthquake warning. Please take cover immediately."

The car lurches forward, and we cross into the other lane. A yell is torn from my throat when we jolt again. I brace my hands on the back of Cole's seat and plant my feet against the floorboards.

"Fuck, hang on!" West yells. He eases the car to the side of the road, away from the overpass we just drove under.

The earth shakes and shakes as West rolls us to a stop on the shoulder. He pulls the parking brake with a quick jerk, and his eyes find mine over his shoulder.

"It's alright, Ames. It'll be over quick," West says. The whites of his eyes stand out against the muddied green of his irises, making it hard to swallow his platitudes.

The contents of our trunk rustle, sliding against one another with clinks and thumps. West tears his gaze from mine and glances behind me.

It feels like we're on one of those Tilt-A-Whirl rides, but at a shitty traveling carnival with questionable equipment. Nausea creeps up as the jerking motion gives me a touch of motion sickness.

I blindly reach out for Sonny's hand, something to anchor me here, to reel in my fear. His long fingers lace with mine, and he tightens his grip.

Cars stop left and right, some pulling over in front and behind us, and some stopping in the middle of the road. I look behind me right as the overpass we drove under buckles. Cracks splinter and pieces of concrete break off, plummeting to the highway below.

Tires screech as cars slam on their brakes on the other side of the overpass. Thankfully, no one was underneath when it fell. But all those cars are stranded on that side of the road.

The small trees on either side of the highway bend like seventy-mile-per-hour winds are pounding against them. The bushes and flowers and vegetation shimmer like a mirage.

I face forward again, my right hand inching over the top of the seat and grasping Cole's shoulder. I don't think about it—or anything else. And when he reaches up and tangles his fingers with mine, I squeeze them in appreciation.

He turns his head toward my hand, his five o'clock shadow scratching my skin. "We're alright, Mia."

"It's almost over," Sonny says. I don't know who he's soothing, me or either of them, but I'll take it all the same.

An eternity passes before the shaking stops. At least, that's what it feels like. In reality, it was probably a minute.

Sixty of the longest seconds of my life. I clutch Cole's and Sonny's hands the entire time. And when the shaking stops, I slip my hand from theirs and exhale a deep breath. A hysterical sort of chuckle bubbles up in my chest, rising higher and higher until it slips free.

I push my hair off my face and grip my head. "Holy shit. I can't believe we made it through that."

"There could be aftershocks, we shouldn't linger," Sonny says.

My hysterical laughter tapers off, and I sober up at that thought. "You're right. Dad said there could be multiple big earthquakes too. We should go. I can drive, West."

He looks over his shoulder at me. "I'm fine, Ames. We'll—"

"I'll drive, man," Sonny interrupts him. "Let's switch."

West's shoulders tense for a moment before they drop, and he nods. "Yeah, alright. We'll need gas soon, probably a couple hours."

"Anyone need anything from the back?"

"I'll take a water," West says as he pushes open his door.

"Me too, Cher," Sonny murmurs as he carefully opens his door and steps out.

Cole half-turns, looking at me over his shoulder. "I'll take one. And a snack if you have something."

I unbuckle my seatbelt, push onto my knees, and lean over my seat to reach the water in the trunk area. Thankfully my SUV has an open-concept trunk, which makes it very convenient in situations like this. I grab two waters and hold them out behind me. Cole snags them, and I grab another two and some snacks.

I turn around and pass up a canister of nuts and an apple. "Here ya go."

"Thanks," Cole murmurs. I don't know what surprised me more—the lack of hostility or the fact that he didn't bring up the hand-holding while mother nature raged her displeasure and shook the earth.

I eye his head, unconsciously looking for any further signs of hurt or damage, but he seems alright. I nod, working to keep my face in a neutral expression.

Sonny sits behind the wheel at the same time West slides in next to me, and Cole pulls his gaze from mine, slowly turning around.

West spreads his legs wide as he settles in next to me. He leans his head back against the headrest as Sonny steers us back into traffic. He scrubs his hands down his face and lets out a sigh I feel in my bones.

Not for the first time, I feel our time apart so acutely, it steals my breath. Gratitude expands inside my chest at our fateful reunion—or union, when it comes to Sonny.

They say emotions heighten in life-or-death situations, and I've been in a few of them in the span of as many days. It'd be easy to chalk everything up to that.

But that doesn't explain the bone-crushing terror that held me captive when my dad told me to ditch them and leave their fates up in the air.

Sonny speeds down the highway, fast enough that our surroundings blur together. With every passing moment that the earth doesn't shake beneath the tires, I concentrate on relaxing my body, one muscle at a time.

It's a little trick I picked up from yoga class—another one of those things Alley dragged me to.

And holy shit—*Alley*!

I lean forward and swipe my phone from the rear cup holders on the back of the middle console.

"Everything okay?" West arches a brow.

I unlock my phone and pull up her contact information. The thumbnail with her smiling face taunts me as I tap the call button and bring my phone to my ear.

It rings over and over and over again.

"C'mon, pick up, pick up."

"Are you calling your dad back? Did you forget something?" Sonny asks.

I pull the inside of my cheek between my molars. "No, Alley."

"Who's Alley?"

"My best friend," I murmur as her voicemail picks up.

"Hey, it's Alley. Don't leave me a voicemail because I probably won't listen to it. Text me instead!"

I clear my throat as the beep sounds in my ear. "Hey, girl. It's Amelia. I'll try to text you too, but you need to take cover if you can." I hesitate, knowing that my dad might kill me for sharing this information. But I can't *not* tell her either. "If you can, drive toward the Midwest. I'm headed to Magnolia Park in Kansas. It's uh, the safest place right now, but call me back."

I end the call and immediately text her the same information from my voicemail. My thumb hovers over the send button, almost afraid to text her.

What if she's hurt or trapped somewhere?

I press send and clutch my phone in my hand, worrying my bottom lip with my teeth.

"Hey," West says as he lays his palm on my thigh. "You okay?"

My lip pops free as I look over at him. "Yeah, it's just—I should've reached out right away. I wasn't thinking properly, but I could've warned her at least." I blow out a breath. "And now it might be too late."

The air feels heavy between us. It's a strange juxtaposition since Sonny has us near flying down this two-lane highway. He expertly weaves into the oncoming lane to pass a little two-door hatchback car packed to the brim.

The guy driving flips us the bird, but Sonny never even notices, his attention firmly on the road in front of us.

31

AMELIA

WE'VE BEEN DRIVING for a half hour, the mood tense but bearable. I think we're all just waiting for another earthquake to hit.

I know Sonny is—he speeds up every time we have to go underneath an overpass. I have a feeling the image of the bridge collapsing will stay with all of us for a while.

We've been lucky though. I thought for sure we'd experience another earthquake, but it's only been little rumblings. Twice now, the earth has hummed for a few seconds. And by the time Sonny slows down, it's over.

Maybe since we're moving east and the fault line runs north and west, we're somehow escaping it?

I don't know. I almost called Dad, but since we're all fine, it feels unnecessary. Our check-in phone call is in a little over an hour, anyway. I can always get him up to speed then.

The highway we're on is in the middle of a desert, all flatland and minimal trees, so it's not a terrible place to be for an earthquake. So long as the earth doesn't crack wide open and swallow us whole.

I flip my phone over again, the screen brightening with the motion. No new notifications.

A sigh slips out before I can hold it in, and I roll my head along the headrest and look at West.

He rakes his hand through his hair, tugging it off of his forehead. "I can feel you staring, you know." His voice is low, meant for my ears only.

I can't help the little smile that quirks up the corner of my mouth. He's so goddamn good-looking it makes my chest ache a little. And when he does things like this, little mannerisms and catch-phrases that I can recall with vivid details, it squeezes my heart a little.

"Just admiring the view," I murmur.

Someone turns up the volume on the radio, loud enough to muffle quiet conversation. And considering Cole's shitty disposition ninety-five percent of the time since I saw him, I'm guessing it was Sonny.

His gaze cuts to mine with a quick jerk of his head, his hand still tangled in his locks. He spots my smirk immediately, and his mouth mirrors mine. "Is that right? A fan of California, are we?"

I arch a brow. "Are we still in California?"

West leans toward the middle and looks at the touchscreen in my dash. Thankfully, we're able to use the GPS system in the car so it doesn't drain our phone batteries.

His leather and crisp linen smell surrounds me, and I didn't realize I closed my eyes until I feel his breath fanning my eyelids. "We're in California for another twenty miles."

My eyes spring open, and I'm not surprised to find him so close to me. I'm tempted to tilt my chin up, to feel his lips pressing against mine again.

But first, a little teasing never hurt. Especially if it riles him up a little. I cock my head to the side and lift a shoulder. "Oh perfect, then. I've always been into California surfers. Maybe we can find a few on our way out of town."

Someone snorts in the front seat, but we don't break our gaze from one another.

"Bullshit," he whispers, never pulling back.

I shift in my seat, feeling the air in the car swell with an entirely different emotion. "Is it?"

He pulls back and reaches up, tugging on the ends of my hair. His gaze ping-pongs over my face quickly.

"Yeah, Ames, it is." He drops my hair and leans back, folding his arms across his chest. This cocksure smirk spreads wide across his face.

A smile that has no business being so . . . *so attractive*.

"You hated those preppy-boy assholes who never shut up about their weekend trips to *catch waves in California* back when we were in school."

I lift my left leg up and tuck my foot under my right knee. "Yeah, well, those were preppy asshole *boys*."

He takes my sass in stride, his smile growing wide just as a grumble sounds from the front seats. A kernel of guilt threatens to worm its way inside my joy. It feels almost too easy to tease him—to *flirt* with him—so soon after everything that happened.

But maybe that's the point.

Maybe that's the silver lining for us.

It's another chance with them—and a fresh one with Sonny.

It's just cruelly offered at the supposed end of the world. Perhaps it's part of the gift. When faced with possible imminent mortality, those hang-ups and bruised egos and festering feelings don't feel as oppressive as they once did.

If my dad's right, then these could very well be the last few days of our lives. And how we choose to spend them is entirely up to us.

I rake my teeth over my bottom lip, letting my thoughts run wild, drafting the biggest *what if* scenarios imaginable. And then flipping them around and seeing if my reaction would be the same.

Our time is never guaranteed, but the tricky thing is most of us are rarely aware of our seconds ticking down. And now? Now the whole world is privy to that fateful clock.

The only choice is: how are we going to spend the rest of our time?

West reaches over and drags his thumb across my jaw. "Where'd you go? You lost your smile."

I lean into his hand, and his palm slides further along my jaw. "I'm right here."

His eyes narrow as they look between mine. The soft brush of his thumb sweeping along my jaw is soothing. My shoulders sink as tension I didn't realize I was carrying releases.

His pink lips twist to the side. It's his telltale move when he's feeling playful.

"Good, because I have a serious question."

Gratitude settles around my shoulders like my favorite sweatshirt, warm and comforting. He let me have my vague brush-off. I roll my lips inward to smother a smile. "Shoot."

"Who the hell is Alley, and why did you let her take my spot?"

Another grunt sounds from the front seat, and I swear I hear some grumbling. Not anything that I can make out over the radio though. There's some slow, jazzy rendition of "Silent Night" playing.

I shake my head, my brows sinking in the center. "*Your* spot?"

He taps his chest twice with his free hand. "I was the best friend, yeah?"

"You and Cole," I murmur with a nod.

Something flashes in his gaze for a moment, like a shadow skirting across his vision. If I blinked, I would've missed it.

Still, it's the truth. They were both my best friends.

Until they weren't.

"Don't," West says, sliding his palm down my neck and into my hair. "I see it in your eyes, but let's not go there. Not right now."

I nod, two small movements. "Okay." My voice is low, my acceptance saturating the space between us now.

His thumb brushes a soft pattern across my neck, pausing on my pulse point. My breath hitches as the air around us shimmers with awareness.

"Do you remember all the shit we got into growing up? The pranks and the little turf spats over the quad?"

I chuckle, feeling my eyes twinkle with laughter. "Of course I remember."

His smile is soft, his thumb never slowing. "Me too. I remember all of them—every second with you."

My chest tightens with his admission, truth ringing from each syllable. Confusion sinks like a boulder in my gut. If he was so *invested*, then why didn't he write me or reach out?

We're dancing around it now, and it only grows by the second. Pretty soon, it'll be unavoidable.

And I'm not sure if I'm looking forward to that conversation or dreading it.

"Like the time Shelley Langston got expelled for turning the pool hot pink even though she swears she didn't do it. She got kicked off the swim team for that one."

I tip my head up and look down my nose at him. "Oh, I remember. Shelley Langston was a bitch. She deserved everything she got."

I caught her talking shit about West one day. She had her entire little posse of girls—a bunch of *yes men*—gathered around like she was holding court or something. As soon as she started spewing lies about West's birth parents, she signed her own fall.

And because she was an equal opportunity dick to everyone, it didn't even take that much legwork to get people to help.

His thumb pauses, and he tightens his grip ever so slightly, tilting my head up a little. "So savage."

When it comes to you and Cole, yes, I think to myself.

I don't say it out loud though, instead, I smirk. "I thought that's what you liked about me."

I couldn't help my jealousy back then, and to be honest, I'm not sure I could weather it any better now.

Though that doesn't even seem remotely like an issue when it comes to Cole or Gray—for very different reasons.

"Oh, Amelia, there are so many things I like about you," he murmurs.

Before I can respond, the volume on the radio is turned up further. Mariah Carey's "All I Want For Christmas" plays loudly through the speakers.

West and I share a look, his eyes twinkling with mischief. It's all the confirmation I need, and before I can stop myself, a giggle slips out.

West nods his head, these drawn-out movements. "You thinking about that one time, Ames?"

I cock my head to the side and close my lips over my laughter. "What time?"

"Gray, did we ever tell you about that time Cole ran for student government?"

Sonny's gaze flicks to mine in the rearview mirror before moving to West's. He twists the volume knob and Mariah gets quieter. "Nah, don't think I've heard that one."

I bite my lip and try to keep my giggles under control. I haven't thought about that in a very long time. "You sure he didn't tell you about the time these song lyrics were on a poster with his face—"

Cole huffs. "I know it was you two who did it, so laugh it up."

West holds up his hands, palms up. "Wasn't me, man. I swear it. I told you that from the beginning!"

Cole rolls his neck from side to side. "Whatever. I don't know why I bother. You covered for her then, and you're still covering for her now."

"Hey, I didn't do anything either, though it was kind of funny—"

"Yeah, it's so funny to have your photo on bullshit fliers with the twisted lyrics to a *bullshit* Christmas song—"

"Hey, I love this song!"

Cole keeps talking, never skipping a beat. "Right around Christmastime in some fucked-up mash-up of this song and the whole *Uncle Sam wants you* message. It wasn't even clever. The only thing that fucking flyer did was make my life harder. That fucking flyer almost made me change my number."

I smirk. "But you won though, so I guess you should've thanked whoever hung up those Armstrong for VP posters."

"I never wanted to be the vice president of our class, so it was a waste of time." Cole reaches over and turns the volume up until Mariah's high note feels like it's rattling inside my head.

I unbuckle my seatbelt and scoot over to the middle seat. West stretches his arm along the headrests, and as soon as I buckle up again, his hand comes down to rest on my shoulder.

"Don't mind him, Ames, he's just cranky because he hasn't had his *special* coffee."

His fingertips twirl little patterns back and forth, his touch so innocent yet my mind conjures up an entirely different scenario in which his fingers softly glide across my skin.

My eyes close at the feeling of his lips on the top of my head, and I let myself melt into his embrace, even if just for a moment.

If I keep them closed, I can almost pretend that this is a normal car ride. Just four friends cruising down the highway and enjoying the ride.

32

AMELIA

"WE'RE STOPPING FOR GAS." Sonny flicks the blinker on and pulls into the parking lot of a deluxe gas station. He follows the small sign with an arrow pointing right toward the six rows of regular gas pumps.

I lift my head from West's shoulder to look out the windshield. It looks nice, not quite brand-new, but probably built in the last five years. Considering it's the first gas station we've seen in fifty miles, it was probably needed.

To the left is a lot of four rows of those special gas pumps for trucks. And in the middle, bridging the two is a sizable building. A sign for a fast food restaurant takes up the left side of the building, and my mouth waters at the thought of a greasy cheeseburger.

I wonder if they're serving food. A couple walks out a second before a woman and two kids and a guy walk inside the building, so it seems like they're open, at least.

Apprehension prickles down my spine, like ants crawling over your feet during an afternoon at the park.

"Where is everyone?" West asks. "We're only a few hours away."

I lean forward and glance around, noting that only half the pumps have cars at them. "That's what I was just wondering. Maybe they didn't hear the news?"

"No," Cole says with a shake of his head. "They were saying online that it was nationwide."

"An earthquake just rocked California a couple hundred miles away. Shouldn't they be—I don't know, *distressed* or something? The gas station outside the pharmacy was *insane*."

"It doesn't seem like there's much urgency here." West's voice is low, his head turned to look out his window.

My gaze strays to a sign in the window advertising their *clean and secure showers*. For those people on a long run or road trip, I imagine. Still, it's not the kind of sign I expected to see.

It's such a sharp contrast to the scene from earlier today. It makes my head spin a little.

"Left side or right, Cher?"

"Uh, left—driver's side," I murmur.

Sonny pulls up to a pump, throws the car in park, and turns off the car. He palms the keys and stays inside the car for a moment. "It seems oddly calm here, but let's not linger, yeah?"

The satellite phone starts beeping and vibrating inside the cup holder. I practically dive for it between the seats and answer it in two seconds flat.

"Dad?"

"Amelia? Hello? Amelia?"

I lean over in my seat, as if the six inches to the left is really going to improve the signal that much. "I'm here!"

Static comes through the phone. I wince at the loud crackling in my ear. "Oh, good. Where are you now? Are you alright? Make it out of California okay?"

"Yeah, we're alright. We felt that earthquake, Dad. It was—" I quiet my voice as I remember how scared we were. It feels like a lifetime ago, not hours. "Scary, but we're safe. Lucky."

"Glad you're alright. We lost communication with our friends in

California, so we lost our lifeline to the west coast seismology center."

The static gets louder, and I push my index finger of my left hand against my left ear. "Where are you?"

"We're somewhere in Utah."

"Utah?" West mumbles from right next to me. He's close enough that his cheek nearly touches mine.

I pull the phone away from my ear and press the button to put it on speakerphone. West doesn't pull away from me though, his brows drawn low over his eyes as he stares at the black phone.

Panic slices through me, a swift line down my sternum. "Why Utah? I thought we're supposed to go to Kansas?"

"We were in northern Nevada the last time we spoke, remember? That's where our site was when we pieced everything together about Burton's journals. I bet they'll make it some sort of national landmark when this is over. If there's anything left when it ends, that is—"

"Dad." I snap his name. His ability to get lost in tangents is going to be the ruin of us one day. I can only hope today is not that day.

"Yes, of course. Well, we couldn't very well pass through Las Vegas to take the Arizona route. Not with the flooding and general hysteria there."

My fingernails bite into my thigh as I clutch my leg. My chest feels tight. "There's hysteria in Las Vegas?"

There's some rustling on his end, and I can't tell if it's static or he's shuffling a newspaper. "It's everywhere, Amelia."

West's warm palm covers mine, and my gaze snaps to his. His expression is open, his eyes look like fresh moss. He slides his fingers between mine, so we're both clutching my thigh, and I release the death-grip on my leg.

In a moment of clear reception, I can hear Dad clear his throat. "I'm sorry, Amelia. I can't—I can't make it to you."

My sinuses sting, catching me off-guard. "It's fine, Dad. I'm fine. We'll meet you in Kansas like we talked about."

He coughs. "Yeah, okay. Okay. Your, uh, new husband and his brothers are still with you, right?"

I flash the phone a watery smile. "Yeah, Dad. We're all still together."

"Good, that's good. Be safe, and I'll call again in three hours."

I sniff and nod, even though he can't see me. "Talk to you in three hours."

He ends the call, and I stare at the phone for a moment. "Do you think they'll be able to make it through the mountains?"

I don't know who I'm asking—them or myself or whatever higher power is listening.

"He'll be fine, Ames. Your dad knows his shit when it comes to weather and natural disasters. Him and Jerry will be fine." West gently squeezes my hand.

I nod, wipe away the stray tear with my finger, and blow out a breath. "Anyone else feel like a burger from the place next to it?"

"Yeah, I could eat. I'll go with you and pay for the gas inside. Let's conserve our cash," West offers.

"Alright," Sonny says with a nod. "Grab a cooler if they have it and some ice. We could use some cold water in this heat."

"I'll stick with Gray, and then we'll hit the bathroom when you come back," Cole says.

We all sort of collectively nod, and the strangest sense of community washes over me. It catches me off-guard, but it's not uncomfortable.

There's a touch of warm nostalgia with it, like when you pull out an old sweatshirt you forgot about from the back of your closet. When you slip it over your head, it still fits perfectly, and memories flood your consciousness without any warning.

I shake it off and push open my door, the boys following suit. Arizona heat slaps me in the face with the force of a frying pan.

"Holy shit, it's hot out." I close the car door with my hip and round the front of my car.

West extends his hand out with a small smile, and I slip my palm against his. He tightens his hold on me, and butterflies spring to life inside my belly.

Who knew that something as simple and innocent as hand-holding could bring those winged beauties to life?

"Burgers first?" He flashes me a crooked smile.

My stomach answers for me and lets out a low growl. I chuckle. "Yeah. Let's see if they're open."

We cross the parking lot hand-in-hand. I'm not even embarrassed about the stupid smile I feel spreading across my face.

Do we have a lot of baggage to unpack? Absolutely.

But I'm also not too proud to admit that I missed the hell out of him—and Cole. And this simple gesture only cements that feeling more.

Besides, I can't think of anyone else I'd rather be with right now than the three of them.

The motion-detected automatic doors open, and cool air pours over us in a wave.

He tugs me to the left, toward the fast food joint, and I follow a half-step behind him. Worry for my dad settles around my shoulders like a scarf, no matter how much I try to shake it off.

I let West order for us, and we lean against the little half-wall behind us while the woman who took our order gets it ready. She's probably in her mid-forties with a shock of bright-red hair tucked under her black baseball hat.

She bustles around behind the counter, waiting on the guy behind her at the cooktop. He hasn't turned around yet, giving our burgers his full concentration.

I have half a mind to ask them what the hell they're doing working like it's a normal day and we're not days away from total destruction.

Allegedly.

My own judgment keeps the words trapped in my mouth. Who am I to rebuke how they want to spend the rest of their days?

Hell, maybe nothing will happen and we'll be the ones with egg on our faces while they keep their jobs.

Even as the thoughts run through my head, I know deep down that my father is right.

Despite practicality and all reason.

A moment later, she slides a large bag with burgers and fries across the counter with a smile. Her lips are painted in a bright coral shade that stands out against her tanned skin but clashes horribly with her red hair.

Still, her smile is wide, genuine. "Have a nice day now."

"Thanks," West and I murmur at the same time.

He grabs the bag with one hand, and we cross through the little lobby into the regular gas station side.

Soft classical music falls from the overhead speakers and goose-bumps race over my skin. The air conditioning in here feels like it's at fifty-five degrees.

The registers are in front of us. To the right is an entire wall of windows. I glimpse Sonny leaning his hip against the hood of the car as Cole fills three red gas cans.

I spot the mom with two little kids a couple rows over from our car. She's hustling them inside, leaning in and buckling one into a booster seat.

A couple more cars have pulled up to the pumps since we came inside, but still, it's not nearly as busy as I thought it would be.

I tug on the hem of West's shirt, and he pauses instantly. "Doesn't this feel a little like the *Twilight Zone*?"

His lips twist to the side as his gaze flicks around the store and out the windows. "Yeah. It feels like a normal day here. No chaos or weird weather, and they all have power."

"Should we tell them?"

"It's been, what, a day? Eighteen hours since the DHS messages went out? If they don't know by now . . ."

He doesn't finish that thought, and I don't know if I could either. Would they even believe us?

He tips his head to the side. "C'mon. I saw coolers over here. Let's grab what we need and get back on the road. We've been relatively lucky so far, and I don't feel like tempting fate today."

I nod a few times, my gaze lingering on the mom driving away in a silver minivan. "Yeah, okay."

33

AMELIA

I SLIP into the driver's seat after West and I unloaded our haul. We now have a little cooler full of Gatorade and water. It fits perfectly on the floor in front of the middle seat.

I turn the car on and adjust the vents so cool air blows against my face as I unwrap the burger. Sonny settles in the passenger seat after he replaces the gas cans in the trunk, and Cole and West file in the back.

"I just need a minute to eat, and then I'll get us back on the road," I mumble, holding my hand in front of my mouth while I chew.

"No worries, Cher. We've got a few minutes to spare to eat."

I nod my head in appreciation and take a pull from the water bottle in the cup holder next to me. Condensation already peppers the plastic, despite the air conditioning being on.

A few minutes later, I crumple up the waxy paper and toss it in the fast food bag.

West balls up his wrapper and drops it into the bag on top of mine. "Damn, Ames. You ate that almost as fast as me."

I arch a brow over my shoulder with a grin. "I was hungry. But really, why did it taste *so good*?"

"You think *all* cheeseburgers taste good," Cole grumbles.

I shrug my shoulders. He's not wrong. "Ready to go?"

Sonny leans forward and presses a button to take our directions off pause. He whistles under his breath. "Still have about a thousand miles to go."

I pull the inside of my cheek between my molars at the reminder. Once we got out of California, it was relatively smooth sailing, and I'm not naïve enough to think it'll be a breeze until we meet Dad in Kansas.

But I am hopeful. And that might be worse.

I GLANCE in the rearview and side mirrors, a little routine I started implementing far more often than usual. I don't know what I'm looking for exactly—trouble, I guess.

"Favorite color?"

Sonny's face scrunches up as he looks at me. "Hm?"

"What's your favorite color?"

"Teal. Like a peacock's feather but softer. Why?"

I nod, already picturing him in the middle of a gorgeous teal-colored ocean. "I could see that. Mine is a bold red, the blue-red not the orange-red." There's something intoxicating about the color red, empowering.

"Okay," Sonny drags the words out.

"Favorite '80s movie?"

"*Dazed and Confused*," he replies with a little smirk.

"Favorite boy band song?"

He tsks. "Uh, uh, I think it's my turn. This is twenty questions, right?"

"Something like that. I thought it could help us get to know one another a little. And help pass the time."

"Ah, Cher, I think we know each other pretty well, don't you?" His smile turns sly.

"Watch it." West leans across the car and stretches his arm out to flip Sonny in the back of the head, but he leans forward and dodges.

"Anyone ever tell you that green's really your color? Brings out your eyes," Sonny says with a snicker.

I swipe my tongue over my bottom lip, hiding the smirk that wants to spread across my face. "Let's all play then. Favorite boy band song?"

Sonny wags a finger playfully in my direction. "Nah, you're not dodging me that easy. Me first, then we can dish on Backstreet Boys versus *NSYNC."

"Okay, okay. What's your question then?"

"Middle name?"

"Rose," West answers before I even open my mouth. "She was named after her grandma, Summer Rose Christensen."

"Grandma's mom and dad were ahead of their time." I lift my shoulders with a smile, turning the wheel to follow the curve of the highway.

Trees blur past us on either side of the highway. I glance at the gas gauge, noting the half tank we have left. We already stopped to use the gas from the cans in the back.

"Before I forget, keep your eyes open for a gas station. We'll need one soon."

"Sure thing, Cher."

"Okay, since I won that round, I think I get to go next," West says, humor laced in his voice. When no one objects, he hums a little under his breath before he exhales. "Okay, this one is serious, yeah? Pineapple and ham on pizza?"

I laugh and a second later, I hear Cole and Sonny join in.

"What? It's a legitimate question, and before you ask me, yes, I'm serious. This kind of shit could make or break a relationship, and you assholes know that."

Cole laughs. "Nah, brother. What I know is that if you base your relationship off of *pizza toppings*, then you've got bigger issues than tropical fruit."

Sonny chuckles. "Sorry, man. Not to pile on, but Cole's right."

West leans forward between the front seats and angles his chest toward me. "Back me up here, Ames."

I pull my bottom lip inside my mouth with my teeth before releasing it with a grin. "I don't know, West . . ."

"Traitors, the lot of you," West pushes off the seat and sits back with a huff. It's too lighthearted to be serious though.

And just like that, it feels like I got a piece of my heart back.

"You good, Cher?"

I blink my eyes a few times and look at him. There's a crease between his brows as he watches me. How does he look so effortlessly sexy in the front seat of my well-loved SUV?

Like that kind of pose shouldn't *do it* for me, and yet when I see any one of them slouched *just so* in my passenger seat, it does.

It really, really does.

"I'm fine."

"Okay. Tell me when you want to switch. Cole's driving next." I can feel his eyes on me, casually roaming over every available inch he can see.

"Okay, I'm good until we need to stop for gas though. Speaking of which, don't you think it's weird that we haven't seen anything else besides a few gas stations and some trees alongside the road? Not even a lot of cars."

"Maybe this is a more remote part of Arizona? I mean, Grand Canyon National Park is over there." Sonny points out my window. "And it looks like some forests to the south." He hooks a thumb out his window. "So, I guess it's possible that this isn't a busy highway right now."

"I don't know. I could see some people going to the Grand Canyon and trying to make a go of it," West says.

"Trey and Clive would totally do that," Cole says with a laugh.

"Trey and Clive?" I arch a brow and look at Cole in the rearview mirror.

For a second, it feels like the whole world stops spinning. Cole's dark brown eyes look lighter than I've seen in, well, years. They're positively sparkling with laughter as they meet mine.

And just like that, I find myself sprinkled with jealousy. I used to be one of the few people in this world who could bring Cole Armstrong to laughter.

But not anymore.

And I'm not sure if we'll ever get back to that place.

"They're some guys we've hiked with a few times. They're totally into living off the land," Cole says.

My gaze flashes between the road in front of me and Cole's face in the rearview mirror. Desperation slicks my gut, quickly followed by a dash of shame.

It's so easy to fall back into those roles we had when we were younger. I hung on every word that fell from their lips, and they always treated me with respect, never crossing that invisible line. A boundary that I never agreed to and did my best to chip away at.

Until eventually, it fell.

And then I had to leave.

West laughs, yanking me from my swirling pity party. "Hell yeah, they'd definitely trek here."

"Let's hope they made it out of Vegas in time." Cole scratches his jaw, some of the light from his eyes fading.

"Yeah, let's hope." West leans into the seat further. "I'm going to try to catch some sleep."

"Yeah, me too. Wake me when we hit the next gas station, and I'll drive." Cole balls up a sweatshirt and tucks it between his head and the window as a makeshift pillow.

"You can close your eyes too, ya know. I'll be fine. It's just a couple of hours until our next stop," I murmur, chancing a glance at Sonny.

"Nah, I'm good."

I lift my shoulders and let them fall just as quickly. "Apparently, they're doing an entire set of Elvis Christmas, so I'm good for a while. You don't need to keep me company."

Sonny laughs and flashes me a smirk. "You secretly love Christmas music, don't you?"

"No, I—"

"Yes she does," West interrupts me.

I don't even have to look back at him to know he's wearing that stupid goofy grin I love so much. It's his signature smile when he's teasing me, a touch too wide and the left side lifting a smidgen higher than the right.

"And if I didn't spend fifteen minutes looking for any other stations myself, I would say she planned it this way," Cole says with his eyes closed.

My lips twist to the side. "I told you the radio was broken when I bought it. It's a simple twist of fate that Christmas songs will accompany us on this cross-country drive."

34

AMELIA

THE UNMISTAKABLE SOUND of sleeping fills the car. It's the rhythm change in their breaths, and one of them is snoring softly. My money's on West. He always did snore a little when he fell asleep during movies.

A silver van is pulled over to the right shoulder about a half mile ahead of us, and I slow down on instinct. It looks familiar, and a moment later, I place it.

It looks just like the van I saw at the gas station, the one a mom and her two kids were getting into before we left. I wonder if that's them.

Sonny inhales deeply before a yawn stretches his jaw wide. "What's going on?"

"I don't know. It looks like the same car I saw a woman get in at the gas station."

I slow down further, easing into the other lane to give the car plenty of room. The shoulders are narrow here, barely enough inches to even *be called* a shoulder.

Sure enough, the messy black bun and oversized black tee pop out of the sliding rear driver's side door. She waves her hands over her head, crisscrossing them in the universal *over here* gesture.

My foot eases from the pedal further, and I pull over in front of her car.

"What are you doing, Cher?" His voice is low, cautious but not angry.

I throw the car in park and look at him. "I'm just going to see if we can help. She had little kids, Gray. I can't just leave them stranded out here like that."

Sonny scrapes a hand over his face. "Alright, I'll come with you."

I place a palm in the center of his chest. "No offense, but if you three approach her, she'll probably run. Let me go first, and then I'll come get you in a minute."

He exhales a noisy breath and nods a few times. Leaning down, he fiddles with his backpack for a moment before he pulls something out and deposits it in my hand. "Take my knife just in case you need it for something—for anything. Remember the motto we talked about?"

"Don't be a hero?" I tilt my head to the side.

"Sure, that's one of them. You've got thirty seconds before I'm out of the car and next to you, yeah?"

"Deal."

He leans across the middle console and captures my lips in a quick kiss that I feel all the way down to my toes. It was such an unexpected move, I never saw it coming. By the time I try to deepen it, he's already pulling away.

"What's going on?" West mumbles, sleep thick in his voice.

"I'll be right back," I answer, pushing open the door and climbing out.

The dry, hot air feels like a brick wall, only much, much hotter. I bet it's close to one hundred degrees out here, and with little respite from the sun, those kids of hers are roasting. It's not safe.

"Hey, are you okay?" I call out as I approach.

"Oh thank god you stopped." Her voice trembles as she emerges from her bent-over position.

"I saw you at the gas station earlier. Do you need help with something?" I stop a few feet away from her, idling by the driver's side door.

"Please, it's my son. The air conditioning is broken, and I think he's overheating or something. Can you help me please?"

The desperation in her voice is real. I would never forgive myself if I didn't help her and her son out.

"We've got ice and some cold water in my car. Let me go—"

"No!" She rushes toward me, grabbing onto my forearm. "Can he maybe sit in your air conditioning for a few minutes? Just to cool him off. I need help carrying him, he's like a limp noodle right now."

The hair on the back of my neck stands on end, and I take a half step backward.

"Mommy?" The small voice from inside the van stops me in my tracks.

Damnit. "Yeah, okay. I'll help carry him."

I close the distance and lean into her darkened van.

WEST

I TWIST around in my seat and stare out the back windshield at Amelia talking to some woman in front of her open van. I watch her take a step backward toward us, and my hand flies to the door handle. "We should go out there."

"She's a big girl, she can handle one conversation without either one of you panting after her like lost little puppies."

I ignore my brother's snark, too preoccupied with the scene unfolding. I can see the woman's mouth moving, but I'm not risking flooding the perfectly cool car with oven-like heat. They're too far away to hear much of anything anyway.

I grip the back of my neck. "Time, Gray?"

"She's got five seconds and we're out there. I promised her thirty seconds, and I see no reason to break that promise."

I peel my gaze from her to look at Gray, my brother from another mother—just like Cole. He's objectively good-looking, and while he doesn't take even a fraction of the women up on their offers, he's not a fucking monk. There's no way he didn't hook up with Amelia. Hell, they all but confirmed it.

Not for the first time, I wonder why I'm cursed to love the same women my brothers do.

Or maybe it's just her. Her magnetism is uncanny, it plants roots inside of you and twines you up in them so much that there's no use in cutting yourself free.

And the most fucked-up thing is that I don't want to.

I never did.

"God damnit, Mia," Cole snaps before a rush of warm air fills the car.

It takes a moment for my brain to catch up, and when I do, I curse myself for taking my eyes off of her. Gray and I are out of the car in a flash, the keys gripped tight in his fist.

We stalk after my brother, who steps to the side and reveals Amelia.

Her hands are up, palms forward, and she doesn't take her gaze from inside the van. The woman with the messy hair and oversized shirt clutches a child to her chest and another one by the hand. I spare her another glance to make sure we're not going to get ambushed if she comes up behind us. But all I see is fear. It permeates around her like a cloud.

"I'm sorry, I'm sorry. I had no choice. He was going to take my kids if I didn't help him. I'm sorry," the woman says between tearful sobs.

"Mia? We're here. Come back to us."

"Cole?" Her voice shakes a little but she doesn't turn her head.

Something inside of me fractures at the sound of the hitch in her voice. I storm up to the car, stopping behind her and look inside.

A man emerges from the shadowed third row. "Give me the keys and no one gets hurt."

He steps over a diaper bag and two kids suitcases as he exits the van, gun-first.

"I told you, I don't have the keys on me. They're in the car."

Pride swells inside my chest at the even tone of her voice.

"Yeah? Well, tell one of them to go get them," he says, gesturing to the side with his gun.

He takes his eyes off of her for a moment, and it's the opening I needed. I reach around and curve a palm around her hips. With one small tug, she's behind me, and I'm between her and the gun.

My brother curses behind me, but I don't give a shit. It's the end of the world, anyway.

Do I have a death wish? Hell no. I still have many, many things on my to-do list, and yeah, a lot of them involve the woman behind me. And sure, a good portion of them don't include clothes, but fuck, I'm not going to hide behind my girl when some asshole waves a gun around.

Besides, I can't think of a better way to go than protecting her.

I don't need to confer with my brothers, we've been together long enough that we sort of developed a rhythm. Bargaining first, then violence.

I keep my palms up. "Why don't you let the women and kids go, and we'll get you the keys?"

He takes another step, on the threshold of the door. "Do you think I'm fucking stupid? *I'm* the one with a gun, you fucking dick. If I say jump, you bitches better ask *how high*. Understand?"

"Got it, man. Let's go get the keys then. We'll walk over there just the two of us," Gray offers.

"Nah, I'll walk with her," he says, gesturing behind me with the gun.

I'm getting really tired of this gun waving around like a miniature flag at the Fourth of July parade.

Amelia steps out from behind me. "Alright."

The asshole reaches out and clamps a hand on her shoulder, and she doesn't hide her wince fast enough.

"You think that's bad? Obviously you've never felt a bullet wound, sweetheart. We can fix that for you," he says with a sneer.

"I'm fine," she says through gritted teeth.

He uses her like a shield, keeping her in front of him with the gun casually pointed at her head as he pulls her backward toward her car. My fists clench, and I take a step toward them.

He tsks, this obnoxious noise and straightens his hold, caressing her cheekbone with the end of the gun. "Tell your boyfriends to stay put, unless you want me to decorate them with bullets too?"

I feel a muscle in my jaw pop out when I clench my teeth hard enough to hurt.

Amelia shakes her head. "It's alright."

She holds my gaze as she lets him walk her backward. I try to convey everything in my gaze, but it's been too long since we've been together. I'm afraid we've lost touch of our silent understanding of one another.

The corner of her lips tilt upward, a small, sad smile. And when the gun lowers from her head and the guy half-turns to open the driver's side door, she strikes.

35

AMELIA

THE PRESSURE from the gun leaves the side of my face as he half-turns toward my car. It's the perfect opportunity, and maybe the only one I'll get. I recall some moves from those two self-defense classes I attended with Alley and figure it's better than not trying.

His arm relaxes further, and I quickly step to the side and link my hands together to make a fist. I exhale a breath and raise them high over my head as he opens the driver's side door.

Now or never.

I hope this works.

It's the last thought I have before everything becomes a flurry of motion. I slam my fist down in a harsh chopping motion, nailing him right in the wrist. I think it's a pressure point or maybe just a weak point—whatever it is, it works.

His wrist buckles under the pressure, and the gun starts to slip from his hand. I snatch the gun, but before his grip totally leaves it, he whirls around on me.

Violence shimmers from his narrowed eyes, his thin lips curling into a snarl. "You stupid bitch."

My pulse is a drumline in my ears, drowning out everything

and leaving only my will to survive. It thunders against my skin, coiling my muscles tighter and narrowing my focus.

Both of us have a hand on the gun, and we grapple with it for a moment. It feels somehow like time speeds up *and* slows down.

I blink, and my hand settles against the handle of the gun, now pointed toward him.

His palms meet the air between us and his scowl deepens, even if his eyes are wide. "Whatcha gonna do, hm?"

Indecision breaks through the fog clouding my senses, and I back up a step. It was the wrong move. My hand twitches as I hold my ground. It's one thing to handle a gun at a supervised range, but it's entirely another thing to point it at someone. Especially in a situation like this.

The asshole with the greasy hair and smug grin advances on me, taking two casual steps until the gun is only six inches from his chest. "Nah, you're not going to shoot me, are you?"

I scramble back a few steps and try to hold the gun steady, but my hand won't stop trembling.

I've held a gun before, but never after one was just aimed at my head.

The whooshing noise inside my head subsides long enough for sound to filter back in. The guys are talking over one another behind me, their voices strained.

"It's alright, Cher. Just take another few steps back. I'm right here."

Sonny's soothing voice comes from right behind me, but I'm afraid to take my eyes off of the guy in front of me.

I adjust my grip and take a step back. When the asshole moves to follow me, something inside snaps. I rush forward two steps and aim the gun with intention. "Stop. Stop moving right now."

His dark eyes narrow on me, but he doesn't challenge me other than that.

"Just follow the sound of my voice, Amelia," West murmurs from behind me.

They're talking to me in low, soft tones, like I'm a spooked animal.

I swallow, my throat feeling drier than the desert we're in. "Okay."

I nod a few times and take a few measured steps backward. Sweat coats the back of my neck, rolling down in distracting rivulets.

"Good girl. Two more, yeah?"

I feel West's heat at my back, and I make another mistake. I take my eyes off the slimeball in front of me for a second to look over my shoulder. West's handsome face comes into view, his expression encouraging and focused on me.

But it's Cole's yell that pulls me up short. "Mia!" He screams my name in a way I don't think I've ever heard before, and that scares me more than anything.

Even more than the two-hundred pound man charging toward me with murder in his eyes. I twist around to face him, gun wobbling in my grip and mentally preparing to pull the trigger.

A hand grips underneath my wrists and pushes my arms up high, the gun now pointing toward the air a split second before Cole tackles the guy in front of me.

West's free arm bands around my middle, and he turns me around and shuffles us back several paces. My chest heaves with nerves and fear and another emotion I can't pinpoint. I gasp these big gulping breaths and bend at the waist, dropping my hands and taking my finger off the trigger.

"Oh my god. Oh my god."

"Shh, it's alright. You're alright," he murmurs against my ear.

"I almost shot Cole. Why—why would he *do* that?" Terror wraps around my confusion, shock and adrenaline soaring through my bloodstream. "Why did he do that?"

"He made a move he thought was right. Just like you did by helping that woman." West applies a little pressure on the gun, and I let go of it instantly.

"You good, Cher?"

I lift my gaze from my shoes to look at Sonny's gentle dark brown eyes. There's no judgment or accusation, just warm understanding.

And maybe that's what does me in. My face crumples like a wet tissue, and in a flash, I'm in a West-Sonny sandwich. They wrap their arms around me and whisper in my ear while I totally lose my shit.

Guilt eats away at my insides. "I never should've stopped." My words are mumbled into Sonny's shirt, damp with my tears.

"Nah, you probably saved their lives. They high-tailed it out of here as soon as they could." West strokes my hair back and buries his face in my neck from behind.

I sniff, the knowledge that she wasn't in on it soothing some of my guilt. "Still. I'm sorry."

"It's a good reminder that this isn't the same world we woke up in a week ago, even if it seems like it is," Sonny says. "You did good, Cher."

"If we're done with this pity party, can we get this over with?" Cole grumbles.

I lift my head from the safe cocoon they made for me, my chest lighter. I swipe a finger underneath each eye to catch any lingering tears. "He's right. Thank you though, both of you." I eye each of them until they offer a small nod.

West, of course, smirks. "Anytime you want to get between Gray and me, I'm game, Ames."

I roll my eyes, but his joke does the trick. I smirk at him. "In your dreams, Campbell."

My chest heats because, you know what? In *my* dreams too. I eye him over my shoulder and his trademark flirty grin is back, but when I look at Sonny, it's his almost imperceptible nod that has my breath catching in my chest.

"You about done now?" Cole snaps.

West's fingers are slow to leave my arm, only dropping when

he's physically out of reach. "Chill out, man. He's not going anywhere, are you?"

He clamps a hand on the guy's shoulder and frog-marches him to the other side of the car, across the little shoulder, and down the small slope of the ditch.

I tug the inside of my cheek between my molars. "What happens now? We can't just leave him here."

Sonny doesn't answer right away. "It's not the same rules as before, Cher. You know that now." His voice is gentle, inconsistent with his insinuation.

Something squeezes tight inside my chest. "What does that mean?"

His palm finds my lower back, gently nudging me. "Go wait in the car, yeah? We'll be right back."

My eyebrows crash over my eyes, but my feet reluctantly take me toward our car. Sonny's hand never leaves my lower back, an anchor in this–this madness. He opens the driver's side door for me and waits for me to slip inside.

"Turn the car on and cool off. We'll be right back." He drops the keys into my palm and curls my fingers over the top of them.

The sun glints off the metal in his other hand. When did he take the gun from West?

I swallow over the lump in my throat, and it takes me two times before I can croak out, "Okay."

Sonny steps back, one hand on the top of the car door frame. "And Cher? Don't look, yeah?"

I nod, but I already know that it's a lie. I have to know what happens.

He waits for me to put the keys in the ignition before he closes my door with a flick of his wrist. I watch, my heart in my throat as he follows the path Cole and West took.

He disappears from view, the ditch steep enough to swallow them whole.

I flinch when a gunshot rings through the night.

36

AMELIA

I GRIP the steering wheel in tense fists, my knuckles turning white. The tension in my body coils tighter and tighter the longer no one speaks. Twenty minutes have gone by since they all slid into the car without a word.

I keep waiting for one of them to speak up, offer an explanation, but I should know better by now. It seems Gray is perfectly content to leave me in the dark like Cole and West have done for years now.

Cole huffs next to me, adjusting the vent in front of him. I glance at him out of the corner of my eye. The air conditioning blows directly on his face, fluttering his soft dark blond hair.

Part of me loathes the fact that I'm still attracted to him. But my libido doesn't care that he bruised my heart.

He looks like the kind of guy who spends a half hour artfully coifing his hair every morning, when I know for a fact he never has. Not like the kind of guy who shoots someone in the middle of the desert either. But the sound of a gun was unmistakable. And only three people walked back up the ditch.

I scan all the available skin for the tenth time since they piled back into the car.

No blood. On any of them.

Could it have been a warning shot?

I squirm in my seat, the question on the tip of my tongue. I swallow it back down in the next breath, my stubbornness digging my heels in.

Sonny and West are quiet in the backseat, but what else is there to say really?

I fucked up.

I thought I was doing the right thing by stopping to help that woman. Instead, I almost cost us everything.

Including our lives.

Cole adjusts himself in his seat, shifting from side to side like he can't get comfortable. I don't know if he's doing it on purpose or if he's genuinely uncomfortable. Either way, it feels personal to me. I don't give him my attention, keeping my gaze firmly on the road in front of me.

Another Christmas song plays, and I have to wonder what kind of fucked-up joke the music gods are playing on us that we need to keep the radio on and the only station that comes in clearly is a Christmas one.

As in all Christmas, all the time. Three-hundred-sixty-five days of Christmas—twenty-four hours a day. I can't imagine how the radio DJs do it all the time.

I exhale a breath as my lights automatically flick on. Dusk settles around us as we cross Arizona state. We're still in the northern part if I remember right from the map.

He finally settles in his seat only to sigh. I swear my blood pressure is rising with each haughty exhale.

"Is there something you want to say, Cole?" If my voice is snippy, I don't really care.

"Yeah, Amelia, I think there is something I want to say."

"Well, here I am," I say through gritted teeth.

He waits a beat, the suspense building. "Just wondering if you forgot your common sense when you fucked off from wherever you came from this time?"

"What?" Indignation coats my words like honey, and I rubberneck toward him in the passenger seat.

"Cole." West drags out his name in warning.

Which in true Cole fashion, he ignores. "Nah, I'm not sugarcoating it for your little princess any longer." His voice is such forced nonchalance as he glances in the backseat toward his brothers, it makes me want to scream.

I scoff. "*Little princess*? What the hell, Cole?"

"When she does something stupid—"

"Hey, watch it," Sonny snaps.

"I'm *not* stupid," I grit out between my clenched teeth, my hands gripping the steering wheel hard.

Cole folds his arms across his chest and glares at me. "I mean, what the fuck were you thinking, Amelia? Not only did you stop, but then you almost got killed!"

"Too far, man," West growls out.

I pull the car to the side of the road, the need to lash out rising like the tide. My tires squeal for a second, and I exhale through my nose. I stare straight ahead and ask, "Do you want to take a second and rethink your approach?" I hold up a hand between us, a preemptive stop to whatever knee-jerk response was waiting on the tip of his tongue. "Think before you spew anymore venom at me. Think about the lines we've drawn. *Together*. Years ago."

We grew up together, and once upon a time, we told each other nearly everything. Which means that he knows all the right buttons to push to trigger me. And if I ever forget that, all I have to do is remember the barb he casually launched at me at The Lodge.

"I am," he grits through clenched teeth. "And if they"—he hooks a thumb over his shoulder—"weren't so far up your ass, they'd be saying the same thing. You were reckless." He looks down his nose at me, a sneer marring those full lips of his. "Wake up, Amelia. Normal societal rules don't apply here. It's kill or be killed now. And you—you're going to get *us* killed."

I suck in a breath at his cruelty. Angry tears fill my eyes, distorting his scowl. "What's your problem, Cole?"

"You," he says without hesitation.

That hollow place inside my chest aches like it's been cleaved in two. I slap my hands on the steering wheel as the tide of anger and frustration and hurt and shame swells larger and larger. I'm suffocating underneath the weight of it.

My belt is unbuckled, and I'm pushing open the car door in a flash.

My shoes kick up loose stones and bits of chipped off concrete as I round the hood of the car and stop dead center. My shoulders feel like they're at my ears, reaching toward the sky with the amount of tension I'm holding.

The waning sunlight casts a golden glow over everything, but not even the gorgeous sunset can catapult me from the shitty headspace I'm in.

It's fine. I'm fine.

I just need a few minutes to breathe, to fast-track process what the fuck just happened.

The night brings a blanket of cool in the desert that the daytime desperately demands, and it's a balm to my heated cheeks. It's a lot like yin and yang. They're opposites in most ways, and yet, one cannot exist without the other.

I used to think that I was like that. That I couldn't live without them, but time and too many pitchers of margaritas has shown me that's not true.

I don't need them to live.

But I *wanted* them.

"You okay, Cher?" Sonny calls from his rolled down window.

I rake my hands through my hair, my nails digging into my scalp. "I'm fine. I just needed some air. I'll be right there."

He's slow to answer, but eventually he acquiesces. "You got two."

He's so calm and understanding that it almost brings a tear to my eye. I didn't know what I was missing—what I *needed*—in this life until it was given to me. Freely, wholeheartedly, and without stipulations.

I blow out a harsh breath and thread my fingers in my hair at the nape of my neck. I let my head fall back and stare into the darkening sky.

Thankfully, the highway traffic has been sparse, so I'm free to experience my little meltdown in relative peace. And since the air pollution isn't as thick, I have a first-row view of the stars.

"Get back in the car, Amelia," Cole yells.

I ignore him, giving the car my back and looking up at the sky. It makes me feel small but in a good way. Like my mistakes don't define me.

But do my successes?

We're on an impossible adventure.

When I think about all the different legs of this adventure we've been on, I'm surprised I didn't snap sooner.

Calling it an adventure in my head feels a lot less scary than what it really is. A race against the clock.

But I've had it up to my eyeballs with Cole's bullshit attitude. I don't know what frustrates me more: the fact that he acts like his anger is justified or the fact that we're all still dancing around it.

We're going to reach a boiling point sooner rather than later.

COLE

I ROLL my window back up when she doesn't respond or turn around.

"She's fucking lucky that this is a slow highway. She's standing in the middle of the damn road." My lips pinch to the side.

"Yeah, well, she wouldn't even be out there if it wasn't for you," West says.

I narrow my eyes over my shoulder at him. He tugs on his dark brown hair, his five o'clock shadow grown out longer than I've seen in years.

"Don't look at me like that, man. You know I'm right."

I face forward and widen my legs. "I don't know shit."

"Yeah, no shit, asshole," Gray says.

I cock my head to the side but don't turn around. All this swiveling is making me feel claustrophobic. We've been trapped in the same car together for hours, so I don't understand why it feels so fucking *small* now. "You got something to say now?"

"Yeah. Why the fuck did you say she was stupid—"

"I didn't," I interrupt him, my voice like a fifty-pound weight—heavy and unyielding. "I would *never* call her stupid. And you both know that. But what she did was reckless, and you'd be saying the same thing if you weren't trying to slide into those little jean shorts of hers."

Gray sighs. "Nah, man. See that's where you're wrong."

Warmth rolls over me, and I look toward the roof with a shake of my head. "No offense, Gray, but you don't know shit about her."

"I know enough."

I bristle and look back at him. "Yeah, well, you don't have all the facts. You'd be singing a different tune if you did."

Gray throws his hands out to the side. "You got something to say, we're all ears, man."

Bitterness swells in my gut, and I press my lips together. Flicking a glance at my brother, I'm not surprised to see his gaze volley between Gray and me, his mouth a straight slash across his face.

Gray nods a few times, mostly to himself. "Alright then. But just remember this, by stopping, she saved that woman and her kids today."

I turn around and stare at Amelia through the dusty windshield. Each second feels like a minute, each minute an hour. Urgency filters in my bloodstream, and my foot starts bouncing at a quick pace.

"It's been more than two minutes," I murmur. "How much longer until she comes back?"

"I'll go get her," West offers.

My mouth opens before I even think about it. "You'd probably be better off just hauling her over your shoulder and dumping her in the backseat with you, though I bet you'd like that. Wouldn't you?" There's a disconnect, the wires between my brain and my mouth seem twisted up, wrong. I normally would have kept that last comment to myself.

There's a moment of silence before Gray starts laughing. It's a genuine laugh, tinged with a little disbelief. My ears get warm, and I cast my eyes low.

"Are you fucking kidding me, bro?" West says. "How long are you going to keep doing this with her?

The flush spreads to my chest, my fingers tingling. The claustrophobia takes root, and I'm pushing open my door in the next breath.

37

AMELIA

"YOU'VE MADE YOUR POINT."

I whirl around at the sound of Cole's voice. He stands three feet away from me, the perfect picture of casual interest. Hands shoved into his pockets, biceps flexing underneath his fitted black tee.

"If you're waiting for me to apologize, don't."

And the boiling point I mentioned earlier?

I think I've reached it.

I point an angry finger in his direction. "You know, you're the most infuriating person I've ever met!"

My voice sounds screechy even to my own ears, but I'm too far into this mess to stop now. I'm a train derailed, only there's no emergency brake, and the conductor is going rogue.

He scoffs. "You should be so lucky."

"What?" His response pulls me up short.

Cole huffs and folds his arms across his chest, his pecs flexing. "I said you should be so fucking lucky to know me. Because you don't, Amelia. You don't know who I am. And you don't get that privilege. Not anymore."

"Yeah, well, it's not like you know me either. Five years is a long time." As far as comebacks go, it's weak as hell, but it's the best I've got right now.

A sarcastic laugh barks from his mouth, echoing around us. "You're right. I don't know you now, and you know what? I never knew you then either."

My face scrunches up, confusion stealing some of my fire. "What are you talking about? Of course you knew me then. The three of us were inseparable, Cole."

"You don't have to remind me. I remember everything."

It's so similar to what West said to me earlier, but the tone and intent couldn't be different.

"Huh. That's strange because ever since I've been back, it doesn't seem like you remembered me at all."

"Where'd you go, Amelia?"

I throw my arms to the side and spin in a half circle. "Who are you pretending for? It's just me and you now, so you can drop the act." My hands drop against my thighs with a slap.

"Pretending?" He laughs, this derisive noise that is the furthest thing from joy I've ever heard. "Nah, that's your move, baby."

My brows lower, and my lips purse at the nickname. The only other times he's ever called me that were tender, intimate. So using it now? It's intentional. Cruel, even.

"Are we doing this now then?"

He lifts his shoulders, the fabric of his shirt bunching with the movement.

He wants to get into it? Fine by me. The sooner we clear this up, the sooner they can *both* get to the groveling.

I lick my lips and square my shoulders, preparing to crack open my chest for him to examine. "I never wanted to leave you—both of you. And I *know* you know that much is true."

He doesn't reply, just stares at me with his impossibly dark brown eyes, the sun sinking low over the horizon behind him.

"But I didn't have a choice."

"Everyone has a choice, Mia."

His reminder lulls my ire like low tide, pulling it back to sea until the next wave strikes.

I nod and look at my feet. "You're right." I meet his gaze, my voice quiet. "I asked you to wait for me. I was going to come back to Vegas when I turned eighteen."

His mouth parts and his brows sink together over his eyes. "What?"

"My birthday is—"

"I remember your birthday." A muscle in his jaw ticks. He looks away, toward the empty road ahead of us for a moment. His Adam's apple bobbing with a swallow. He brings his gaze back to mine. "Why. Why did you leave me, Mia?"

There's vulnerability in his entire demeanor, like his very molecules have shifted and shed his armor. I didn't realize I had been waiting for this until now. And just like then, something inside me responds in kind.

"Cole." His name comes out a choked whisper, and I take a step toward him. My eyes plead with him to meet me halfway, a step toward the way we were back then.

He bites the inside of his cheek, but he doesn't move to meet me in the middle. "I need to know why. Was it . . . was it something I did?"

I thought I'd be cracking open my rib cage for his perusal, but instead, he's handed me everything with careful hands. I knew he would blame himself—I *knew* it.

That's why I called them and sent letters. Over and over again. I left countless voicemails and texts, and my letters never came back undeliverable, so I know they made it.

My bottom teeth sink into my top lip and pull it inward as I shake my head. "No, never. You were perfect. You always have been. That's part of the problem."

He looks over my shoulder, his mind far away from the Arizona highway. "Do you love him?"

My thoughts falter, my lips parting with an exhale. "Ask me the question you really want to know the answer to."

His gaze snaps to mine. "I do want to know."

I shake my head, a sad little smile on my face. "Let's go. It's getting dark."

I pivot on the ball of my foot, but I don't take a step before his hand is curled around my bicep, his touch gentle. He pulls me back around to face him, and in the next breath, his hands are in my hair.

He angles my head back, the tips of his thumbs underneath my jaw as he cradles my head.

"What are you doing?" My whispered words hang in the miniscule space between our mouths.

"I—I don't know."

He sounds so tortured, I do the only thing I can do. I eliminate the space between us and press my mouth against his.

There's a moment of suspended time, the stars pause their twinkling and the world slows until it's only the two of us. The feel of his soft lips on mine unlocks the last piece of my heart, and I shudder in relief.

I swipe my tongue across his bottom lip, and he groans into my mouth. His lips part, and he steps into me further. I sneak my arms around his neck and arch my back, pressing the length of my body against him.

Tears prick my eyes from all the emotions coursing through me right now. Euphoria dances on my nerve endings with every roll and swipe of Cole's tongue.

I push onto my tip toes and yank him closer still with my arm around the back of his neck. We're so close I don't know where he ends and I begin, and the overwhelming feeling of *rightness* floats over me.

A horn honks behind us, and I jump. Cole tightens his hold on me and buries his face in my neck.

His mouth skims over my neck, his tongue peeking out to flick over the thundering beat of my pulse. "I think they're ready to go."

A giggle bubbles up inside my chest, and I exhale it into the night. "Yeah, okay. How's your head? It's your turn to drive."

"I'm fine, Mia. Do me a favor? Sit in the front," he says against my skin.

I don't bother smothering my smile, no one bears witness to my giddiness except the moon. And she's rooting for us, I just know it.

We part at the hood of my car and slip into the car at the same time. He presses the button on the side of the driver's seat, and it reclines and shifts toward the back.

I reach over and buckle my seatbelt, hiding my smirk dancing on my lips.

"Are we going to talk about the fact that you two just made out in the middle of the road?" West asks with more bite to his voice than I anticipated.

"Nope," Cole says, popping the p.

I let my smirk fly free as I peek at Sonny in the side mirror. He's sitting behind me, a small smile tilting up the corner of his mouth.

"If you're waiting for me to choose, don't."

Sonny swipes a palm over his mouth, but I don't miss his widening smile.

A cover of "Christmas (Baby Please Come Home)" fills the silence, and I take it as a sign. I've never felt more at home than I do with the three men around me.

38

AMELIA

THE EARTH SHAKES, and I jerk forward.

"Hey, hey, it's just me."

I blink several times to clear my blurry vision. West's face is in front of me, his dark hair looking wild like he just ran his hands through it. His eyes look more brown than green today. I always thought they changed depending on his disposition, like some fancy mood ring.

I used to think I could tell what he was thinking, even behind the smile that he always plastered on for other people's benefit.

"Hey." My voice comes out scratchy, thick with sleep. I sit up a little in my seat and scrub my hands over my face, looking around. Sunshine filters through the windows, making my eyes water a little. West fills in the space between the open car, the hot air wrapping around me like a warm hug. "What time is it?"

He smooths some of my hair back. "Six."

I wipe underneath my eyes and blink a few times. "In the morning? Why didn't you guys wake me up?"

"You and Gray both knocked out after we talked to your dad."

That was at least four hours ago!

"Oh, shit. I missed the check-in call. He must be so worried." I pat the seat around me, looking for the familiar black rectangle.

His hand rests on my shoulder, his touch soothing. "Relax, Ames. Cole answered it when it rang about an hour and a half ago."

"Cole?" I shake my head a little. "Why would he answer?"

West's gaze flies around my face. "You didn't even stir when it rang. I was going to get it, but he said it should be him. Since he's your husband and all."

The word husband falls from his lips like the letters are poisonous.

My chest flushes, and with a clarity I didn't know I had on such little sleep and no caffeine, understanding dawns.

He's jealous. Of a fake marriage.

I cover my hand with his and squeeze, the initial panic subsiding. "Hey, you do know I made it up right? Cole and I didn't run off into the sunset."

He nods, but he doesn't laugh like I expected him to. Instead he leans his forehead against mine and whispers, "It should've been me."

His minty breath wafts over my lips on an exhale that tugs something inside my chest. My lips part, but I snap them closed in the next instant, shaking my head and acutely aware that I'm not as minty fresh as he is.

"I don't give a shit about your morning breath, Ames. I want to kiss you, feel the way your breath hitches when my hand slides here." His palm slips out from under mine and slides across my collar bone to settle at the base of my throat. "Relish in the way you lean into my touch."

My chest rises with deep breaths as I close my eyes and angle my head to the right a little. His words are soft and slow, backed by desire. His fingertips smooth up the side of my neck, trailing along my jaw.

"Just like that," he murmurs against my lips.

My mouth parts, and I arch my back, pushing up against his hand. A thrill runs through me at the pressure, and I flick my tongue across his bottom lip before I sink my teeth into it. I tug his lip a little, and his fingertips flutter over the base of my neck.

He groans into my mouth, the sound sending a shot of lust straight to my core. I drag my teeth over his lip, and he groans again, deeper this time. With a knee on the seat between my legs, he angles himself over me.

It's such a dominant move, my core clenches. I would've expected this from Cole, but not West. Though now all I can imagine is what it would be like with Cole and West.

And Sonny.

Fantasies play across my vision like a movie, flashes of hands and mouths and cocks, all the while, West dominates my mouth.

And I fucking love it.

I squeeze my legs together, trapping his knee between them. He leans into me further, but we're restricted by the seats, and I don't get the pressure or the friction I need.

Someone pounds on the hood of the car, scaring the crap out of me. I jump and pull back from West, but he doesn't even flinch. His kiss-swollen lips curve into a sinful smile, and his thumb softly brushes against my skin.

"Unless you want to give everyone a show, reel it in, asshole," Cole yells.

"As much as I want to keep that sweet mouth on me, he's right. Raincheck?"

I press a hand to my racing heart. "Absolutely."

He lets go of my neck to lace his fingers with mine, tugging me gently out of the car. "C'mon, stretch your legs for a few minutes."

Raising a hand to shield my eyes from the sun, I glance around. Nothing but flatland for as far as I can see. The same hard-packed red dirt of the desert, but dotted with more trees, mostly in clusters down the road.

The wind blows, whipping my hair across my face. Before I can push it off, West tucks it behind my ear.

"Where are we?"

"Just crossed into New Mexico. Had to stop for gas and to stretch our legs. I wanted to see what they knew here too, maybe there's a national update we missed somehow."

"Did DHS send another emergency message?"

"Nah, nothing like that. But your radio is busted, so I thought . . ."

"Yeah, I know. It came like that. But I get what you're saying. Wait. What did Dad say?"

Nervousness tightens my gut and a dash of guilt. I should've asked about him first, not let myself get swept up in his kiss.

He fiddles with a lock of hair, his knuckles brushing against the shell of my ear. "He's fine. They ran into a little snow in Colorado, but they're alright. Wanted to make sure you remembered the deadline."

"What deadline?"

"The bunker closes June first. Regardless of a *golden ticket*."

My brows furrow. It's hard to remember what he said through my haze of panic. Clarity shines through my memories. "That's in nine days."

He nods, his expression solemn. "Plenty of time to get there. We've made good time, and we've been lucky, all things considered."

I swallow, my throat suddenly dry. I don't want to ask the question, but it's beating against the back of my teeth, demanding entrance into the world. "And if we don't make it in time?"

He just shakes his head slowly. "We'll make it, Amelia."

I blow out a breath. "Okay. Okay."

"C'mon, let's go get an icee or something. This doesn't look like the kind of place that has a lot of fresh food, but maybe they have some good snacks."

I look around then. The gas station looks worse for wear, like it's not maintained as often or as well as others. If not for the neon red open sign, I might think it was closed.

We're the only car at the pumps, but I see two older model trucks parked along the far side of the building. Employees, maybe.

"You good?" Sonny calls over the hood of my car.

My gaze snaps to him. He's standing next to Cole, who's bent over, probably filling up the gas cans.

I tug West behind me and walk around the car until I'm next to them. "I'm sorry I crashed."

"Me too." A genuine smile tips up the corners of Sonny's mouth. He leans in closer and brushes my hair off of my forehead with the back of his index finger.

"Both of you bailed, but West and I stayed awake for one another," Cole says. There isn't any annoyance in his voice, just relaying the facts.

"I grabbed a bunch of electrolyte sachets from my backpack for all of us too. We should down those before we get back on the road," Sonny says.

I nod and untangle my fingers from West's to stretch my arms up high above my head. "Sure. I'm going to find a bathroom quick. And I'll take the next shift."

"I'll ride shotgun," West says.

"You should catch some sleep, and you might have more room in the back."

"And miss talking to my girl for a few hours? I would never." His voice is low and smooth, like freshly melted chocolate.

West Campbell has always been too charming for his own good. Looking at him now, talking to him, it'd be so easy to fall back in love with him. All too easy.

And if I'm halfway there with three different men?

The thought makes my heart race, and it's not from fear.

Okay, maybe a little fear. But mostly excitement—hopeful.

And if Dad's right and Mother Nature decides to throw in the towel, then I better make the most of the time we have.

I nod to myself, proud of my little pep talk.

"We have a lot of catching up to do, Ames. Don't think I forgot about the first *gun in your face* thing either." He pauses and glares at me. It doesn't pack the same punch when the laugh lines around his eyes wink at me.

I hook a coy smile at him. "It was fine. I was totally badass. You should ask Sonny."

"I'd rather hear it from you." He tosses an arm around my neck, and I reach up to hold his hand as we cross the cracked pavement to the small building.

39

AMELIA

IT'S QUIET HERE, like eerily quiet. I don't even hear the quiet hum of nearby traffic. "Where are we again?"

"A remote part of New Mexico, I guess."

"Huh. I should've studied harder in geography—and maybe history too."

"Instead you were too busy hanging around with two punks." He flashes me a cocky little smirk and lets his arm fall off my shoulders. He opens the door for me, standing to the side to let me pass by him.

I separate our hands reluctantly, already plotting to hold his hand while I drive.

I'd forgotten what it feels like to hold hands with West. His palm dwarfs mine, but instead of it feeling awkward, it makes me feel protected, cared for.

The weather in this part of the country is pleasant enough, if not hotter than hell. But at least it isn't storming or hailing or shaking.

I smother my smile at his chivalry in my shoulder. "Thanks," I murmur over the bell tinkling above the door.

"Of course. You need anything?"

"Nah, I'm going to go to the bathroom and then take a quick look around. I'll meet you at the register."

"Okay. We leave in ten, okay? We're right on track, but you never know."

"I'll be quick."

I flash him a smile and then weave in and out of a few short aisles until I find the restroom in the back corner of the store. The lightbulb is buzzing above like it's on its last leg before it burns out completely.

There's only one bathroom back here, and when I check the knob, it's locked. I stand back a few paces and look around, seeing if I can spot any snacks to beeline to when I'm done. I thought I saw some of those starlight mints. I haven't had those in years.

They remind me of my grandma. She always had a bowl of them out. *For company*, she'd say.

Their selection in general seems pretty lacking, but maybe I'll get lucky. There are six aging cooler cases, two with beer, an empty one with a sign for ice, and three more with water and soda and what looks like a few energy drink options.

The chipped metal shelves lean toward bare. Maybe they don't get restocked often since it seems like we're off the beaten path.

The door creaks as it opens behind me, so I pivot on the ball of my foot and turn around. I feel the awkward face everyone makes when you realize someone was waiting for you to be done, only the bathroom door didn't open. The employees-only one did.

And standing in the doorway are two very tall, very broad, very mean-looking men.

"Well, well, well. Look at what wandered into my shop."

"Oh, uh, I'm just waiting for the bathroom." I hook a thumb toward the closed door to my left. The hair on the back of my neck stands up, and I let the eerie sensation wash over me.

"It's broken," one guy says around a toothpick in his mouth. His hair is jet black, cropped short on the sides, and his eyes are just as dark. He looks like he spends all of his free time in the desert sun, his skin golden brown that looks older than his years.

"Been meaning to put a sign up," the other guy says. He's just as suntanned as his buddy, but his hair is light brown with eyes to match.

"Right, well, okay." I flash them a brittle smile and spin on my heel.

"Not so fast, girlie." The black-haired guy clamps his meaty hand above my elbow. His fingers dig into my skin, and I already know he'll leave bruises. "We've got an employee bathroom in the back you can use."

I glance from his hand around my arm to his face, which is much too close to mine. He leans in closer, flashing me his teeth in a smile too cruel to be anything but a sneer. He takes an exaggerated inhale, and I jerk back on reflex.

"No thanks. My boyfriend and his brothers are waiting for me," I grit through clenched teeth, yanking my arm.

He tightens his hold as the other guy laughs. "The dark-haired one your boyfriend or a brother? Doesn't really matter, he's otherwise occupied."

My stomach roils, and I bend over, my shoulders curling inward. Dread pools in my gut like oil, slick and toxic.

"West! West! I'm back here!" I scream as loud as I can. Maybe Sonny or Cole can hear me from outside. I wasn't paying enough attention when I walked in, so for all I know, there's a window nearby that opens up to the parking lot, right where my car is parked.

I struggle in his hold, wiggling and wrenching my arm to the left and then right, screaming their names. "Cole! Gray! West!"

And these fucking assholes behind me just laugh. They laugh like they just saw their favorite stand-up comedian. It's a surprised sort of delighted sound, and that might be what pushes me over the edge.

My heart hammers inside my chest, demanding to leave my

body. A massive wave of fear crests, flooding my system with the urge to fight or fly. I was holding it at bay, secured in the fact that West was waiting for me at the register.

But there's no way he didn't hear me, which means they were telling the truth.

They did something to him.

My heart hitches, a suspended moment in time where my fear escalates into full-on terror. It holds me hostage, freezing my thoughts but not my body. I'm flailing, scratching at everything I can reach.

At some point, he grabs my other arm and pins my arms behind my back. He holds the spot above my elbows, which pushes my breasts out.

Too many new fears have been unlocked in a short amount of time. But this one? This takes the cake—over being stranded by flood water, buried under debris from an earthquake, even being taken out by a volcano eruption.

I will die before I ever let these disgusting, vile men take what I will *never* offer them.

With that gauntlet, a sort of clarity showers over me.

I know enough from true crime shows, that I *cannot* let them take me somewhere. I shift my feet and widen my stance. I don't have a weapon or anything nearby that I can use, but I'm determined and scrappy as fuck.

And I've survived too much already to give up now.

I have to try something.

I lick my lips and stop struggling. My chest heaves with labored breaths, and I struggle to clear my vision. It's fuzzy with panic and fear.

"Ah, see, girlie, we're not going to hurt you. We just want to spend some time with you. We don't get many visitors around here," the brown-haired guy says as he steps in front of me. He brushes a lock of wild hair behind my ear, and I jerk out of his touch. Which has me stepping into the guy holding my arms behind me.

I glare at him, packing all the hate and promise of retribution I can.

"Ooh, she's feisty, Trevor." The brown-haired guy gets in my face, breathing his sour breath all over me.

"I don't mind a little fire, Doug."

They want fire? I'm going to burn them to the fucking ground.

40

COLE

"WHERE ARE THEY?" Deja vu tilts the world on its axis. The sun-warmed metal heats my skin through my pants, and the air shimmers in the heat.

The desert is brutal on her kindest days.

My nerves feel raw after Mia and I kissed last night. I feel like a fucking thirteen-year-old boy thinking about a kiss like that. But I can't help it. She felt so—so *perfect* in my arms.

Secrets still stand between us though, and it's holding me back. I'm a man at war, constantly vacillating between throwing her over my shoulders and saying *fuck it* and walking away without turning back.

I already know I won't walk away from her. I couldn't, not even when she physically walked away from me. Left me just like everyone else in my life has.

Everyone except for West and Gray.

They're my family now, have been for years.

The acute ache inside my chest, perfectly sized for her, throbs. I've fucking missed her, more than she knows. Hell, probably more than West even knows. And Gray never knew about her at all. By the time we met him, she had been gone for three weeks. Without a trace. There was no point in bringing up some girl we used to know when we were just trying to survive.

So that's what I've been doing—fucking surviving. Existing. Going through the daily motions.

Then she floats into my life like a fluffy cloud of everything good in the world. And I don't know how to turn it off, this constant pang that I've just been living with for five years. I kept waiting for it to go away, to ease.

But I guess it's true what they say. You never forget your first.

"Give 'em a minute, man." Gray's voice snaps me out of my funk, and I look at him.

He's wearing a heathered charcoal-colored short-sleeved tee with black utility pants, standing next to the hood like it's a casual Monday. His lack of urgency only ramps mine up further.

I check my phone and note the time. "I have. It's been seven minutes."

Gray sighs and leans against the front of Amelia's SUV next to me. "Look, West is right there, at the register."

I flip my baseball hat around so it shields the sun from my vision. West places some chip bags on the counter, and I chuckle. It's good to know that even when the world is allegedly ending, West didn't lose his craving for processed and fried potatoes.

Gray pushes off the car and stands at attention. It's the only way to describe the way he shifts and stills.

"Can we help you?"

My brow dips low, and I look around Gray. I don't know what I was expecting, but whatever it was isn't him. I bet he's pushing seven feet tall, built like a brick wall.

I step next to Gray to face this guy, but movement from the corner of my eye catches my attention.

I shift to keep the brick shithouse in my line of sight and eye the inside of the gas station.

Where the hell are they?

I eye Gray. "You good?"

He nods and jerks his chin toward the building. "I'm going to get to know our new friend here. What did you say your name was again?" He leans forward, his hands stuffed into his pockets, a smile that promises pain on his face. I bet he's already flipping open his knife in his pocket, just waiting for the right moment to strike. He's like a fucking cobra, only more deadly.

"I didn't," the guy snaps.

He doesn't sound scared yet, but he will be by the time Gray is done.

Everyone always assumes that I'm the loose cannon in our trio, but they've never seen the real West *or* Gray. They use their friendliness as a mask, wielding their charm like a fine-tuned blade when it suits them.

I'm not worried about leaving him with the guy out here. I'm more concerned about where the fuck my brother disappeared to.

As my hand closes around the metal handle of the glass door, I'm hit with a chilling realization that makes my head feel weightless, like it's floating ten feet above me.

Where's Amelia?

I yank open the door and fling it behind me. I stop a foot inside, breathing through my nose like a bull, these big, deep breaths that have my chest heaving.

I scan the register area where I last saw him. Bags of chips and chocolate bars and bottles of water are on the counter, but West isn't anywhere in sight.

I cock my head to the side, trying to hear anything over the music blaring overhead. It's one of those instrumental covers of some heavy metal song.

It's fucking with me. The music swelling into a crescendo that seems to steal my breath.

And then I hear it.

A shuffle and a groan.

I stalk across the faded red all-weather rug with some company's black logo stretched across the middle. I keep my feet light, determined to keep what little surprise advantage I might have.

The groaning gets louder as I walk along the register, coming from my right.

I huff and shove down my annoyance. There's nothing around me that I could use as a weapon, unless you count high cholesterol.

I flex and fist my hands.

Fuck it.

I'm not afraid to use my hands. I push onto the balls of my feet and shift my weight as I round the end of the register, behind the cash wrap.

There, surrounded by fallen packs of cigarettes and tobacco containers, is West.

"Goddamn it," I curse under my breath and crouch down.

He groans as he sits up, clutching his head by his temple. "What the fuck."

Blood pools between his fingers, but not too much, thank fuck.

"Are you okay? What the fuck happened?" I reach behind him to a package of unopened paper towels. I rip it open in an instant, the roll popping free and falling to the dirty mat beneath us. "Shit."

I unravel several sheets and toss them to the side.

"God damnit," he groans, pulling his hand back to inspect his bloodied fingers.

"Would you stop that? Here." I press a wad of clean paper towel to the side of his head.

"Thanks." He grasps it and holds it tight.

"What happened?"

He adjusts the paper towel, blood slowly seeping in. "I don't fucking know, man. I was sucker-punched, I think. My head is killing me. I was just waiting for—oh fuck. Fuck, fuck." The color leeches from his face further, turning his skin a pale shade.

He pushes up to his feet, and I jump to mine a second after him. He reaches out and grips my bicep as he sways a little on his feet.

"What, West!" Panic sloshes inside my gut, burning me up from the inside.

He doesn't answer me, just pushes around me and screams, "Amelia!"

He sways again, and I place a hand to his chest, shoving him to sit down on the small stool behind the counter. "Sit down. I'll go get her."

He pushes up. "Fuck that, I'm fine. Let's go." His pupils are blown, his jaw set.

I grip him by the shoulder and stare at him.

"We're wasting time, man! The last thing I heard was her screaming for us." His eyes are wide, and he shifts from foot to foot.

"Fine, let's go. But I'm not stopping, so if you need a break, you fucking sit down, yeah?"

"I'm fine," he says, brushing me off and stepping around me. He stumbles and shakes his head a little, like he's trying to clear it.

One of these days his stubbornness is going to bite him in the ass. But until then, he's got me at his back.

"Stay behind me before you fall down," I grumble, skirting around him and running down the first aisle. Black creeps in around the edges of my vision, and my breath sounds loud in my head. I frantically look around, desperate to see any sign of her and half expecting to find her in the middle of one of these candy aisles. She always did have a sweet tooth.

"Where is she?" I snap, urgency and frustration boiling together.

"In the back. Bathroom."

The world shifts again, and I experience that sense of free falling like that stupid fucking drop rollercoaster Amelia and West forced me to go on one year. I almost puked, but the elation on her face had me riding that fucker two more times that night.

It always comes back to her. If five years apart didn't change that, then I don't think anything will.

I skirt the end of an end cap, clipping my hip on the metal corner.

"There," West says, pointing toward the opposite corner.

I push off, the old linoleum floor creaking in protest as I pivot and run down the aisle. In my peripheral vision, I see West slow down and grip his head, shaking it a few times.

Despite what I told him, I slow down and look over my shoulder.

"Don't stop, asshole. Go get our girl," he yells at me. "I'm right behind you."

It's all the encouragement I needed. My vision gets hazy like looking through a smudged lens. I skid to a stop in front of the bathroom door and pound on it.

"Amelia!" Her name is a vicious plea, but she doesn't answer. Though I don't know how anyone could hear anything over the music pouring through the overhead speaker. It's some heavy metal song I've never heard of with enough percussion to drown out any sound.

I fuck up then and allow a sliver of fear to embed itself inside of me. It takes root, and I know myself well enough to know that I'm a minute away from losing control.

I push off the doorframe to the bathroom and take a step back. I lift my right leg up and bring it down against the door. The lock snaps, and the door swings open to reveal a dingy single bathroom.

The light above flickers like some ominous warning system, and I whirl around in front of another door.

And then I hear it. It's faint over the pounding drums, but I'd recognize that sound anywhere.

It's Mia.

And she's screaming for me.

41

AMELIA

THE BLACK-HAIRED ASSHOLE, Trevor, walks me backward with his grip on my arms behind my back. I become dead weight, dragging my feet and wrenching my arms out, throwing my body to the side. Anything to stop them. Or at the very least, make it fucking difficult to drag me to whatever hell they have planned.

"Let go of me, you motherfuckers," I grunt each word. "West! Gray! Cole!" I scream for them, desperation hollows out my stomach and claws at me with her sharp talons. I twist my body and kick out when the brown-haired guy, Doug, steps close to me, anything to dislodge his hold on me.

He bats my legs down like they're nothing but annoying flies buzzing around, and the momentum sends me leaning to the right. At the same time, Trevor lets go of me, so I catch the doorframe on the side of my face.

Everything goes white for a moment as blinding pain ricochets through my body. My cheek screams in pain, and my body shuts down. I can't make my limbs cooperate, and I land in a heap on the ground.

"Ah, not so feisty now, are ya, girlie? Haul her up, Trev."

Fingers dig into the already tender flesh around my bicep and jerk me to my feet. The guy holding my arms adjusts his grip to smash both of my wrists together in one fist. My bones protest the crushing grip, but it's nothing compared to the way his other hand squeezes my breast. I flinch at the pain and throw my body backward without thinking.

Trevor shakes me hard enough I can feel my teeth rattle together. I can feel my heartbeat in the right side of my face, a throbbing reminder, but I do my best to shove it aside. To breathe through it and not let it interfere with what I might have to do to survive.

Because that's what matters now.

Not bruises or black eyes or even a broken bone. It's about survival.

And I've already decided that I'll do whatever it takes. They like 'em feisty, prepared for it even. I don't even want to think about what that means—or how many times they've done this before.

So I'll play the part of the docile woman for a few minutes if it gives me an opening I can use. And if a little piece of my soul withers at my faux acceptance, then I'll just have to deal with that later.

I stop struggling altogether and let Trevor lead me into the oversized closet masquerading as an employee lounge.

Doug kicks out the legs of a metal chair in front of an old desk, and Trevor pushes me until I'm sitting down in it. The desk is old, made from that cheap particle board crap and painted to look like real wood. It's chipped in places, fading in others, and there's absolutely nothing suitable for a weapon on it.

Except for a vintage glass ashtray.

It's green glass with a big enough lip around the side that I can use as a makeshift handle. And it probably weighs five pounds.

Trevor lets go of my wrists but clamps a hand on my shoulder, sinking his fingers into the sensitive area around my collar bone.

I don't hide my wince, and they both chuckle. I look at the floor, gritting my teeth and swallowing the urge to reach for the ashtray. I need to wait for the right opening. I can do that. I can be patient.

"So, here's how it's going to work," Doug says as he places a gun down on the desk in front of me.

My gaze flies to the firearm a foot in front of me and then to Doug. He smirks like he knows exactly what I'm thinking. Hell, maybe he does. I wouldn't be surprised if he gets off on this—giving women hope knowing full well he's not going to let them achieve it.

Well fuck that and fuck him.

I'm a recent supporter of hope, a fact I can thank my three men for. So I'll be damned if I'm going to let these vile men take that from me too.

Doug holds my gaze as he deliberately unbuckles his belt, pulling the leather strap through the buckle slowly.

"Hurry up, man. We don't got all day," Trevor whines behind me.

"Chill. Phil was taking care of the one at the pump, probably knocked 'im out cold. But alright, we can get this party started." Doug pulls his belt free from his belt loops and takes a step toward me.

Bile crawls up my throat, and I breathe through my nose so I don't vomit. How much farther can I let this go? What if I don't get the opening I need?

Hopelessness threatens to drown me, tiny tendrils of terror wind around my ankles, rooting me to the spot. I lower my head, keeping my gaze on my shoes. There's a scuff on the toe of my left sneaker that snags my attention.

"Bitch, are you listening?" Trevor fists my hair at the back of my head and yanks my head up.

Doug's pants are unzipped, his dingy white underwear showing. He grabs himself and grunts. "You better not bite me, bitch, or I'll find another hole to start with."

Rage simmers beneath my skin, and I exhale a quiet breath. *This is it*, I think. There wasn't an opening for me to make my move, so I'm going to have to make it myself.

Maybe vomiting all over him is a good distraction.

No sooner than I commit and let the nausea swell up, the door flies open. I shut everything else down. The commotion at the door distracts Trevor enough that he loosens his grip on me, and I dive for the ashtray. My stomach hits the edge of the desk as I stretch out and curl my fingers over the lip of the heavy glass.

With a battle cry Alley would've been proud of, I pull myself off the desk and grip the makeshift weapon in two hands, swinging it in a wide arc that catches Doug in the side of the face.

"You stupid bitch!" he roars, his hands flying to his face as he sinks to his knees.

My heart is an oppressive beat in my ears, and I can feel how wide my eyes are. I drop the ashtray to the floor with a thump and scoop the gun off the table next. I flick the safety off and whirl around on Trevor behind me.

Only he's not the only one there.

Cole looks like a man possessed. He stands over Trevor, his fists flying against his face and torso, pummeling him at a frightening speed. His tattoos look like living creatures winding over his corded muscles as they bunch and flex with each hit.

"Cole," I choke out his name.

He pauses, one hand fisting Trevor's collar and holding him off the floor. He lets go, Trevor's head hitting the floor with a resounding thump.

Cole eyes me then, his gaze scanning me from head to toe and back again, but he doesn't rush me like I thought he would. No, his gaze stills on the tear along the collar of my shirt.

"Which one?" he grits out.

"I don't know. They both . . . put their disgusting hands on me, took liberties." And I have half a mind to cut them off. I don't tell him that though, not yet, at least. I'm not sure I have the right temperament for that kind of punishment, even if it's deserving.

Despite the precarious situation I'm in, that slippery emotion that feels a lot like love slithers into my veins. Worse, it fills me with hope.

He's here.

"Oh, this must be the boyfriend then." Doug says with a psychotic laugh. He eyes me then and licks the spot of blood on the side of his mouth. "I can see why. I bet she's an animal in the sack, huh. I can't wait to find out."

I changed my mind. I think I could make an exception and liberate both of their hands from their bodies.

"You're fucking dead." West stands in the doorway, blood dribbling down the side of his face as he delivers three words that sound more like a promise than a threat. He looks impossibly big, just like Cole, all heaving muscles and cold, calculated rage and determination.

West's gaze flies to mine as he crosses the room, scanning me much like Cole did.

"I'm alright." I don't know who I'm reassuring, me or them, but either way, West nods.

He shifts his focus and lunges for Doug on the floor. He winds back and hits him with a jab that has Doug rocking back on his ass.

It's the flint to the flame, and energy explodes.

Cole kicks Trevor at the same time West lands another punch, but despite the ass-kicking they're receiving, the rage doesn't settle inside of me.

It's oxygen to the rising inferno inside of me.

So I let it out.

"Wait!" I scream. "Enough."

"Amelia," West hedges.

"No—*no*, West." I shake my head, reading his sentiment all over his expression. "No, I'm not going to go wait in the car."

"It's her revenge too," Cole says as he shuffles Trevor to the other side of the room by West.

They hold their positions, their arms still and their chests heaving. If I look closely enough, I can see the fine trembling in their limbs. But not from exertion or injury—no. I've seen them both like this before, not much but enough to recognize the fury sweating from their pores. It permeates the small room, and I know I'm not the only one who feels it.

For the first time, the two strangers look genuinely afraid. Good. I want them to feel what I felt. What every woman they've dragged in here has felt. The kind of bone-deep terror that women just live with on a day-to-day basis, always looking over their shoulders, always going to the bathroom in twos.

It's because of men like *these*.

The gun trembles in my hand, my arm shaking with effort to hold it steady this whole time.

"Men like you two are all the same! You take and take and *take*!" Rancor drips from my words.

It feels like my ribcage is cracking open, no longer able to suppress my overwhelming righteous indignation. I don't take my eyes from the two men in front of me. "Well today *I* am the one who takes."

Cole and West witness my unraveling, but they don't interfere.

West stands behind Doug, wrenching his arm high behind him. I remember this move from one of my classes. It immobilizes them because if they move, they dislocate their shoulders.

Cole's next to Trevor, who sways on his feet, face swelling already.

But it's not enough.

"Get on your knees." My voice is rough as my mind fractures a little bit. I don't allow myself to spiral completely, I can't. I can't even entertain the nightmare thoughts of what could've happened had Cole and West not found me in time.

"What's a little thing like you gonna do, huh?" Doug taunts me.

"Why don't you put my gun down, and my brother and I will sort it out with your boyfriend here. A proper match, not some amateur ambush. Winner takes *you*." He takes a step toward me, and I widen my stance.

"Amelia."

My shoulders sag at the sound of Sonny's voice behind me. A second later, his palm slides down my spine, pausing on my lower back. I feel him behind me, close enough that I could lean into him if I needed to.

"Are you okay?" My voice is low, but the room is small, and not even the blaring metal music from the store conceals my question.

"Right as rain, Cher." He smooths his palm back up my spine and rests it gently on the back of my neck, underneath my hair. His fingertips rest on either side of my neck, grounding me. "You good?"

I nod, too quickly. "I'll be fine." And I will be, once I settle the score.

Doug laughs again. It sounds like nails on a chalkboard, all derision. "Now I get it. You're fucking all three of them. Seems like you're real accustomed to sharing, girlie. So how's about you let me and my brother have a taste?"

"I said get on your knees," I snap.

Cole kicks the back of Trevor's knees, and he crumples like yesterday's newspaper.

West yanks Doug's arm, angling it higher and forcing him to his knees. "What the fuck do you think you're doing, asshole? Don't talk to her—don't even fucking look at her."

Doug grunts. "Or what?" When West doesn't answer him right away, he smirks. "That's what I thought."

"You don't get to just take what you want!" I yell at them, startling everyone in the room. Angry tears welling up in my eyes. I blink, setting them free to roll down my cheeks in a testament to the collective pain of every woman they've forced. "How many? How many women have you done this to?"

Doug looks up at me from his prone position on his knees. His left eye is already swelling and his lip bleeds from West's brutal right hook. He grins, flashing me a sinister smile, and pointedly looks from the trembling gun to my face. "I've lost count."

I pull the trigger on an exhale.

42

AMELIA

IT'S A PUZZLING SOUND, a gunshot. It's unmistakable when you think about it, yet it's so foreign at the same time. How can such a recognizable noise sound so *strange?*

Or maybe it's the sound it makes when it hits a person and not a piece of wood or paper. Or even a tin can like you see at some gun ranges.

I think I'm experiencing some sort of break from reality. It's the only explanation for it. One second, I'm standing in front of two men who think they can take something that doesn't belong to them.

And the next, one of Sonny's arms wraps around my middle, and the other one slowly lowers in front of me until his palm covers my hands wrapped around the gun.

White noise fills my ears, like I've got a conch shell placed up tight against both of them. He gently applies pressure to my hands, and I don't put up a fight, letting him lower the gun until it's pointing at the floor.

"That's it, Amelia. Just breathe for me, baby."

His voice sounds far away in my ear, like he's in a tunnel or something. I inhale as my lashes flutter, reflexively blinking to clear the haze from my vision. The scratch of Sonny's scruff prickles my cheek, pulling me back into myself even further.

"I shot someone, Gray."

"I know, baby." His thumb sneaks underneath the hem of my tee, brushing slow strokes along my abdomen.

"I shot him. *I* did that."

"I'm proud of you." I feel his chest rumble with his words in my ear.

It might seem like a strange response to my admission, and maybe I'll look back on it and think differently, but right now, it's exactly what I needed to hear. My chest expands, and my lungs fill with his alluring deep-amber scent.

"I—" I lick my lips, my throat parched with understanding. "I wanted to make him hurt."

"You did good, baby. Let me handle it now, yeah?" His voice is a smooth, deep tenor, rolling over me in soft waves. He slips the gun from my grip but doesn't move.

I nod and tilt my head back to ghost my lips across his jaw. "What now?"

He turns his head so our lips just barely graze. He murmurs against my mouth, "Why don't you patch up one of the boys?"

My gaze snaps to West first, eyeing the faint trail of blood on the side of his face and then to Cole. Blood speckles his face and shirt, but I don't think most of it is his. His knuckles, however, are a mess. A glance at West shows his hand in a similar state, probably from teeth on those wicked punches.

I make myself look at the guy I just shot, Doug. He's not dead, but he is hurt pretty good. I don't think I should feel so . . . indifferent toward his demise.

No, that's not true.

I'm not indifferent. I'm *pleased* that he's suffering. That he's experiencing an iota of the countless amounts of pain he's inflicted.

Sonny's whole hand skates underneath the hem of my shirt. "Cher?"

I come back to myself with a blink. "Yes. Yes, I'll go get supplies to patch up the boys."

His fingers are slow to leave my skin, only separating once I step away. "Good girl."

I pause in front of the only window in the room and survey the carnage. I know I should feel something, remorse, maybe.

But I don't.

I look at my men, their chests broad, their gorgeous faces downturned in rage, their protectiveness a palpable thing filling up this small room. An emotion bigger than I've felt before wafts down like a gift from mother nature herself and settles on my shoulders.

I allow the corners of my lips to tip upward in a small smile. I hold each of their gazes for a moment, trying to convey everything I don't think I can even voice yet before I stalk out of the room without a word.

COLE

MY EARS still ring from the gunshot, but my eyes never stray from the woman in front of me. Backlit from the sun piercing through the cloudy window, she looks like an angel.

An avenging angel.

Her hair sticks to her sweaty neck, her slate blue eyes wide as she stares at the rapist motherfucker bleeding from his shoulder. He lays sprawled out on the dirty concrete floor, gasping and pleading with Gray like he's going to help him.

I grab a handful of the guy's hair and yank it backward. I want her face to be the last thing he sees before he descends into hell. To witness her retribution.

Gray wouldn't help him even if he wasn't too busy whispering in my girl's ear. He's standing behind her, one arm banded around her middle and the other slowly pushing her hand with the gun down. She sags into him, not enough for him to take her weight. More like relief that he's there, watching her back.

Like he won't let anything happen to her.

Jealousy curdles in my gut, this sticky tar of discomfort. Despite everything, I can't stop the knee-jerk reaction that *I* should be the one behind her, offering her understated comfort.

My muscles lock up and relax, over and over again in the matter of a few seconds as I fight the urge to go to her. The guy on his knees in front of me starts blubbering, so I cuff him in the side of the head without taking my eyes from her.

"Shut up, asshole."

It's an inconsequential tap in the grand scheme of the violence today. He'd have to be an absolute idiot to not realize that they're not walking out of this building today.

I see it then. The moment a film of distance shudders over her eyes. She blinks and peels her gaze from the guy she shot to me. Panic flickers behind the faux-blank expression, her brows scrunching up.

Gray murmurs something too low for me to hear over the goddamn heavy metal music still blasting through the speakers.

She tilts her head to the side, brushing her lips across Gray's jaw and mine throbs, bereft.

She steps away from him then, pausing in front of the window. Again, I'm hit with the vision of her as an avenging angel. My chest hitches at the sight.

She allows her gaze to fall to each of us before she smiles. It's a soft sort of expression, one I wouldn't normally associate with the violence that erupted.

And then she stalks out of the room without a backward glance.

I wait for two seconds to see if she's coming back, and when she doesn't, I whirl on Gray. "What did you say to her?"

He lifts a shoulder. "I told her she did a good job and that she needs to patch you two up." He pins both of us with alternating glares.

"What about these two?" I push the guy in front of me forward, and he hits the ground like dead weight with a groan.

"I'll take care of them," Gray says.

West steps forward. "I'll help you, let her patch up, Cole."

I bristle at the insinuation. "I'm fine. You're the one who got a head wound—"

"A *minor* head wound. I barely even feel it," West snaps.

Sonny turns to us. "Are you fucking kidding me right now? You do realize that you're arguing over who gets to *take care* of the problems, right?"

West folds his arms across his chest and glares at me. "It's my right. I'm the one who was sucker-punched by one of these assholes."

"Yeah, well I should've been there and protected both of you. That's on me." I slap my chest with my palm. "That's my responsibility. And I fucking clean up my messes."

West's arms drop to his side and scowls at me. "What the fuck is that supposed to mean?"

"That's not your burden, Cole. We take care of each other," Gray says at the same time.

I tip my chin up and roll my shoulders back. "Yeah, well."

West's eyes narrow, and he pins Gray with a look. "Why don't you leave Cole and me to clean up the mess?"

Gray rolls his eyes. "I'd be happy to play nurse with our girl, let our girl fawn all over my injuries. But unfortunately for me, I know neither one of you has even been in this kind of situation before."

Now it's my turn to roll my eyes. Gray's not usually the one for dramatics, but it's an unpredictable situation. "Oh and you have so much experience burying a body?"

"We're not going to bury them, Cole. We're going to send them straight to hell in a blaze of condemnation."

I still as realization dawns. My attention hyper focuses on my brother. West and I claimed him as our own five years ago, shortly after Mia left us. But like most foster kids, we didn't talk a lot about our pasts, where we grew up. Or how.

And as I look over at him now, I discover that there's so much more that I don't know about Gray. He's deceptively calm, no eye twitch or shaky hand. Just casually talking about turning a gas station into a bomb like we're chatting about what to make for dinner.

My brother and I share a look, and as one, we turn to our other brother.

"We're in a gas station, Gray. You can't just blow it up."

He lifts a shoulder. "I'm not."

"Oh, good. For a second there, I was worried," West says.

"I'm going to look for any security tapes, though I doubt this kind of place has any. And then I'm going to shoot that motherfucker who left bruises on our girl." He points to the guy who doesn't have a bullet hole in his shoulder. "And then I'm going to lock them in this room." He pauses a beat. "After I start it on fire."

He sinks his free hand into his pocket and rocks back on his heels, all the while, the neutral expression never leaves his face.

My mouth opens and closes at his even tone. He's so matter-of-fact about it that it takes a full five seconds for me to respond. I nod a few times. "Okay. I'll take Mia and get her to the car."

He holds up the gun, gesturing to it. "Once I pull the trigger, we'll have less than a minute until she burns. So make sure to get whatever we need from this place now."

"See if they have any of those red gas cans. I don't want to stop at any more gas stations if we can help it," West adds.

I cross the room but pause with my hand on the doorframe. "Make it quick, boys. It's a desolate road, but still, we don't want to take the chance of anyone stopping until we're long gone."

"You sure we'll have enough time to put enough distance between us?" West asks.

I tilt my head. "Retribution?"

He dips his chin. "Yeah, that and our own demise. I don't know the range of a gas station explosion."

West gestures toward the guys with the borrowed gun. "We'll be fine as long as we leave as soon as I light it."

"Got it. And Gray?" I eye the scum still on their knees with contempt. "Make them suffer."

He smiles, a twisted slash across his face. "With pleasure, brother."

Gray doesn't call us brother too often, and he rarely does anything without purpose. I can only imagine his reasoning for using the moniker now.

I tap the doorframe three times as I pass through it and hunt for my girl.

43

COLE

I FLIP the lock on the glass doors and stalk the aisles for my girl. I don't want to tempt fate too much today, and leaving it unlocked seems like a stupid way to invite more trouble.

"Mia?"

She springs up from the end of the aisle I'm in, her arms full of stuff. "Cole."

It's been five years since I've heard her sigh my name like that, the four letters a prayer falling from her perfect lips. My chest aches at the lost time between us, at the possibilities of where we would've been had she not left.

She must read something in my gaze or the way I'm damn near prowling toward her. She angles her body toward me, her lids lowering and her tongue peeking out to swipe along her lower lip. I have no idea how I look, but I know that I can't deny the urgency any longer.

I stop in front of her, crushing the things in her arms between us, and sink my hands into her hair, cradling the back of her neck.

I hover a few inches in front of her, giving her time to pull away and praying she doesn't take it.

I shouldn't have worried.

Everything in her arms clatters to the ground as she drops it. Something hard lands on the top of my foot, but I don't feel it. Every single molecule inside my body focuses on the way her hands feel wrapped around my wrists, anchoring us together.

We crash together in a kiss that's more teeth than tongue, more aggressive than tender. It's a physical manifestation of heightened emotions.

It's over almost as soon as it begins.

She keeps her eyes closed and rests her forehead against mine, both of us breathing heavily.

I lick my lips, still tasting her on my tongue. "Don't leave me again, Mia."

She pulls back enough that I can see her face clearly. Her lips are a brighter shade of rose, plush from my mouth. Her eyes soften as she looks at me. "I would never willingly leave you."

I straighten up and put a little more distance between us, sliding my hands from her hair. How can someone still smell good after the long journey we've been on? Like strawberries or something equally sweet. My mouth hooks up on one side. "You said that before too."

AMELIA

I PRESS the button to unlock my car and open the trunk, tossing the bags of things we grabbed from inside. Not too much, just some bottled water, three more gas cans we need to fill up, a few lighters and whatever Cole snagged when I wasn't looking.

I walk around the side and open up the passenger door, looking at Cole with an arched brow. "Sit down, Cole."

He inclines his chin and falls into the seat, keeping his feet planted on the ground. "What're you doing, Mia?"

Déjà vu slithers down my spine when I crack open a bottle of water and lean in, setting the plastic bag of bottled water on the floor of the car. I hear his sharp intake of breath as my breasts brush against him.

I straighten up and look down at him. At this angle, I have a few inches on him, but that's not what makes me feel powerful.

No, it's the way he's looking up at me like I'm the light in his darkness.

He plays with my fingers, skimming his fingertips up and over my knuckles and back down again. My hand runs through his hair softly. It's something my grandma used to do to me when I was younger. It's one of my fondest memories, the simple affection she gave so freely and often.

Now I run my fingers through Cole's and West's hair as often as I can.

Cole groans when I apply a little pressure along his temple. "Where have you been my whole life, Mia?"

Outwardly, I chuckle but inside, I'm a sunflower opening under his attention. "Well I'm here now."

"You can never leave, you know that right?"

I roll my lips inward to smother a smile. "I'm sure you could find someone else to play with your hair. I bet you'd have a line of girls waiting for their turn."

Am I fishing? Absolutely. But sometimes a girl's gotta cast a line.

"I don't care about them." He waves his hand in the air, his gaze on the movie playing in front of us. But I can't take my eyes off his face. "When you're around, everything is lighter. I've been treading quicksand in the darkness for years, Mia. Years. And then you show up, and suddenly, there's a brightness in my life."

My heart squeezes painfully in my chest, like someone spins a vise tighter and tighter. What's worse is that West said something similar to me last week. He even made me promise I'd never leave.

And then he kissed me.

I still, and Cole gives me his attention instantly. His eyes are guarded, his body tense. I smooth some hair back and promise, "I'll never leave you or West."

His lips part on an exhale, but whatever he was going to say never reaches my ears because West saunters into my living room. He's pulling a black hoodie over his head. He stops in front of the TV and stares at Cole and I sprawled out on the couch. He ruffles his damp hair, a faux pout on his lips. "No fair. It's my turn with Ames."

I giggle and sit up a little and pull my hand from Cole's fingers to pat the cushion next to me. "I saved you a seat."

Cole grumbles a little and scoots down.

"That's my girl," West says as he plops down next to me. He tosses a velvet green throw pillow on my lap and swings his legs over the arm of the couch. He lowers his head to my lap, looking at me with a goofy grin and puppy-dog eyes.

I know exactly what he wants, just like he knows his puppy-dog eyes work on me every time. At least that's what I tell myself and not the startling truth: I'd do anything for both of them.

I sink my fingers into his hair, and he lets out a happy hum.

I blink myself out of the flashback playing before my eyes. "I'm taking care of you," I murmur.

He places his right hand in mine, and I make short work of cleaning it the best I can with a roll of paper towels and water.

I blow on his knuckles one more time before releasing his hand, but I don't step back from between his legs. "There, now at least they're clean. We'll have to find somewhere to get washed up soon."

He nods, his gaze soft and pensive on me. I feel it like a physical caress.

"You have blood on your shirt though." I point my finger at the worst of the stain in the middle of his chest.

He reaches behind his head, grabs a handful of fabric, and tugs it off in one swift, stupid-hot movement. It's not really the time to entertain any kind of lusty thoughts, but I can't stop them from flitting across my consciousness.

His full sleeves stand out against his sun-tanned skin, and my fingertips ache to trace them. Grief sinks into my lungs, catching my breath at all the designs I missed. The three of us were supposed to get our first tattoo together when I turned eighteen.

I open my mouth, the question about the letter on the tip of my tongue when Sonny and West come running out of the building.

"Time to go, Cher. Hop in the back and toss me the keys, yeah?"

"What's the rush?" I ask.

"We'll explain everything in the car. Hop in, Ames," West says, ushering me in the backseat. He follows behind me, slamming his door just as I hand Sonny the keys.

Sonny throws the car in drive and squeals out of the parking lot.

I swallow over the lump in my throat. "What the hell is going on? Did you . . . did you kill those guys?"

"Nah, just made them wish they were," West replies, propping his arm along the backseat, his fingertips swirling a pattern on my shoulder.

"The fire will take care of them for us," Sonny says.

I cock my head to the side. "Fire?"

A loud boom answers for them, and I twist in my seat to look out the back windshield. It looks like the gas station just exploded!

"Did you guys blow up the gas station?" My voice hits an octave reserved for incredulity.

Sonny punches the gas, and the car speeds up. "Well, I started a small fire in the room where you last saw them. Guess it spread."

I face forward and sit back in my seat. "Okay."

Sonny's eyes flick to mine in the rearview mirror. "I did what I had to do, Cher."

I blink and touch my fingertips to my small smile. "Thank you. All of you."

"You don't have to thank us, Ames," West murmurs.

"I am all the same," I say.

Sonny doesn't slow down, not even twenty minutes later, weaving around slower cars on the highway like we're auditioning for *Fast and the Furious*. I don't question him though. If there's anything I learned about Gray Walters, it's that he has a reason for everything he does.

I clear my throat, my voice hoarse, and pinch the dirty, torn shirt away from my body. "I need a shower."

I can't take it anymore. The urge to scrub myself raw from their touch hasn't gone away. It beats down on me like the hot desert sun through my window.

I spent the entire time with my head leaning against the window, letting the sun warm my skin while my gaze wandered to the dozens and dozens of advertisements along the side of the highway.

Gentlemen's clubs, real estate agents, tourist attractions, and new neighborhoods. Lots of new neighborhoods are being built around here.

"No gas stations." I slowly twist around to look at the men in the car around me. "I saw some that offer *safe and secure showers*, but I—" I lick my lips. "I can't do it. Not yet. Tomorrow, maybe."

"We'll find somewhere else to stop," West says. His palm covers my thigh, and I shift toward him, my knees leaning against his.

I lean my head against his shoulder with a sigh. "Alright."

"A couple hours to clean up and rest wouldn't hurt," Cole agrees.

Sonny's gaze meets mine in the rearview mirror. "Maybe we can find a diner too. I don't want to dip into our reserves unless we have to."

I slip my arm through West's on a sigh. "You know what sounds so good right now? A basket of French fries with aioli and ketchup and—"

"Nacho cheese," Cole interrupts, looking over his shoulder at me. The area around his eye is starting to darken with a bruise already. I wouldn't be surprised if he had a black eye by morning.

"You remember," I beam, tightening my arm around West's.

West chuckles. "How could we forget? You ordered it every time we went to The Spot."

"And you ordered it at Tennessee Pete's," Sonny says.

A silly grin slips over my face, pleasure soaking into my soul.

"There," Cole says, tapping his window. "It looks like a new fitness center. I bet they have showers we can use, probably some couches we can crash on too."

I look out the window and see a giant building in the middle of what looks like a construction zone. It looks like they're building condos or luxury apartments, but the fitness center went in first.

There are four buildings being framed out, only steel beams and piles of lumber.

"Let's check it out," Sonny says as he exits the highway.

44

AMELIA

"WAIT HERE," Sonny murmurs as he rounds the corner of the building.

Wind whips my hair, the strands stinging my face with the force. I'm not sure if it's just this area or if a storm is coming, but the wind has definitely picked up in the last thirty minutes.

The fitness center is a modern color block design, charcoal on the bottom two-thirds and burnt orange on the top-third. The front corner of the building is floor-to-ceiling windows with a few modern-style orange loveseats around an oval low-profile wood coffee table.

I look around again, but there's no one here. A few neighborhoods sit about a mile or so down to the south, but it's hard to tell if they're lived in or still under construction.

I bite the corner of my bottom lip. "Are you sure this is a good idea? What if someone comes?"

"We'll be fine, Mia. Worst-case scenario, they ask us to leave and we do."

"True." I can't shake the unsettling feeling though. Maybe I'll feel better once I can clean up a little, put on fresh clothes.

Sonny pushes the metal door open, greeting us with a smile. "Good news. They have power, and they have a mini kitchen area. Not much, but they have a cooktop and a microwave, so I thought we could do something with that."

We follow behind him, toward the back of the building, passing a few empty lounge rooms and some that look like they'll be fitness class rooms with wood floors and floor-length mirrors on one wall.

We find the kitchenette to the left, but there are a few more doors down this hallway that I want to look in. "I'm going to check these last few rooms out."

"Don't stray too far, Mia."

"I won't," I say as I walk out the door and to the left. I don't bother covering my smile from his protectiveness. I could get used to that again.

A conference room, a yoga studio, and bingo. A bathroom.

"Found the showers! It's like a spa in here," I yell over my shoulder.

I flip the switch and dim lights turn on overhead, barely offering any light in any of the six shower stalls in the room. Three on each side with modern metal sconces strategically placed every few feet above the shower stalls.

The floor is big square beige marble tiles, and the showers are a slightly darker shade of beige and much smaller squares.

Someone whistles behind me, and I turn to see West filling the doorway. He jerks his head toward the wall. "Wow. And power too?"

I grin. "Looks like it. You want to take a shower?"

"You go first, Ames. I know you're eager to wash off."

"Come check them out at least," I say, walking to the middle shower on the right.

The shower curtains haven't been installed yet, so it's completely open. A small bench takes up most of the right side, and the left side has built-in shelves plus built-in dispensers.

I lean closer and sure enough, they're already filled with shampoo, conditioner, and body wash. The logo doesn't look familiar, but it looks nice. And judging by the general finishes in the building, I'd bet it's a luxury brand.

The shower head is one of those wide rainfall ones with five or six different settings. Plus, there's a bonus detachable shower head a foot lower.

I press a button next to the built-in shelves for the floor warmer and kick off my shoes. I hop on one foot as I peel off my sock, repeating the same thing for my other one.

West doesn't offer to help, he just watches me with soft eyes and a grin on his face.

"What?" I ask, tucking my socks together and stuffing them into my shoes.

"Nothing, Amelia. I'll be outside until you're done. Holler if you need me." West raps his knuckles on the tile frame and turns around.

"Wait."

He stills instantly. "Need something? I can try to find a washcloth or something."

Nervousness sloshes around in my veins, and I suddenly feel seventeen again. Desperately trying to tell him I liked him—*loved* him even—but so unsure of what to do or say.

You're not seventeen anymore, I remind myself. *Time to take what you want.*

I swipe my tongue over my bottom lip and pull my shoulders back. "You. I need you."

West turns around, his eyes going from soft to intense in a nanosecond. "I'm here, Amelia."

I reach out, lace our fingers together, and gently tug him into the shower stall. "I want you here. With me."

He exhales a long breath, and the air around us starts to steam up without the shower on yet. His gaze ping-pongs between my eyes. "Tell me why."

I swallow hard, my ribcage contracting over the vulnerability I know I'm going to lay out for him right now. "Because I've missed you. Because I used to dream about what it would feel like to be with you, to feel you inside of me. Because I loved you."

He cocks his head to the side, a gasp slipping past his lips. "You loved me?"

"You had to have known," my voice trails off, and I look to the side to cover my discomfort.

But he doesn't let me get away with that. His fingers come up to my chin, and he applies gentle pressure until I'm facing him again. "Why didn't you tell me?"

"I dropped a million hints. I thought you knew and I don't know, never felt the same."

"Ames, why would I try to kiss you all the time if I didn't feel the same?"

I roll my eyes and swat at his chest. "Psh. You didn't try to kiss me all the time."

He captures my hand and holds it against his heart. "I did. Every time I thought I could get away with it. I wanted to kiss you all the time, Amelia."

I shake my head, memories of him with a new girl every couple weeks bombard me. "But you had a revolving door of women."

He covers his mouth with his free hand, swiping it a few times. "I was an idiot who got some bad advice."

"I don't understand."

"I thought I could make you jealous enough to . . ."

"To, what? Date you?" My brows furrow as I stare at him.

His cheekbones pinken. "Look, I already admitted it was terrible advice, but in my defense, I was only thirteen."

"Wait. Thirteen? But you guys were thirteen when I moved across the street."

He nods. "I know. I've loved you for as long as I can remember."

My chest caves in at this terrible what-if game thrust in my face.

What if he told me when we were younger? What if I never had to leave? Or my personal torture: what if they sent a different letter instead?

As easy as it is to play this game, sometimes I like to remind myself of what's at stake.

If I was exclusively with West, then *there'd be no* me and Cole. If I never had to leave, I would've never met Alley, and I probably would've had a different relationship with Sonny. If they sent a different letter, then they might've made me choose.

He steps closer, the tips of his sneakers almost brushing the tips of my toes. "The only real question left is: how do you feel?"

"I think falling in love at the end of the world would be tragic. Reckless, even."

A half-smile tilts up the corner of his mouth, the angles of his face highlighted in soft yellow light from behind me. His thumb ghosts the underside of my bottom lip. "Jump, Amelia. I'll catch you."

My lips part, and my eyes gloss over. "I meant what I said earlier though. I won't choose."

I search his gaze, hoping that he won't bow out. I would understand if he did, but that doesn't mean that I don't want him to stay.

"As long as I get you, then nothing else matters."

I push onto my toes, and he meets me halfway, placing his mouth directly in front of mine. "Take off your clothes, West."

45

AMELIA

WEST'S BICEPS flex as he reaches behind his head to grab his shirt. He pulls it off in one smooth move and tosses it behind him. My mouth salivates when I take in the shirtless vision he makes. Colorful tattoos paint his arms and chest in vibrant whorls. And just like with Cole, a spike of grief spears me in the chest at the lost time between us.

I blink it away just as quickly as it comes.

Time is no longer this fluid concept. It's as absolute as it has ever been. Tomorrow truly isn't guaranteed, not for any of us.

So I'm going to start *living* each day.

My palms meet his warm chest a second later, and I take my time smoothing them over his pecs, around his shoulders. His fingers curl into fists by his side as he lets me explore.

I drag my fingertips lower, over the grooves of his abdomen and tuck them inside the waistband of his pants. His breath hitches, his fingers flexing in my peripheral vision.

I swipe my tongue over my lower lip to stifle my smile. It's a powerful feeling to have him like this, it's a charade of control, but I don't mind. I want to give up control to him, but I want to play a little first.

I unbutton his pants and drag the zipper down with an almost cruelly slow pace. My knuckles barely skim his cock—his very hard, very large cock.

"Ten, Amelia."

I pause, my fingers on the silver pull of the zipper. "Ten?"

"Ten more seconds, and then it's *my* turn to play." His voice becomes a deep rumble, and I shiver as it rolls over me, peaking my nipples.

I look at him from underneath my lashes, watching the way his eyes grow darker. I slip my hand inside his black boxer briefs, and he hisses out a breath. I drag my palm over the length of him, my fingertips barely touching as I grip him hard. I stroke him once, loving the way he feels in my hand and desperate to feel him inside of me.

He's big and even though it hasn't been that long, before him, it had. A speck of worry punctures my lust. It's gone in the next second.

"Three, two, one," he says in a rush.

With a delicate touch, he catches my hand and brings it up to his face. He places a soft kiss on the inside of my wrist, right over the spot I always said I wanted my first tattoo.

"My turn." He skims his nose along my arm, pausing once his face is buried in my neck. His tongue flicks against my pulse point in a distracting rhythm.

He palms my thighs and hauls me into his arms, encouraging me to grip his waist.

But I've dreamed of wrapping my legs around West Campbell for years. I've fantasized a hundred different ways I'd fuck him and dozens more where we'd make love.

I'm one step ahead of him, squeezing my legs above his hips, rocking my core against his hardening cock.

"Goddamn, Amelia," he moans into my neck. His breath

feathers over that special spot behind my ear that has my toes curling.

I tilt my head to the side to offer him a better angle. He follows my wordless cue, laving his tongue over that small patch of skin that has my breath stalling in my lungs.

I have no idea how he knew right where to drag his tongue, but I'm eternally grateful. My eyes close, and my head thuds against the tile behind me.

He pushes his hips into mine, slides one hand up my side, and grips my chin between his thumb and index finger.

My eyes are slow to open, my body strung tight already and we've just begun. He tilts my chin down as his lips move up my neck and crash into my mouth.

His tongue is relentless in his pursuit to claim my mouth. I wrap my arms around his neck, rolling my hips on instinct, matching the tempo of his tongue.

I'm lost to the pleasure his mouth can give, desperate to see what other talents his mouth has. I break the kiss to mumble, "More, West. I want more."

He stares at me, pupils blown and lips parted. I reach up and nip at his bottom lip, tugging it a little before releasing it. "I want to feel you inside me."

He groans this low noise in the back of his throat as he captures my mouth once more, carrying me over to the bench on the other side of the shower. He sets me down and reaches over to turn on the shower.

The showerhead points away from us, but we're close enough that we feel a misting. The water is cool against my feverish skin. I push to stand up, intending to take off my clothes, but he stops me.

He places a palm in the center of my chest. "Let me take care of you first."

I nod, my words stolen by the intense look he gives me. He kicks off his shoes and socks, tossing them out of the shower stall by his shirt.

Then he sinks to his knees.

I hold my breath, anticipation thrumming inside my veins, making my fingers tingle.

His hands skim up my legs, carving a path along my thighs. I don't spare the kernel of insecurity that tries to slither its way into this moment, squashing it under my lust. He taps my hips. "Lift."

I raise my hips off the bench, and his fingers slide underneath the waistband of my shorts. He pulls them down my legs, and my ass crashes back to the bench. Whatever material it's made of, it feels smooth against the bare skin of my ass, my cheeky panties not offering much coverage.

My shorts join the rest of the clothes, and then his mouth follows his fingers, pausing to place soft kisses along my inner thighs. "So smooth."

His breath teases me, my muscles damn near quivering underneath his touch.

"I, uh, had that laser hair removal thing—" I fold my lips inward, trapping the rest of the nervous chatter inside my mouth.

He smiles against my skin. "Shh, baby. Don't be nervous. I'll take care of you."

I release the death grip on the edge of the bench and slip off my tee and unhook my bra in record time. I throw them blindly, too focused on the way West's lips tease me, getting closer and closer to my pussy.

His tongue flicks out, trailing a wet path along the space where my hip meets my pelvis. It's deceptively sensitive, and my breath hitches in my chest. I can feel myself grow wetter with each swipe of his tongue, and he hasn't even touched me yet. Not really.

Like he heard my plea, he palms my knees, widening my stance and bringing me closer to the edge. He looks up at me then, his dark brown hair looking deliciously disheveled and nearly black from the steam.

My fingers curl between the slats in the bench, and I shift back, opening my legs even further. West doesn't miss the invitation, lowering his head until his mouth hovers right over my core.

"What do you need, baby?"

I shift my hips, aching to feel his mouth on me. "Your mouth, West. I need your mouth."

He seals his mouth against me, tonguing my pussy through the cotton separating us. His nose nudges my clit, and I wiggle my hips.

"What's the matter, Amelia?" He speaks right against me, his breath warming me.

He's toying with me, smiling into my pussy through my panties. I've never been so turned on from so little foreplay before.

Though if you counted all the years of lingering glances and sly touches between us—*and between Cole and I,* my brain helpfully supplies–we've spent years in foreplay.

I slide my hand into his hair, curling my fingers around the soft strands. He groans into me again, but he doesn't lift his head. "I changed my mind. I can't wait any longer. I want you inside of me."

He hooks a finger around my panties and pulls them to the side. "I've been waiting years to taste you, Amelia. You sure I can't convince you to wait a minute longer before I slide inside this perfect pussy?" he says, his lips dragging across my hypersensitive skin with each syllable.

My eyes screw up tight, and I arch my back further. I keep my grip on his hair, holding his face against me. We both know that he could move if he wanted to, but I appreciate the façade of control he's offering.

"Yes, yes. Please," I beg him.

He puts me out of my misery and licks the length of me, from ass to clit. My chest heaves, my breath stalling as he pulls my clit into his mouth. *Hard.*

"Oh my god," I hush out, my legs closing on instinct.

His free hand curls around my leg from underneath my thigh and gently tugs. "Open up, baby."

I relax my legs and arch into his mouth as he fucking feasts on me. He slips two fingers inside of me, stretching me and fucking me with slow, drawn-out strokes.

I roll my hips in tune, my body feels like a live wire, sparking with pleasure from every nerve ending.

It's too good—*he's* too good. And all too soon, I feel the telltale tingles in my toes.

Like he can read my mind, he pulls back with one final swipe of his tongue. "No, why did you stop?" My words fly out in a whiny exhale.

He sits back on his heels and looks at me with an expression of raw lust I've never seen on anyone before. His lips and chin are shiny with my arousal, and my core clenches on his fingers still slowly pumping inside of me.

His face awash in desperate hunger, a primal sort of need. "I thought you couldn't wait, that you needed me to fuck this tight pussy."

"Yes, yes, I do." I've become a bobblehead, nodding too quickly. But I don't care. Ecstasy is so close I can taste it on my tongue. I reach out and palm the back of his neck, bringing him close so I can kiss him.

He moans into my mouth, shuffling closer and deepening the kiss. His fingers keep up their leisurely pace, and I roll my hips, encouraging him to go faster, harder.

With my free hand, I slide my palm inside his boxer briefs and stroke his cock. He's impossibly harder, his hips unconsciously rocking into my palm.

He pulls back and drops his gaze to watch where our bodies connect. "Such a good girl."

His praise washes over me, and heightens my arousal even further. I'm dripping onto his hand, down my thighs.

I buck my hips, a last-ditch effort to give me what I want. "Please, West."

His arm bands across my hips, stilling me. "Please, what, baby? I want to hear your words."

His fingers scissor inside of me, before slowly sliding out. A noise of protest flies from my lips, and that bastard chuckles. "I want you to fuck me."

He thrusts his fingers inside of me, his fingertips hitting that special spot that makes me see stars. "I am fucking you."

I close my legs, a poor attempt to trap those long, talented fingers inside of my pussy. My chest heaves, steam blanketing us in a fine mist. I arch my back a little, so only my shoulders touch the tiled wall behind me, and spread my legs wider.

His gaze climbs up my body slowly, pausing to look at my tits before he meets my eyes. I look into the eyes of one of the few men I've ever loved. "I want to ride your cock, West. And then I want you to fuck me like you'll die if you don't get inside of me. And then I—"

He leans forward and seals his lips to mine, his fingers slipping from my pussy. He shuffles off his pants and boxer briefs with quick movements and picks me up for the third time. I don't have time to wrap my legs around his waist before he sinks to the bench with me on his lap.

He palms my waist, raising me up as I fist his cock with one hand and grip his shoulder with the other.

"There's no going back after this," he murmurs, his dark-green-eyed gaze bouncing around me with a stark possessiveness. "I won't be able to hold myself back from you."

"I don't want to go back." I sink down onto him slowly, taking him inch by delicious inch.

46

COLE

I LEAN my hip against the marble countertop in the kitchenette and look around. It has that sort of never-been-used cleanliness, like no one's really used the microwave yet or sat at the small square table in the corner or used the fifty-inch flatscreen TV in the middle of the wall.

Thankfully it has power. I keep waiting for the other shoe to drop, for Amelia's Dad's prophecies to come true and the world to descend into darkness.

Though I suppose you could make a case that we're actually on our descent now—as humanity. I've done more fucked-up things since Mount Charleston started coming down than I've done in my entire life. I was ready and fucking willing to end that motherfucker's life earlier today, and I didn't even think twice about it.

Still, I can't shake the doom that looms over my shoulder. Like some sort of specter just out of reach in this realm.

But until then, I'm grateful for this boon. It's functional and safe enough.

I jerk my chin toward the overstuffed and extra-long couches in the corner. "Let me ask you something."

Gray slides a box he nabbed from the trunk onto the marble island countertop. "Hit me."

"Do you believe what Mr. Christensen said? That we're all doomed?"

He pulls out a bag of rice, a small bag of beans, and a set of campfire pots. "I think the outcome of him being right far outweighs the outcome if he's wrong."

I help him get everything together, measuring out water for each. "How do you figure?"

He turns the knob and the gas ignites, a flame licking to life. "Well, if he's right, then we at least have a shot at survival. And we have her."

"And if he's wrong?"

He leans against the small sink next to the stove and folds his arms across his chest. "Then we get to take our time driving back to Vegas. Maybe we turn it into a proper road trip with our girl. Speaking of my girl, you good here?" He pushes off the island and hooks a thumb over his shoulder toward the stove.

I fling my arm out, stopping Gray from going down the hallway. "What about taking watch?"

His eyes narrow on my hand in front of his chest before they switch their target to my face. "What about it? We're only stopping for a couple hours. Not sure if we need it."

I run my hand across my lower jaw, my five-o'clock shadow prickling. Another sharp reminder of how life has derailed since Amelia Christensen waltzed back into it.

"What about how you got in? Someone could come in the same way. I don't want to be caught off guard."

He nods slowly, his gaze too intrusive for his own good. "Okay. Why don't you take the first shift then?"

"We should really do watch in pairs."

He cocks his head to the side. "What's going on with you?"

I hold his gaze, wondering which way this is going to go. All I know is that I don't want it to come to blows with my brothers.

She'd never forgive herself. So it's best I give him fair warning of what he's walking into.

"Nothing. You might want to wait a little bit, that's all." My words practically fly from my mouth, tripping over one another in my haste.

"Nah, I'm good. I found some towels we can use." He pushes my hand down with two fingers.

I adjust my stance, shuffling back a foot. "No, I don't think you get it. I don't think you want to go in there."

He straightens up, shoulders rolling back as he regards me. There's a shrewdness in his gaze, something I haven't seen aimed at me for a very long time. He doesn't trust me right now.

I rock back on my heels and shove my hands in my pockets with too much force. Disbelief and anger war inside of me, and I land somewhere closer to a sneer. "Hey, you want to go inside and see your girl with our brother? Be my guest."

"Our girl, Cole. She's *our girl*." He cocks his head to the side. "Or did you think we missed the way you two look at each other when you don't think anyone's looking? Or maybe you think West and I didn't see you kiss her? You looked like you were starving—for *her*."

I bristle at his insinuation, shame solidifying in my gut. Like I went back on everything I said about her—like I'm a liar.

I don't fucking like it.

"How long have I looked out for you, huh?"

"Since the day after we met," he replies without hesitation.

I nod, the move measured. "Exactly. Since the day West and I strolled into that group home and saw you take down a kid twice your size."

"He was stealing from everyone, and I caught him stealing from my bunk."

"I know, I remember. Just like I know you remember that West and I kept our mouths shut when the questions started."

Gray sighs through his nose. "What's your point, man?"

"My point is that I've always looked out for you, and that's exactly what I'm doing right now."

He looks at me with a smirk tipping up the edges of his mouth. He waits a beat, and then the smile spreads. "Nah, that's not it. Why don't you just admit that you're jealous?"

"I'm not. I don't want you to make a mistake," I grit through clenched teeth.

He laughs, this caustic noise that grates against my nerves. "A mistake?" He flings his arms out wide and spins in a half circle. "Look at everything we've been through in the last week! We're in a newly finished fitness center in the middle of New Mexico, on the way to a government-funded bunker because the end of the world as we know it is imminent. And you're telling me we shouldn't celebrate every moment we have left? That we shouldn't seize the motherfucking day?" He's breathing heavy by the time he finishes his little speech.

He runs a hand through his hair, bunching it together at the back of his head before he lets it fall down again. "And you've got it all wrong. Amelia would *never* be a mistake."

My chest swells with indignation. I shouldn't be shocked at my reaction, but it catches me by surprise. I've spent years layering bitterness and dislike over my deeply-rooted love for the girl next door.

I stare at Gray, irrationally angry that he misunderstood me. "I didn't say that. I meant that you're going to walk in on our brother fucking our girl, and I wasn't sure how that would play out. I didn't want any violence to happen. Not so soon after . . ."

I trail off, but I don't need to finish that thought, he's already nodding.

He takes a few steps toward me and claps my shoulder a few times. "I appreciate your concern, but I'm good, man."

I arch a brow. "You sure?"

His face transforms when he flashes me a genuine grin, laugh lines deepening the corners of his eyes. "Yeah. Trust me, I'm good."

Something about the way he said it has me pausing. Have Gray and West shared women before? The question is on the tip of my tongue, but I trap it behind my teeth at the last minute.

"Huh. I didn't know you were into sharing."

"I'm not," he replies without missing a beat. "I'm into *her*."

He taps the wall as he walks out, whistling under his breath.

47

GRAY

I HEAR them before I see them. Muffled by the sound of a running shower, his grunts and her moans float across the locker-room-style bathroom.

I don't think I'll ever forget the way her voice hitched in my ear every time I hit a sweet spot. Blood rushes to my cock just thinking about the way her tight pussy clenched around me.

Despite my attitude toward Cole, I had my reservations about sharing. I'm not a fucking saint. I'm sure I'll get jealous from time to time, but I'm also a patient man.

I wasn't fucking around when I told her I never planned on it being a one-night thing. I had plans of going back to Tennessee Pete's and using some creative incentives to get her information.

Some might call that unethical, maybe even a touch on the psychotic scale. I don't disagree.

But those people don't have all the facts. The truth is, our connection is one in a million, and never, in all my time across the states, have I ever connected with someone so easily and so strongly before.

So, yeah, if I have to share my girl with anyone else, I'm okay with it being the two assholes I consider brothers.

I find them in the middle shower stall, the water running but not really touching either of them. Steam billows into the rest of the room, ascending to the ceiling and getting sucked out by a fan.

West sees me first, his dark eyes nearly feral with pleasure as he palms our girl's waist while she bounces on his dick. He holds my gaze as he leans forward and wraps his tongue around her right nipple.

She moans, long and low, and it goes straight to my dick. I lean my shoulder against the tile dividing wall, one hand clutching a couple gray bath towels. I watch as she arches her back, tipping her head toward the ceiling and bracing herself on his knees. Her hair falls down in soft, damp waves. She thrusts her perfect tits in his face while she smoothly rotates her hips.

He smirks at me, even as his tongue flicks her tight nipple. But he wasn't prepared for my answering one.

I arch a brow for good measure and then let my eyes roam over the two of them. Objectively, watching them fuck is turning me on. I'm a master of being still, and I call on those reserves right now. There's nothing I want more than to storm in there and claim her mouth and then her pussy.

But this is new territory for all of us, and I'm not going to fuck it up on day one by being a total jealous asshole.

So, for now, I curb my jealousy that I'm not the one balls-deep inside what I know is the prettiest pussy I've ever seen. And instead, I focus on the way she must feel.

Her chest is flushed, and I trail the soft pink color spreading up her neck, pausing at her mouth. I imagine what her voice feels like when she moans against my skin. I glance around her features, until finally, her eyes blink open, her gaze on mine.

"Gray," she breathes my name on a sigh.

I cave and palm my aching cock, but it's a poor imitation of what I really want.

"Oh, fuck, baby, just like that," West says, his fingers tightening around her waist.

She rolls her hips, but she doesn't sit up or stop. She holds my eyes, a challenge.

Or an invitation?

I don't have to wait long for the answer.

"Are you going to watch or are you going to join us?"

I jerk my chin toward West. "I don't want to overstep."

West slides his hands up her ribcage, down her back, over her ass, disappearing underneath. My mouth salivates at the thought of tasting her again.

I feel like a goddamn junkie when it comes to her. I don't think I'll ever get enough.

She stills and faces West, cradling his face in her hands. "I want him to join us, but only if you're okay with it."

He nips at her lips, palming her ass. "It's your show, baby. I'm just the supporting actor."

She smiles at him, and I can't see her expression from this angle, but I get a front-row seat to his. West's face softens, and I imagine her smile is sweet, much too innocent for all the ways I want to dirty her up.

He murmurs something against her mouth, too low for me to hear. And then those hauntingly blue eyes are on me, stealing my breath from my lungs with one look.

Cher holds out her hand to me, and it feels like so much more than an invitation to turn their twosome into a threesome. More than desire and a temporary fix for the constant ache that's been my constant companion for far too long.

It feels like *more.*

I saunter across the shower stall and slip my hand into hers. She laces our fingers together, and I bring our hands up to run my lips across her knuckles. "You have no idea how exquisite you are, Amelia. And that might be one of my many favorite things about you."

Her face softens. "Gray."

"I know, baby girl," I murmur, trailing my fingers down the side of her face.

She tugs me down by our hands, a wordless request for my mouth, I'm sure. I lean down, and she lifts up to meet me halfway. Her hand wraps around the back of my neck as her tongue tangles with mine.

West groans next to us. "Why the fuck is that so hot?"

He sounds dazed, drunk on her, no doubt. An odd sense of camaraderie seeps into my skin, bonding West and I further. A brotherhood of sorts.

I feel the moment she sinks back onto his cock, her hips swiveling and her tongue mimicking the same movement in my mouth. I let her play a little longer, practically tasting the way the control heightens her arousal. It's intoxicating—*she's* intoxicating.

She pulls back, gasping for breath and fisting my shirt in her hand. "Take off your clothes, Sonny. I want to watch you."

I take a step back, the spray from the shower soaking me from the thighs down. I barely feel it, my blood heating at the way her gaze devours me. I reach behind my head and fist my shirt, tugging it off and tossing it out of the stall in a flash.

"Watch me do what?"

"Touch yourself. I want to see what you like." Her tongue swipes over her lips, and her gaze zeros in on my fingers tugging my zipper down.

I let my pants hit the floor with a slap and hook my thumbs over the waistband of my navy blue boxer briefs. I take another step back, letting the water slide over me.

"You're getting wet, Sonny."

"A little water only makes things more fun." Lust thickens my voice, sending it lower than normal.

I watch her as she watches me peel off my boxer briefs, stepping out of them. I hear her gasp as I fist my cock, stroking slowly with a tight grip.

"Do you like what you see, baby?" West asks on a groan,

trailing open-mouthed kisses along her chest. "Do you like seeing Gray stroke his dick as he watches me fuck this perfect pussy?"

"Yes," she hisses, rolling her hips faster. "Come closer, Sonny, please."

I step out of the shower and stop next to her. Tendrils of hair stick to her sweat-dampened skin, her lids low over her gorgeous eyes, she's sin incarnate. And I'll spend the rest of my days worshiping her.

She rises up and falls back on West's cock, her hands behind her on his knees again, offering herself up to us.

I drag my finger down the side of her face, still keeping my torturous pace stroking my cock. "I can't wait to have those thighs wrapped around my head again."

West moans, his hands wrapping around her waist. "Damn, she likes it when you talk like that."

I let the wide grin spread across my face, knowing she loves it when my *dimples come out to play*, as she says it. "That right? You like hearing about all the ways I want to fuck you, Cher?" I press my thumb to the middle of her bottom lip, tugging it down. Her eyes glaze over as she stares at me.

West starts thrusting up from the bottom, since her movements slowed, her rhythm rocky.

Her tongue peeks out, flicking gently against the tip of my thumb, pulling a breath from me. "Or maybe you want to hear about how I've dreamed of how beautiful you look with your lips stretched wide over my cock. How your pussy squeezed the life out of me over and over again."

She's not moving at all now, letting West do all the work. But he's not complaining either. A vein throbs in his temple, and we're all covered in a thick layer of steam.

"Sonny," she murmurs, sucking my thumb into her mouth and swirling her tongue around and around. She releases it with a soft pop, her lips wet and swollen. "Kiss me."

I rest one hand against the base of her throat, the other on the back of her head to support her neck, and bend down to capture her mouth. She wastes no time, kissing me like a woman on a mission. I feel it in the gentle tremble in her muscles, she's close.

I take my time kissing her, reacquainting our lips, tongue, teeth. Her muscles flex then relax several times, and I have a sneaking suspicion she's holding off her orgasm.

I pull back, staying close. "Do you trust me?"

"Yes," she answers without hesitation.

"Good girl." I flash her a smile that feels a lot more sinful than normal. I keep my hand on the back of her head, but my other hand slides down her body, pausing to tease her nipples. My fingers continue their descent, hovering above the place where West's and Cher's bodies connect. I look at West. "And you, do you trust me?"

"Yeah. She's got a vise grip on my dick, man, I don't know what you had in mind, but she's already close."

"I know. Let's make our girl scream, yeah, brother?"

She must squeeze him again because he groans. "Goddamn, baby."

My fingers tiptoe down, hovering over her clit. When West pulls back, I slip them between her folds. Using my index and middle fingers, I open her up a little so every time West grinds against her, his pelvis offers the friction she's desperate for.

"Yes, more, Sonny. I need more."

"I got you, baby girl," I murmur against her chest, right in front of my face. I pinch her clit just hard enough that I know she's riding the fine line between pleasure and pain.

Her muscles lock up, and her eyes snap closed as she comes on a long, low moan. West stills a moment later, coming with a shout.

Cher slumps forward, catching herself on my arm. Her hands fly to my forearm when I try to slip my hand free. She looks up at me through her lashes and runs her tongue across her teeth.

"I'm feeling greedy, Sonny. I want to come again, from your hands." Her voice is breathy, like the orgasm stole some of her oxygen.

48

AMELIA

"WHEN YOU COME, it's going to be on my cock," Sonny breathes against my mouth.

"Or West's," I taunt. I don't know why I'm poking him other than this rising tide inside of me keeps growing and growing. I keep thinking it's going to recede with every orgasm, but it's not.

It's only getting worse. This vicious yearning for my men—all of them, really. I fantasize that Cole's going to stroll through the door next and take my mouth.

But that's all that is—a fantasy.

Cole's barely allowed himself to touch me, there's no way he's jumping right into the inferno.

"No, baby girl, you're going to come for me on my cock. And if you're a good girl, you'll get his mouth *and* my cock."

My mouth drops open and my eyes roll back a little, imagining how delicious it'll feel. "Promise? I'm a very good girl. Aren't I, West?"

West smirks and thumbs his bottom lip. His eyes blaze a path of intention and lust across my body, heating every available inch of skin, and I feel his cock harden inside of me.

I brace my hand on West's shoulder and slowly slide off of his cock just to torture us both a little more.

"Damn, baby," West grunts.

I preen under their praise, twisting and pushing onto my toes to take what I want from Sonny. I brush a kiss across his lips and fall back on my heels.

"You trying to tease me, Cher?" His voice is low, husky even.

I watch him as I curve my hands around my tits, pinching my nipples between my thumb and index finger. I feel the sharp tug in my core, my clit pulsing with surprising need.

I'm a little shocked at my insatiable lust. I've never done anything like this before, but I already have plans to repeat it again and again.

"I'll take that as a yes," Sonny murmurs more to himself. He catches my hands and tugs me close. He palms my thighs and hoists me up. I loop my arms around his neck, my legs around his waist, trapping his cock between us.

The head of his dick bumps against my clit with every step, and before I give it conscious thought, I'm grinding against him.

"Goddamn, Cher. You know how to bring me to my knees."

"I can't help it, Sonny. I've been thinking about this since the moment I left the motel room. I almost didn't, you know."

I don't know why I tell him that. I wasn't planning on it, not here at least.

He doesn't miss a beat. "I wish you would've stayed. Though I have a sneaking suspicion I wouldn't have been able to willingly let you go."

"Why's that?"

"I'm a man of many flaws, and addiction isn't one of them. But with you, all bets are off. You've turned my world upside down, Cher, and I can no longer see anything but you."

"Gray Walters, you're a sweet-talking romantic."

"Only for you." He sets me down on a towel covering a wide

bench in the middle of a lounge area with lockers. "Hands and knees, baby. Give our boy a show, yeah?"

I get on all fours and look across my shoulder at West. He stares at me with an unmatched intensity. He fists his cock, but he doesn't stroke it. Not yet, at least.

I bet by the time Sonny's balls-deep, hitting that perfect spot, he'll be just as desperate as I currently am.

Sonny strokes down my spine, and I hear him move around, the creak of the bench as he gets situated. Anticipation is thick on my tongue, my arousal climbing higher and higher with his innocent touches, skirting where I really want his hands.

A warm, wet mouth meets my pussy and I almost sink into the bench.

"Oh my god," I moan.

"You should see her face, man. She's in fucking heaven," West says.

"Open up for me, baby girl." He speaks into my pussy, the vibration sending a slew of goosebumps

I widen my stance, and Sonny's tongue flicks out to tease my clit. He offers light pressure, not enough to send me into euphoria, but close. His tongue worships my pussy, alternating between dipping inside of me and toying with my clit.

I'm a panting, sweaty mess. My pussy aches to be filled by him, and I'm near desperate to come.

"Please, Gray. I need to feel you inside of me."

He leaves my pussy with one last lick, and much to my surprise, skims his lips up my ass cheek. His hands spread my ass cheeks a little, and his mouth drags across my curves in open-mouthed kisses.

My breath hitches and I hold it, afraid to exhale in case I spook him. I don't know where this is going, but I have a feeling. And if I'm right, it's going to be another first for me.

His tongue flicks around my asshole, these soft almost tentative strokes. It feels so incredible I can barely describe it. I snake a hand between my chest and the bench and sink two fingers inside my pussy. I slide them out and encircle my clit in tandem with Sonny's tongue on my ass.

"Oh fuck, fuck. I'm going to come soon."

They're the magical words, but unfortunately, not the kind of magic I wanted. He pulls back, and I miss his warmth immediately.

"What did I say, Cher? Where are you going to come first?"

"On your cock," I pant.

"Good girl," he says as the tip of his cock nudges my entrance. "Ready?"

"Yes, yes, yes," I chant.

He pushes inside of me in an achingly slow thrust, letting me adjust to the sheer size of him. He pulls out and slides back in slowly again, and I clench around him.

I press my cheek to the bench and look over at him. My easy-going man looks a hair away from losing control, and I want to watch him fall over that cliff so bad I can taste it.

I arch my back, sinking my shoulders against the bench. The towels he threw down pad it a little, but it's still hard against my cheek.

I'd fuck Sonny on the pavement if it meant I got to experience this.

I wiggle my ass. "Move, Gray. Please."

His hands explore my curves in slow strokes, almost reverently. "You know I love it when you beg, baby girl."

His thumbs sweep up my ass, dipping closer and closer to my asshole.

My eyes close as my breath hitches when he grazes the sensitive, untouched skin.

"Do that again," West demands.

I blink open my eyes and stare at him. He's sitting on a bench to the side, shoulders against the wall, legs spread wide, cock in his hand. Lust flares at the picture he makes.

Dark hair wet and tousled over his forehead, tattoos wrapped around cut muscles, and those goddamn forearm veins popping. My mouth practically salivates as he strokes his cock.

They're getting along better than I anticipated, both of them giving and receiving direction. It's giving me all sorts of ideas for the future.

Sonny's wet fingers circle my rim, and my core clenches.

"You like the way that feels, Cher?"

"Yes," I hush out, nodding quickly. "Please, Gray. I need you to fuck me now." I wiggle my ass again, arousal and anticipation stealing my words.

His index finger brushes around my asshole again, the nerve endings firing with enough pleasure to almost send me off that cliff again. Sonny chooses that moment to slide out of me, but before he's completely out, he thrusts back inside of me.

I don't think I'll have enough of him—of any of them, really. The way they play my body like they've been doing it for years is almost alarming. If it didn't feel so fucking good.

"Yes, just like that. Harder, Gray," I beg.

"Good girl," he murmurs before he fucks me harder, his fingers never stop playing with me.

I'm climbing too quick, I screw up my eyes and think of anything to stave off my orgasm for another minute. I want this to last as long as possible.

Sonny moans, and I take quick breaths to prolong the pleasure. I'm not going to last much longer, I feel the tide swelling bigger and bigger. And I fear this one is going to knock me on my ass.

Rough fingertips brush my clit, and my eyes snap open. West is crouching next to the bench, his face right next to mine. "I can see you holding off, so I figured I should help you out."

The corner of his mouth tips up on the side, but I don't have time to tease him about his prideful smirk. In the next thrust, Sonny hits that magical spot inside of me, his finger presses against my asshole, and West pinches my clit.

I free fall, white splotches of light exploding behind my closed eyes. Everything inside of me freezes and stretches, my orgasm going on and on and on.

My core clenches Sonny, and I hear him grunting and saying something, but I'm lost to pleasure. He stills inside of me with one final thrust, running his hands over as much of my skin as possible.

West pulls his hand out and shoves two fingers in his mouth with a smack.

I just need a moment to rest, to close my eyes and let the feeling of gravity sink back into my bones.

49

AMELIA

THE FOUR OF us sit around the small table in the kitchenette area. My damp hair air-dries into frizzy waves down my back, but I'm too busy shoveling food in my mouth to toss it up in a ponytail. The best I could do was throw on clean clothes West brought me to change into. I sort of crashed. West and Sonny fucked me straight into a disco nap, and then I took a record-fast shower.

"Damn, I never thought I'd be so happy to have beans and rice," West mumbles around a mouthful of food.

I scrape a few grains of sticky rice off my fork tines and smile at him. "You're right. It does taste good. Thanks for making it, Cole."

"Someone had to keep watch while the three of you fucked around like we're on spring break," Cole grumbles without looking up.

I let his surly attitude roll off my back and instead go for a surprise counterattack. I place my now-clean fork down next to my plate and sit back. "You should've joined us."

His head snaps up, a scowl already in place. But his eyes are too wide with shock to really sell it.

"I wanted you to." I work to keep my expression neutral.

His eyes flick around my face before he meets my gaze once more. "Yeah, well, I never shared well growing up. Don't think that's changed much."

One side of my mouth lifts into a sly grin. "I seem to remember you sharing quite well with me. You always let me have the last bite of everything we split, too."

"That was French fries, not you—"

"My what?" I ask after he cuts himself off mid-word.

The TV behind me crackles, and I jump a foot into the air. I whirl around and stare at the black screen with my hand pressed to my thumping heart. "What the hell?"

Cole pushes his chair back and nabs a small black remote control off the island. He points it at the TV and presses a few buttons, but nothing changes, just the light staticky snow of a dropped connection. "I turned it on earlier. I thought I might be able to catch the news or something since our phones stopped working. But it doesn't seem like the TV is set up to a provider yet."

"Let's finish eating and pack up, get back on the road." Sonny pushes his chair back and brings the paper bowls we ate out of back to the kitchen.

I slide my chair back and stand up, reaching my arms up high to stretch. I relish the tightness in my muscles and the low ache in my core. I watch my three men out of the corner of my eye, silently plotting the next moment I can convince them to play again.

The TV speakers crackle again, followed immediately by the familiar high-pitched tones preceding an emergency broadcast. "The following message is from the New Mexico emergency system. A tornado warning has been issued for your area. Please take cover immediately."

My fingertips start tingling as panic sinks its hooks in me. "Does this place have a basement?"

A wailing siren splits the air, and I slam my palms over my ears. "Oh my god!"

"The following message is from the New Mexico emergency system. A tornado warning has been issued for your area. Please take cover immediately," the message repeats itself again.

"We gotta move, Mia." Cole grabs me by the bicep and pulls me out of the kitchenette.

"Wait, wait!" I twist away from him, dropping my arms and dashing back into the kitchenette.

"We can't stay in here, Cher. It's too dangerous!" Sonny yells from right behind me.

"We can't leave without our backpacks. Everything we have is in here—including the satellite phone," I yell over the repeating message.

I loop my arms through two backpacks and shoulder the other two. They're heavier than they look, which is good. It means we'll have some things if we lose the car.

The wind gusts against the side of the building, rattling the windows on the other wall. I'm distracted when Sonny grabs two of the backpacks by movement from outside.

Across the parking lot, one of the framed-out buildings sways to the right. "Holy shit," I whisper.

I stare in horror, my feet rooted to the floor when another gust of wind lifts two-by-fours, orange cones, metal poles, and a bunch of other things I can't make out.

My chest compresses, like my ribs are constricting over my lungs, and I feel like I can't breathe. The materials and debris get swept up, lifting at least twenty feet off the ground.

Sonny grabs my hand and pulls me toward the hallway, but I can't tear my eyes from outside. "C'mon, Amelia. Stay with me, baby girl."

I twist around just as the glass breaks behind us. Sonny pushes me to the ground and lands on top of me in the next second. He shields me with his body as the wind whooshes through the broken windows.

The siren gets impossibly louder. Or maybe that's just the thundering of my pulse inside my ears.

He eases off me and grabs my waist to hoist me up. He doesn't give me any time to turn around and survey the damage. "We gotta go find the boys. Stay with me, yeah?"

I adjust the backpack on my shoulder and grab his hand with both of mine. "Like glue."

"Good girl," he murmurs distractedly. We pause once we reach the mouth of the hallway, scooting to the right of the doorframe.

"Where did they go? Cole? West?" I yell, though I doubt they can hear me over the siren and the wind. My shoulders hitch up toward my ears. "Is the warning siren in the parking lot or something? Why is it so loud?"

Cole pops out from around the corner to the right and waves us over. "Down here."

Sonny and I turn and run down the short hallway, and right before we reach Cole, the lights go out.

"Oh fuck." Sonny tightens his hold on my hand.

A second later, emergency lights flicker overhead, offering us the barest amount of amber light. But at least we can see where we're going now. We reach Cole in a few steps, and he takes the backpack from my shoulder without a word.

Cole eyes the lights above us. "What happened?"

"Broken window," Sonny says.

I quicken my pace to keep up with Cole. "Where's West?"

"Down here, Ames," West calls from beyond the darkened doorway to our left. "Found the basement."

I follow Cole down the stairs, descending into darkness. A hysterical sort of humor flits across my consciousness at the irony. I trap the comment behind my teeth. No need to freak them out, even if it is true.

I already know I'll follow them anywhere.

50

AMELIA

THE BASEMENT ISN'T MUCH MORE than a square cement room with a small closet-sized room off to the side. Inside the closet are two water heaters and some electrical boxes.

I glance around. "What now?"

Sonny leads me toward the little nook underneath the stairs. "Now, we wait. And pray, if you're the praying type."

He ducks under the stairs, slips off his backpack, and sits down. I mimic him and plop onto the cold concrete.

I sit as close to Sonny as I can without physically sitting on his lap. "I'm not. The praying type, I mean."

He throws an arm over my shoulder as Cole and West settle in across from us. Cole snags a small fabric square from his backpack. He unfolds it into a blanket, the lightweight kind that's surprisingly warm.

He shakes it out and drapes it over me. "Your hair's still wet."

It's four little words that shouldn't pack as big of a punch as they do. I pull the blanket higher on my torso. "Thank you."

He only nods, stretching out his legs so they bracket mine.

"I should call Dad. Let him know." I pause, refusing to give the terror another foothold. "Just in case."

I fumble around in my backpack, plucking the satellite phone and dialing my dad. It doesn't ring, just static air before it beeps three times and drops the call. I try again, and the same thing happens.

I bite my cheek and end the call and tuck the phone back into my backpack. "It wouldn't connect."

"There's no signal underground, Ames."

"Right." I nod a few times, distracted by the howling noise from somewhere above. "Tell me something."

It's a frantic plea, anything to not focus on the tornado most likely coming for us. I'm not as smart as my dad, but just living with him my whole life has afforded me knowledge by osmosis.

I know the likelihood of a tornado hitting the one building standing for miles is high if we're anywhere near its path. And I know the wind speed must be insane if it can bend and bow the framed-out building.

Which means it's probably a category three—maybe four.

"What do you want to know?" Sonny asks. His fingertips dance along my shoulders in soft strokes.

"Tell me something true."

"You fishing for secrets, Cher?"

"Yes, yes I am. Got any to share?" My voice trembles, and I have to clear my throat.

Sonny rakes his teeth across his bottom lip. "Alright. I got one. My granddad used to read romance novels, real bodice ripper types, right. Said it made him a better friend. I was only twelve at the time, so I didn't really get what he was insinuating. But then I snuck one from his bookshelf the following year, hid it under my bed and waited until he went to sleep. I threw my sheet over my head and turned on my favorite blue flashlight and cracked the spine on *Rogue Gentleman*. I understood exactly what he meant by page twenty."

A surprised giggle flies out before I can stop it, my shoulders shaking with mirth. "Did you read the whole thing?"

He turns to me, his lips brushing the top of my head. "Nah, I snuck it back in his bookshelf the next morning. A few years later I picked them back up out of curiosity."

"That explains so much." Cole grins at him, laugh lines winking at me from around his eyes.

I lean my head further against his chest. "There's so much I don't know about you."

"We have time, Cher."

I look at the space between the four of us, our legs outstretched and tangled. The wind howls and something above us creaks. Fear drips down my back. "But what if we don't?" I lift my eyes and look at West, then Cole, and finally turn to look at Sonny. "What if this is it? If this is when it ends?"

Sonny smooths his thumb between my bunched brows. "Then I'll find you in the next life."

"And in the one after that," West vows.

"In every life," Cole promises.

My sinuses burn, and my eyes well up. Their admissions give me courage to voice something I'd been holding onto for years. I look above, avoiding their gazes even though I can feel them on my skin.

"I don't know if I've ever really believed in love, ya know? It always felt like a fairy tale sort of thing, something manufactured by Hollywood. I didn't have the best role models growing up, outside of my grandma, but I—" I sniffle and blink my eyes, setting a tear free. I look at West first. "I just want you to know that I've never felt more at home than I did when I was with you." I look at Cole. "Both of you."

He visibly swallows, his face a mask of seriousness.

I look at Sonny. "All of you now."

The building trembles beneath my back, and the whooshing sound gets louder.

"I loved you. Both of you." I alternate between the two men in front of me. "And I regretted not telling you for five years. So if this is it, then I wanted you both to know. I don't expect you to say it back, or say anything really. I just . . . I just wanted you to know."

I look at Sonny next as another tear rolls down my cheek. "You're the closest thing I've ever experienced to love at first sight, Gray Walters. And it would have been an absolute pleasure to love you."

"Loving you would be the greatest honor of my life, Amelia." He runs his nose along mine in the gentlest touch of affection we've exchanged yet. Somehow it makes our declarations all the more bittersweet.

"Why?" Cole croaks.

I look at him then, surprised to see a shell of a man. Like he's been wearing a Cole-sized mask this whole time and he's finally shed it. He sits forward, his hands braced on his thighs.

"If you loved me—us—why did you leave? Why didn't you come back?" He looks at his hands.

"I didn't want to leave—"

"But you did!" he interrupts me. "Fuck, Mia. I waited for you."

I'm shaking my head before he even finishes talking. "I told you. I had to leave, I—"

"Why didn't you tell us?"

"I did! I left you countless voicemails and texts, I even wrote you letters. You *know* this, Cole."

He shakes his head, a sad smile tipping up the corner of his mouth. "Yeah, well that weekend we were gone? Some asshole tripped and knocked our backpacks over the edge of the mountain. Wayne couldn't afford new ones until the following weekend, when his check came."

I search his gaze, glancing at West for any indication of where this is going. West folds his arms across his chest and looks away.

"I don't understand."

"Wayne passed away in his sleep a week after we got home. Two days later, we were in the group home," Cole says.

I press a hand to my chest, right over my heart as tears well up. "I'm so sorry, I had no idea. If I had known, I would've . . . I don't know, asked my dad to help or something."

"Yeah, well, you disappeared off the face of the planet, remember?" Cole says. "I even drove back to your house and tried to get that property manager to give me your address, but she claimed she didn't have it."

My nose scrunches and I shake my head, three small movements. "It doesn't matter anymore, I've forgiven you."

He rears back. "You've forgiven me? For what?"

I lick my lips. "For writing to me and saying that May eleventh was the worst day of your life."

"What happened on May eleventh?" Sonny asks.

There's a pause, a moment suspended in time where Cole and I lock eyes. I open my mouth, but it's not my voice ringing through the room. It's West's.

"Cole took Amelia's virginity." West stares at me, his suffering barely concealed behind contempt.

51

AMELIA

MY MOUTH DROPS open and memories I try not to revisit too often play in my mind.

Color drains from Cole's face as he cuts a look at West. "You knew about that?"

"Of course, I fucking knew. My room was right next to yours."

Sticky webs of shame hold me hostage, and tears of disbelief prick at my eyes. "You heard us?"

He shifts his glare from Cole to me, his expression never softening. "It about killed me to hear you with him."

"I don't understand. Why didn't you say anything?" I ask.

He tips his head back and scoffs a laugh. "And what? Knock on his door while he's fucking the love of my life and ask for next?"

I bristle at his tone but not his words. "Yes."

Whatever West was going to say gets stuck in his throat and he chokes.

"You should've *talked* to me, West."

He concedes with a nod. "Probably, but I was a seventeen-year old with a chip the size of Texas on his shoulder."

The wind gusts, a loud noise barreling closer and closer. If I close my eyes, it almost sounds like the crescendo of the emotions inside this room.

I fiddle with a loose thread on my pants and recall *the letter*. I read it so many times I have it memorized.

"What about the letter you wrote me then, Cole?"

He sighs. "For the last fucking time, I never received or sent a letter to you, Amelia."

My brows slam over my eyes. "That's not true. You wrote to me and said, 'I'm sorry, I can't. My brother has feelings for you, and I would never forgive myself if I stepped in between us. We're over.'"

Cole stares at me in shock, lips parted and eyes wide.

"Tell me you didn't," Sonny murmurs.

It takes me a few more seconds to catch up, but when I do, my sinuses burn for an entirely different emotion now.

"Before you say anything, know that it's one of my deepest regrets." He swipes his tongue across his lips, his eyes pleading with me to listen.

I'm trying to understand, but I'm struggling.

"I was an idiot. I was the asshole who was in love with his best friend and didn't know how to tell her. I heard you in Cole's room that night, and something just snapped. I planned to talk to you, but then you just vanished, and then Wayne died. And then one day, I got our forwarded mail and there was a letter. The return address was some little town in Nebraska."

"I remember that town." We didn't stay long enough to get a PO Box, but I had mailed my last letter to them from our rented house.

He nods. "It was addressed to both of us, so I tore it open and read it. And in my jealous, love-twisted brain, I thought the best thing would be for Cole to write you back and tell you it was a mistake."

"Why?" I don't realize I'm crying until a tear slides onto my lip.

West looks at me, shame washing his features in anguish. "I was so in love with you that I would've done anything to get you to look at me the way I saw you look at him."

"You're an idiot," Cole rasps.

"What?" West looks at him.

"I said, you're a fucking idiot."

West hangs his head. "I know. I'm sorry."

"No, you don't get it. She looked at you exactly the same way."

"What?" West's head whips to stare at me.

"You're an idiot," I confirm.

West holds my gaze, his eyes getting glossy. "I'm so fucking sorry."

Sonny's fingers never stop swirling patterns, and whether he realizes it or not, he's giving me the strength and support I need.

"Okay."

"Okay, that's it?" Cole asks, a touch of incredulity in his voice.

"We can't change the past, Cole. And who knows how long our future will be. I—I don't want to be angry anymore."

Cole tips his chin up. "I've spent the last five years manufacturing guilt for one of the best moments of my life. But I can't just get over it so easily."

"I understand. I'll make it up to you, brother—"

"No, you'll make it up to *her*," Cole interrupts him.

"I swear it," West says.

"Good. Now stand up," Cole demands as he pushes to his feet.

West follows behind him without a word.

I lean forward. "Wait a minute. You can't go out there yet. It's not safe."

"They're alright, Cher. They need to work it out between themselves."

I don't understand what he means, but I don't need to wait long for clarification. They face one another just outside the little alcove we're in.

And then Cole punches West in the face.

THE SIREN STOPPED a few minutes ago, and the winds have died down a little, but we can still hear them whipping around.

"Alright, West. Let's go find some ice for that eye, yeah?" Sonny says, standing up.

I grab his hand. "Wait. Are you sure that's a good idea?"

"We'll be careful, Cher. Besides, I think you two could use a few minutes alone. West dropped a bomb today."

"Oh, okay. Be careful."

"Always am," Sonny says.

"West," I call out after him. He pauses just outside the alcove. "Come back to me."

He's been quiet, withdrawn since the truth came out. I understand why, but I don't want him to pull away.

"I always will, Ames."

He doesn't offer a smile or crack a joke, but I'll take it all the same.

The stairs creak as they ascend, and then it's just Cole and me.

"After all this time, it was a misunderstanding?"

"A miscommunication," I say.

"Still, what kind of fucked-up shit is that, huh?"

"Now that we know, does it change anything? For you, I mean?" Nervous butterflies careen inside my stomach.

His dark eyes meet mine. "It changes everything."

My lips quirk up in a smile. He used my words, and that's practically a declaration from him. I shift to my knees and shuffle toward him. He snags my wrist and meets me halfway.

His mouth descends on mine, and a hunger unlike anything I've ever felt grows low in my belly.

I wrap my arm around his neck and pull him into me. It feels both familiar and foreign, like I'm rediscovering chocolate after not having it for five years. I can't get close enough, small noises of protest slipping through our kiss.

My back arches, and my hands roam across his broad shoulders. I'm aching to see what he looks like now, to see how he compares to my memories.

He palms my ass through my pants, encouraging me to continue my slow grind against his hardening cock.

I pull back on a gasp, staring at the ceiling. He drags his mouth down my neck, pausing to suck hard on my fluttering pulse.

"We don't have a lot of time, so you have to be quick," I say between panting breaths.

"I feel like there's a hidden insult in there somewhere," he murmurs, the vibration of his voice sending a shot of lust straight to my core.

"There's not. I just don't know when the next opportunity will come, and I don't want to waste another second without you inside of me."

I don't say what we're both thinking: we have no idea how much time we have left here.

"Jesus, Mia," he groans before crashing his mouth to mine.

We undress each other in a frenzy, only breaking our kiss to help each other out of our shirts. My heart hammers inside my chest, drumming a beat that's only for him.

Giddiness twirls around with my lust, heightening everything.

Cole flattens the blanket on the ground before he lays me down on it. I lift up and reach for him, but he places his palm in the center of my chest.

With gentle pressure, he pushes me to lie on my back. "I've waited a long time for this. And since I can't take my time right now, I want to look my fill, yeah?"

I nod a few times, suddenly shy, which doesn't make sense considering the things West, Sonny, and I did only a couple hours ago.

He covers my body with his, chasing the chill from the floor away instantly. He kisses me with reverence, like I'm something he cherishes.

His hand runs over my stomach, dipping across my hip bone, and descending to my pussy.

I widen my legs to give him better access, and my eyes close when he swirls his fingertips around my clit. He doesn't tease me at all, applying gentle pressure as he goes around and around.

I moan into his mouth, rocking my hips into his hand. I'm too close too soon, revved up by our ticking clock and pent-up lust. My thighs tremble, and my toes curl into the blanket. I gasp, reaching for the promised oblivion.

Before I get there, he withdraws his fingers, pulling back.

"What the hell, Cole?" I grumble.

"I've thought about the way your tight pussy feels squeezing my cock more than I'll ever admit. And I'm desperate to feel it again—to feel you."

I grab him by the back of his neck and pull his lips back to mine at the same time he lines himself up. I reach down blindly, wrapping my fingers around his cock and guiding him inside me.

I can't resist stroking him a couple times, relishing the feel of him in my hand.

I wrap my legs around his back, nudging his ass with my heels to get him inside of me.

He groans as he rocks his hips in, slowly gliding right back out. He stills after the third time, bottoming out.

"Fuck me, you feel even better than I remember."

"Fuck me, Cole. I want to feel you come."

He captures both of my hands in one of his and holds them above my head. My tits rise with the new angle, pressing against his chest.

He groans my name, the same way he did when he made love to me five years ago.

And then we're a tangle of limbs and tender kisses. Reignited flame and heightened passion.

It's everything I've been dreaming about and more.

52

AMELIA

"CHECK YOUR PHONE AGAIN," West says, weaving our car around the aftermath of the tornado.

I still don't understand how we were virtually untouched. There was a ring of destruction around the fitness center but outside of a handful of broken windows, the building stayed strong.

The same can't be said for the luxury apartment complexes. I take comfort knowing no one lived in them, since they were in the construction stage. The emergency lights stayed on, but the power never came back.

The wind probably took down some trees, knocked out a bunch of power lines. It didn't matter much to us, once we were able to leave, we piled into the car and started making our way through everything.

"I already told you it's useless. There's no cell towers around here, so I don't have a signal. And before you ask me about hot-spotting my phone, I already tried it three times. I got nothing," Cole says.

"Damn, bro. I thought you'd be a little less snippy since you finally—"

"Don't you finish that statement, Gray, or I swear to god, I'll give you a black eye to match our brother."

My gaze flies to West, but I can't see anything from the rear passenger seat. I press my fingertips to my lips, applying enough pressure to feel a bite of pain.

"I'm fine, Ames. A punch is the least of what I deserve," West says softly like he can read my mind.

"We all make mistakes, West. And we have enough people who want to hurt us, we don't need to hurt each other." I look out the window, letting my mind wander.

I have whiplash from the last twenty-four hours. From the last week, really.

The moment I stepped into Tennessee Pete's, everything changed. I find it hard to regret it, though.

I mean, I could definitely do without the constant threat of mortal danger.

But I try to live my life without regrets, really. A lesson that was hard-learned five years ago, and only after I carried a suitcase full of regrets around with me from city to city.

I pull my phones from my backpack on the floor in front of me. I started keeping track of the days in my calendar app. It's easy to lose track of time when you're in a car for ninety-five percent of a cross-country dash.

My phone doesn't update anymore, something about the cell towers, I'm sure. But it eases my anxiety to physically see the countdown to showtime.

A bit macabre of a nickname for the alleged end of the world, but that too, eases my anxiety.

It's easier to swallow the concept of the possible destruction when I think of it like a play.

"I never did get to see a musical on Broadway," I mumble.

"Want me to bust out some showtunes, Ames? We can pretend we're in the Christmas Carol," West says, twisting the volume knob on the radio.

Christmas music fills the car, and I can't help but laugh.

"Yeah, you know what? I kind of want to sing too. Elvis Christmas wasn't what I had in mind, but I think we can make it work."

I elbow Cole next to me, flashing him a wry smile and singing the chorus of "Blue Christmas." He indulges me, just like I'd hoped, and the four of us belt out our best Elvis impressions as we cruise down the highway.

"DAD? CAN YOU HEAR ME?"

Static fills the line, and I can hear his voice, but I can't make out his words.

"Hang on, Amelia. I have to go somewhere higher to get better reception," he says.

I wait for the sounds to quiet, my knee bouncing in anticipation and anxiety. This is it. We're only five miles away from the site, from meeting up with Dad. There's a pit of snakes in my gut, writhing around.

For the last five or ten miles, we've seen cars abandoned on the side of the road. I didn't think anything of a few of them. I figured they ran out of gas or a tornado came through here or something equally as bad. We passed huge, uprooted pine trees along the side of the road a few miles back.

But with every mile closer to the bunker, more cars litter the highway. And now, Cole can barely maneuver the car around them. I'm afraid that we're going to get trapped soon.

The shoulders aren't wide and there's a solid dropoff too, so we don't have much of a choice but to try to go around them. For as long as we can, at least.

"Hello? Amelia? Are you there?"

I lean toward the middle console and press the speakerphone button. "We're here, Dad. I can hear you now."

"Oh good, good. Look, I can't talk long today. What's your eta?"

"We're only four and a half miles away, but we ran into a problem. We can't get through, there's a crazy amount of abandoned cars on this road, and I don't think we can go around them."

"I've never seen anything like this," Sonny murmurs.

"Yes, well, about that. You're going to have to leave your car there and walk the rest of the way."

Alarm bells ring inside my head. "Leave the car? Why?"

"Like you said, there's only one route here, and that automobile graveyard stretches for miles. About five miles on either side of the bunker, actually."

"I don't understand. What's going on?" I ask.

"Just grab what you can't live without, leave the car, and I'll meet you at the front entrance in two hours."

He disconnects the call. I lift my gaze to look at West and Sonny in the backseat. "I guess we need to pack up."

ONE HOUR and thirty minutes later, we find out the reason behind the abandoned cars.

A mob of people swarm a double barbed-wire fence surrounding what I assume is the bunker. It's unassuming from the outside, which is probably the point. Only some strategically placed cellar doors would alert anyone to its presence, outside of the barbed-wire fence.

My footsteps drag until I stop about ten feet away. Disbelief and dread coil tightly in my gut. "What is this?"

West pulls up short on my left and Sonny and Cole on my right. The four of us make a united front as we stare at the thousands of people surrounding the fence. Armed guards patrolling seem to have everything under control, so there isn't any violence. Not yet, at least.

We still have a week left. And we already know firsthand what can happen when people feel pushed to the brink. When they think they have nothing left to lose.

As it is, there's a tangible energy swirling around, something dark and primitive.

Survival.

Men, women, and children cluster in small groups, clutching their suitcases and backpacks. Some have carved out a bit of space within the masses, while others press tightly together against the fence, arms gesturing wildly and obscenities filling the air.

It's loud, louder than I anticipated.

But all I can think about is what are these people going to do if another tornado carves a path right through here? There's nowhere to go for miles and miles.

The startling realization crests, and my gut clenches.

They would face Mother Nature's wrath for the slim chance they're allowed inside the bunker.

Despair swells inside of me, empathy thick in the back of my throat.

West nudges me with his elbow. "Call your dad, Ames."

"Yeah, okay." I reach back with my right arm and snag the satellite phone out of the side pocket. I dial his number and he answers on the second ring. He must've been waiting for me.

"We're here."

"I'll be right out. Go to the door on your right, not the main one," his voice sounds tinny in my ear.

"I'll see you soon." I end the call and stuff the phone back in my pocket, my gaze straying to a woman with a double stroller. She's closer to us than the fence, a few duffle bags and a suitcase around her feet. She's kneeling down, brushing the hair off one of her three young children and giving them what looks like a snack.

"What now?" Cole asks.

I jerk my head to the right. "There's a door over here, I guess. He's coming out to get us."

"Stay alert, boys. We're about to walk through the fire," Sonny says as he slips in behind me.

Cole takes the lead, and I follow behind him. West slides in to my left, and it doesn't hit me until we're almost to the crowd of people.

They're protecting me.

53

AMELIA

THE NOISE GETS LOUDER the closer we get.

"This is my corner of the fence. Get the fuck out of here," one man yells.

"Fuck off. I was here first," another one yells back.

"Hey, how do you sleep at night knowing you're condemning us," a woman hurls at the closest guard.

The hair on the back of my neck stands on end, and I tuck my index finger through Cole's back belt loop. West closes in beside me, his right arm pressing against my left one. And Sonny places a palm on my shoulder.

We move as a unit through the crowd, trying to make as little waves as possible.

"Hey, you can't just get to the front of the line," someone yells.

"There are no fucking lines, asshole," someone else snaps.

There's some shoving and it sounds like flesh hitting flesh, but I keep facing forward. I know that if I catch someone's eye—or the wrong someone—violence will erupt. It's shimmering in the air around us like a mirage.

I don't doubt my men or their ability to protect themselves and each other, but we'd be so severely outnumbered, I don't want to think of the possible damage.

A ring of people three-deep surrounds the fence, and Cole has to barge his way through. I catch an elbow to the left side of my face, but I don't stop. A yelp comes from that direction a second later, and even though Sonny didn't lift his hand from my shoulder, I have no doubt he did something in retribution.

We make it to the fence, and there, flanked by four armed guards is my father. I push onto my toes and wave my hand in the air. "Dad!"

He leans toward a guard and points in my direction, but he doesn't come any closer. I understand the armed entourage a moment later when they try to open the fence door. People rush it, and the guards step up to block their entrance. They wouldn't get very far since they'd still be trapped in the space between the two fences.

Cole reaches back and grabs my hand, so I grab West's, and Sonny keeps his hand on my shoulder. After a few touch-and-go moments, we make it through both doorways.

The crowd surges again, but the guards bat them back and lock it up again. People scream and yell, and I feel the violence thickening in the air, glittering on every molecule around us.

"Follow me," Dad says when we're a few feet away. He spins on his heel and strides toward one of the cellar-style doors.

I don't let go of West's hand, Cole and Sonny take up their previous formation, and together, we descend into the earth.

"SO, here are your quarters. I'm right next door, rooming with Jerry and Cheryl. It's the only way I could get your, uh, husband and his brothers in." He points to a slate gray door, the kind you would see in a gymnasium, horizontal push handle and everything. A white ornamental plaque with the number 1985 sits to the right of our room.

So far, everything is varying shades of gray. The walls are slate gray concrete with large horizontal lines. I'm not sure if it's to add texture or design or how it was literally poured.

The floor is light gray speckled concrete, the kind that has an epoxy coating to make it shine. Lightly textured charcoal gray rug runners are evenly spaced down the many, many hallways.

The sconces look custom-made. Metal twisted into an industrial-style design and dual upper and lower bulbs.

"Thank you, Dad." I rest my hand on his forearm, squeezing gently.

"Of course, of course. Let's take a quick tour and then I'll let you get settled. I've got a meeting to go to soon as well."

"A meeting?" I skip a few steps to catch up to him. The boys make a protective wall behind us.

"Yes, well, we have very limited communication with a few other government-made bunkers in the US and some others from around the world. There are currently fifteen hundred volcanoes on land and an immeasurable amount under water. Our best hope is that the submerged volcanoes don't activate."

"Why?" Cole asks.

Dad pushes up his glasses. "Good question. If they erupt, then we can safely estimate it'll wipe out the entire underwater ecosystem. The water will be too acidic, and it'll set us back further than we'll ever be able to recover from."

"But can't the same be said for the above ground volcanoes?" West asks.

"Yes and no. Some of the volcanoes we estimate will have minor eruptions while some others will have effusive eruptions. That's when there is slowly churning magma that flows out. And then some will have devastating eruptions, with ash clouds so thick, the sun won't be able to penetrate it. Which will lead to another collapse of our ecosystem."

"Jesus," I hush out. My chest feels tight with anxiety.

"But don't worry, we're in the safest place you can be: underground," Dad says, turning down a hallway.

"But what about everyone else? All those people out there." I look at Dad, his shoulders tight and his head facing forward.

"C'mon, I'll show you the cafeteria," Dad says, ignoring my question.

I let him off the hook and follow behind him. The cafeteria is the size of the one from high school, with probably a hundred tables taking up the majority of the space. They're a cross between picnic-style and dining room table, and it looks like each one seats at least ten.

"Over there is where you can order food. There will always be a couple options available, plus snacks and drinks. I don't know exactly how it works yet, since I've taken all my meals with Jerry and Cheryl in our room."

There are a few people milling around behind the glass counter, and it looks like one of them is using a cooktop stove.

"And how do we have food they can actually cook with? I kind of thought it would be MREs," West asks.

"Excellent question. Now I can't show you because it's not public, but I've been inside there and it's magnificent. There are several greenhouses on one end, where we have some of the best and brightest minds down here with us. Not only growing our food but teaching a few others how to do it too."

"Let's look at the rec center next."

My brows hitch upward. "Rec center?"

Dad grins. "It's important to be active so we don't lose muscles. There's a couple basketball hoops, every sporting ball you can imagine, a volleyball net, and so much more."

I trail behind Dad this time, taking everything in with a critical lens.

For a luxury sanctuary underground, where are all the people?

DAD SHOWED us around for an hour before he dropped us back at our room and went to his meeting, wherever that is. He didn't show us that area yet.

It's a giant maze down here. I don't know how many people it houses, but I'd guess thousands, at least. It's utilitarian in a way, gray concrete floors, walls, and ceilings in the hallways and common areas. But the living quarters are warmer, softer.

It's one big room sectioned into smaller spaces. Only the bathroom has a door.

There are four bunk beds pushed on opposite walls, a small couch and a TV, a kitchenette area with a refrigerator and microwave. The walls are a soft cool beige color, and a few charcoal gray tapestry art pieces decorate the walls.

A soft gray circle rug covers most of the floor, and the lighting is adjustable. There are three options for light: halogen, daylight, regular.

"Want to unpack, Cher?"

I've been laying down on this bottom bunk for the last twenty minutes, my mind tripping over the images of all those people outside the gates.

Something is brewing inside of me, an idea taking shape. It feels crazy, reckless even. But it also feels right. I don't think they're going to like it though.

I roll my head along the pillow and look at Sonny with a soft smile. "No."

His eyes narrow briefly as he studies me. "Something on your mind?"

"Yeah," I sigh and push to sit up. "I—I don't know how to say this. But I can't stay."

West and Cole freeze, then they both whip around to look at me. I love it when they have the same mannerisms like that. It makes me think of easier times.

"What's that now, Mia?"

I lick my lips and look between the three of them. "I can't stop thinking about it. About all those people outside. What do we have that those people outside don't? What do I offer that they can't?"

"I don't understand," West says, shaking his head and crossing the room to sit next to me.

"She wants to leave," Sonny murmurs.

All eyes snap to him. A moment later, they shift their intensity to me, and my shoulders hit my ears with tension.

"That true, Mia? You want to leave this place we just spent the last however many days getting to?"

My shoulders fall and I sigh. "Why us and not them?"

"I don't know," Sonny murmurs.

"I don't know either. But it just doesn't feel right, leaving them out there. There were kids out there, Gray."

"I know, Cher." His voice is low, his eyes soft.

"We don't make that choice, Ames."

"You can't save them all, Mia," Cole says, his voice softer than before.

I nod, raking my teeth across my lip. "But what about those three little girls in that double stroller? They couldn't have been older than four. I can save them."

"What are you saying?" Cole asks, taking a seat on my other side.

"I could do it, you know. I'm smart and resourceful. I could go, find another bunker to hide out in."

"Not without me," Sonny says. "I'd never let you leave without me, Cher. You should know better by now."

I shake my head. "I can't—I'm not asking you to do that. You can stay here. I'll clear it with my dad—"

"You can't get rid of me that easily, baby girl." Sonny flashes me those lethal dimples.

Cole folds his arms across his chest. "And what's your plan then?"

"My granddad was a prepper," Sonny says with a grin, rocking back on his heels. "He has a pretty sweet bunker in Wisconsin. I can get us there."

Hope blossoms like a deadly flower. "You can?"

"Absolutely, Cher. Why do you think I packed my Wisconsin maps?" He winks at me.

"Are you two so quick to die that you'd leave guaranteed safety for a possibility," Cole hisses.

I twist to face him, tucking my left ankle under my right knee. I brush some of his hair off his forehead, relishing in the softness. "I'm not afraid to die, Cole."

"Then why the fuck are you always trying to leave me?" He can't disguise the hurt in his voice or the anguish in his eyes.

I place a kiss in the corner of his mouth. "If you need me to ask you to come with me, here's your formal invitation. Come with us, Cole."

"God damnit, Mia." He steals my lips in a harsh kiss and pushes off the bed. "I guess it's a good thing I didn't unpack much."

"And what about me, hm?"

I look over my shoulder at West. "We both know you're coming with us."

He only grins, and I guess that's the only answer I need.

54

AMELIA

"DAD! DAD, WAIT UP!" I holler, jogging to catch up with him.

Dad pauses halfway down the hall and turns to look at me. "Oh, Amelia. Did you need something?" He cranes his neck to look around me. "Where are your . . . friends?"

I blow out a breath and scoot to the side to let a pair of older men walk down the hallway. It's the first time I've seen anyone since I started searching for my dad ten minutes ago. Neither one greets us, but I wait until they're out of earshot before I speak.

"They're back in the room. But I was hoping to talk to you more about a few things."

He inclines his head. "Alright. What's on your mind?"

I tuck my hands into my pockets, concentrating on the way the fabric pinches around my knuckles. I glance around the hallway. "It's nice, down here, I mean. It's very . . . industrial."

"Yes, well, I don't really know how long this has been here. Or who designed it if that's what you were wondering."

I shift my weight from foot to foot. "I wasn't, not really."

Dad huffs a breath. "Is there something else because I wanted to check and see if there's any word from California."

My head snaps up. "What happened in California? We've been in the dark since we left Vegas."

"I . . . I don't know. I don't want to fear the worst, but no one has heard from anyone west of the San Andreas Fault."

My chest feels heavy with grief. "I'm sure it's just because the cell towers are down."

Dad offers me a grim smile. "Maybe."

I clear my throat. "Listen, I wanted to ask you about all those people up there. How'd they even find this place?"

He rubs the back of his neck. "I really don't know. I'm still not sure how they found out about the location, someone must've leaked it."

"What's going to happen to them?"

He shifts uncomfortably, alternating his weight from foot to foot. "It's not up to me, Amelia."

Translation: nothing. Nothing is going to happen to them. And when June first rolls around, they'll all still be standing there.

Until they just *aren't*.

I shake my head. "I don't understand why they can't come in though. I've explored this place for the last few hours, and Dad, there's so much room down here. You can fit thousands of people." My voice rises a little, and I exhale, trying to rein in my frustration.

"The rooms are all spoken for."

The way he said it has me pausing. I tilt my head to the side. "But I've barely seen anyone around. Are people actually in all these rooms or are they just being *reserved*?"

Pink darkens his cheeks and he glances away. "I honestly don't know. They don't include me in all that kind of stuff."

"Are you kidding me?" I scoff. "There are people up there begging to be let in, and you have so much room—"

"It's not that easy, Amelia. It's all very scientific, you know. There's a finite amount of space—the rooms are built without little room for expansion. Everything is calculated right down to the water and food. Even the air!" He shoves his glasses up his nose with a violent push. "I had to threaten them to get three more people in for you. I did that *for you,* Amelia."

I swallow around the lump in my throat. "Why can't you do it again then?"

"Because there are forty-seven children out there, Amelia!" He shouts, throwing his hand out wide. "Three or four, maybe, but there just isn't room for that many."

I take a hasty step toward him, my heart hammering inside my chest. "Then you make room, Dad! You make some hard choices because a bunker full of old men with room to spare ignoring fathers *begging you* to save their babies is wrong. It's wrong and immoral and—and you're better than that." A tear tracks down my cheek. "I know you're better than that. You're a good man."

His shoulders slump. "I already tried to bargain with them."

"Then try again. Barge back in there and you *tell them.* You have to take the children!" I feel out of control, bordering on hysterical.

"I can't, Amelia!" he yells. He swipes his palm down his mouth and turns away from me.

I allow him his moment of privacy. He so rarely raised his voice to me in all my years that it stuns me speechless.

The air between us thickens with accusations and hopelessness. I look at the concrete walls around us, the custom metal sconces every few feet with special sunlight bulbs on the top and bottom. The soft sunray ones, like when the sun shines through the clouds on an overcast day.

I clear my throat, keeping my eyes on my shoes in the half-circle of sunshine shining on the floor. "I've never asked you for anything, Dad. Never. Not when we moved around all the time, not even when you tore me from the first real home I've ever had in Vegas."

I lift my head and look at him. He slowly turns to face me, grief cutting deep grooves between his brows. "I'm sorry, Amelia."

I sniff back tears. "I know, Dad, I know. I found my way back home."

He nods, his eyes glossy. "With them."

It's not a question. He already knows.

He chuckles then, a sad, watery sort of noise. "Did you really get married to Wayne's boy?"

I lift both shoulders and let them curve forward a little. "Does it matter?"

He looks at me then, a soft smile on his face. "No, I guess it doesn't."

There's so much distance between us, my heart aches. In three steps, I'm in front of him, wrapping my arms around his shoulders and hugging him hard. His arms clutch me closer. He smells like he always does, clean mint soap.

My gut clenches as pain lances through my heart. How cruel is it that it took the end of the world for us to embrace so tightly, so freely affectionate?

"I love you, Dad," I say through tears. I blink and they spill over my lashes, soaking into his shirt underneath my cheek.

"Don't, Amelia. Don't go." He tightens his hold on me.

I don't give him enough credit. He's more perceptive than I ever realized. He already knows what I'm going to say.

"I needed you then, and some part of me will always long for you. But I'm okay now. I've found my family, people who care for me and look out for me. But those kids out there, they need you. I'm asking you to help them."

He sniffles and rubs my back with one hand, never loosening his embrace.

"You can't leave them out there to die," I choke out the last word on a sob.

"You can't ask me to sacrifice my daughter for strangers."

"I'm not asking you, Dad. It's my decision."

"I love you so much, Amelia," he chokes out.

"Make them listen. Make them find room."

"Alright. Alright. I'll convince them," he says.

I try to pull away, but he tightens his hold on me. "Just another moment longer."

For the next twenty minutes, that's exactly how we stay.

55

AMELIA

I SCOOT to the middle seat, shoving the cooler to the passenger side. West raises his right arm, and I huddle underneath it. My nerves feel like live wires, sparking and hot.

We're in a literal race for survival with the highest stakes imaginable. The only thing that makes it bearable is knowing that three little girls and their mom are safely tucked away in that bunker next to Dad and Jerry.

Even if this ends terribly for us, I don't regret it.

The mob of people standing outside the fences, begging and pleading to be let in will haunt me for the rest of my life.

"Next right," Sonny says, gesturing to the exit.

Cole exits the highway, the mood somber as we try to outrun Mother Nature.

We've been driving for twenty-two hours, only stopping for the bare minimum: gas, restroom breaks, and any hot food we can find.

Sonny's been filling us in on what to expect with his grandpa's bunker and what we might need still. It's been a few years since he's been there, but from what he remembers, there are six different rooms. A bedroom with two beds, a sizeable bathroom, a full kitchen, two living rooms, and a den. He explained cooking and cleaning and the water system.

Apparently, his grandpa was big in the prepper community, and he had this plot of land for years. It's close enough to a fresh water source that it makes the water filtration system easier. Sonny swears the water tastes better this way, without all the chemicals we're used to. I've reserved my judgment until we get there.

Dad hooked us up with four cans of gas and an entire wagon filled with supplies. He snuck us out one of the two emergency tunnels that open up a mile away from the fenced-in area.

We trekked back to our car, which by some divine intervention was untouched, piled in, and haven't looked back since.

There's a collective gasp in the car, like we're all holding our breath, waiting for it to end.

Not even the Christmas songs play anymore.

Cole flies down another road, this one smaller.

"We're almost there, fifteen minutes," Sonny says.

The car shakes, a jerky motion that sends me leaning into West.

"We get a flat?" West asks.

"No. I think it started," Cole says through clenched teeth.

I sit up quick. "What started?"

"The end of everything."

I twist around and look out the back window as a huge mushroom cloud covers most of the skyline. "Holy shit. Something big erupted."

"Faster, man," West encourages.

"I'm going as fast as I safely can," Cole snaps.

"Here, turn here." Sonny points to the left.

Cole yanks on the wheel, and the car skids across a gravel road, if you can call it that. It's more like a path of rocks off the side of the road.

The shaking continues, but now I don't know if it's because of the first volcanic eruption or the gravel underneath us.

"Stop," Sonny says, bracing his hand on the dash.

Cole slams on the brakes, and we all look around. I don't see anything but the woods. Tall pine trees, giant oaks and maples, small flowering bushes and big wild ones.

Sonny jumps out of the car and runs between two pine trees. He disappears from view for a moment. Then I see his waving hand. "C'mon, over here!"

The three of us start grabbing our stuff and run toward Sonny. He's bent over, two hands on a metal handle, and wrenching open a solid metal door with a grunt.

He looks at us with a manic sort of smile. "Welcome home."

56

AMELIA

"WE'RE GOING TO MAKE IT."

"You don't know that, Gray," West murmurs from next to me.

Everything from my car haphazardly lays around the bunker. I didn't have it in me to unpack if we're all going to simply cease to exist in a couple days.

It's June first.

The first volcano erupted three days ago when we arrived. And it's been nonstop since. Or so we theorize.

"I do," Sonny says as he looks at me. "We'll be fine in here."

I nod but doubts plague me, drumming up the worst-case scenarios.

Sonny extends his hand to me. "C'mere, baby girl."

I slip my hand in his and allow him to pull me into his lap.

"Remember what I said?" Sonny asks, running his hands through my hair.

"Remind me," I whisper against his mouth.

I shut out the vision of the orange-colored cloud rolling closer and closer to us and focus on him.

"Loving you is the greatest honor of my life."

My breath hitches at the heartbreak in his eyes. My throat burns with unshed tears, catching any words I might say. So I crush my mouth to his in a tender kiss full of every what-if I could imagine.

What if we met a year ago or what if he was one of Wayne's boys too?

What if we fell in love—the three of them and me—and we lived in peaceful bliss?

What if the world didn't end in fiery destruction?

He pulls back, and I crawl into West's lap. His expression is regret and bone-deep sadness. "I'm so fucking sorry, baby. If I could go back and change everything, I would."

"Shh, it's alright. And I wouldn't change everything. Some things happened exactly as they had to." I tip my head to the side toward Sonny.

"Still. It's my deepest regret, only furthered by the fact that I won't be able to spend a lifetime making it up to you."

"Maybe not this one," I concede. "But in the next?"

It's a tease, a playful reminder of the very real possibility that we're going to die today.

His palms press into my back, crushing me closer to his chest. "In every lifetime, baby. I'll find you in every single one, and I'll never stop."

Tears pool on my lashes in a thick line, and I offer him a watery smile. "Promise?"

He brings us closer still, his lips brushing mine with every letter. "I guarantee it. You're the love of my life, in every life."

I swallow his last word in a kiss, putting every emotion we never got to act on in this one moment. We pull back at the same time, our gazes mirrored with sadness and love.

Cole's hands slide around my waist, and he hauls me onto his lap. He crushes his mouth to mine in the next breath. His kiss is demanding, full of anguish and love. I pull back on a sob, resting my forehead against his.

"We wasted so much time, Mia. So much fucking time, I—" His

voice cracks, and he presses his lips against mine in a bittersweet kiss.

I taste the salt from our tears, and I clutch him tighter.

Everything on the shelves around us rattles, and I pull back.

I stare into his eyes, the amber bursts vibrant against the dark brown. "I love you, Cole. I have for a long time."

"I've loved you since the moment I saw you fall off your pink-and-yellow daisy skateboard."

Surprised laughter huffs out of me. "I was a terrible skateboarder."

He smiles. "You we're."

I exhale a breath and nod. "It'll be over soon and then we'll know."

West and Sonny scoot in close behind me. West's arm bands around my middle, and he rests his forehead against my shoulder. Cole covers my back with his front, always protecting me, even until the very end.

The four of us huddle together in a bunker, murmuring words of love and affection as the world ends twenty-five feet above us.

EPILOGUE

AMELIA

I SET my favorite green mug on the desk and tap the keyboard to wake the screen up. The mug says "I'm a romance reader" in black cursive font and keeps my tea warm for ages. I still remember when I found it tucked away next to some well-read bodice ripper romance books from a few decades ago. We were exploring the bunker, taking stock of what we had and what Sonny's grandpa had stockpiled here. I'll never be able to repay him for this, and I hope that wherever he is, he knows how grateful we all are.

The screen blinks to life with the camera feed for the security system topside. We lost six of the twenty cameras when the initial blast happened, and another four this past winter. But we're coming up on the nine month mark, I'm not the only one who's eager to see something.

I know Dad said minimum a year, but I'm hopeful. At this point, I'd be happy to see a chipmunk running across the forest floor.

Well, what used to be a forest.

The volcanic eruption didn't take out all plants and wildlife, but the thick cloud of smoke that blanketed the sky for months nearly did.

I press a button and toggle between the feeds, noting nothing new.

Hands slide over my hips from behind and a cold nose nudges my hair to the side. "Wanna try your dad again?"

I smile and arch my neck to the side to give West room. "I already did. Still nothing. I know, I know. Our phone won't work so far underground, but I still keep it charged every day. Just in case."

I cling to that knowledge that it's a connection issue on our end, refusing to acknowledge the other reason for a failed connection.

His breath fans across the sensitive part of my neck, eliciting a shiver. "We still have three more months before we can go topside, you know."

I hear the chastisement in his voice, but I take it in stride. "I know. Just like I know *you* know that I check every day, regardless of the countdown."

He spins me around to face him, his hands smoothing up my sides to rest underneath my breasts. His thumb brushes back and forth, just enough to tease me and he knows it.

I tilt my head to the side, suspicion sneaking in. "What are you doing?"

His brows hit his hairline in a faux-innocence. "Who, me? I'm not doing anything. Just enjoying the company of my girl."

I grin, knowing exactly what happened. "You sure it's not because Cole kicked you out of the den again?"

His brows crash down over his eyes and a scowl too playful to be serious tips up one side of his mouth. "It's total bullshit. I'm trying to learn something new, the least he can do is be supportive."

"I was for the first three months, but it's been nine months, man.

Give the guitar a rest. Not everyone is musically inclined," Cole yells from down the hall.

"Harsh," I mock-whisper with a laugh.

He flashes me a coy smirk. "You see the way they treat me, Ames? Savages, the lot of them."

"I love you, man, but if I have to hear you butcher "Something In The Way" one more time, I'm going to lose my mind," Sonny says.

"I'm learning by ear, asshole. And your grandpa only stocked the place with a random vinyl collection," West grumbles.

I hop onto the table behind me and tug him close. He steps between my legs, his hands roaming underneath Sonny's shirt I snagged this morning when I rolled out of bed.

"Don't listen to 'em. I think you're great."

"That's because you love me," he mumbles, ghosting his lips across mine.

"That's true." I smile against his mouth.

"Hands off, bro. She's mine today," Cole says from nearby.

A second later, Cole clamps a hand on West and shoulders him out of the way, stepping into my open legs.

Sweat dots his bare chest, his tattoos glistening. We turned one of the flexible rooms into a makeshift workout area two weeks in.

Cole flashes me a wolflike smile, and it's all the warning I have before he pecks me hard on the lips. He pulls away before it goes anywhere, drops his shoulder to my belly, and hauls me up, fire-man-style.

My hair hangs down, blocking my vision, but the only thing I do is laugh when he parades me around our home.

"Put me down, Cole. I can walk just fine." I playfully swat at his firm ass.

He taps me on the ass, sliding his palm under the hem of the shirt. "No panties today, Mia?"

"I didn't get a chance to get dressed yet."

He hums under his breath. His palm smooths over each cheek,

pausing to tease me with a featherlight touch. He flips me over and carefully lays me on our bed.

I blink away the spotty vision from the head rush and smile at him. "What was that about?"

He climbs on top of me, and my knees fall to the side to make room for him. "I'm ready."

My brows scrunch and I shake my head. Understanding dawns a moment later and my brows arch toward my hairline. My teeth sink into my bottom lip, pulling it in my mouth to take the excitement down a notch.

"Really?"

"Really," Sonny says from the doorway.

Excitement rushes my veins like a shot of vodka. I run my hands across his chest, marveling at the muscles he has. "Are you sure? You don't have to."

"He's sure," West says. He's standing next to Sonny, both of them wearing matching grins.

Cole rolls his eyes, but his smile grows wide. "For you, I'm willing to share."

"Thank you," I breathe.

"Don't thank me, Mia. I love you."

"I love you—all of you. But today, I want you to fuck me like you don't."

***

KEEP TURNING to read some bonus scenes from When It Ends!

A NOTE TO READERS

You didn't think I was going to leave you on Chapter 56, did you?

I mean, I gotta be honest. I low-key thought about it. There's something so deliciously tragic about Amelia's journey with her men, that I thought it might be a fitting ending. But then I remembered that at the end of the day, I love love. And I'm enamored by the idea of love persevering.

Amelia, Sonny, West, and Cole get their HEA, and hey, you never know. Maybe we'll see them again one day.

Keep turning for three bonus scenes!

This story has been on my mind for over a year, and I am so, so excited that you get to read it now. I hope you enjoyed reading it as much as I loved writing it. I know it's not my spiciest story, but I hope you enjoyed all the angsty tension!

And if you feel so compelled, slide into my DMs or my FB group, Penelope's Black Hearts and tell me your favorite scene or character! Those kinds of messages are like fuel to my little author heart. Plus, I love seeing people's favorites in the harem!

Oh, and did you see The Wren is coming soon too? It's book 1 in our King sisters world! Do you have any guesses which sister is first?

Grab it here!

As always, my DMs are always open if you need to slide in there and chat—or proverbially throw your kindle at me! ;)

I would be honored if you had the time to leave a brief review of this book! Reviews are the lifeblood of a book, and I would appreciate it so much.

xoxo

—pen

Stay in the loop!

Join my newsletter

Join my Facebook group, Penelope's Black Hearts

Follow me on Instagram @authorpenelopeblack

ACKNOWLEDGMENTS

Thank you to my readers! Thank you for hanging in there with me on all those cliffs on just about every book I write, sending all of you air hugs for that!

Thank you to my husband who's always the first one to champion me. And I love that you're always shouting, "My wife's a romance author!" with pride to anyone you pass on the street. You're the best, and I love you so much.

To my tiny humans: I love you both more than all the stars in the sky. And you have to wait until you're older to read Mommy's books.

To all the bookstagrammers and bloggers and readers that send me messages and create beautiful edits for my books—I'm still in awe. Thank you so, so much. On my most insecure days, I pull up your edits and kind words and never fails to reignite my spark.

To my wonderful family who's encouraged and supported me—thank you, thank you! And thank you to each and every one of you who read my books. I'm looking at you, Grandma + Grandpa!

To my beta besties: Tracey, Dorothy, Elaine, Erica, Jen, and Megan, I'm so thankful for each of you. Your kindness and support mean the world to me.

To Christine for jumping right in with a smile! I'm so grateful we met!

Thank you to the amazing babes on my ARC team! I'm so grateful to have you in my corner!

To my Songbirds—I'm so lucky to have you all with me on this journey! Thank you for being a safe space!

And finally, I want to thank my author besties! I found y'all this past year, and trust me when I say, I'm never letting you go! I'm forever grateful for the ease in which you fix crowns, champion one another, and become a safe haven for me.

BONUS SCENES

THEN
Cole, 9 years old

"I'll be right back, okay, sweetie?"

I blink at the woman in front of me, but I don't say anything.

She sighs, her mouth tipping downward. She looks sad. It reminds me of the way Mom always looked, like she could cry at any second.

Thoughts of Mom makes my stomach squirm, so instead, I turn to look across the street. The houses in this neighborhood look bigger than the one I used to live in.

"Alright. I'm going to go inside and talk to Wayne. You're going to like it here, sweetie." She pats me on the shoulder, and I flinch, ducking out from under her touch and looking at the houses down the street.

She sighs but a moment later, I hear the clacking of her shoes on the cement before a door creaks.

It's quiet then.

I take a deep breath and adjust the straps of my backpack.

They're digging into my shoulders and something is poking me in the back. The wind picks up, blowing hot air across my face.

"Hey!"

My head jerks to the side at the shout. A girl skips down the driveway across the street from me, her blonde hair a mess on the top of her head.

I stare at her.

She's wearing a black t-shirt that's too big for her, jean shorts, and the whitest sneakers I've ever seen. She grins at me, showing missing front teeth. She must be younger than me, because I lost my front teeth two years ago. "I never see any kids around here. You just move in or something?"

I look down the street instead of answering, hoping she'll get the hint and leave me alone.

"I'm here on vacation visiting my grandma for a week."

I look at her from the corner of my eye. She's still smiling at me, skipping down her driveway.

Geez, she talks a lot. I shift from foot to foot, my stomach feeling uncomfortable again. Mom used to get stomach aches a lot, said something about too much sugar, but I know that can't be why my stomach is hurting. I can't remember the last time I had dessert. It feels like I've been at the group home for weeks, and they don't have sweets like that.

"Wanna ride bikes? I have an extra one you can borrow."

I can hear the scuffs from her shoes against the pavement, but I keep facing away from her. The hair on the back of my neck prickles when I see a car driving toward us.

It's one of those cars that's too loud with smoky gray exhaust.

It's hard to tell, but it doesn't seem like they're slowing down. My stomach does a somersault as I look from the girl to the car.

She's in her own little world, skipping and staring at me with that toothless smile.

My heartbeat gets loud in my ears, and I glance from the car to the girl again. My backpack hits the driveway with a thud and my feet move before I even think about it.

"Is that a yes?" She doesn't look both ways before she skips into the road.

It feels like my chest is caving in, and I don't take my gaze from hers as I run as fast as I can across the road. I don't have time to flinch before I collide with the girl. I sweep her off her feet and push us both out of the road. I palm the back of her head and wrap my other arm around her back as we land on her driveway. The impact makes my head ring and my teeth rattle.

A horn honks but the car doesn't stop.

Which is fine because I don't think I could talk right now even if I wanted to. My head spins, but it's nothing compared to the way my stomach dips when the girl looks at me.

Her eyes look like the sky, that kind of blue-gray right before a storm. And right now, they're wide and focused on me.

"Holy shit," she whispers before she winces. "Shoot. Don't tell my dad, okay? I'm not supposed to swear."

I nod, my tongue thick in my mouth.

"Are you okay? That was like something out of a movie! Where did you learn to do that?"

She's talking fast again, like she has to cram all the words into ten seconds or she'll explode or something.

I clear my throat and stand up, dusting my hands on my shorts. "I'm fine."

I haven't said a word in weeks, not to anyone. Not since the police showed up at our house and took my parents away. But she doesn't seem to care.

She sits up and springs to her feet, stepping toward me and throwing her arms around my neck. My neck feels hot and I'm not sure why. Probably because the last person to hug me was my mom the morning she died.

"Amelia?" A deep, masculine voice yells a second before a screen door slams. "C'mon. It's time for dinner."

The noise wrenches through the air and I jump away from her in a second.

The girl, Amelia, looks over her shoulder at her house. I follow her gaze and see a man with a bushy beard and glasses staring at me. I jerk my gaze away and shuffle backward without another word.

"Hey, wait! You didn't even tell me your name," she yells.

But I'm already jogging across the street. I scoop up my backpack with one hand and keep jogging until I reach the porch. There's a plastic chair in the corner, behind a bunch of spindly bushes. I don't bother brushing off the spiderwebs before I sit down.

My heart hammers inside my chest and sweat rolls down my temple. I steal a glance across the street through the small gap in the bushes just in time to see Amelia going inside. She pauses and looks across the street, but then that guy calls her name again, and she goes inside.

I exhale a breath and focus on my shoes.

THEN

Cole, 12 years old

The box fan whirs two feet away from me, ruffling my hair with hot air. Sweat beads on the back of my neck, even with the fan blowing on me. But Wayne won't turn the air conditioning on for another three weeks. Something about the electric company increasing their prices.

As hot as I am, I don't complain.

Being at Wayne's is infinitely better than the group home. I spent two weeks at there before I came here. Those memories have stuck with me for years, even if they're mottled with confusion. Wayne's been good to both me and West, treats us well. I keep waiting for him to take in another kid, but it's only been West and me.

Speaking of my foster brother, he'll be looking for me soon. I promised him I'd go hiking with him and the rest of the Spring Mountain Explorers. We have to leave in twenty minutes if we want to get there in time.

But I can't stop looking out the window.

There's a moving van in the driveway across the street. The same driveway that I tackled some girl onto three years ago.

Amelia.

I never told anyone what happened. I wasn't much for talking then, and it would be weird to bring it up all these years later. I kept thinking that I'd see her again, but for three years, only her grandma came and went.

Until today.

She looks different than I remember, like maybe my memory is distorted. Her hair is lighter now, more blonde than brown. The wind picks up the long strands and blows them in front of her face for the third time in five minutes.

She shoves it off of her forehead for the fifth time, not that I was counting, and repositions her feet on her skateboard. She falls off it more than she stays on, giving me a glimpse of the daisies on the bottom of the board.

I shift in my seat, my butt going numb from sitting in the same position for too long. She's looked at our house a few different times, and I can't decide if I want her to knock on the door or not.

Part of me thought I imagined her as what my state-appointed therapist called a coping mechanism. A response to how out of control I felt when everything happened with Mom and Dad.

But I didn't. She's real and she's right in front of my house.

My palms feel clammy the longer I look at her. I wipe them on my shorts again, and shake my head at myself. I'm acting like I've never talked to a pretty girl before.

Man up, I tell myself.

I exhale a breath and push to my feet.

West's footsteps echo off the hardwood floor in the kitchen a second before I see him.

"What's up, man? Ready to go?"

I jerk my gaze from the window and focus on my brother. "Yep. Let me grab my things."

He crosses to the window and leans in. "Damn." He whistles under his breath.

I shift from foot to foot, my neck feeling hot. "What?"

"Did you see this?" He doesn't look at me, keeping his gaze trained outside. On her.

"What?" If I sound snappy he doesn't call me on it. He's too busy staring out the window.

"There's a girl skateboarding in front of our house. Well, trying to at least."

I lift a shoulder. "Yeah."

"You think she's moving in?"

I roll my eyes. "Well, there is a moving van in the driveway."

"I'm going to go out there."

Something uncomfortable churns in my gut. "What about the hike today?"

He waves a hand behind him, tapping me on the arm. "Let's go tomorrow instead."

I huff. "I don't think you can just reschedule a whole group like that. C'mon, man. Let's go meet the guys."

"Yeah, I'll be right there." He steps back and flashes me a wide smile. "But first, I'm going to go talk to her."

He's out the front door before I can get a word in. I sink back into the chair in front of the window and watch my brother jog over to the girl with hair like gold and daisies on her skateboard.

I can't hear what they're saying, but she stops when he reaches her. And then she's smiling at him. He probably told her some self-depreciating story. That always gets the laughs at school.

Just when I decide to go out there and do something embarrassing and see if she remembers me, West turns around and jogs back into the house.

I stand up and hover in the foyer like I wasn't watching the entire time. The front door creaks, and West practically skips inside. A big, goofy grin stretches across his face.

"Oh, man, she's totally moving in. I told her we had a pool and invited her over to swim tomorrow."

"Yeah?" I perk up at the news. This is perfect. I won't need to go to her and ask if she remembers if she'll be in our backyard.

He turns around and walks backward down the hall, toward the mudroom door. "This is going to be our best summer yet. I can feel it."

His enthusiasm is infectious, and my smile mimics his without conscious thought. "If you say so. C'mon, Wayne's probably already in the car waiting on us."

I grab my gear off of the kitchen counter as we pass through it and follow my brother into the garage. Sure enough, Wayne's ready and waiting on us with his favorite Chicago Cubs baseball hat low over his eyes.

"You boys ready?" Wayne asks as he taps the button, and the garage door starts to ascend.

I know he means to go on a hike, but it almost feels like he's asking if we're ready for this summer—if we're ready for her.

I pause at the rear passenger door and look into the street. "Yeah, I've been ready for a while."

NOW

Amelia

Cole tosses me on the bed with a smirk.

A giggle slips out as I bounce a little on the mattress. Like most things in this bunker, it's surprisingly comfortable.

I feel rather than see West and Gray close in on me, but I keep my eyes on Cole. He's the wild card—and it has to be his decision to move forward. We've gotten very creative in the last nine months in this bunker, and for the most part, we've been able to give each other some semblance of privacy.

But I'd be lying if I said I wasn't excited to finally have all three of my men at the same time.

My teeth dig into my bottom lip, my veins buzzing with anticipation. I stretch my arms up high, the hem of my oversized tee rising high on my thighs. Another inch or two, and Cole will get a front-row seat of my panties.

If I was wearing any.

I'm grateful for my dad's warning to pack all those months ago, because I have no idea what kind of shape we'd be in if we weren't as prepared. Even still, there are only so many times I can wear the same dozen clothes before they start to wear thin. We've all adopted the less is more mentality.

Cole stares at me, his chest rising and falling with pent-up emotions. He reaches behind his neck and fists the collar of his tee. He pulls it over his head and tosses it to the floor in one smooth movement.

"We need some ground rules," he says.

My toes curl as the authority in his voice. "Alright."

"You tell me if it's too much or if you need a break," he says.

My brow lifts. That's not where I thought he was going with this. Tenderness warms my heart as I look at him. I reach out and hook a hand around the back of his neck. He comes closer willingly, still holding his weight off of me.

"You don't have to worry about me," I murmur.

"I'll always worry about you." He sinks to his elbows, his hips sliding in between mine.

But it's not enough. I want to feel the weight of him pressed tight against me. I apply a little pressure on the back of his neck and he finally gives me what I need.

My breath hitches at the feeling of his hard cock pressing tightly against me. We've barely begun and already, I'm feeling desperate.

His hands slide up my thighs as I wrap my legs around his waist, locking him against me. I nip at his bottom lip, tugging it into my mouth before swiping my tongue along the spot.

Cole groans against me, the vibration sliding down my body and settling against my core. He captures my lips in a bruising kiss as his hands wander higher on my thighs before resting on my hips.

I know the moment he realizes what's not underneath my tee. He rolls his hips into me further, and I swallow his groan.

He moves my tee up my ribs with eager fingers, and either West or Sonny makes a low noise in the back of his throat.

I live for those low noises from my men. I smile into Cole's mouth, and he takes it as an invitation to deepen our kiss.

Time loses all meaning when his mouth is on mine. His hips roll and his cock slides along my core. I'm certain there's going to be a wet spot on his shorts soon—if there isn't one already.

Cole pulls back, and my eyes are slow to open. I have to blink a few times to focus, and the look on his face makes me suck in a quick breath.

An intensity I've only ever associated with him heats up the space between us.

"You trust us?"

I don't have to think about it. "You know I do."

Warm fingers trail along my jaw, sliding up to skate across my swollen lips. I glance over at West. He's shirtless, his athletic shorts low on his hips. That goddamn vee is inches from my face, a certified arrow to his cock, as if I needed help locating it.

His eyes darken to a muddy green, his pupils already wide. His fingers dance along my jaw, pinpricks of pleasure left in their wake. He skates his thumb across my bottom lip, and my tongue chases his touch before I've even given it conscious thought.

Cole slides down my body with long, teasing touches in all the right places. I'm a panting mess by the time he settles between my thighs.

West slips his thumb in my mouth, and I swirl my tongue around and around, my attention distracted by the way Cole's breath brushes against my exposed pussy.

Cole teases me with light, brushing strokes of his fingers along my pussy. He plays with my arousal, touching everywhere but where I'm throbbing for him.

West replaces his thumb with his mouth the second Cole finally —finally—bridges the gap. He sucks my clit into his mouth with a hard pull, and my back arches off the bed. West swallows my moan of pleasure, swirling his tongue against mine.

Cole feasts on me, moaning into me like he's enjoying it as much as I am.

My orgasm hits me hard and fast, my muscles tensing and my eyes slamming shut. Cool air hits my overheated skin and I barely open my eyes to see why Cole's pulling away so soon.

His mouth is magical, but I wanted his cock too.

My brow arches high over my left eye as Cole steps back and West slips in front of him. I blame the fog of lust for how long it takes me to put it all together. I smirk at them, casting my gaze to the right to see Sonny standing a foot away.

"What was the bet?" My voice is low, heavy with lust.

"No bet, Amelia," West murmurs as he trails his fingers through my folds, stealing my attention. Three fingers sweep through me in slow, almost lazy patterns. His touch is light, teasing.

My chest rises faster still. "So you're all playing musical chairs today just for fun?"

West lifts a shoulder. "There may have been a conversation."

I breathe out a laugh. "I knew it." I flick my gaze to Sonny. "You're sitting out?"

He rakes his teeth over his bottom lip and shakes his head. He jerks his head to the man currently tormenting me with his feather-light touches between my thighs. "Not me, Cher."

West smirks. It's a smile I'm used to seeing on Cole's face—another testament to our time underground together. "Fine. I lost rock paper scissors—"

A laugh slips out of me before I can stop it. Little competitions are just another way we stay sane. I hated the idea of a rotating schedule for who sleeps in my bed, it felt too much like a task, something scheduled. So they started playing little games with stakes.

So I really shouldn't be surprised.

He plunges two fingers inside me and my laugh turns into a groan. My eyes slam shut, my legs widening impossibly further.

A heady sort of desperation infuses my bloodstream. I already came, but they make me feel greedy. They always have.

"And I'm not sitting out. I'm going to sit right there and watch," West says, tipping his chin toward the bed on the other side of the room.

Clarity pierces a hole in my fog, and I understand. Cole said he's ready to share, but that doesn't mean we're all ready to dive into a four-way. Baby steps and all that.

West curls his fingers inside of me, pressing against that dangerous spot. And that's all it takes. I explode in an eruption of pleasure. If I wasn't flying so high, I might be a little embarrassed about how quickly I just came.

The bed depresses next to me, but I need another moment before I open my eyes. Cole murmurs next to me, his hands trailing down my arms. He gives me the space I need to float back down to earth. And when I open my eyes, it's to Sonny at the end of the bed.

He smiles, his dimples winking at me. "Flip over, Cher."

My head swims with pleasure, my body oversensitive.

Steady hands span my hips as I turn over and place a knee on either side of Cole's waist.

"Hey," Cole murmurs. He reaches up and tucks some hair behind my ear. His grip pauses on my neck, his thumb sweeping back and forth over my pulse point.

"Hey," I whisper. "You okay?"

"I'm perfect." He leans up and kisses me. It's soft and chaste.

Sonny's hands settle low on my hips, and my back arches into him.

I feel wanton in this position, exposed for their perusal.

But never self-conscious. There might have been a time where I would've closed my legs or shied away from all of them seeing me on display, but not any longer. It's hard to feel insecure when you have three gorgeous men worshiping you and bringing your body unimaginable pleasure.

Sonny's hands smooth over my curves in soft, sweeping strokes. "You ready, baby girl?"

I nod against Cole's mouth. Nerves dance in my belly at the thought of both of them inside me like this. "I want to feel you both. Like this."

"C'mere, Mia." Cole guides my mouth to his, distracting me from Sonny's fingers circling my asshole.

My lashes flutter closed as sparks of pleasure ripples down my spine. I arch into Sonny's hold, and he rewards me with something infinitely better than his playful fingers.

His tongue.

The things these men can do with their tongues should be illegal.

Hands wander and tongues swirl, and all too soon, I find myself climbing that peak again.

"Oh, oh—I'm going—"

Sonny pulls back, and I rip my mouth from Cole's.

I send him a harsh glare over my shoulder. He's lucky I love him and his adorable dimples winking at me. "Why did you stop?"

Sonny drags his mouth down my spine, and I arch further. Movement from the corner of my eye catches my attention, and I look over my shoulder at West. True to his word, he sits on the bed across from ours, legs spread wide and hand palming his cock through his shorts.

"Patience, baby girl," Sonny says against the curve of my hip.

The last vestiges of my patience crash into the bed.

"I don't want to be teased anymore."

I reposition my knees on the bed, sliding down Cole's body until I hover over his cock. I wrap my fingers around him in a tight fist. I pause for a second, exhaling at the feeling of Cole in my hand before I guide him just inside.

"Now who's teasing." Cole's voice is low, strained, his fingers flexing on my ribs.

My lips quirk up on the sides, and I tilt my head, letting my hair fall down my shoulder. Sonny takes the invitation and drags his lips along that sensitive spot underneath my ear.

Goosebumps scatter down my body, and my lashes flutter closed. I slide my hands up his chest, reveling in the way he feels beneath my palms.

Cole takes advantage of my momentary distraction and snatches the control from me. He thrusts upward and uses his hold around my ribs to press me down onto him.

We groan together, both of us falling still for a moment.

West grunts, and I turn at the sound of it. His shorts are gone and his cock is in his hand. I lick my lips and watch as he strokes himself with a light, slow grip.

"God damn, Mia. How do you always feel so good?"

"Magic," Sonny says with reverence.

CONTINUE READING FOR AN EXCERPT

Continue reading for an excerpt from

Wolf:
The Brotherhood book 1
Available now on Kindle Unlimited

WOLF

THE BROTHERHOOD
WOLF
PENELOPE BLACK

PROLOGUE

"Congratulations, Class of 2020! It's been my absolute pleasure to watch you ladies achieve your goals these last four years."

I tune out the words from the principal of St. Rita's All-Girls Academy as my gaze zeroes in on the reason I'm here: the redhead with doe eyes in the fifth row. Judging by the way she's searched the stands every sixty seconds for the last twenty minutes, she's waiting for someone to show up.

Lucky for her, I did.

The air conditioner closest to me hums to life, adding to the low murmur of the crowd around me. A makeshift stage sits in the middle of the gym, red and silver balloons framing all four corners. A bead of sweat rolls down my back as the New York City heat-wave bakes everyone inside this glorified tin can.

I tug my ball cap lower to shield my face and tuck my hands back in my pockets as I lean against the wooden accordion bleachers. The last thing I need for someone to recognize me, and with a face—and hands—like mine, it's inevitable. Technically, I'm in neutral territory, but I don't put it past those weaselly fucks to jump on an opportunity while I'm alone. And I don't want to spill blood here today.

My gaze tracks her every movement, and when they call her name, she glides across the stage, her smile wide and bright. She waves to a group of familiar faces cheering for her in the stands, but her shoulders never lose their tension.

Ah, so my little bird wasn't waiting on any of them, I muse.

She tips her chin higher as she poses for a photograph at the end of the stage, and my black heart squeezes at the sight.

She's the most stunning creature I've ever seen.

And she will be my queen.

CHAPTER ONE

ALAINA

"Kiss a stranger."

An involuntary cough wracks my body as my strawberry wine cooler gets caught in my throat. "Sorry," I say as I put a hand to the base of my throat and set my drink on my desk. "It went down the wrong pipe when I thought I heard you say I have to kiss a stranger." I pin my cousin, Madison, with a glare.

"That's because I did." She quirks an eyebrow at me and flips her long, straight red hair over her shoulder. "Although I'm not sure why you're surprised, because this isn't my dare."

"Well, it's not my dare, so . . ." I turn to look at Madison's twin sister, Mary, with new appreciation. "Color me impressed," I murmur.

"What?" Mary huffs and crosses her arms over her chest. "We're eighteen now—"

"Ahem." I point at myself with a wry smile.

"Well, *we're* eighteen"—Mary gestures to herself and Maddie—"and your birthday is in like a week. I thought we could step up the game a little." Mary's cheeks are pink by the time she's done talking. "Plus, we just graduated!"

Mary and Madison are fraternal twins, and while their differences are minor, they have different styles. Mary wears her red hair in a lob—a longer bob—that she straightens every day. With matching ice-blue eyes, they're total knockouts. And they're my best friends.

"I think it's a great idea, but you guys are going to be disappointed because I definitely added 'binge-watch *Vampire Diaries*' in there last week," I tell them with a laugh.

Mary's stiff as she sits on the end of my twin bed in our shared dorm suite at St. Rita's All-Girls Academy. Technically, we're no longer high school students here, but since we're enrolled in the sister school—St. Rita's College, we're opting to keep the same living arrangements.

Mary's arms are still crossed tightly across her chest, and she stares at the cream-colored carpet as if it's holding all her secrets.

I glance at Maddie and nod toward her sister. With a sigh, she sets the colored popsicle stick with the dare on it on my dresser and crosses the room to her sister.

"Babe. It's totally fine. And you know I'm all for you kissing whoever you want—whenever you want."

"Yeah, you can have this dare if you want, Mary," I offer.

"No take-backs, Lainey. You know the rules," Maddie interjects.

Mary lifts her head, a wry smirk on her face. "No worries, all five of my dares last week were 'kiss a stranger.'"

A giggle escapes my lips before I can catch it, and Maddie joins in. After a few seconds, Mary loosens up a little, and before long, she's giggling right along with us.

"Who knew we'd still be playing the silly game we made-up with an extra mason jar and colored popsicle sticks when we were twelve?" I muse as I take a drink of my wine cooler.

"Me. I did," Maddie sasses, lifting her chin and leaning back.

"That's because you came up with the idea," Mary says with a roll of her eyes.

"And what a good idea it was! Besides, what else were we going to do? We couldn't leave the dorm, and we needed something fun to look forward to since they dumped us in the city and left without a backward glance." Maddie's smile is hard and forced, her eyes narrow.

"Ah-ha! I knew you cared that Mom left us here and went to Europe that summer!" Mary exclaims, her earlier tension long forgotten.

Maddie tilts her chin up. "Don't be ridiculous, Mary. I did not. I was only making a point. And Mom brings us with her to Europe every summer now."

Watching my cousins trade quick retorts is like watching a tennis match. I sip my drink and settle back into my chair.

"Exactly! Because you pitched a fit that one summer, so now Mom's afraid to leave us here. Honestly, I don't even know why you want to go over there anymore. Being a *wingwoman* to your middle-aged mother while she picks up guys fifteen years younger lost its appeal years ago." Mary practically sneers the word wingwoman, and I do a double-take. The expression is more Maddie than her. I feel like I'm missing something here.

"That *one* summer? You mean the one where we were attending summer courses, and you got your period in the middle of ceramics, but I pretended it was me, and Becky Parsons made fun of *me*" —Maddie jabs a finger into her chest—"for months. That summer?" Her lips flatten, and a flush of anger creeps down her neck.

This is a familiar discussion they've had many, many times over the years. The thing is, Mary always apologizes—again—and Maddie always accepts, they hug, and then, they move on. I'm not sure what it is about that one instance that has Maddie still hung up, but it's time for me to step in, like usual.

I stand up and face them, hands on my hips. "Alright, girls, are we going to kiss some strangers tonight or what?"

Both girls stop and turn to face me, their cheeks pink, arms crossed, and eyes guarded. I swear, they're so alike sometimes, it's like they're the same person.

This time, it's Mary who deflates first. She turns to face Maddie. "I'm sorry, Maddie."

Maddie turns toward her. "I'm sorry too. Don't worry about it. I'm just getting hangry, I guess." Maddie leans into Mary and wraps an arm around her shoulders. "Okay, let's pick our dares for tonight."

Maddie leaves her twin on the end of my bed and walks to the mason jar on my dresser. Somewhere along the years, we decided to start keeping the dare jar in my room. The colorful popsicle sticks nearly fill the jar. We pick from the jar once a week, sometimes more, but always when we're together. Now that I'm working at the coffee shop a few blocks away, tutoring a couple of middle school kids in the afternoons, and singing for fun with the girls nearly every Friday, we have to be a little more strategic.

Maddie closes her eyes and pulls a stick from the jar. "Alright, tonight, Mary's dare is *dance with a stranger*." Her voice rises higher with each word, her eyebrows following suit.

My lips tip up in a smirk. I added that dare months ago. Ever since I started noticing the same guy show up to open mic night at O'Malley's Pub. Tall, chestnut-brown hair, and a cloud of danger surrounding him. He watches my set every time I sing, but he never stays afterward, and he's always alone.

I thought I'd give myself the push to approach him and ask him to dance, but it looks like Mary will be tearing up the floor tonight. I look at her to gauge her reaction to her dare.

"Fun. I have just the outfit for tonight." Mary's eyes sparkle as she claps her hands together in front of her chest and bounces on her toes.

"Okay then." Maddie eyes her sister with a knowing grin. She closes her eyes again and pulls another popsicle stick from the jar. "And tonight my dare is *sing karaoke . . . in a lime-green tutu*."

Maddie's eyebrows hit her hairline, and her mouth opens slightly. And I can't hold back my grin.

"Ah, I was watching a lot of *Sex and The City* re-runs when I added that dare," I offered. Maddie looked at me with her mouth open. "You know, where she wears the pink tulle skirt and looks badass walking down the city blocks? That's what I was going for, but I thought lime-green would be fun."

"Lainey, we're three fair-skinned, freckled, redheads. Lime-green is not *our* color, babe," Maddie says as she looks at me, head tilted and eyebrows drawn together like I actually need a fashion intervention. Just because I like to wear old band tees doesn't mean I don't have a good sense of fashion. I just know what I like.

"Exactly," I say with a smirk.

Mary laughs as she gets up from my bed. "Ooh, you're good, girl. Nice subtle hit on all of us—I like it. Let's eat some dinner and then get ready. I'll check what the dining hall has on their menu for tonight." Mary heads to the kitchen, where we have the month's dining hall menu tacked up on a corkboard.

"But . . . we don't even have a lime-green tutu—so, ha!" Maddie yells, thrusting a finger in the air.

"Except." I cross the room to my closet, open the closet door, and shift my clothes around so I can reach the three brightly-colored items in the back. Curling my fingers around the hangers, I wrangle the items out. "Ta-da!" I shimmy the hangers, causing the tulle skirts to swish around.

Maddie looks at me for a moment before she starts laughing. "Oh my god—Mary, come here and see what your crazy cousin did!"

I hear Mary's footsteps in the hallway, and she speaks before I can see her.

"Coming! Oh, and before I forget, tonight it's spaghetti bolognese"—Mary freezes in the doorway, her mouth falling open—"and what the hell are those?!"

"Why, our outfits for tonight, of course!" I answer cheerfully.

"But only Maddie has to wear the lime-green one!" Mary whines.

Maddie doubles over on my bed in laughter. "You put two more tutu dares in the jar, didn't you?"

I smooth the tulle down on the neon-orange skirt as a smirk tips up the corners of my mouth. "Sure did. And because we love you, we're all going to wear one tonight."

I untangle the lime-green tulle skirt and toss it to Maddie. I turn to Mary, who's still standing in the doorway, and hold out the remaining two tulle skirts. "Neon orange or hot pink?"

"I can't believe I'm going to wear a neon orange tulle skirt while dancing with a stranger tonight," Mary mock grumbles.

"Good choice, Mary. Might I suggest wearing a solid color to really make the orange pop?" I ask with a laugh. I unclip the neon-orange tulle skirt and toss it to her.

"We're going to look ridiculous at O'Malley's tonight." Maddie sighs dejectedly.

"Nah, we'll look amazing. They love us, and Jack would never let anyone say anything bad about us," I assure her. "Besides, we just graduated, let's celebrate!"

Jack is the owner of O'Malley's Irish Pub. I met him sort of randomly a couple of years ago. I was supposed to meet someone there to see a band, but the guy never showed up, and I ended up chatting with Jack for a while. Two weeks later, I showed up with Mary and Maddie in tow for their open mic night and never looked back. Now, O'Malley's has become our go-to place for a night out.

I know they know our fake IDs are bullshit, but they never call us on it. We almost always order vodka cranberries, Long Island iced teas, and Baby Guinnesses—which does not actually have Guinness in it.

I still remember the look of disgust on Mary's face when she tipped the glass back and took a huge sip of what she thought was just a small-sized Guinness.

I thought for sure she was going to spew Kahlua and Bailey's all over the bar top that day. But by some miracle, she didn't. It took her like six months to even drink a latte again—something about the smell of coffee triggering her gag reflex.

"What are you laughing about over there?" Mary asks, eyes narrow and head tilted. "Because I draw the line at footwear, Lainey."

"Actually, I was remembering the time we discovered what a Baby Guinness was." I smirk, quirking an eyebrow. "Do you remember that—"

Mary fake gags before I can finish my question. "Ugh. Yes. Don't remind me, or I won't be able to look at a latte again for months," she whines.

I laugh. "Good times, good times. Now, shoo"—I flick my fingers in her direction—"and go change for dinner. We're celebrating tonight!"

"Yeah, yeah. I'm going," Mary mutters as she walks out of my room.

I hold up the neon-pink tulle skirt in front of me, twisting and turning it, and stare at my reflection in the mirror. The corners of my mouth curl into a mischievous smile.

Tonight is going to be unforgettable.

CONTINUE READING FOR AN EXCERPT

Continue reading for an excerpt from

Gilded Princess:
The Five Families book 1
Available now on Kindle Unlimited

GILDED PRINCESS

gilded
PRINCESS
AN ITALIAN MAFIA ROMANCE
PENELOPE BLACK

PROLOGUE

Sweat clings to the back of my neck and underneath my arms, but I don't move to wipe it off. I'd rather suffer the persistent itch than incur the wrath of my father.

He's on a warpath tonight.

Earlier at dinner, he told me to lay out my Sunday best and be ready at midnight. It was time for me to step into my role as a member of our family. Ma started crying, and then Dad got mad, and they started arguing—per usual.

I don't understand why she's so upset. I'm old enough to help out the family now, and it'll be good for me to learn how to do more stuff and make Ma's life easier.

Plus, the more focus I keep on me, the less time my father has to terrorize anyone else.

So here I am, baking in my black suit I wear to church on Sundays in my father's office. The air feels heavy this time of year, but this room doesn't have any windows to open. It's all dark wood and dark rugs. Intimidating and lightless, just like him.

My uncle Abram and my cousin Nico sit in the chairs across from my dad, who's reclined behind his massive oak desk. He's staring at the two men in front of him as he puffs on his cigar, his posture deceptively calm, shoulders loose.

It's a demeanor I've seen all too often.

Tension simmers in the air, so thick I can almost see it. Dad asked me to stand behind him to the right and stay against the wall, no matter what. I'm not entirely sure what will happen tonight, but I can't imagine it's anything good.

Uncle Abram adjusts his tie and cranes his neck to the side to release the tension as the silence continues.

Without a word, Dad slides open his top desk drawer and pulls out a gun.

"Half-assed murder plots are for boys. In this family, you act like a man. So, let this be a lesson to you, son. If you want to be the king, you have to kill the king."

My eyes widen as I glance between the gun my father placed on the desk and my cousin. He's eight years older than me, so we didn't exactly grow up together, but I always looked up to him. My palms feel clammy, and I stifle the urge to wipe them off on my pants. I know he hates it when I fidget.

"Do you understand why this is necessary?" Dad looks over his shoulder at me, waiting for my answer.

I nod, even though I don't understand. The memory of Dad making me watch *The Godfather* years ago flashes before my eyes. He told me this is what I should expect from our family, and at the time, I thought he was being sarcastic.

I was wrong.

He turns toward Uncle Abram. "The choice is yours, brother. Either you or him."

If he's surprised, Uncle Abram doesn't show it. He stares back at Dad, unflinching. "You know my choice, Angelo." He turns toward Nico. "I love you, son. No matter what."

Dad nods twice before he picks up the gun and points it at Uncle Abram. He fires two shots. Uncle Abram's body jerks violently, tipping over the chair.

I jump with each crack of the gun, unable to stifle my shock.

He shifts his hold to point it at Nico. His eyes look like saucers, bloodshot and wide.

"Uncle Angelo, please. D-d-don't do this. My dad—"

A gunshot splits the air.

Nico's eyes shine with tears, disbelief slackening his jaw. He pushes a hand to his chest, and bright red blood oozes out between his fingers.

Another shot lands in between his eyes, Nico's head jerking back in a swift, violent motion.

"I don't give second chances." His words are slow and contemplative like he's wondering if there's rain in the forecast today.

I bite my lip hard enough to draw blood, desperate to keep my fear inside. Anything to keep my dad's focus off of me.

It's selfish. A coward's move. But at twelve, I know I can't win against him.

Not yet.

CHAPTER ONE

MADISON

"I can't believe you're ditching me again, Mary. You agreed to go with me."

I shouldn't be surprised that my sister, who prefers books to humans, is abandoning me during event season, but I am.

She sighs, the noise loud in my ear as I squeeze the phone in my hand and press it against my face to hear her over the busy streets of New York City. "Don't be so dramatic, Maddie. You'll be fine. I don't even know why you asked me. You know I hate those things. Besides, they only ever invite me because of you anyway."

Now it's my turn to sigh. I shove my irritation down to the bottom of my stomach and exhale a calming breath. "You know that's not true. Clara Vanderbilt and Isobel Chambers specifically invited you to the masquerade ball."

"Yeah, well, I'm not going. Why don't you ask Lainey like you usually do?"

The scorn in her voice has me fumbling over my thoughts for a moment. I shove the concerning reason behind my cousin Lainey's impromptu cabin visit down deep and bury it alongside all the other things Mom said are wrinkle-inducing. It's easier for me to ignore it now that we don't have honest-to-god bodyguards following us around anymore. It only lasted for a few days, and I know it was more for Lainey's peace of mind than anything, but it was strange.

My cousin Lainey is more like a sister than an extended family member. Sometimes she's closer to me than my actual sister. I like to think of her as the perfect balance between me and my twin, Mary.

Lainey's mom, Lana, and my mom are twins too—apparently it runs in the family. But outside of their looks, they're not that similar. It's kind of how I feel about Mary and me. Even though we're fraternal twins, when we were younger, we'd dress alike and it was hard to tell us apart.

These days, Mary and I couldn't be more different.

Where I wear my dark-red hair long and in waves, she cut hers short into a long bob and religiously straightens it. Mascara and lip gloss are about all she wears—*not* that she needs makeup. She's gorgeous, and sometimes, I think she's the only one who doesn't realize it.

You're more likely to find her in cardigans and sneakers than dressed up in a gown fit for a ball. I don't know why I'm surprised that she's backing out of this event.

I clear my throat to get myself back into the conversation, looking both ways before I cross the street. "You know why. Lainey's recovering—"

"Yeah, yeah, yeah. Tucked away at some cabin with a bunch of dudes, I know. I guess she should think about the company she keeps, huh? Maybe she won't end up in those shitty situations then."

I stop in the middle of the busy sidewalk, the flow of people swerving to move around me. "What the hell, Mary! I cannot believe you said that."

My sister scoffs. "What? It's true. Anyway, I'm not going to your stupid gala. So I guess you should find some other friends." She mock-gasps. "Think of what they'll say if you go solo?"

My jaw drops at her cruelty, and I clear my throat, swallowing down the emotion. "Wow. Are you going for a record of below-the-belt hits today, sister? Because I gotta say, you're hitting your marks."

She knows damn well how I feel about stuff like that. I don't have a problem with being alone, but who wants to go solo to those kinds of events? It's like daring someone to jump into shark-infested waters wearing Lady Gaga's 2010 award show dress—you know, the one made up of raw meat.

You need a buffer to these sorts of things—a plus one.

With a mother who offered to buy me a boob job, a nose job, and lip fillers for my twelfth birthday, is it any wonder why I have these sorts of thoughts?

If you're told most of your life that your only value is your appearance, after so long, you start to accept it as gospel.

She sighs, the exhale long and somehow sounding irritated. "Whatever. Sorry. I have plans, okay?"

My ears prick at the change in her tone. "What kind of plans?"

"None of your business."

I can just picture her folding her arms tight across her chest and shifting her weight. It's her tell when she's hiding something.

I gather my hair and twist it over my shoulder to let the hot summer breeze roll over my neck as the proverbial lightbulb goes off. "Oh my god. You have plans with a guy! You sneaky little—"

"Just drop it, Maddie. It's probably nothing, okay? And anyway, I don't want to talk about it."

I pause, sorting through my initial hurt. Her unwillingness to share picks at my decades-old insecurities and wounds. I know it's more to do with her than with me, but it still takes me a moment to wrap my mind around it.

"You used to tell me everything, Mary," I murmur.

Mary huffs. "Yeah, when we were like eight. You tell Lainey everything now, so don't act like it's *me* who has changed."

Shock stills my tongue. I'm not sure what's going on, but I have a feeling my sister is going through something. My heart pangs at the hurt in her voice. "I'm sorry if you've felt left out. You're my sister."

"Yeah, okay. Look, I've gotta go. I'll see you later."

As soon as the last word leaves her lips, she ends the call. I pull the phone away from my ear and feel my eyebrows reach my hairline. She didn't even give me a chance to reply before she hung up.

The summer sun feels heavy as it beats down on my back. I love summertime. It's the season of possibility and spontaneity. And this was supposed to be our summer. The one we'd been dreaming about for years.

We survived high school at one of the most prestigious all-girl academies in the country, and we had three months to revel in our accomplishments until we had to buckle back down and get to work on our degrees.

St. Rita's All-Girl Academy is a tradition in my family. All the girls attended, and for the most part, I didn't mind. I lived in a luxury dorm suite with my cousin and sister for years. And since we're all attending St. Rita's University, we're staying in the same suite. A perk of being a legacy member, I guess.

I tap my phone against my lips as I walk toward my favorite coffee shop. It's not too far from our dorm suite, and they have a new iced tea flavor every week from May to September. If I wasn't busy teaching adorable little girls ballet three days a week, I'd work here just for the free coffee perks.

I know I can't ask Lainey to go with me. Not only is she out of town, but she just went through some seriously scary stuff, and she needs time to rest and recharge. And honestly, I'm proverbially eating popcorn and watching her romantic entanglements play out.

And Mary's out, obviously.

I guess I could go alone. Despite the masks required to enter the event, I have a good idea of who will be there. It's generally the same group of people my age who attend every year. One of those legacy things. Lots of girls from St. Rita's—high school and college. Plus, the school has a lot of affiliations with other private schools around the country.

Every year, the private school board council throws a masquerade ball to raise money for a different charity. This year they're focusing on saving the rainforests, which is something I can get behind. The music's usually good and the food is always excellent. I could do without the monotonous small talk from random adults who don't actually care about the answers to the questions they ask.

Plus, there are only so many times I can binge-watch shows on Netflix.

I roll my eyes, annoyed with myself. It's not like I don't have other friends, just none as close as Lainey and Mary. I suppose now is as good a time as any to strengthen new friendship bonds, though.

With my mind made up, I quickly tap out a text to Blaire Hawthorne. If anyone knows the theme, it's her. That girl is like a real-life *Gossip Girl*, but without all the secrecy—she lives for drama.

I slide my phone into the pocket of my cream and light green linen skirt. The breathable fabric swishes against my thighs as I walk the last few feet to the cafe.

A blast of air-conditioning greets me as I walk inside and get in line. I wave to Amanda, the barista at the counter, just as I feel my phone vibrate with an incoming text.

Blaire: Madison, babe! I hope I see you at the Enchanted Forest masquerade tomorrow.

Enchanted Forest. Okay, I can swing that. A flicker of excitement blooms. I do love a good theme.

Madison: See you then!

I pocket my phone again as the line moves forward, my mind

already spinning. I'm going to have to call my favorite designer and seamstress and see what she has in stock. Dolores is in her mid-sixties, but her eye for fashion is incomparable. And luckily for me, she took a liking to me when she volunteered for our middle school theatre production. She did the costuming, and we bonded over our shared love of high fashion and French truffles.

"Hey, girl. Surprised to see you here. I thought you'd be in Europe still," Amanda says, pulling me from my thoughts.

My answering smile feels tight. "Ah, yeah. Change of plans. Turns out, I'll be in the city all summer."

"I guess you'll get to try all the flavors this summer then, huh." Amanda smiles. "What'll it be today?"

That gets a wide smile from me. I've been coming to this coffee shop for a long time, and just about every time I'm here, Amanda is working. We've gotten to know one another over the years. "Too true. Busy today?"

Amanda nods and adjusts her daisy-printed apron. "Yep. Just getting over a little rush. And we have blueberry green tea today. I know that's a favorite of yours."

I chuckle and adjust the strap of my crossbody purse, peeling it off my sticky skin. "You know me so well, Amanda. Okay, I'll take one of those, large, please."

"You got it." Amanda turns around and pours my drink from the carafe on the counter behind the register. A few seconds later, she spins to face me and slides the to-go cup and straw on the counter. "That'll be four seventy-four," she says with a smile.

I shove my hand into my purse to grab my wallet, but I come up empty-handed. I open it wider and peer inside, moving a few things around as if my pink wallet will magically appear behind my lip gloss.

My heart settles in my throat and a flush that has nothing to do with the heat rolls over me and settles in my cheeks. My shoulders hitch toward my ears, and I flick my gaze back to Amanda. "I, uh, seem to have misplaced my wallet. Probably left it on my kitchen table or something." I force a laugh that sounds strained even to my ears. "Let me go grab—"

"Here." The deep, smooth voice comes from behind me at the same time a hand extends past me and places a black Amex card on the counter. "On me."

A shiver of awareness skates down my spine, and the small hair on the back of my neck stands on end. Amanda stares over my shoulder without reaching for the card.

Okay, so it's not only me then.

The man behind me chuckles, the noise soft and rich like melted dark chocolate. He steps forward again, his arm just barely grazes mine as he pushes his card further toward Amanda with his index finger. My gaze zeroes in on his veins like a homing beacon. What is it about those veins on a man's forearm?

"And an Americano, please."

The movement snaps Amanda out of her daze and she licks her lips before taking his card and ringing his drink up. "You got it. Seven eighty-four."

I snag my iced tea off the counter and take a step to the side so I can get a better view of the kind stranger. He tilts his head to meet my gaze, never shying away from my blatant stare. Taking a sip of my drink, I let the taste of crisp blueberries and tart lemongrass quench my thirst as I give him a proper once-over.

The corner of his pouty lips tips up on the side as he holds himself still, almost like he's encouraging my perusal.

He's tall—I'd say six-two or six-three with broad shoulders and a tapered waist. Colorful ink peeks out from underneath one sleeve of his black polo shirt, swirling down his arm and stopping at his wrist. I spot a familiar logo on the pocket, and a pair of Ray-Bans hang on the open top two buttons.

Light-brown hair with what look like natural highlights from time spent in the sun. And with the way his biceps strain the sleeves of his shirt, I'd bet he spends a lot of time either on a field or at a gym.

Long sooty lashes frame big dark-green eyes that currently have mirth dancing in them. Something low in my belly clenches when he sinks his teeth into his plump bottom lip and stares at me with an intensity that wasn't there ten seconds ago. It should be illegal for a man to have lips so plump.

"Here's your Americano," Amanda says, breaking the connection. He reaches for it and murmurs his thanks, never taking his gaze from me.

"Thank you. For the drink," I say after I take another sip.

"It's my pleasure." He trails off, and I know he's subtly fishing for my name.

"What's life without a little mystery?" I let the mischievous smile I've been holding back spread across my face as I spin on my heel and walk toward the exit. I pause with one hand on the door and flash him my most flirtatious and inviting smile. "See you around, Americano."

I don't wait for a reply and push open the door and let the thick, humid air greet me.

I swear I hear him murmur, "Count on it."

Slipping my sunglasses on, I pull out my phone and see that Dolores is ready for me. With a renewed sense of excitement, I make my way across town to pick out a show-stopping dress.

ALSO BY PENELOPE BLACK

THE BROTHERHOOD SERIES

Wolf

Rush

Sully

THE FIVE FAMILIES SERIES

Gilded Princess

Twisted Queen

Vicious Reign

Fractured Dynasty

STANDALONES

When It Ends:

A Dark Apocalyptic Romance

THE KING SISTERS WORLD

The Wren

Coming this Summer

Printed in Great Britain
by Amazon